SUSANNE DIETZE
ANITA MAE DRAPER
DEBRA E. MARVIN
GINA WELBORN

Austen
~ in ~
AUSTIN

WhiteFire

IF I LOVED YOU LESS © 2016, Gina Welborn
ROMANTIC REFINEMENT © 2016, Anita Mae Draper
ONE WORD FROM YOU © 2016, Susanne Dietze
ALARMINGLY CHARMING © 2016, Debra E. Marvin

Cover image of historical Austin, TX courtesy of AustinPostcard.com
Cover images from Shutterstock.com
Cover Design by Roseanna White Designs

WhiteFire Publishing
13607 Bedford Rd NE
Cumberland, MD 21502

ISBN for Austen in Austin, Volume 1:
      978-1-939023-77-3 (print)
      978-1-939023-78-0 (digital)

Table of Contents

IF I LOVED YOU LESS

GINA WELBORN

And let us not grow weary
while doing good,
for in due season we shall reap
if we do not lose heart.

Galatians 6:9

Seldom, very seldom does complete truth belong to any human disclosure; seldom can it happen that something is not a little disguised, or a little mistaken.

~ Jane Austen, *Emma*

Pecan Street & Congress Avenue
Austin, Texas
February 1, 1882

"**M**y ability to recognize one's true love, and I say this in all humility, surely must be a gift." Emmeline Travis stopped at the front of the new desk she'd insisted would fit perfectly in Noah's office. She sat her open-top wicker basket next to the NOAH WHITLEY, PRESIDENT, WHITLEY-CRAWFIELD SAVINGS & TRUST nameplate, and then without taking care to remove her white gloves, she withdrew a handkerchief-covered china plate. Paused. Waited. She looked expectantly at the man across from her, sitting behind his desk, as handsome as ever in his ebony, high-buttoned coat.

Noah stopped reading what looked to be another dreadfully dull banking contract, although he didn't put down the papers. His light brown brows rose to convey a silent *finish what you came here to say.*

Emmeline grinned. She adored how accommodating he was. "If you had asked—and I forgive you for not—I would have told you Anne Fairfax was unsuitable for you. Trust me, Noah. I *know* suitability."

He leaned back in his chair, a slight indent along the left side of his mouth. He bore not the disposition of a man recently spurned by the love of his life. He appeared quite delighted. Amused, vaguely so, at her announcement. Nothing could be more suspicious. In Noah's case, looks were deceiving at times because she knew him and knew what he thought. That seemingly amused look was really one of *pray tell me why Anne Fairfax isn't suited for me.*

A myriad of reasons why rolled around in Emmeline's mind.

The most obvious being—

"Her heart is too cold to love," she said, still smiling because talk of Anne Fairfax would not ruin her high spirits. "And yours is... Well, for generations Whitley men have been known for their passionate devotion. Anne Fairfax has the emotional range of a block of ice. I know the most incomprehensible thing in the world to a man is a woman who rejects his offer of marriage"—he winced as she'd expected a man with a broken heart would do—"but you, my dear friend, are best to forget her."

And forget giving her any more flowers, replacement violins, or bushels of beets because you heard she likes them.

Not wanting him to think she was jealous—and she wasn't— Emmeline withheld those thoughts from the man she considered an older brother, though they shared no blood ties, only the fortune of having siblings wedded: his younger brother to her older sister. Theirs was the first of two true love matches brought about by Emmeline's insight into marital bliss potential.

Noah's lips parted and—

Emmeline added, "And do not say this insight of mine stems from the jealousy you think I have of Anne Fairfax, because it does not."

Whatever he muttered under his breath, she could not decipher.

Nor did she wish to.

If something wasn't worth saying aloud, it wasn't worth being heard. Which was why she kept silent her grumbles about Anne Fairfax. Anyone with reason would agree that Austin Abbey's instrumental music teacher was merely too cold of a person *to* like. And how could Emmeline like Anne Fairfax, considering they had not a single thing in common other than them being females with brown hair? That was not completely true, for Emmeline's hair was more red than chestnut. Instead of Anne Fairfax for a wife, dear Noah deserved someone less...

Emmeline paused as she balanced the luncheon plate on her upturned palm and gave her thoughts a good dose of concentration.

Perhaps instead of someone *less,* he deserved someone *more.* Of course, *more of what* she wasn't sure at the moment, and she may have to spend a day fasting to gain clarity. Doing so would not be the first time she sought the Lord on Noah's behalf. Nor would it be the last, she suspected. Of what she was confident, was that if anyone were to know the best woman for Noah, she, Emmeline LeNoir Travis, his closest and truest female friend, would be that person.

Anne Fairfax was not suited to Noah Whitley.

Since Noah wasn't adding anything to the conversation—not that she expected him to since he generally waited a good five minutes to speak after she began any conversation with him—Emmeline rested the luncheon plate in the only spot on his polished-to-a-shine desk free of banking papers. How he found anything, she would never know. She deftly removed the linen handkerchief, exposing the leftover food from the book club gathering last night at her home. *Leftover* because her father and Noah elected to have a lengthy dinner elsewhere.

Without notifying her ahead of time.

Noah's lips parted again, and he looked like he might speak.

"Well," she prodded, "have your say. I am all ears."

His left brow rose. Smugly.

Emmeline did her best not to growl.

"Noah, do not look at me as if you know my thoughts, for I promise you do not." She snatched three silver utensils from the basket. "Cucumber mint sandwiches, raisin scones, and strawberries." She leaned over his desk to neatly set the silverware in their proper place settings. "Mrs. Collins shared her grandmother's recipes. Hattie and I made everything with our very hands. The sandwiches and scones, that is. Not the strawberries. Father had them shipped in from Florida." She straightened, smoothed the long-waist bodice of her emerald moiré gown, and waited for Noah to start on his meal.

A warm grin teetered on the edge of his lips.

If Noah wanted too, he could charm the rattle off a snake or, considering he was a bank president, Scrooge out of his last dime. Any female would thrill to have his finely sculpted elegance turned upon her. He was not angelically handsome like Garrison Churchill, but Noah's looks combined with his height, rugged independence, kindness to all, and that deep-seated contentment in who he was, was enough to draw notice whenever he entered a room.

He merely continued to watch her.

Emmeline reached up to pat for stray curls (none). She checked the placement of her hat (pinned straight). Nothing askew in her appearance, which could only mean he was trying to rattle her.

"Would you please eat?" she pleaded, even though she knew he'd only eat—or talk—when he was good and ready. "I vowed to our concerned siblings that I'd ensure your recovery."

"My recovery from what?" he finally spoke, his tone and face perfectly bland.

For a moment she could do nothing but stare. He wasn't the type to drift away in his thoughts. "Did you pay attention to anything I said?"

He gave her a cheeky grin. "You *think* you know true love."

"I do."

"Have you ever been in love?"

"No." Emmeline couldn't quite manage an offended tone in time to cover how clever she felt at adding, "I've never been a bird, yet I can recognize one."

Noah burst out laughing.

Emmeline plowed on. "Food always heals a broken heart, or so Mrs. Collins often says. Yes, you would be correct to assume by my figure that I've never experienced a broken heart either. Still—I grieve for yours."

He gave her a look to say *my heart isn't broken.*

"You may deny all you wish," she continued, "but your well-being speaks to me. And if you aren't going to see to its care, then as your dearest friend and almost sister, I shall."

He blinked several times.

Emmeline clasped her hands together before her. "I do not fault you for denying your inner pain. You, after all, aren't the first man to have his attentions spurned by the block of ice named Anne. Like many, you may need more than a meal and a bottle of wine to forget your heartache." She paused as the idea blossomed. Why hadn't she realized this sooner? "What you need is—"

"Don't," he warned.

"—a party."

Emmeline's heart fluttered over the brilliance of her idea. No one in Austin organized parties like she did. Of course, she would invite the most jovial and engaging people in town to ensure Noah was well cheered and heart healed...even if he boasted his dislike for parties. And dancing, which further emphasized his predilection toward dullness.

"On that note," she announced, "I received a letter from Mr. Garrison Churchill."

Noah slapped the papers he held onto his desk. "A true knight in shining armor."

Emmeline did her best not to glare at him. "I show compassion for your heartbreak *and* bring you lunch, yet you offer cynicism toward the very man who lost his precious mother the day I lost mine. Garrison and I share a bond."

"So I've heard ad nauseam since you were twelve. You don't need to remind me he is a loving and dutiful nephew either." Noah frowned slightly as he turned the plate of food, the strawberries now in the twelve o'clock position and the triangular cucumber sandwiches at six. "Thank you for the lunch."

"My pleasure."

He lifted a bread wedge to expose the thinly sliced cucumbers.

"You will eat it all," she ordered. "Without complaint."

"That may be impossible. What is the point of making these this small?"

"They were for ladies."

He bit into the cucumber sandwich. His upper lip curled, yet he chewed then swallowed. "You too often assume attachments which don't exist. That is a flaw, not a gift."

"Oh Noah." Emmeline walked around his desk. Considering her in-heels height barely reached his shoulder when he was standing, that he still sat put them closer to eye-level. She rested her hands atop his immaculately combed light brown hair.

She released a weary breath. "Ye of wee little faith."

"This isn't about faith. It's about—"

"How you exasperate me!" she cut in. She paused for a dramatic moment. "I have been your closest friend since I can remember. My father should not be your sole confidante."

"He's a good listener," he said promptly.

"Better than I am?"

His brow furrowed. "What do you know about anticipatory hedges?"

"Nothing," she answered in all honesty, "and I prefer to keep it that way, but I do know last night you two did not discuss banking hedges all two hours of dinner. Papa told me this morning you were distraught about a recent proposal that did not end as you'd wished."

"You immediately *assumed* that referred to Anne Fairfax."

"There's no need to get into a snit."

"Em..." Noah released a loud sigh.

He claimed her hand and cradled it between both of his, surprising her with his action. Other than when he'd assisted her in or out of a carriage or a streetcar, she couldn't remember a single time he'd ever held her hand. That thought left an ache deep in her chest, which made her want to cry. Even her eyes felt warm and watery. Only she wasn't the type to cry. Or flutter. Or faint. Or do any of those silly things that Hattie had done when she thought she was in love with Mr. Martinez and now as she loved Mr. Belton.

Love shouldn't be dramatic.

Love should not make a person giggly or weepy or blind.

It should make a person feel...

Well, she had no idea. She supposed there had to be a hundred different ways to be in love, yet in all her twenty-three years, she'd never experienced deep passion, a distracting attraction, or even an unspoken *tendre*. It was sad, really. She'd like to know love once.

"Emmeline?" Noah squeezed her hand.

Blinking to regain her focus, she knew she'd needed to say something, yet her mind was blank. She looked at him, his familiar blue eyes intent on her. All air disappeared from her lungs, and she stood there feeling, seeing, and knowing with all certainty the thoughts in Noah's mind.

He'd say, *I am sorry I confided in your father instead of you.*

Then she would respond with, *Apology accepted.*

And all would be as it normally was between them.

"Some things," Noah said, breaking the silence with that melodic voice of his that oddly couldn't carry a tune, "are best left unsaid, even between friends. Thank you for caring enough to see to my welfare. I would not survive without you to feed me minty cucumbers." He winked. "I may also not survive eating them."

She tried not to smile. And failed. It was difficult not to in his presence. "Do you think being charming will sway me to forget how exasperating *you* are?"

"It always does."

Emmeline responded with a *pffft* and a withdrawal of her hand from his. "You are insufferable."

He grinned, and Emmeline couldn't believe Anne Fairfax had actually spurned his proposal. With his classic features, strong chin, and as-blue-as-her-dress eyes, Noah Whitley would give any woman beautiful babies. Just not Anne Fairfax.

"Would you like to hear about Garrison Churchill's letter?" Emmeline blurted to redirect the conversation. She couldn't help grinning in delight over the news.

Noah shifted in his chair, turning to where he could directly face her. "What does Churchill have to say?"

"Seems his ailing adopted aunt, Mrs. Churchill, has agreed to allow him to attend Austen Abbey's Saint Valentine's Ball."

"And on Monday, February thirteenth," Noah replied in that patronizing older-brother tone of his, "Mrs. Churchill's health will turn for the worse, and your beloved friend will have to cry off visiting Austin again."

"Oh, no, he'll be here this time. Any day, in fact."

"People don't change."

"The depth of your cynicism truly astounds me."

The corners of his mouth indented ever so slightly. "It is not cynical to call a duck a duck or to say a duck will return to the pond it calls home."

Emmeline ignored his comment, letting her silence be all the response he'd get.

"The clever girl you are knows I'm right."

Despite his smugness, she still said nothing. Unlike Noah who prided himself on his analytical abilities, she did not always feel so entirely convinced that her opinions were right and her adversary's wrong, but now was not the time to concede him the victory. Mr. Garrison Churchill *would* attend Austen Abbey's Saint Valentine's Ball, and when he did, she would be gracious to Noah and not gloat like he would over the victory.

Emmeline motioned toward the food she'd set out. "Eat, please."

Leaving him to attend to his meal, she stepped to the French doors leading to a small, two-person balcony. She drew open both doors, exposing the rich blue sky of winter, allowing in a pleasant afternoon breeze. The second-story view enabled her to see all the traffic, people, and businesses on the corner of Pecan and Congress. Directly across from Whitley-Crawfield Savings was the Imperial Restaurant where she, her father, and Noah enjoyed dinner every Monday night, instead of their usual meals at Papa's hotel. Beyond the restaurant, she could see in the distance the empty Capitol Square where construction would begin soon on the new Capitol building. In the opposite direction was the beautiful Colorado River.

Was there anything she didn't love about living in Austin?

Emmeline glanced up at the weather thermometer attached to the bank's white limestone wall. Sixty-two degrees. In February! She breathed deep and smiled. Her favorite type of winter, indeed. There was nothing like staying at home for real comfort.

She looked over her shoulder. Noah sat on the edge of his desk, facing her. He held his plate, ate a strawberry without using a single utensil, and looked completely uncaring that all could walk by his open office door and see their distinguished bank president behaving like his eight-year-old cousin. Emmeline tensed.

The very cousin who wasn't anywhere in Noah's office.

The very cousin who Noah should be keeping an eye on.

The very cousin who couldn't attend school due to his ailing stomach and who Emmeline was to take home and attend to his "illness." This wasn't good. Not good at all.

"Where's Hank?" she said, her heart beginning to race.

Noah's gaze shifted to the wall clock. He finished another strawberry. "At this moment, he's in Austen Abbey's dining hall."

"He's supposed to be ill."

"He was hungry, and Miss Fairfax's music lessons begin a quarter past noon."

"Austen Abbey is a finishing school for young ladies, Noah. Ladies."

"To be polished and shined to perfection," he muttered as if it were something she said ad nauseam, and she knew quite well she did not. He tossed the strawberry's leafy top onto the plate. "I sent him over to the Abbey early so he would have time to eat first."

"Why? He is not a student nor taking lessons."

"I didn't know you were bringing food."

Emmeline gave him a pointed look. "Noah."

"Emmeline."

"I do not care for your patronizing tone. You did not answer my question."

He ate a cucumber sandwich in response.

Emmeline let out an irritated exhale. "Let us set aside the fact Hank is supposed to be ill, and yet clearly isn't. The last time he was at the Abbey he tormented—"

"Hank has seen the errors of his ways."

She doubted that. "People don't change—you said that yourself."

"People don't." He bit into the last strawberry. With the side of his hand, Noah wiped the juice off his bottom lip. "Children will, with the right and firmly placed motivation."

"Did you check his pockets for crickets, ferrets, or toads? Did he have his slingshot with him?"

Noah shrugged. "He'll be fine. I sent a note with him to give to Mrs. Collins." At her *he will not be fine* look, he added, "Hank knows better than to incite the headmistress's wrath a second time. I told him you'll meet him at the Abbey in an hour to take him home." He took another bite of the cucumber sandwich and grimaced before swallowing. "Music calms Hank. There's no harm in him sitting in on a music lesson this one time. Besides, he's in love with Miss Branch."

"Miss Branch!" Emmeline closed the distance between them, which wasn't much because the balcony was barely six feet behind his desk. "Miss Eliza Branch? The very girl who sat next to me last night during the book club gathering and had an opinion on *everything*? That Miss Branch?"

Noah finished his sandwich then grabbed another. "She's a lovely young woman," he said between bites.

"Yes, but..." Emmeline hesitated. Noah Whitley was the last person she would ever accuse of being a romantic. "Eliza Branch?"

"She plays the lyre," he said in a tone conveying *this* was enough of a reason for his young cousin to be in love.

"The lyre?" she repeated even though she knew full well what instrument Eliza played, which was probably too generous of a word. Eliza definitely showed more enthusiasm than skill, yet she played out of love for music, and this Emmeline found quite admirable.

Noah picked up the last of his sandwiches. "Hank needs a woman who knows a lyre from a harp. I say he chose wisely." He resumed eating.

"He's eight."

Noah pointed the triangular sandwich at her. "But he won't stay eight forever, my dear. One day he's going to find a woman who will make him want to charge the castle, slay the dragon, and leap across parapets. I'd rather he learn *now* the difference between a Maid Marion and a Jezebel. Eliza Branch is a lady of the finest character."

Emmeline blinked repeatedly. "Eliza is ten years older than Hank. Ten!"

He shrugged again.

"Hank's parents entrusted you with his safe-keeping until they return from their tour of the Mediterranean," she said without pausing for a breath. "You're foolish to encourage a relationship which will come to naught but heartache for a child who yearns for nothing more than to be loved by his parents."

His gaze bored into hers. "Age should never come between true love. I would have thought with your *gift*, you'd know that." Sarcasm dripped from his voice.

"This isn't about Hank and Eliza. It's about putting me in my place."

"Only because you need it."

Emmeline opened her mouth and shut it as quickly. In one look he could win an argument. A trait she admired in him—when the *look* wasn't cast upon her.

The silence between them deepened, intensified.

Noah lifted a scone to take a bite, only to return it to the plate. "Would you rather I give you flattery or honesty?"

Emmeline stiffened. She wanted neither when he was being so disagreeable. "You did not believe me when I insisted Hank was pretending to be ill in order to skip school. Therefore, whatever ill befalls us today because of Hank is your fault."

"Nothing will befall us," he said with that swoon-inciting (according to Mrs. Collins) smile of his.

Emmeline rolled her eyes.

Oh, she was aware of his charms. Not that Noah was a flirt, at least not that she'd ever seen. What she *had* seen was the way he looked at a woman with undivided interest, even when she was speaking of fashion, afternoon tea, or the latest thing she'd read. He listened and encouraged, never judged. No one was better than him at changing the conversation when it verged upon gossip. If his contentedness with his bachelorhood wasn't so well-known throughout Austin, women would be clamoring over one another to garner his attention.

Noah shifted on his desk, and the toes of his boots brushed against her skirt. Despite the layers of silk and muslin, she didn't merely feel his boot. She felt him. And she wanted to move. Or not move. Or perhaps rest against his shoulder. He would say all would be well with Hank. He would say he was sorry for being critical of her. He would say love was the most wonderful feeling in the world and that someday she would know grand passion.

Or maybe that wasn't it at all.

Maybe she had the autumn doldrums. Only, she didn't feel melancholy.

She felt... She wanted...

Emmeline released a ragged breath. Well, she really had no idea what this was or what she was feeling or wanted or why or how. Later... tonight...when she was alone, she'd sort it all out and decide it was nervous expectation over the upcoming Saint Valentine's Ball and Mr. Garrison Churchill's arrival. Yes, that had to be it.

"Something is bothering you," Noah said.

She met his concerned gaze. "I was thinking of the Saint Valentine's Ball. You are coming, whether you wish to or not."

He grimaced.

"Miss Travis!"

At the wail in her protégé Hattie's voice, Emmeline looked past Noah, who was also looking over his shoulder at his open office door.

Standing at the threshold, with her blond curls springing erratically from her chignon, Hattie held her hand to the bodice of her favorite calico dress as her chest rose and fell. Her bonnet dangled down her back, held on by the haphazard knot at her neck. A month of personal instruction on decorum by Emmeline gone in a moment's outburst. Sophistication clearly didn't come as naturally to Hattie as being pretty did. While Hattie chose to continue wearing Mrs. Collins's cast-off calicos despite the elegant dresses Emmeline had bought her (which Hattie insisted on saving for special occasions), Hattie also had a teachable spirit and extraordinary ability to be dedicated to those she bonded with. In summation, Hattie's strengths were far superior to her minor flaws, which Emmeline found quite admirable.

"Good afternoon, Miss Smith." Noah spoke politely as he always did.

Miss Smith finally looked to Noah. Her hazel eyes widened. She blushed then immediately curtsied as if he were a British aristocrat instead of a man who spent his day denying and approving loans. "Mr. Whitley," she said, her tone heavy with surprise, "I didn't realize you would be here. The receptionist said I could find Miss Travis in the navy and gold office at the end of the stairs. I've never seen such a magnificent room except at Miss Travis's hotel."

Noah put the luncheon plate down on his desk, right next to his nameplate. "The odds of finding me in here are rather high. Why do you think that could be?"

Emmeline pinched his thigh. He didn't flinch.

Hattie's gaze shifted to the nameplate. "Oh." She cringed. "It's your office."

"Hattie, why are you at the bank already?" asked Emmeline in concern. "You're supposed to be delivering the remaining book club food to Miss Gates and her mother."

Hattie twisted her hands together. Her gaze nervously shifted to Noah then back to Emmeline. "Mr. Belton"—her voice caught—"has returned."

Emmeline released a sigh in both delight over the news and in relief it wasn't as dreadful as she'd first thought. While the good headmaster's attentions toward Hattie had diminished prior to his departing for San Antonio, with his return two weeks sooner than expected, absence clearly made the heart grow fonder. By Saint Valentine's Day, Hattie would be engaged to a respectable, God-fearing man. Emmeline would see to it. Just as she would see to it that Noah married any woman besides Anne Fairfax.

She moved around Noah to reclaim her basket; he grabbed the back of her gown just above her bustle, stopping her. She glared at him. His attention never wavered from Hattie.

Emmeline returned her gaze to her protégé. "What wonderful news!"

"It's dreadful," Hattie countered.

Emmeline's smile fell. "Why?"

"He returned..." Her shrilly words increased in volume, drawing the attention of what looked to be every person on the second floor of the bank. "With a *wife!*"

Two

If things are going untowardly one month, they are sure to mend the next.
~ Jane Austen, *Emma*

As Emmeline's usual golden glow drained from her face, Noah pieced together the chain of events that had occurred since she'd decided to make Miss Smith her paid companion. With one hand, he gripped Emmeline's dress tighter. With the other, he motioned to his secretary who stood in the hallway looking into his office. "Please escort Miss Smith back down to the lobby." When Emmeline stepped away, he yanked her back next to him. "I need a word in private with Miss Travis."

The words hung like cigar smoke about a room.

At a level only Emmeline could hear, Noah said, "*You* aren't going anywhere."

Miss Smith looked beseechingly at Emmeline, who recovered from the shock of the news with an, "All is well, Hattie. I'll be but a moment." She grinned as if she wasn't being restrained from leaving. "Do wait for me downstairs."

Miss Smith nodded and left his office, trailing behind Noah's secretary.

With her square-shaped face, large hazel eyes, and distractingly full lips, Miss Hattie Smith would never be overlooked in a crowd. Noah was aware of what had captured Joe Martinez's interest. The few conversations Noah had had with Emmeline's orphaned protégé testified she was not a great wit but neither was she a simpleton. What she'd learned about farming during the summer she boarded with the

Martinezes actually impressed Noah. That Emmeline, in three weeks, had "improved" Miss Smith enough to rid her of her schoolgirl giggle proved Miss Smith had a teachable spirit. He'd been confident Emmeline, even with her partiality to Miss Smith, would think a gentleman-farmer a good match with her protégé.

Yet the curvaceous blond's refusal yesterday morn of Martinez's marriage request—even though both Martinez and Noah had been convinced she'd reciprocated Martinez's feelings—made no sense. Until now. Hattie Smith's intellect wasn't so much as poor as her will was pliable. The blame for the refusal of Martinez's offer lay at another woman's manipulating little feet.

Keeping his hold on Emmeline, he stepped around his desk and walked to his office door, her in step.

"I'm not a puppet," she ground out as she reached around her back to repeatedly slap at his hold. "Release me."

With his free hand, Noah closed his office door with a force that stilled Emmeline's action. "You encouraged Miss Smith to reject Joe Martinez's marriage proposal. Don't lie," he warned.

Her eyes narrowed. "Why would I lie? She asked for my counsel and I gave it."

"Miss Smith is good-tempered and well-mannered, but—"

"In this we agree," she cut in.

"—beyond this she brings nothing to a marriage, which is what I told Joe Martinez when he sought my advice."

"You told him that?"

"It's the truth."

"From your perspective."

"From anyone's perspective...except yours and his," he said in exasperation. "I could not reason with him. He loves her."

"He proposed through a letter, Noah. A letter!" she shouted, as if volume equaled mortification. "No true gentleman proposes through a letter. I saw her response. Hattie was far more gracious than I would have been."

"Saw it? Em, you *told* her what to write."

That earned him a glare.

"You have been a mentor of the worst kind to Miss Smith."

She flinched.

Noah didn't smile in pleasure over finally getting through to her. Not that he expected her to concede to his rightness and her wrongness.

The woman was too stubborn, too resistant to change, too content in believing she knew what was best. No one, except for him, resisted giving her what she wanted. As her gaze centered on the closed door, her lips pursed tight, brown eyes narrowing. Noah gritted his teeth, his patience wearing thin. He knew that look. He knew she was calculating the finest justification for her role in what caused Joe Martinez heartbreak deeper than what Emmeline was imagining Noah recently endured over Miss Fairfax. Doubtful she would host a party to soothe Martinez's heartache.

Noah released his hold on her dress. "You owe both Martinez and Miss Smith apologies."

Emmeline raised her chin. "Mr. Martinez is a respectable young man," she said in a calm, reasonable tone reminding Noah of his mother when she'd lectured him, "but Hattie is seventeen, with the sweetness of temper and manner of any young graduate of Austen Academy. She is, in fact, a beautiful girl and would be described so by ninety-nine of a hundred people. Hattie should not—" She paused, restarted. "No woman, not even Hattie, should be obligated to accept the first offer of marriage."

"If she has no family, no income, and the offer is from an honorable man, then she very well ought to accept it."

She looked up at him then brushed an auburn strand from her face, a perfectly feminine action yet one devoid of flirtation. "Noah, you're being insufferable."

"As you are," he retorted.

"I am not—" Emmeline cleared her throat. "This is not about me. Hattie should be allowed to consider her options."

"Options?" Noah stared at her in disbelief. "Until you decided to make her your friend, Hattie Smith had no options, any more than she had a sense of superiority. But now, thanks to you, she still has none of the former and yet a gulf-filled amount of the latter."

"I've done nothing more than see to it that my protégé marries well."

"To Belton?" Noah stepped forward, and she stepped back. "Is he your grand aspiration for Miss Smith?"

With both hands, she pushed his chest until *he* had to take a step back. "I will not cower to your attempts of intimidation." She rested her white-gloved hands on the hips of her blue gown whose silkiness and black lace trim made Miss Smith's calico appear dowdier than it was. "Yes, I intended to marry Hattie to the esteemed headmaster. That he has married another woman is rather an unfortunate complication, which I cannot alter. I shall now have to find another suitable man for my protégé."

"Joe Martinez is more than suitable," he reminded her.

Her mouth gaped for a moment. "What's the point of my *improving* Hattie if she's only going to be a farmer's wife?" she asked yet gave him not time to answer. "My first trip outside of Austin will not be to a beet farm. I don't even like beets!"

Noah groaned. "You wouldn't be marrying Martinez. Miss Smith would."

"I thought you, of all men, would have the sense not to believe a woman is so desperate to marry that she will marry anybody who asks her. Nor is a woman obligated to marry a man because he finds her figure appealing or because he writes a tolerable letter."

"He loves her!"

She rolled her eyes, a silent indictment of her belief that love was a necessary cornerstone for a marriage. "Hattie's beauty and kind disposition makes her a desirable match for someone better than a lowly beet farmer whose father fought in Santa Anna's army during battles at the Alamo and San Jacinto. His father killed good men who were defending Texas's right to be free from tyranny."

She sounded like a politician.

"Joe is as much a native Texan as we are," he countered.

"Yet that Hattie grew up in a Christian orphanage is a negative in your eyes, while Mr. Martinez's disrespectable ancestry is insignificant," she said in a near shout. "How is that fair?"

"Martinez is a taxpayer, a contributing member to society," he argued. "Miss Smith is an unwanted child, likely from one of the prostitutes outside of town. Were it not for the compassion of Mrs. Collins and generosity of an anonymous benefactor, Hattie would have left the orphanage for a life of—"

"Don't say it," she warned.

He didn't.

"Why do you assume the worst of her birth?"

"There is no evidence to assume the best."

She squared her shoulders. "Unlike you, I prefer to focus on the best in people, something I instruct Hattie to do."

"Yet you ignore Joe Martinez's best qualities."

"I do not ignore what is not there."

Noah stared at her in disbelief. "He's a gentleman, and you know it."

"He's a beet farmer," she retorted.

"An excellent beet farmer!"

"Why is it I am the only person you lose your temper with?"

Noah raked his hand through his hair. "Because you are the only one I know who refuses to admit when you've made a mistake."

She didn't wince, flinch, or shed a tear in response to his gruff manner. Doing so would show she was intimidated by him, or at the very least distressed at arguing with him. He knew her too well to know she believed her actions—and views—were in Miss Smith's best interests. He could always count on Emmeline to be honest with him, even if he had to prod the honesty out of her.

She looked at him, her heavily lashed eyes capturing his full attention. Her eyes were the same dark brown with gold flecks as the seal brown quarter-horse he'd given Hank for his eighth birthday. She was a sight when riled up. Her eyes sparkled. Her cheeks boasted a rosy glow. He could feel himself being reeled in again. He'd apologize for losing his temper with her, and all would be right again between them. Except...her thinking-she-knew-what-was-best had hurt someone—Joe Martinez... and Miss Smith, even if Miss Smith wasn't aware of it yet. Noah knew what being in love felt like, even though it'd been years since he'd been in love. He could remember the desperation he'd felt and the heartache and anger when his proposal had been rejected before he could even voice it. That same hurt was what he'd seen in Martinez's eyes when he showed Noah Miss Smith's response to his proposal.

The man had looked crushed.

Love did that to a person.

Noah looked to the crystal chandelier hanging in the center of his recently remodeled office. He'd allowed Emmeline, as his birthday gift to her, to have it installed for no practical—no sensible—purpose other than she thought it was pretty. Emmeline was as obsessed with sharing pretty things as she was with collecting them—Miss Smith included. Men didn't need pretty things. If it weren't a waste of money, he'd have his office restored to the rugged simplicity it had been prior to Emmeline's intervention.

This time Emmeline wasn't getting what she wanted.

Noah owed that much to Martinez.

"Em," he said as calmly as he could muster, "you will have Miss Smith tell Martinez she's reconsidered his proposal and accepts."

Emmeline stared up at him with the familiar, wide-eyed *that's the most ridiculous thing I've ever heard* stare. "Why?"

"Because it would show good sense."

"In me?"

"In her." He let out a sigh. "Good sense is the quality men most value in a wife. I wish you would teach *that* to Miss Smith." *And demonstrate it more in your own life.*

"Good sense?" She laughed, yet when she spoke again, her voice held a bitter edge. "Most men would be quite content to have a wife as striking and personable as Hattie.

"Men of sense do not want silly wives."

Her eyes flickered heavenward. "I can only fathom that Mr. Belton was coerced into marrying someone else."

"You actually think that?"

She nodded.

Noah shook his head. "You were wrong to think Belton would have married Miss Smith. He is obsessed with marrying for money. That's why he wanted to marry you."

"He never expressed interest in me," she said with an impressive amount of revulsion in her tone.

"Why do you think he's been paying attendance on Miss Smith?"

"She'd garnered his affections," Emmeline answered. "I noticed how he looked at her."

Noah groaned. He, too, had seen how Belton looked at Miss Smith. What the man wanted her for was more carnal than matrimonial. Belton wasn't the only man Noah had seen looking at Miss Smith that way. For her protection, she needed to marry quickly. Best to a man who loved and could protect her.

Noah spoke gently. "Belton paid attendance on Miss Smith in order to spend time with you."

She stared at him blankly.

Noah stared back. He couldn't seem to stop. That look of naiveté in her eyes held his attention. Emmeline had no idea the lure she was to a man who wanted not only a beautiful wife, but a rich one as well.

"Have you forgotten how much you stand to inherit?" he asked.

Emmeline stepped forward. "Why must you make everything about me?"

"You always make things about you!"

She whirled around and walked back to his desk with the calm of one strolling in the park. She returned the unused silverware and his plate with the two scones into her basket, before removing a sealed mason jar of strawberry lemonade. She sat it on his desk. She turned to face him, gripping the basket's handles with both hands.

They stared at each other a long, silent moment.

Noah waited. Emmeline's silence was nothing but a momentary reprieve for her to collect her thoughts and reform her argument. God had blessed Emmeline with beauty, quick-wittedness, and a happy temperament. Her father's keen mind for investing ensured her a life of affluence. She was used to doing what she liked, when she liked, and with whom she liked. Save for the death of her mother a decade ago, Noah couldn't think of anything in Emmeline's life that hadn't gone in her favor. Until now. Until Mr. Cornelius Belton, headmaster of the Austen Boys' Academy, married a woman not of Emmeline's choosing.

"Share your thoughts," he said. "I want to hear them." Heaven help him, he actually did.

Emmeline gave him a cat-with-cream smile. "I will admit Joe Martinez, despite his unfortunate paternal relations, can hold his own in a conversation and dotes on his mother and sister. The proposal letter he wrote Hattie was, in fact, the most impressive words I have ever seen put to paper. All of which I find quite admirable."

Having read the letter himself, Noah agreed.

"However," Emmeline said walking to him, "men, in their courtship of women, will speak the most grandiose words they believe a woman desires to hear because they believe a woman cares more for flattery than with receiving honest words of love, may they be simple or even stumbling. Love, should it be real, must be more than that which one writes or speaks."

Noah blinked in stunned shock at her admission. "You believe Martinez's words were *too* eloquent to be sincere?"

"Yes." Without looking at him, she softly added, "Don't forget tonight we are playing cards with the Sharps. Dinner at six. Captain Sharp is bringing smoked ribs. Miss Tarleton—Mrs. Sharp—will be bringing little Travis." She opened his office door.

He waited for the reminder that her former governess and Captain Sharp would not be married were it not for her *gift*, which even the Sharps would acknowledge since they named their son in her honor.

Instead, she walked away.

Something he'd never heard before in Em's voice kept him from responding—bitterness. Since he could remember, he'd never heard any direct or indirect criticism of Emmeline from anyone in Austin. Everyone loved her. Everyone. She lived in the largest home in Austin, if one could call Hotel Brunswick a home. She knew almost everyone in town. Since Austen Abbey's founding two years ago, Emmeline had chosen it, of all the schools in the area, on which to bestow the largest amount of her love, finances, and support. Noah knew her actions were not motivated out of vanity or need for acclamation. Being involved in the lives of the young women attending the Abbey filled the void caused by her sister's marriage and subsequent move to College Station. She'd taken on a protégé to replace the absence of her governess, Miss Tarleton, who in the last three years had been more of a paid companion than an actual governess.

Yet she was routinely praised by the girls. By instructors. By grateful parents. Emmeline was *always* praised. Enough to make any person weary and suspicious.

Especially one with as calculating a nature as Emmeline had.

Noah swiveled around in time to see her disappear down the stairs and out of sight. He confronted her when she was wrong because he cared about her. She had to know that.

Noah took off running to the marble staircase, determined not to let her leave until she knew he only wanted the best for her. He descended two steps at a time until he reached the bottom, turned the corner, and ran right smack into Brandon Tabor.

"A bit undignified for a bank president," Brandon remarked in the soft, raspy voice of his as Noah steadied them both and noted Tabor wore a tan suit instead of his usual ranch foreman attire. With the month's continued warm weather, Brandon's scarred and sensitive-to-the-cold right hip didn't require the former Texas Ranger to use a cane.

"Em and I had words," he answered.

Brandon nodded as if he wasn't surprised to hear Noah's admission. "What did Austin's Cheery Tornado do to annoy you this time?"

Noah looked over the leaner man's shoulder to the bank's lobby.

Emmeline and Miss Smith exchanged a lengthy hug before Emmeline spoke to her taller yet less dignified companion. He expected Em, though he wasn't sure why, to look not quite herself. For her posture to be not quite perfect. For her to look vulnerable. For her to glance his way and need him to make thing right between them, and he would, because he enjoyed making her happy.

She didn't look his way. She gave her attention to the mayor's curly-blond sons.

"Emmeline's the reason Miss Smith refused Martinez," Noah replied in a hard, unbending voice.

Brandon gave him a quizzical look then turned to face the marble-floored lobby. "Does Martinez know?"

Noah shook his head. Nor would he share the information and give the Martinez family any reason to think ill of Emmeline. Unless Noah could guilt her in to admission of wrong, she would never make things right.

"You have to admit," Brandon remarked, "Emmeline Travis is easy on the eyes."

"Too easy," Noah muttered. Yet he wasn't amused.

Emmeline was a vision of loveliness. Since his parents' deaths four years ago, every conversation they'd had couldn't begin until he'd taken a good five minutes to appreciate the flecks of gold in her dark eyes, the ease with which she smiled, the exuberance she had for including him in her thoughts and feelings. Truth was—he flat out loved to look at her. Even when she spouted such rubbish as her "gift" to recognize true love, she amused him. He enjoyed her playfulness, wit, optimism, and generosity to and concern for others. Emmeline Travis was a clever girl...who needed to keep her mind distracted from meddling in the real and imaginative affairs of others.

"For all of her beauty," he added, "I'm thankful she has no obsession with it."

"Will you look at the Hampton twins?" Brandon said in disgust.

Noah did. The pair weren't even trying to hide their lustful glances at Emmeline and her protégé. Course, were the ladies dressed like trail-worn cowboys, they'd still attract stares. Miss Smith because of her curves. Emmeline because of the contrast between her porcelain skin and auburn hair...and that infectious smile and laugh and her ability to charm even the most cantankerous of characters. She had a definite sensuality in her walk, too. He'd seen other men notice. But none had publically ogled her as the twins were doing now.

He took a step forward then, remembering why Brandon was at the bank, stopped. "They'd be fools to try anything."

Brandon didn't look convinced any more than Noah felt. "If she were my woman, no man in Austin would be—"

"Emmeline can take care of herself," Noah groused. "She knows how to use a gun and wears a knife I gave her strapped to her right calf."

"*Hmmph*," Brandon muttered. "She doesn't seem to notice the way others admire her."

To Noah's delight, one of the twins looked his direction. He scowled. The twin then elbowed his brother, whose attention immediately shifted away from Emmeline's chest.

Emmeline waved good-bye to the pair. The twins nodded. Without looking in Noah's direction, she grabbed her protégé's arm and resumed her path to the bank's entrance.

Noah moved to the left so his friend could use the hand-rail as they climbed the stairs.

"Emmeline's vanity lies in another way," he said, taking slow steps up to the second floor for Brandon's benefit. "She often mistakes the meanings of others' actions and greatly over-estimates her matchmaking ability."

"Then I *shouldn't* ask for her aid in finding a wife?" Brandon said with a grin. Or at least Noah thought it was a grin underneath his heavy mustache.

One day Noah might find amusement in the situation. He didn't now.

"Em is blind to the dangers of meddling in others' lives, so don't even hint to her you're interested in..." Without missing a step, Noah stopped climbing and grabbed Brandon's elbow. He stared at the man who'd been his friend since their days at Baylor University. "*Are* you interested in marrying again?"

Brandon paused, let out a sigh, and then continued up the steps. "Noah, as long as I can read my Bible and walk on my own, I'm content."

Noah knew what he'd heard. Knew Brandon Tabor never lied. Yet he also knew what he'd seen flicker in the widower's green eyes in the split-second before he'd answered—loneliness. Despite Brandon's occasional gripes about "being old," he wasn't. Nor was he a cripple. But as long as Brandon saw himself as too much of a burden for a wife to have, then single would he remain. Yet there had been that flicker of loneliness. Noah hadn't mistaken seeing it. What Brandon needed was a woman to love him. To remind him he was worth being loved.

Feeling a tug at the corner of his mouth, Noah hurried up the stairs.

They reached the landing and crossed the wooden floor to enter Noah's carpeted office. While Brandon limped over to one of the chairs near the desk, Noah closed the office door to give them privacy while discussing Mattie McDermott's loan request.

"I had thought," Noah said as he walked to his desk, "that experiencing a heart break herself would cure Emmeline of her matchmaking-gift delusion." He sat and, with forearms resting on his desk, leaned forward and focused on Brandon's rugged face. "A better cure is marriage. Once she has a husband to entertain, she won't have time to think of meddling in others' lives."

Brandon nodded as if that made sense.

Encouraged by the response, Noah said, "Would you court her?"

Brandon's eyes widened. His skin-tone took on a decidedly green cast. "Me? I could have sworn..."

"Sworn what?"

"I, uhh..." Brandon shifted awkwardly in his chair. "That *you'd* eventually marry her."

Noah felt his own eyes widen. "Me?"

Brandon nodded.

Noah frowned at that. "Why would I want to marry Emmeline? I've known her since I was ten and she was a screeching newborn."

"Have you *looked* at her since then?"

Of course he looked at her. Noah saw her every day. After he moved out of the Whitley mansion three years ago and took a room in Hotel Brunswick to give his brother and her sister privacy after the wedding, sharing breakfast, dinner, and holidays with the Travises in their expansive private apartments in the hotel had seemed the thing to do since they were all now family. He could have moved back home after John and Isabelle moved to College Station, but staying at the hotel seemed more convenient. And with Martinez needing somewhere to stay when he came into Austin to see his mother and sister at the Abbey, Noah hated to cease providing the Martinezes a house when the Abbey was out of session during the summer.

Most men would be quite content to have a wife as striking and personable as Hattie.

Most men would be quite content to have a wife as striking and personable as Emmeline. Until she began her meddling and matching and manipulating. That would drive any man insane. It'd drive Noah insane.

Noah broke the silence, a strange weight pressing on his chest. "Would you marry a woman solely because you loved to look at her?"

"No." Brandon's answer came quick. "How a woman hooks a man is how she will keep him. Beauty fades, but a woman who loves God and loves others grows lovelier with every passing day." Brandon paused, a

V deepening between his brows. "Emmeline Travis is more than a pretty face, yet she's never had a suitor. Ever wonder why that is?"

Noah ignored the question. "I'm content with how things are between me and Emmeline. No sense changing a good thing."

Brandon looked at him curiously. "If you aren't going to pursue the woman, then you need to stop coiling at her feet like a rattler warning others away."

That stung his pride. Noah had been accused of many things but never of keeping Emmeline from marrying. He wanted her to be happy. If she wanted to marry, he would support her. Help if needed. He drew the line, though, at Garrison Churchill. That man was the snake.

Noah grabbed the loan contract he'd spent the morning double-checking the numbers on. "Everything is in order. Have Mrs. McDermott sign these, and I'll have the money transferred to her account on Monday." He offered the papers to Brandon.

Only Brandon didn't take them. "Emmeline isn't your sister."

"What does that have to do with anything?"

The corner of Brandon's mouth eased up. "Didn't want you thinking of her as a younger sibling who needs an older sibling's protection like you treat your brother."

Noah hadn't taken John into his confidence in years, not since his brother had married Emmeline's sister, Isabelle. Nor had he ever had long, serious talks with Isabelle like he had with Emmeline. Neither John nor Isabelle understood him like Em did. She was as much his confidant as her father was. When something troubled him, she was the one he sought out to help him gain perspective or to soothe his frustration. They always spoke freely with each other. He valued her womanly insight. He loved how she made him laugh.

"I support Emmeline as I do all my friends," Noah said with a smile, although he was still accountably irked at the implication Emmeline had no suitors because of his interference. "Now about this loan..."

Brandon regarded him carefully. Whatever he saw must have convinced him to change the subject. "About the loan...I need you to deny it."

Noah leaned back in his chair. "Why?"

"Taking out a loan she doesn't need will put the ranch at the mercy of her brother. The older Mattie gets, the less wary she is of her brother's schemes." He shook his head. "Unlike her, I don't trust him."

"She's fifty-three years old. If it's what she wants—"

"No," Brandon grumbled. "I've agonized over this in prayer. This is the only answer I have from God."

"She'll go to another bank," Noah put in.

"You're the only banker she trusts." Brandon leaned forward in his seat, elbows on knees. "Mattie McDermott's become family to me. When you love someone, Noah, wouldn't you do all you could to stop her from ruining her life?"

Noah nodded.

"Help me stop her."

Three

You need not be afraid of unwholesome preserves here.
~ Jane Austen, *Emma*

New mission, same objective: to find Hattie a husband.

Emmeline gripped one of Hattie's ungloved hands, pulling her close, as they stepped outside the bank onto Pecan Street. They walked to the nearby intersection. Pausing, they waited for a lull between the various horses, buggies, wagons, bicycles, and pedestrians. Usually when circumstances vexed her, Emmeline found solace perusing the merchandise of Bennet's Boutique. This moment, of all moments, called for shopping.

"There is no cause to fret, Hattie." Emmeline tightened her grip on the basket and Hattie as they finally crossed Pecan to head north up Congress. She glanced at Hattie and noted the desolate expression. Emmeline felt terrible. Mr. Belton's character was clearly duplicitous. To run off and marry while having spent a month courting another woman...well, he was an actor of the highest caliber and lowest character.

"Mr. Belton's marriage is a minor set-back," she remarked. "I shall find you a suitable husband."

"How I wish I had your confidence." Hattie's tone edged on wailing.

"Now, now, we must stay optimistic." Emmeline had never seen anyone this desolate. Recognizing her protégé's nearness to the precipice of despair, she gave Hattie's hand an encouraging shake. "In times of woe, it is best to remember our successes, which breed confidence for future endeavors. Ever since the day Miss Tarleton and I dashed inside the livery because of the rain, and Captain Sharp gallantly fetched two umbrellas for us to use, I planned their union. Five months later it occurred. Now it is your turn."

Hattie sniffed. She blinked at the water in her eyes.

"Go on," Emmeline prodded.

Hattie released a ragged breath. "Uhh... Well..." She smiled somewhat. "As you also orchestrated Mr. Whitley's brother, John, marrying your sister, Isabelle."

Emmeline couldn't help smiling over Hattie's keen memory. While her protégé could not claim the quickest of wits, neither was she dense, as Emmeline was sure Noah thought her to be. "Yes, and when such success has blessed me twice," she told her, "you can be sure I shall not leave off matchmaking after one minor set-back."

"Oh, Miss Travis, what would I do without you?"

Emmeline smiled and squeezed Hattie's hand. A better day was always on the horizon. "It is such happiness when good people get together," she instructed, "and they always do. Have faith, Hattie."

"Yes, Miss Travis."

They continued down the street, acknowledging those they passed. Once they reached Bois de Arc Street, they turned left then immediately entered the first shop. Bennet's Boutique was Austin's premier woolen-draper, linen-draper, and haberdashery, all united. If one was fortunate to visit on the right day, batches of Mrs. Bennet's prize-winning nut brittle were available for purchase, and her adorable daughter, Eva, would insist on playing hide-and-seek.

Emmeline glanced down the counter. To her chagrin, Bennet's had no nut brittle and no three-year-olds to be seen. She acknowledged Mr. Bennet. "Good afternoon, sir. Any—"

"Oh, Miss Travis, new ribbons!" exclaimed Hattie, who was easily tempted by what first caught her eyes—and was swayed to buy by half a word regardless if she needed the item. She selected a purple ribbon. Held the spool up for Emmeline to see. "This is perfect to wear for the ball."

Emmeline cringed. She set her basket on the counter then walked to the ribbon display. "As lovely a purple as this is, it will still never match the yellow pattern of your gown." She deftly removed the ribbon spool from Hattie's clutches and replaced it with an ivory one. "The colors one wears should blend, not clash."

Hattie frowned. "I like purple."

Emmeline couldn't help but admire a woman who knew what she

liked. "Then buy it to wear with a purple dress. Buy the ivory to wear to the ball."

"That's perfect! Oh but..." Hattie's smile fell, shoulders slumped. "I don't own a purple dress."

"Then don't buy the purple ribbon," Emmeline answered with a smile. She laid the spool of purple ribbon on the display rack. "You do, however, have a yellow dress which would look lovely with ivory ribbon in your hair."

Hattie glanced longingly at the ribbon display. "But I like the purple ribbon."

Emmeline gripped her protégé's shoulders and turned her away from the ribbons. "Hattie, look at me." *And not at what tempts you.* "If you wanted plain muslin, would you look at printed fabrics?"

Hattie's gaze settled on Emmeline, a flicker of uncertainty in their blue depths. When she started to nod, Emmeline shook her head, which caused Hattie to follow suit. "I would only look at muslin. Plain muslin."

"Correct," Emmeline replied. "Now with that in mind, would it be wise to purchase purple ribbon when you have nothing to wear it with?"

"It wouldn't. But, Miss Travis, don't you think the purple is pretty?"

"Miss Smith," Mr. Bennet said, stepping forward, "several new calicos arrived yesterday, including a purple one with ivory flowers. You could were either ribbon with a gown of it."

"Oh!" Hattie scooped up the purple ribbon spool and handed him it and the ivory one. "Then I shall take the calico, two lengths of white muslin for Mrs. Collins, and one length each of these ribbons."

He nodded, his grin broad. "Would you like your goods sent to the Abbey? My delivery boy has several other orders to take there today."

"Yes—no—yes," Hattie rushed out. "My gown for the ball is with Miss Travis's. To Hotel Brunswick, if you please. But—Mrs. Collins needs the muslin immediately and my pattern gown is at the Abbey. You could make it two parcels, could you not? Oh, three, for I'd like to take the ribbon myself."

"Hattie," Emmeline cautioned, her patience waning, "is it worthwhile to impose upon the delivery boy the trouble of making two deliveries?"

"I suppose not." Hattie nipped at her lower lip. "Well, if you please, send it—oh, I don't know." Her brow furrowed most unbecomingly. "Miss Travis, what do you advise?"

Emmeline patted Hattie's hand. "I advise you not give another thought to the subject." She turned her attention to Mr. Bennet. "All to

Austen Abbey, please."

After a mental note about giving Hattie lessons on being more decisive and prudent, Emmeline then checked on buying replacement buttons for Noah's formal frock suit. Even though she knew he wouldn't dance, she preferred he purchase something new to wear to the Saint Valentine's Ball, but, unlike with Hattie, getting Noah to part with his money was easier if one were asking him for a loan or to donate to a mission cause or to help a widow in need.

"Bankers," she muttered under her breath.

Five minutes later, with buttons bought, Emmeline perused the new fabric arrival.

Ring-a-ling came the door bells. The boutique's door then jingled close.

Emmeline peeked around the rack of summer linens. She gasped. Oh dear. Inside, not three yards from where she stood, walked none other than Joe Martinez and his lovely sister, Vicente, who wore a beautiful wine-colored gown, a waterfall of ruffles down her bustle. Emmeline adored Vicente, who never said a critical word about the books chosen for reading by the book club. Even when her dislike of the novel was evident, she always finished the book, never criticized the person who'd selected it to be read, and contributed to the conversation—things Emmeline found quite admirable. That, and the fact Vicente never seemed resentful over being a cook at the Abbey and not a student. Vicente was destined to be Emmeline's next protégé.

What business, though, could a beet farmer have in Bennet's?

Although Mr. Martinez wore no coat, the charcoal-striped trousers and matching vest he wore over a perfectly pressed white shirt fit his form almost as well as Noah's clothes fit his. Almost. Joe Martinez's shoulders and chest were too brawny. Too elemental. His nose too large, too crooked. He had none of Noah's elegance. He probably came home from the fields smelling of sweat and dirt.

She grimaced, muttering "*ick*" under her breath. He would never do for the refined lady her protégé had become. Hattie, no one could deny, was merely too beautiful for Joe Martinez. That Noah could think otherwise...

Mr. Martinez walked directly to Mr. Bennet. Vicente smiled then waved at someone outside of Emmeline's line of sight. She walked to the left.

Emmeline froze. *Hattie!*

"Joe," Vicente called out, "look who's here!"

Mr. Martinez stopped talking to Mr. Bennet and turned around. For a second, his heavy black eyebrows came down ever-so-slightly. He looked...devastated. He removed his black Stetson. Held it to his chest. Yet he didn't move a step away from the counter. "Miss Smith," he said, his voice all polite and friendly, "fancy meeting you at Bennet's."

"Uhh, hello," Hattie answered, yet Emmeline still couldn't see her protégé.

Vicente waved at her brother to approach. "Don't just stand there."

Mr. Martinez walked slowly toward his sister, as if he wasn't sure what he should do, as if he was nervous about conversing with Hattie.

Vicente wrapped her arm around her brother's. Emmeline wouldn't be surprised if it were to keep him from fleeing. "Momma mentioned this morning after breakfast how she rarely sees you anymore since you've become Miss Travis's paid companion. When you didn't visit her in the kitchen after breakfast, she wondered if she had done something to offend you."

Emmeline eased a bit more around the stacks of fabric. Hattie and the Martinezes were standing in a close circle, yet Hattie's gaze was only on Vicente.

"I thought"—Hattie twisted her hands together—"she wouldn't want to see me anymore after I...umm..." She glanced at Mr. Martinez. Her cheeks colored pink. "I'm sorry, Vicente, I should go. Uhh, good day, Mr. Martinez." She started toward Emmeline, and Vicente immediately nudged her brother. He hurried after Hattie.

Emmeline backed farther down the aisle. She immediately focused on a bolt of brown twill, fingering it as if she were seriously considering buying some.

"Will you be attending the Saint Valentine's Ball?" came Mr. Martinez's deep voice.

Hattie stopped, turned around, and nodded. "With Miss Travis."

From the corner of her eye, Emmeline could see Hattie but not Mr. Martinez—which meant Mr. Martinez couldn't see her. She breathed a sigh of relief.

"She does a fine job organizing social events," Hattie added.

"Yes, she does," Mr. Martinez answered with not the least bit of mocking in his tone. "You are blessed to have Miss Travis mentor you." He shifted his stance. "Mrs. Collins asked me to attend the ball, to dance with her students. She is in great need of male attendees. Vicente's been giving me lessons. Might I impose on you for a dance?"

"Oh, I don't know. I'm supposed to...umm, well, Miss Travis...uhh—yes." She nipped at her bottom lip. Her gaze lowered, and she repeated a little more softly, "Yes, you may."

"Good. *Good*," he said with a bit more emphasis and a bright smile.

Emmeline felt her mouth gape open. Not only did Joe Martinez have perfectly aligned white teeth, but how could she have ever thought him unattractive? Because she'd never seen him smile before. Could he actually be in love with Hattie?

He nervously twisted his hat. "I need to see about my suit. It's been a pleasure, Miss Smith." He walked off.

Hattie hurried down the aisle to Emmeline. As she touched the bolt of gray tweed next to the brown bolt Emmeline was still fingering, her hands shook.

Emmeline covered Hattie's hand with her own.

"His behavior was quite gentlemanly, wasn't it?" Hattie whispered, meeting Emmeline's gaze.

"It was," she answered in all honesty.

"Dear me! I shouldn't have agreed to a dance, should I?"

Emmeline smiled as best she could. Hattie was one of those, she feared, who, having once begun, would always be in love. The poor girl! If Mr. Martinez weren't a beet farmer... If his father hadn't served in Santa Anna's army and murdered many brave Texans at the Alamo and San Jacinto... If love were actually enough to base a marriage on... Emmeline's chest ached. As much as she wished to change her thinking about Mr. Martinez—and even about love—doing so would only give Noah one more reason to gloat about his being right and her being wrong. Again.

Love wasn't necessary to begin a successful marriage. Her parents had proven that. Love did not lead to a life of prosperity and happiness. Garrison Churchill's parents had proven that. As had Captain Sharp, who had made a fortune in the years following his wife's death. He now owned a mansion in Austin and the largest dairy farm in all of Texas. Captain Sharp hadn't seemed interested in marrying again until Emmeline intervened. Were it not for her insight, Captain Sharp would have remained a lonely bachelor and Miss Tarleton a lonely governess, both eventually dying alone. Yet now they had a son born last month. For a man of forty-six years, Captain Sharp couldn't be more delighted to be a father.

Were it not for Mr. Belton's rash wedding to a woman who could clearly not be as suitable to him as Hattie, he and Hattie could be married and working on having their own babe.

Impudent man!

"It's only one dance," Hattie mused, breaking into Emmeline's thoughts.

Emmeline refocused her attention on her troubled protégé. She gave Hattie's hand a consoling pat. "What's done is done. We will make the best of it, for propriety's sake."

Hattie nodded. "You are correct, as always."

"I've never seen such pretty tweeds," Emmeline said to distract Hattie.

Hattie perused the fabrics, touching each one, sighing repeatedly. Every so often, she glanced toward the counter. Her cheeks blushed most becomingly. And Emmeline thought all the harder of who she could match Hattie with. Sadly, Mr. Belton was the best of the gentleman lot here in Austin. The only other bachelor of education and character whom she could endorse was Brandon Tabor, the former Texas Ranger and Noah's friend. Yet even he wasn't suitable for Hattie. He lived on a ranch miles and miles outside of Austen. Miles from civilization. Miles.

He would never do either.

Oh, how she wished to raise Hattie above the level of her birth! To introduce her to a world beyond orphanages, beet farmers, and living on the charity of others. But what if—

The thought struck, and Emmeline frowned. What if Hattie was well suited to becoming a farmer's wife?

He loves her.

Or so Noah had insisted. If Joe Martinez had sincere affection for Hattie, would that not be in Hattie's benefit? Possibly. Yet Hattie could not truly know the sincerity of her feelings for Mr. Martinez when she had experienced little beyond the walls of the orphanage and of Austen Abbey. The course of true love could never run smooth when a lady's marital options were so limited by geography. Perhaps the man most suited for Hattie lived in Waco or Houston or even as far away as—inconceivable as it may be—Shreveport.

The only way to know would be to travel.

It wasn't as if Emmeline could go from town to town interviewing eligible bachelors and observing how they interacted with Hattie...could she? This was a good excuse as any for a reason to travel beyond the city limits. She'd read Mrs. Livingston's journals. Females could travel un-accosted.

The shop door opened with a *ring-a-ling-a-ling*. It jingled a second time as the door closed. A clock struck the top of the hour. Noon.

Emmeline gasped. Hank! She'd forgotten about him.

"Come," Emmeline said, grabbing Hattie's hand from a bolt of red wool and pulling her to the register, "we need to get on to the Abbey."

"Why?"

"Hank's there."

Hattie gave Emmeline a blank look. "But I thought Mrs. Collins forbade him from setting foot on Abbey grounds."

Emmeline sighed. "Noah's precocious cousin has decided he's in love with Eliza Branch." She snatched her basket off the counter. "I fear his love for her will not dampen his love for mischief."

Hattie quickly paid for her goods.

They exited Bennet's. As they stood on the bricked walk near the gas street lamp, waiting for traffic to pass, Emmeline pondered, frowned, and gripped her basket tight, but she could think of nothing to confirm which city she should visit first in hopes of finding a suitable mate for Hattie. She would begin by visiting a church to find a God-fearing man. But which one?

"I wish I could ask Noah," she said, feeling oddly weary.

Hattie looked at Emmeline. "Ask Mr. Whitley what?"

"Nothing, for Noah's words are as predictable as his actions." A wiser course was asking the Lord for guidance. Emmeline crossed the street and headed in the direction of Austen Abbey. "Unlike me, he is too set in his ways. Noah doesn't care for change. He's stubborn and resistant."

They fell into mutual silence for some minutes, leaving Emmeline to enjoy the soft breeze as she acknowledged the many Austinites who wished her a good day.

Until Hattie broke the silence with, "I'm surprised, Miss Travis, that you're not married."

Emmeline glanced at Hattie. What an odd comment. She shifted her basket to her other arm. "Since I have yet to meet a man superior to any I've met thus far, frankly, I doubt I shall *ever* marry."

Hattie's eyes widened in surprise. "Never marry? *Ever?*" Her head shook, voice filled with concern. "Every woman dreams of getting married. You must have, I just know it."

Emmeline ignored the comment. If she had dreamed of marriage when she was younger, she couldn't remember. During all the years Miss

Tarleton had been her governess, they had never discussed marriage or any dreams of a husband and children that Emmeline had had. Nor had Miss Tarleton encouraged her to dream.

Emmeline stayed silent as they crossed the north-south intersection, waited for the mule-drawn streetcar to pass, and then crossed the east-west intersection. Even though they were two blocks away, it was impossible not to notice the round turret and stately central tower in the distance. While the three-story school wasn't as stately a building as her father's hotel, she considered it one of Austin's most eclectic landmarks. Dormers. Towers with decorative metal finials. Second-floor balconies. Red brick and cream limestone.

What girl would not want to attend finishing school there?

After waving at more passing Austinites, she finally said, "I have none of the usual inducements of a woman *to* marry."

"What about love?" Hattie blurted.

Emmeline muttered *hmmph* under her breath. Love—she'd rather forgotten about that. "Were I to fall in love," she said as she weighed the possibility, probability, and desirability of love interfering with her perfectly laid-out future, "I suppose it would be a different matter altogether." She shrugged. "But I have never been in love, nor do I think I shall ever be." Truly after seeing Hattie suffer the symptoms and sufferings of love, she couldn't see why anyone held falling in love with such high repute.

They passed under an overhanging tree.

Hattie's head wagged back and forth for a good long minute. "I don't know what to say," she muttered, head still wagging. "Truly, Miss Travis, I've never heard anything so odd. So very *odd.*"

She should be offended by Hattie's response. She should.

Only something shifted within Emmeline. She felt...left out. Like everyone understood the passion, power, and bliss of all that love was—except her. But she was a realist. She knew better than to waste time dreaming for what she didn't have, because doing so only stirred up discontentment. Let it never be said Emmeline LeNoir Travis was dissatisfied with her life. She wasn't. She had no reason to be. She was blessed with so many things and in so many ways that to feel anything less than content had to be wrong. Perhaps even a sin.

Emmeline swung the basket as she walked down the gravel sidewalk.

"Well, I don't think it's odd," she argued, finding comfort in the rightness of her opinion. "I have everything I wish for in our suites at the hotel. I live in the most beautiful town in the best state in the Union. I do not desire employment or need opportunity to increase my wealth."

Hattie stared at her as if she were an imbecile. "Don't you want babies?"

"I have two adorable nephews on which to dote at my leisure, and when they are not-so-adorable," Emmeline added with a laugh, "I can give them back to their mother."

"But...but..." Hattie released a loud sigh. Her head wagged again. "I do not know what to think."

Emmeline smiled. "Besides, I doubt I could ever be as beloved, as needed, as first, or as always right in any man's eyes as I am in my father's."

Hattie appeared to consider her words. "You will become a disagreeable old maid like Miss Gates," she said, her tone matter-of-fact. No, more than that. Confident. Gone was any of uncertainly of what to think or deference to Emmeline's opinion. She looked at Emmeline in disbelief. "I cannot think of a more dreadful fate. She's pitiable. You must agree."

Emmeline restrained the impulse to laugh at Hattie's naiveté. "A single woman of good fortune is always respectable. Always. Poverty alone is what makes celibacy contemptible to a society which decries that a single woman, with little income, must be a *disagreeable old maid*." Spying the entrance to Abbey grounds at the end of the block, she quickly added, "I know poverty can often make a man or a woman bitter and contemptuous to those with wealth, but while Miss Gates can be too good natured and too silly at times, poverty has not hardened her heart. If she had only a dollar to her name, I am convinced, she'd give away seventy-five cents to someone else in need. No child is afraid of her. She spends more time than anyone I know in prayer. I find much about her to be admirable."

Hattie's brow furrowed in a most unbecoming manner. She stopped at the entrance to the Austen Abbey grounds and turned to Emmeline, her face shaded somewhat by the massive oak's overhanging yet naked branches, the very tree Hank claimed was his personal castle.

"Still, Miss Travis, I refuse to believe you will never marry. Dear me!" she exclaimed in additional horror as if Emmeline's not marrying was a fate worse than death. "What shall you *do* when you are old?"

"Anything and everything."

Hattie didn't look convinced.

"If I draw less, I shall read more. If I give up music, I shall take up needlework."

"You do host exceptional parties," Hattie put in.

"When there isn't a party to plan, I shall adopt another charity to aid."

Clunk. Then after a series of *dink, dink, dinks*, a walnut dropped out of the tree and landed at the base only inches from where Emmeline stood. Hank used walnuts in his sling.

She looked up the moment Hattie did.

There, several gnarled branches overhead, was Frank Mallory's Norwegian cat, Thor, not Hank as she'd feared. The cat's variegated long gray hair rose on all sides like that of a porcupine. Hissing, it shifted on the branch that bent under its hefty weight. Then, suddenly—

Clunk. Hiss. Dink, dink, dink.

Clunk. Hiss. Dink, dink, dink.

Clunk. Yowl. Dink, dink, dink.

The cantankerous feline—Emmeline swore he needed to have his diet monitored—hissed, swatted, wobbled, growled, shifted, turned, then fell...right down on Hattie's head. The more Hattie screamed, the more Thor clung to her head, the more Hattie ran in circles swatting at him, the more Thor yowled. Emmeline dropped her basket. She grabbed Hattie's flailing arms and yelled at her to stop, which only made Hattie cry and scream more.

"Thor, home!"

Thor immediately jumped to the ground and darted underneath the evergreen hedges lining the Abbey's perimeter.

Emmeline stopped wiping the blood off Hattie's neck and cheeks to look in the direction of the commanding voice. Her heart pounded in her chest. Her lungs grasped for air. Garrison here? Today? Truly, it was a dream come true. Yet—

Her mouth gaped as the ginger-haired man dismounted the palomino in the Abbey's bricked, circular front drive. She pressed her fingers against two large, bleeding scratches on Hattie's temple while Hattie continued to cry.

He smiled. "Hello, Emmeline."

Emmeline studied his black-suited form half-expecting him to be an apparition. In the last sixteen years since their mothers had died— since Garrison Churchill had left Austin to live with, and be adopted by, his maternal aunt in Waco—they'd exchanged letters every month. They visited once (usually), sometimes twice (rarely) a year when he returned to spend time with his father, Mr. Mallory, who was the jack-of-all-trades at the Abbey.

With his blue-gray eyes, artfully combed hair, and ever-ready smile, he was *very* good-looking, even more so than she remembered from dancing with him once at John and Isabelle's wedding three years ago.

"Is it *really* you?" she couldn't help asking as he stopped next to her and Hattie.

"It's me all right." He removed his riding gloves and stuck them in the V-neck of his tan waistcoat. "Let go of her." Once Emmeline did, pushing Hattie's blond curls back from her forehead, he examined her wounds and his smile faded. "I have never seen so lovely a face scarred so unfairly. Miss, do you live at the Abbey?"

Hattie nodded. Her eyes fluttered, and she fainted...right into Garrison's arms.

His twinkling gaze met Emmeline's. "Good to see you again, Emmy." Then he leaned close, kissed her cheek, and whispered, "Would you do me the favor and grab the Crawfield boy on the other side of the hedge?" He winked. "First, walk with me inside the gate so he doesn't know we're onto him."

Although she was readying to tear Hank life from limb, Emmeline nodded. She reclaimed her discarded basket.

As Garrison lifted Hattie in his arms, Emmeline stood frozen, transfixed, mesmerized by the way his coat molded perfectly to his shoulders. Her chest felt a bit hollow, her mouth dry, her eyes unable to look away. Garrison was sensible, quick-witted, and lively, had a well-bred ease of manner, was diligent with his correspondence, and she liked, indeed, everything about him.

Giving in to the smile she felt grow from her heart, Emmeline tilted her head because she thought she heard music. A symphony. Indeed, an angelic chorus.

It had never happened this way before, but she knew in that moment, she'd found the perfect match.

For Hattie!

Four

As to men and women, our opinions are sometimes very different; but with regard to these children, I observe we never disagree.
~ Jane Austen, *Emma*

Headmistress's Office
Jeannette C. Austen Academy for Young Ladies

Noah patiently sat in a tufted brown velvet chair across from Emmeline and Hank on the matching settee, as Hank had an extended "moment of reflection" on his actions. Emmeline's bloodied white gloves lay on the coffee table between them, her basket on the fancy green rug. He should be livid. Furious. Justifiably so at Hank's willful disobedience. Truth be told, Emmeline was enflamed enough for the both of them. Hank didn't need two angry substitute parents.

Hank sat as far to the right edge of the settee as he could. His left ear and cheek were smeared with blood—Miss Smith's blood from Emmeline's right glove, which Em had deftly pointed out when he questioned it. Served Hank right to be dragged by the ear into the Abbey and through the corridors to the headmistress's office. He wouldn't be surprised if Em had taken the long way through the three-story building.

Noah looked to Emmeline. She sat straight-backed in the middle of the settee, legs crossed at the ankles, hands primly resting on her lap. Her jaw set in a hard line, she was watching him, expecting him to deal with his young cousin in the appropriate manner, which—Noah's best guess—would be five months of extreme misery until his parents returned from their European tour. Emmeline would make an impressive prison guard or supreme overlord. She wore the same severe expression as Mrs. Collins's portrait of Queen Victoria.

He waited for her to speak.

Her lips pursed, just a touch, like they did when she was thinking—and Emmeline was *always* thinking. She sighed.

For as lovely as Emmeline was, she had the most remarkably ordinary set of lips. A bit too wide. A bit too narrow. Not the least bit noticeable to him until this moment. She'd yet to kiss a man; Noah knew this with certainty because Em had told him every eventful, embarrassing, and awkward moment in her life since she was twelve. A man could take pride in knowing he was the first to taste the sweetness...and the last. His pulse increased, his heart was pounding.

That's what he needed—more aptly, what she needed.

A kiss to awaken her heart to love.

And once she understood how engulfing, distracting, frustrating, and complete love felt, then she'd understand the dangers of matchmaking and meddling. Once she was in love, she could manage her husband and their babies with the same efficiency she managed her father's household, Hank, her charities, and the book club. Her husband, in return, would manage ensuring her mind and body would stay passionately distracted from interfering in others' romantic lives.

After a loud expel of breath, Hank said, "If I admit I did it and say I'm sorry, can I leave?"

Noah reluctantly turned his attention from Emmeline to his young cousin, whose dark hair hung over his eyes as he bowed his head in, what Noah hoped was, shame. "Admission of guilt is a start," he said in a gentle tone. "Then we make it right."

Hank looked up. "Fine," he said begrudgingly.

Noah raised his eyebrows.

"Fine, *sir*," Hank corrected. His shoulders stiffened. "I shot at Thor even after I promised Mrs. Collins I wouldn't do it again. It's my fault Thor hurt Miss Smith." Hank withdrew from his inner coat pocket the slingshot Noah had given him for Christmas. "Here, since I know you're gonna take it away." After he tossed it onto the coffee table, his icy blue eyes narrowed at Emmeline. His mouth tightened with anger. "I bet you're pleased now you got what you wanted."

"Pleased?" Her head tilted to the side at she met his glare with one of her own. "I daresay a slingshot is not a toy to—"

"Em, the boy doesn't need another lecture on the dangers associated with slingshot usage, or any other lecture." He gave her a pointed look. "He knows he was wrong."

"Noah," she said with a sweet smile, "I was merely—"

Noah raised his eyebrows. When Emmeline didn't say another word, he turned to Hank, whose glare eased up as he looked to Noah. "We need to discuss the appropriate discipline for your actions."

"Sir, I'll take my whippin' like a man."

"Hank," Noah said, leaning forward and resting his elbows on his knees, "I love you as if you were my own son, and I don't enjoy paddling you."

His eyes glinted with hope. "Then I won't get 'em?"

"You'll get them all three because I told you the consequence if you terrorized Thor again. First, you're going to write an apology to Mrs. Collins for breaking your promise, to Mr. Mallory for attacking his cat, to Miss Smith for her injuries, and lastly to Emmeline."

"Apologize? To her?" Hank looked ready to spit. "Why?"

Emmeline wore her own *why?* expression.

Noah released a weary sigh. "Because we both know you were hoping Thor would fall on Em, not Miss Smith."

Hank's face paled.

Emmeline's did too.

Noah collected the slingshot from off the table and slid it in his coat pocket. "Why did you do it? Emmeline loves you. She ensures you have clothes to wear, food to eat, and a bed in which to sleep. She pays for you to have the finest riding lessons, assists you with your schoolwork, and prays for you daily. If it weren't for her intervention, Headmaster Belton would have expelled you from the boys' academy."

Hank stood. "May I go write my apologies, sir?" he drawled out.

"Answer my question, and then you may."

Hank stared blankly—angrily—at something behind Noah's chair. His jaw shifted, his stance hardened.

Emmeline's gaze shifted back and forth between Noah and Hank.

A long minute passed.

Hank shoved his hands in his pockets.

Noah doubted Hank would ever answer.

When he did, his response was so low and mumbled, Noah couldn't hear. Even Emmeline who was two feet away from Hank frowned as if she hadn't understood either.

"Speak up," Noah ordered, "and look at me."

Hank's enraged gaze settled on Noah. His chin jutted out. "I hate her," he exploded. "You love her more than you love me. You should have sent me away to military school like my parents wanted. I hate you, I hate her! I wish you were both dead!" He turned and ran to the office door, jerking it open so hard it banged into the wall. He stopped abruptly.

Mrs. Collins looked down the tip of her nose at him.

Hank dashed to the right.

"Parenting well is never easy," she said in that crisp British accent of hers. "He will be in the front foyer when you are ready to leave. It is not my policy to leave a gentleman and an unmarried lady unattended." She looked at the watch pinned to her white shirt, and Noah would swear she was trying not to smile. "I will return in precisely fifteen minutes."

She left, and the room went quiet.

Noah looked to Emmeline.

"That he hates me is a bit of a surprise," she said matter-of-factly, yet he heard the underlying anguish in her tone.

He saw the strained expression. Saw the anguish lurking behind her eyes. And he couldn't think of a single person who ever hated Emmeline, certainly not one who vocalized it as succinctly—and ungratefully—as Hank had.

She sat there strong and proud, blinking at the tears in her eyes. She untied then retied her hat's black satin ribbons in preparation to leave. Her gaze settled on her blood-stained gloves, yet she made no move to pick them up.

Noah moved from the chair to the settee. "Hank doesn't mean it."

Her lips tightened slightly at the corners. "I fear he does." She sighed, such a dejected sound. "I do love him."

Noah scooted closer. He leaned back against the settee and, with his arm around her waist, drew her against him. "Keep loving him, Em. Tell him daily, and in time he'll return the sentiment."

She rested her head against his chest. "Hank needs his parents."

"I know," he muttered. "Until they return, we're all he's got."

"I should spend more time with him."

Noah kissed the top of her hat. "Good thinking."

Several minutes passed in silence.

He watched as Emmeline wound a loosened string around a button on his waistcoat. She then fiddled with the button, the movement causing a strange unease. He took her hand in his to stop her from moving. She smelled like flowers. She sighed, and he felt the rise and fall of her chest. Every curve. He'd only meant to comfort her after Hank's hurtful words. Warmth slithered up his arm, the very one wrapped around her waist, and down his back, uncomfortably increasing his pulse.

In the last few years as she moved from childhood into womanhood, he'd been able to recognize her beauty, her appealing figure, and not react to it. He'd been able to look at her and his mind not flood with lustful thoughts. But now, feeling her breasts pressed against his chest—he could pull her onto his lap and kiss the very breath from her lungs. He could. He wanted.

For the love of God, he wanted.

Noah cleared his throat. He shook his head to dispel the image of his hands on her. He shifted in order to put a bit of space between them. The movement did nothing to decrease the burning heat on his skin. He could feel beads of sweat on his forehead. A breeze. Yes, he needed to open a window.

"What's wrong?" Her voice held genuine concern.

For a moment he was speechless.

"You're crowding me," he grumbled. "This room is warm."

"Oh, I'm sorry." She eased out of his hold and then smiled up at him.

All he could do was look at those concern-filled brown eyes and imagine what he shouldn't. One kiss. Then another. Nothing would do but his lips on her remarkably ordinary ones. Only that would change everything right and good between them.

Yet his mind wouldn't stop imagining.

"I had a thought." Emmeline moistened her lips, and Noah couldn't look away. "With the return of Mr. Belton and his new bride, the right and proper thing to do is welcome the new Mrs. Belton to Austin by having a party."

Party. The word was enough to sour his mind. He met her hopeful gaze. "The Saint Valentine's Ball is in thirteen days. You don't have time to organize another party."

"True," she conceded with a shrug, "but I could manage a croquet match here on the Abbey's grounds with Hank as my partner. He loves croquet. Maybe this would help him see how I do love him. We shall do it this Saturday, barring inclement weather." She gasped, placed her left hand in the center of his chest, and leaned closer, completely oblivious to her effect on him. Her smile brightened everything about her. "You won't believe who's here."

Noah kept his gaze on her eyes, yet he felt the lightness of her touch and the increased beat of his pulse. He had to clear his throat again before he could speak. "Surprise me."

"Garrison Churchill."

Not sure if he was more irritated at the delight in her eyes as she said Churchill's name or at wanting to kiss her until she couldn't remember Churchill's name, Noah removed Em's hand from his chest. Right now he needed distance from her to sort out his feelings—all right, his desires. No sense lying to himself.

He stood, muttered a quick "You don't say," then fled—as slowly as he could without making it look like he was running from her—to the gold-plated Louis XV foyer table by the office's entrance.

Emmeline shifted on the settee to face him, a giddy expression he'd never seen before on her face. "I saw him, and, oh Noah"—she laid her hands over her heart—"for the first time in my life, I heard music."

Heard music? He grabbed his Stetson off the foyer table. "I need to return to work," he ground out.

"He's the ideal match, in every way."

Noah rolled his eyes heavenward. Charming, loving, dutiful—did she have to add *ideal match* to Churchill's list of virtues? He wanted to ask who she thought Churchill was the ideal match for, but, right now, he was in no mood to hear her admit she'd fallen in love with the man. He didn't like Churchill. Didn't trust him. Certainly had no inclination to spend another moment in conversation with a man who wrote letters in the soft penmanship style of a woman.

"I'll attend to Hank before dinner," he said to change the subject.

Her gaze fell to her hands. "I must invite Garrison to join the croquet match," she muttered to herself, "and Hattie." She counted on her fingers. "With the Beltons and Hank, that still leaves us with seven. I need another female."

"I'll invite Miss Fairfax."

Emmeline's beautiful eyes narrowed on him. "Were you not listening earlier today when I said you and Anne Fairfax would not suit?"

That he and Miss Fairfax wouldn't suit wasn't something he'd deny. He'd never once had a lustful thought about her, but he wasn't about to let Emmeline know she was right about his and Anne Fairfax's lack of suitability. Doing so would only stoke her belief in the existence of her *gift*.

Noah shrugged because, really, that was enough of a response.

"I will not allow you to invite Anne Fairfax," Emmeline ordered.

"I'm not obligated to attend your croquet party," Noah retorted with equal fervor.

"*Our* party," she corrected, because if someone was going to correct something he said Emmeline Travis would be that someone. "Noah, be reasonable. We always do things together."

"There are many things we don't do together," he muttered. Some quite pleasurable.

"Oh Noah, stop being so contrary."

"I'll be contrary if I want."

"What has gotten into you?" She gave him no time to answer. "Besides the book club, name one thing we don't do together?"

Noah wisely didn't. Truth was, that they often did things together was something he needed to change. If it didn't, he'd end up marrying her, and he didn't want to marry her and spend the rest of his life being managed by her or having to manage all *her* whims and meddling. He liked his freedom. That's what he wanted—what she wanted. Only he couldn't stop thinking about what he wanted more at this moment, which began with giving into his baser urges. And now that his mind had begun the journey, he couldn't make it stop.

God, help me.

He wanted to return to the moment earlier today when he viewed her as a friend. When he didn't want to strip every stitch of fabric—

Noah groaned. He needed to talk about something—*anything*—to distract the direction of the very appealing yet dishonoring thoughts.

A trio of Abbey girls hurried past the opened door.

Common sense said close the door. Right now he didn't care if all of Austin heard.

"You're wrong about Miss Fairfax," he said without hiding his darkened mood. "You also don't know as much about people as you think you do."

Emmeline chuckled. "I doubt that, for I am an excellent judge of character."

"*You* may be, but your creative imagination isn't."

"That wasn't nice."

"But it's true."

She jumped to her feet, her eyes flashing with sudden anger. "My creative imagination did not imagine into existence the flowers you gave Anne Fairfax in the middle of the bank for all to—"

"Stop! The flowers were for Mrs. Collins as an apology for Hank's actions last week. Miss Fairfax was at the bank attending to business. She offered to take them back to Austen Abbey, saving me the trip." He pointed his hat at her. "If you had asked—*and I forgive you for not*—I would have explained all that to you." Noah placed his hat on his head. "Instead you created something out of nothing."

She placed her hands on her hips. "What about the replacement violin that arrived for Miss Fairfax at the Abbey? It came from an unnamed admirer."

"Wasn't me."

She coughed a breath. "Why should I believe you?"

"Trust me, when I want a woman, she doesn't wonder—she won't... uhh—I wouldn't admire and not—" Did she have to look so interested in his answer? Noah removed his hat and pointed at her again. "I don't do anything anonymously."

"You've given in secret to many needy Austinites."

"That's different!"

"Why are you so angry?" She walked over to him. "Good heavens, Noah, you're sweating. Let me see if you have a fever."

"Stop," he positively snapped, and she didn't take another step. He didn't want her compassion, any more than he wanted her to touch him. Not now. Not when he was on the edge of losing all control. "I'm fine."

Her head tilted as she gave him the once over. "You don't look fine."

"Looks are deceiving."

"What has put you in such a huff?"

"I'm fine."

"No, you're not!"

"Don't tell me what I am or am not," he ground out. He put his hat back on his head. "I need to go."

"Fine, go." The moment he took a step, she said, "Of course, I certainly didn't imagine sitting next to you at church on Sunday and hearing you tell Miss Fairfax you'd send her the last bushels of beets Mr. Martinez gave you after she mentioned she likes them."

Noah rested his left palm against the doorframe. There was no way she was going to let him leave until he heard her out. That didn't mean he'd have to turn around and look at her again, because between feeling like he wanted to throttle her or kiss her—

Since he wasn't about to pluck his eyes out for causing him to lust, staring at the wooden floor seemed the least painful option.

"Did you want the beets instead?" he asked wearily.

"No! I hate beets."

"Then it shouldn't matter that I gave them to her." Noah waited for an answer, and when it didn't come, he asked, "When did it become wrong to do something nice for someone?"

"She rejected your proposal of marriage!"

Noah didn't speak for a long moment. This jealousy Emmeline had for Anne Fairfax was twisting her perspective. He'd have to talk to her about it. Just not now.

"That," he said, his voice low, "is another thing you're wrong about."

"Did you propose to her?" she demanded.

Noah caught sight of his knuckles, turned white by the force of his grip on his hat. "Can you accept your wrongness so we can end this argument? I have banking to attend to." And praying. Maybe even fasting, because until he could get control of the desire he had for Emmeline, he needed distance from her.

"How fascinating it is," she said with a crisp edge to her tone, "that any discordancy between us must always arise from *my* being wrong."

"Not fascinating, Em, but true." Noah stepped into the hall and stopped. Somewhere down the corridor someone was crying. Hank. Shame evaporated his anger. "I think Hank heard us."

"We're as bad as his parents," she whispered. "We should go talk to him."

Noah shook his head. He couldn't parent Hank right now. Not with her. "He needs a mother right now. I'll talk to him tonight. I need to get back to the bank."

"I feel like you are running away from me."

Noah's shoulders slumped as he let out a tired exhale. "I'll let you know what Miss Fairfax's response is to my invitation to the croquet tournament." Before she could answer, Noah walked away. Time and distance would return things to normal.

He was sure of it.

Five

These were charming feelings, but not lasting.
~ Jane Austen, *Emma*

Three days later
Abbey grounds

"I dare say I'm in a pickle." Holding the end of her croquet mallet like it was a cane, Emmeline knelt next to Hank. She evaluated the various colored balls scattered about the double-diamond rectangular court she'd put together on the Abbey's grandiose back lawn. She didn't have to look to know every student stood at a window of the three-story, bricked Victorian watching the match, waiting for it to end so they could begin a tournament. Mrs. Collins sat in a rocker on the screened back porch. One did not have to presume she was enjoying a book and a spot of tea.

Anne Fairfax's yellow ball sat to the right of the northwest wicket. One hit would send it out of bounds. But one hit of her blue ball through the wicket would score Emmeline another point, and even if she roqueted Miss Fairfax's ball and earned another strike, she'd lose her prime offensive position. Whatever move she made, Noah would play after her and Hank after him. As far as the rest of the players, they would continue whacking their balls with no rhyme, reason, or slightest degree of strategy. The question was—would Noah continue to play offensively for his "hot" team or defensively against her "cool" one? This was the first time they'd ever played on opposing sides. It felt like he was less concerned with winning and more with ensuring she lost.

She wanted to hit him—or at least his red ball—with her mallet.

"Any suggestions, partner?" she whispered to Hank even though no one was near them. Without her asking, he'd worn the three-piece olive suit she'd bought him to match Noah's. He must have overheard her asking Noah last night at dinner to wear his olive suit today, which Noah did even though he said he didn't need her to be his valet. This February day was more pleasant than his attitude.

Hank touched the crimson velvet hem on the sleeve of her sage green gown. "You want to play nice or play to win?"

"Play nice?" she said in her most affronted voice. Then she winked. "This, sweetie, is croquet. We vanquish the competition to become supreme overlords."

"Then roquet Miss Fairfax." He pointed to where his black ball sat near Noah's red one. "Even if Cousin Noah scores on the wicket this turn, I'll do it too."

"Two against one. We can't lose."

"Cousin Noah shouldn't have chosen Miss Fairfax over us."

Emmeline leaned closer, touching the brim of her straw hat to the brim of his gray Stetson. "Noah does as Noah wants." She softened her voice. "Thank you for choosing me as your partner. You made me feel special."

A broad smile covered his face.

She smiled, too.

Delighted with the camaraderie she and Hank had developed since Wednesday's altercation—even though the camaraderie she'd had with Noah had diminished—Emmeline brushed her gloveless palm across the close-cut lawn to feel the density and angle of the grass. She calculated the trajectory (south-southwest) and degree of force (quite hard) she needed to hit her ball in the slight north wind. She knew Noah was playing to win, despite his lackadaisical attitude. Unlike her, who played for the mere enjoyment of the game, he had a most vicious competitive streak.

She stood.

Hank stood, too. He then tipped his Stetson back further on his head. "What do you think Cousin Noah is talking to Miss Fairfax about?"

Emmeline stopped practicing her side swing and looked to the sideline of the impromptu court Noah and Hank had prepared prior to the luncheon that everyone had enjoyed in Austen Abbey's garden. Hattie, Garrison, and the Beltons clustered together, leaving Noah and Anne Fairfax to themselves. Although they stood a respectable distance apart, the *tête à tête* between Noah and the Abbey's music teacher annoyed her to the tips of her toes. With him in his olive suit and her in a simple navy gown, they looked compatible.

"Since she plays after you," Emmeline answered, hoping her words were true, "Noah is merely coaching his teammate on strategy."

"Aren't you bothered that he talks to Miss Fairfax so effeves—effervet—"

"Effortlessly?" she supplied.

"Yes, that."

It bothered her, indeed! Noah's attitude toward her over the last three days was nothing short of polite avoidance. As if she had the plague. While conversing with Hattie and Hank had its joys, she missed talking with Noah—missed his counsel, comfort, companionship. And since she was on an alliterative spell, she even missed his cynicism. And charm.

Life seemed less bright without him around.

At that thought, her chest ached. No, ached was too weak a word. There, in the deepest recess of her heart, she felt cold and alone. Paralyzed.

Emmeline released a ragged breath. This was the worst feeling she'd ever felt. Later...tonight... hen she was alone, she'd sort it all out and decide it was exhaustion over planning the croquet match while overseeing preparations for the Saint Valentine's Ball. With a bit of missing Noah added in. That had to be it. What else could this misery be? Since her mother's death, her father had never spoken of emotional pain. The only person she'd feel comfortable asking was Noah, and he, for all practical purposes, wasn't speaking to her.

He wouldn't even look her way.

Everything in her life was changing, and it scared her. She liked order. She liked how perfectly acceptable her life had been before, well, before Noah changed. She'd been happy. She'd taken care of her father, Noah, Hank, Hattie, and everything in her life just fine, and all was well. Only, the most important part of life wasn't right or good or well anymore.

She wanted back what she'd lost.

She wanted Noah to be her friend again.

"Hank," she said with a sigh, "your cousin lives to exasperate me."

He thumped the head of his mallet on the ground. "I don't know how he can look at her. She's ugly."

"Who?"

"Miss Fairfax. She's so pale she looks dead."

Emmeline frowned as she looked at Anne. Pale as death? How could he think that? There was a softness and delicacy in her skin which gave a particular elegance to the character of her face. Add to that the contrast of her dark hair and pale blue eyes—why, she was the most beautiful woman in Austin. And accomplished! There was not an instrument she could not play. She relied on her own efforts for employment, and not on any inheritance. If Anne Fairfax married Noah, any discordancy between them certainly wouldn't arise from *her* being in the wrong. She'd never heard Anne voice a contrary opinion on anything.

Emmeline shifted her attention to Hank. "Her fine complexion is in the glow of health."

His upper lip curled. "You're prettier, and better in all things."

Since she didn't feel qualified to debate the merits of her appearance verses Anne Fairfax's, Emmeline responded with, "Miss Fairfax surpasses me in both vocal and instrumental performance. My accomplishments are no more like hers than a lamp is like sunshine. She speaks three languages to my one. And I doubt there is a book she's started and never finished, whereas I've never finished one I've started. Please don't share that with my book club. Miss Fairfax is perfect in most every way." *I find her quite admirable* languished on the tip of her tongue, yet she could not speak upon realizing the depth of the jealousy she felt toward Anne.

Jealousy that existed from the moment she met Anne two years ago.

Jealousy Noah not-so-kindly pointed out too many times.

Emmeline glanced at Hattie, who was smiling at Garrison Churchill as he spoke to the Beltons. The lack of attention Noah had given Emmeline the last three days had been remedied by Garrison, who'd been a doting friend to her and admirer to Hattie despite the cat scratches on poor Hattie's neck, cheeks, and forehead. A small smile teased at Emmeline's lips. Soon the marriage bells would ring for Hattie and Garrison. Another marital success to her credit.

Emmeline retook her position parallel to her blue ball, aiming the head of her mallet to the ball's back. She eyed her target, eased back into her swing, and—

Hank blurted, "Do you think he's in love with Miss Fairfax? I do."

—she whacked the ball.

It went sailing toward the yellow ball just as her mallet went sailing from her hands toward where Noah and Anne Fairfax stood.

"Fore!" she yelled, cringing as it cartwheeled through the air.

Garrison Churchill gallantly shielded Hattie while Mrs. Belton screamed. Mr. Belton immediately covered his wife's head even though the mallet landed a good six feet in front of Noah, who held Anne Fairfax behind his back. Noah glared in Emmeline's direction. He gripped Anne's elbow and walked with her to Emmeline's mallet. He scooped it up and continued toward her like a warrior enflamed.

Hank's hand clenched Emmeline's. "I bet he thinks you meant to do that."

Emmeline swallowed the lump in her throat.

"What do you think you were doing?" Noah yelled, swinging the mallet as he approached. Once he and Anne reached where Emmeline and Hank stood, he tossed the mallet to the ground, where it hit a fair distance off to her left. "That was badly done, Em."

Hank's hold on her hand tightened.

Mr. Belton nudged his garishly dressed wife into walking to the Abbey. "Agatha, how about some lemonade?"

"That sounds delightful." She looked down her nose at Emmeline before wrapping her arm around her husband's and walking off.

Hattie hurried over. "Miss Travis, are you well?"

"She's perfectly well," Noah grumbled.

Hank blurted, "Why are you treating her like she's—"

"Shh, Hank." Emmeline bent down to speak next to his ear. "Sometimes it's best not to speak. Stand tall and take the lecture." She straightened and met Noah's angry gaze.

Garrison joined their small circle. Anne gave him a nervous glance.

"Em," Noah started, "what do you have to say to Miss Fairfax for your actions?"

She was all ready to offer an apology when Anne touched his left arm.

"Truly, Mr. Whitley," Anne said in that breathy voice of hers, "it was an accident."

Noah's glare softened as he looked at her.

Emmeline took that as an opportunity. "It was," she insisted. "I do apologize for losing my grip. I wasn't giving my mallet my full attention."

Noah didn't seem a mite placated by her show of remorse. "How could you be so unfeeling to Miss Fairfax? This petty jealousy of yours needs to end."

"My petty jealousy is not what caused—wait, you think I actually intended to wound her?" Before he could respond, Emmeline laughed. "If your accusation weren't so absurd, Noah, I'd be offended. Surely you know me better than that."

"I thought I did. You've changed."

"Me?" she repeated. "You're the one who has changed!"

Garrison moved next to her side. "Emmy darling, don't be offended." His gaze flicked to Anne before turning back to Emmeline. "It's only upon seeing a woman in her own home, among her own set, as she always is, that a man can form an honest judgment for her actions." He gave his head a sad shake. "Too many men committed themselves after a short acquaintance and rued it the rest of their lives."

Anne, who had seldom spoken in Emmeline's hearing, mumbled, "Such things do occur, undoubtedly, yet—" She was stopped by a cough that left her covering her chest with both hands. Noah moved to help her, but she waved him off. She breathed deep.

Garrison gave her his full attention. "Miss Fairfax, it seems you have something to interject. We're all ears."

She recovered her voice. Looked him straight in the eye. "Although hasty and imprudent attachments can arise between couples, love that is real does not waver regardless of the circumstances. It is patient. It is kind. It is not selfish or demanding its own way."

Garrison's face colored. With anger? With embarrassment? Emmeline wasn't sure.

Noah's gaze shifted from Emmeline to Anne. As his frown deepened, so did the V between his brows.

Hattie touched her throat and eased toward the Abbey. "I believe I could use another cup of tea. Would anyone like to join me and the Beltons inside for a drink? Miss Fairfax? Hank?"

Garrison's bitter laugh bellowed across the lawn. "Seems Miss Fairfax has shown me to be a fool." He gripped Emmeline's arm. "We've been friends for fifteen years, and you have a gift for matchmaking. Why don't you find me a wife? She must be lively. Very lively because I don't think it's possible to love a reserved person."

Emmeline glance at Anne, whose complexion had paled to the degree of actually making her look near dead.

"Hattie," Anne said in a tight voice, "tea sounds delightful." She brushed past Garrison, wrapped her arm around Hattie's, and all but ran with her inside Austen Abbey.

Garrison glanced around the makeshift croquet court. "Seems that leave three 'cools' to one 'hot.' Emmy darling, your strategy to win played out brilliantly."

His flattery and merriment fell flat. Still, Emmeline offered a meager smile. Nothing today had gone as she'd planned. She wished herself to be sitting alone in the top floor of the hotel, and quite unattended to, in tranquil observation of the beautiful views of her beloved city. Alone—where she didn't have to explain her actions or listen to a lecture on her *you are in the wrong* behavior. Only she would not leave Hank to the mercy of Noah's foul mood.

"Garrison," she said, focusing on Hank's gray Stetson, "would you aid Mr. Whitley in tearing down the court? I need to return home and see to—well, I should go." With a tug on Hank's hand, she led him to the Abbey's drive and then onto the sidewalk. Neither Noah nor Garrison followed.

"I'm sorry," Hank said, breaking the silence.

"For what?"

"I thought he was in love with you."

Emmeline spared him a quick glance, still holding his hand as they walked. "Who?"

"Cousin Noah."

She laughed before she could stop herself. "I'm sorry. That sounded mocking, and I did not mean to demean your opinion." Her heart began to pound. "Why would you think he is in love with me?"

"Because of how he looks at you." He grimaced. "It's embarrassing."

A hot blush crept up Emmeline's neck. What had Hank seen that she hadn't? Besides in the last three days, Noah hadn't looked at her at all.

She nodded for no good reason, feeling more wretched with each passing moment. "Why did you say you thought he was in love with Miss Fairfax?"

"I don't know." He looked over his shoulder. "He's not following us."

She glanced over her own shoulder. Her chest tightened with longing to see him chasing her down to make things right between them.

"Does it bother you that he isn't?" she asked, refocusing on the sidewalk.

"I'd hoped..." Hank shrugged.

When he said no more, Emmeline looked back again to see if Noah was running after them. No, that was foolish to hope. Noah was too dignified. Too controlled. If he loved her, he'd do it in a quiet fashion. 'Course, if he loved her, he certainly wouldn't point out her failings. If he loved her, he wouldn't avoid her like the plague. If he loved her, being the honest and forthright man he was, he would have told her, and he would have also shown it until she was convinced.

No, he wasn't in love with her. Couldn't be.

Because if he was, he'd insist on marrying. *That* was equally unlikely. Noah was as happy as possible by himself. He had his bank, vast library of books, and lease properties to occupy his mind. He was extremely fond of his nephews and of Hank, who he was more of a father to than Hank's biological one. Noah had no reason to marry.

Except for love.

Just as she had no reason to marry except for love.

Yet he had proposed to Anne Fairfax, hadn't he? Now that she thought about it, she couldn't ever remember him confirming he had proposed or even hinted that he was in love.

Love?

Emmeline blinked at the tears clouding her view and, with her free hand, wiped away the ones escaping down her cheeks. Her lungs constricted. Throat tightened. She was vexed beyond what could have been expressed, beyond what she could conceal. She'd never felt so agitated, mortified, or grieved at any circumstance in her life because she'd never before felt this way. As the truth forcibly struck, her tears increased.

Emmeline stopped at the bench in front of Lundberg's Confectionary. She gripped the iron armrest, closed her eyes, and gasped for breath. Her legs trembled. Knees ached. She sank onto the seat. She tried to stand, but the pain so palpable in her chest kept her gripping the armrest for support.

This was *not* how she expected love to feel. Where was the joy? The harps and angels singing? The completeness?

This—what she felt in her heart and knew in her mind—*hurt*.

Oh, how she'd been so arrogant and vain thinking she knew marital bliss potential when she couldn't even recognize what was in her own heart.

"I love him," she whispered.

Hank sat next to her. He wrapped his arms around her. "It's gonna be all right."

"I've been such an utter fool." Emmeline dried her cheeks and drew in a settling breath. "I have erred greatly in thinking too much of my matchmaking skill and too little of the influence of love. Noah was right."

"He always is," Hank muttered.

Emmeline nodded. Noah was downright, decided, and commanding, yet she loved him anyway. She needed him to help her be wiser, kinder, and more generous than she was. If Noah was correct about her lack of a true matchmaking gift, what other things...?

Emmeline winced. Noah had insisted Joe Martinez loved Hattie. Had she done Hattie a disservice in dissuading her interest from him? Hattie had been more distraught over meeting Mr. Martinez in Bennet's than over the news of Mr. Belton's sudden marriage. Mr. Martinez's beet farm—the land he leased from Noah, with all its rich pastures, spreading flocks, and orchards in blossoms—was beautiful...according to Noah. Emmeline had never seen it. She couldn't imagine seeing it with anyone save Noah.

She had brought evil on Hattie, on Mr. Martinez, on herself, and, she feared, on Noah.

She straightened her shoulders. Gripping Hank's hand, she stood. "Up."

He obeyed.

Emmeline led him to the busy intersection. "Hank," she said as the mule-drawn streetcar came to a stop in front of them, "when you make a blunder, hurt someone, or damage something—whether accidental or intentional—is an apology enough?"

"Yes—umm, no."

"If you're truly sorry, you'll apologize *and* do what you can to make the situation right."

He looked back toward the Abbey. By the disappointment on his face, she knew Noah still wasn't chasing after them. "What are you going to do?" he asked.

"First, I'm going to see my father and then write a letter."

"Is that all?"

She forced a smile. "It's the beginning at fixing what I broke."

Her affection must have overpowered her judgment.
~ Jane Austen, *Emma*

Hotel Brunswick
Later that day

"Are you sure you want to leave tonight?" Mr. Henry Travis sat at his office desk, on the first floor of the hotel, his attention on what Noah knew were stock reports, giving Noah a prime view of the top of his gray head. Even on weekends, Emmeline's father worked. A behavior in direct response to his wife's passing. "I've never known you to make spurious decisions, which this is."

Noah didn't reach inside his coat pocket for the rail ticket he'd bought on his way from Austen Abbey to the hotel. "I haven't seen my brother since Independence Day." *True.* "Seems a trip to College Station is in order." More like *timely.* But now was not the time to deal in semantics. "I haven't visited the A&M campus since John began his professorship. Wouldn't you like news on your grandsons?"

Henry's head nodded slightly. "A photograph would be nice. Isabelle is always promising images of the boys yet never sends them. She's not as organized as her sister." He turned a page in the report. "Emmeline's ball is in ten days. You will be back."

Noah swallowed despite the tightening in his throat. He'd have shifted in the chair, but it wasn't accommodating to a man of his height. The only way to sort things out was for him to leave town. For an extended stay. Specifically to miss the Saint Valentine's Day Ball so he didn't have to watch Emmeline dancing with other men, in particular Garrison Churchill.

As far as answering, since Henry hadn't technically asked a question, Noah elected to stay silent and allow Emmeline's father to assume what he may.

"You will be back," Henry repeated.

Noah stared at his black Stetson resting on the desk next to the brass Bouillotte lamp Emmeline had insisted her father have in his office even though it was more for décor than function. The command was clear. To honor the man he considered a second father, he *had* to return for the ball.

After a moment of awkward silence, Noah conceded, "I would say so."

"You're still young. A dance would be good for you."

Noah cringed solely because Henry wasn't watching him. "Sir, it may be possible for society to do without dancing entirely. Instances have been known of young people passing many, many months successively without being at any ball of any description, and no material injury accrued either to body or mind."

Henry looked up enough for Noah to see his dark brown eyes over the top of his spectacles. "You don't say."

Noah felt a grin tug at his lips. "The *Texas State Gazette* had an article on it last month."

Henry nodded. "I see. How did Emmeline respond when you gave her this reason for why you wouldn't be dancing ever again?"

"'All work and no play makes Noah a dull boy,' were her exact words."

"Our girl is a clever one."

"That she is." Noah touched the pocket holding his rail ticket, the slip of paper weighing like a rock on his side. "I would rather Emmeline be without sense than to misapply it as she often does."

Henry removed his spectacles and laid them on his stock report. "Most people go through their entire lives without anyone, ever, speaking honest, loving, direct words to the most damaging issues in their lives. You're one of the few people who can see faults in Emmeline, and the only one who has ever told her of them."

"You used to. Why did you stop?"

Henry was staring at him, with a compassionate yet pointed gaze. "You came along."

"I care too much for Emmeline to turn a blind-eye," Noah acknowledged, since it was the truth. "I pray daily for wisdom to tell her the truth in the best possible way for her to hear, just as I pray for a teachable spirit to hear what you have to share with me."

"Yet something has changed in you."

Noah nodded just enough to agree.

"I thought so." Henry's straggly gray brows drew together in confusion. "You two have been as close as brother and sister. What happened earlier this week to make you cold to her?"

Cold? The very nature of his problem was the opposite temperature he now felt for Emmeline. He couldn't admit *that* to her father.

Frustrated, Noah walked to the window on his right facing the street-side of the hotel. He leaned heavily on the sill. "Tomorrow you will attend worship, share luncheon with Miss Gates and her mother, and then spend the evening watching Emmeline and Hank paint. We do the same thing every Sunday, unless your daughter makes other plans." He turned his head enough to see Henry still watching him intently. "Don't you ever grow weary of Emmeline managing every aspect of your life outside this office?"

Henry relaxed in the high-backed chair that only emphasized his short stature. "It makes her happy."

Noah rubbed at the tension in his forehead, yet the action did little to ebb the growing ache behind his eyes. He hadn't slept in days. At least not through the night. Snatches of sleep left him tired and cranky. He couldn't focus on work.

Emmeline had made his life miserable.

They lived in the same hotel. He wouldn't be surprised if they spent more time together than most married couples. Except at night. Now he couldn't even enjoy those hours of reprieve from her presence.

"You don't even choose what you want to wear each day," he said, loosening his tie. "She leaves your clothes out for you—suit, tie, socks. How can you live like that?"

"It makes her happy," Henry repeated as if the answer was obvious.

Only it wasn't obvious to Noah. Was this how things were with Henry and his wife? He'd been tamed by a woman, all wildness domesticated until he'd become as pliable as the family dog.

Noah groaned. "Wouldn't you like to choose what *you* want to eat for dinner?"

"I do on Mondays at the Imperial even when she tries to order the veal for me." Henry tapped his spectacles on the top of his desk. "If you generally didn't care what clothes you wore each day or what you ate," he said, gesturing with his spectacles as he spoke, "but it mattered to someone else, wouldn't you let her have her way? It's only food, only clothes."

Noah released an exasperated breath. "But I do care. I want to choose what I eat and what I wear."

"*Hmmph.*" Henry's expression softened. "You took longer than I expected to reach this dilemma." He checked his pocket watch then looked at Noah. "Son, it's time you moved out of the hotel and back to the Whitley estate. You can manage your own affairs and not have to deal with Emmeline mothering you."

Noah stared at him in disbelief. "I can't move home. Mrs. Martinez and her daughter stay there when the Abbey is out of session. If I were there, she'd insist on cooking for me, and I don't want to burden her."

"A woman who loves to cook wouldn't mind."

"Hank wouldn't want to be away from Emmeline," Noah insisted.

"Children adapt easily," Henry countered.

"I'd have to start riding to the bank instead of walking like I do from here." For good measure, Noah added, "I like walking. It's good for the heart."

After a quick nod of his head, Henry reclaimed his spectacles and slid them on his face. "Seems to me you have a lot of reasons not to leave the hotel yet no good one for why to stay." His attention turned back to his stocks report.

"That's it?" Noah staggered into his chair. He leaned forward, elbows on knees. "You're supposed to tell me what I need to hear even if I don't like what you have to say."

Henry's brows rose. "I tend to do that, don't I? I would say pray on it, but I know you're already doing that." He waved toward his office door. "Go catch your train, Noah. Once you decide what you want most, come home."

With a pinch to raise the gold-fringed hem of her ivory skirt, Emmeline hurried down the hotel's front staircase to the lobby. She held the matching velvet-lined evening cape over her left arm. She hated leaving Hank alone, but she didn't want to keep Garrison waiting at the Imperial. Besides, Noah would be home soon to take Hank to dinner with her father. Tonight the hotel special was meatloaf, boiled potatoes, and asparagus—Noah's favorite.

Emmeline nodded and smiled at those milling about the marbled area as she made her way to the concierge desk. She waved at the prematurely bald man in the navy suit.

He smiled. "Yes, Miss Travis?"

She stopped in front of the counter. "Is my driver ready?" she asked, straightening the gold fringe on the end of her sleeves.

"Yes, ma'am."

"Good. Mr. Whitley should be returning any time to—"

"There he is right now." He pointed behind her.

Emmeline swirled around.

Focused on the hotel's entrance, in a manner decidedly graver than she'd ever seen before, Noah strode across the lobby with a purpose... and a frown. She was sure he hadn't forgiven her for the croquet match. He looked unlike himself, so she tried to smile to appear cheerful despite the pain in her heart. Paralyzing pain. It was odd, actually, to hurt when she'd expected to feel—well, she wasn't sure exactly how she expected to feel upon seeing him again. This agony wasn't it. She loved him.

If he truly desired to marry Anne Fairfax or any other lady, from here on out, she would accept his decision.

"Noah," she called out, walking to him.

He stopped. Whatever card he held, he immediately thrust it in his coat pocket. "I didn't expect to see you." He glanced about the marble foyer. "Where's Hank?"

"He's upstairs reading a book and waiting for you to accompany him to dinner."

His blue eyes shifted from the pearls she'd woven through her auburn hair then narrowed and lingered at the low neckline of her silk faille gown.

"Where are you going in that gown?" he grumbled.

"I'm having dinner with Garrison Churchill at the Imperial, and then we're going to the opera." She motioned to the settee in the empty parlor. "Can we talk?"

His lips tightened, his gaze strayed to the hotel's entrance. "I don't have time. I need to catch the train to College Station to spend a few days with John and Isabelle. Have you anything to send or say?"

Since he still wasn't looking at her, she tilted her head and studied him. His hat was missing. He must have forgotten it somewhere, which was odd because Noah never forgot anything. His usually immaculately combed hair was mussed.

"Give them my love," she answered. "Of course, this is all so sudden. Why tonight?"

"I've been thinking of it for some time now."

"Oh."

While he stood, as if meaning to go but not going, her father exited his office carrying Noah's black Stetson. "Emmeline, my dear, there you are." Papa walked toward them with a slight hitch to his gait from the arthritis in his hips. "Did you get your letter to Mr. Martinez dispatched? Rather generous of my daughter to invite the man and his family to join us and Miss Smith for a Saint Valentine's Day luncheon, wouldn't you say, Noah?"

Noah frowned at Papa. "Why didn't you tell me this earlier?"

"It wasn't relevant to our conversation." He handed Noah his hat. "You forgot this."

Noah placed it on his head. He turned to Emmeline. "What are you scheming now?"

She winced yet didn't take offense. His question was fair. She'd given him too many reasons to presume the worst. "I'm not scheming. Not anymore," she amended. "I've learned my lesson."

"Then why invite Martinez and Miss Smith to lunch?"

"You were right about Mr. Belton."

His brows rose.

"He was never in love with Hattie." She paused to give him time to gloat about being right. When he said nothing, she continued, "Mr. Martinez is in love with her, and I now believe Hattie is in love with him too. She's been all along. I'm sorry I didn't listen to you."

"So you're trying to match them now?"

Emmeline winced at the hardness in his tone. She looked to Papa, who gave her an encouraging smile to continue. "Noah," she said meeting his gaze, "I'm trying to repair what I broke. Saying I'm sorry isn't enough. I have to confess to Hattie and Mr. Martinez where I interfered. What they do after that is up to them."

His hand reached for hers. Or maybe her wishful thinking imagined his action because he stood there unmoving. His gaze absently focused on the staircase behind her. "That's good. Good," he muttered.

Moments passed in silence.

Emmeline looked to her father.

He shook his head. Because he didn't know what was wrong with Noah? Or because he was warning to give Noah some space?

Papa patted Noah's back. "Have a safe trip and bring me back images of my grandsons."

"I will."

Papa kissed Emmeline's cheek. "Enjoy your dinner, sweetheart." He winked. "Try the aged rib-eye over the veal. You will be pleasantly surprised at how much better it suits your palate."

Emmeline absently nodded. How else was she to respond to such odd advice from her father? He'd never made food recommendations before.

As Papa walked away, Emmeline stepped to the left to where she was in front of Noah. He frowned. She smiled.

"Will you return in time for the ball?" she asked in a most casual manner.

"I don't know." Either because he did not dance himself, or because she'd claimed a Saint Valentine's Day Ball was the ideal occasion for adorably besotted men to propose to their ladies, he seemed determined to be indifferent about attending. His gaze focused on the entry doors. For someone who seemed ready to flee, he'd yet to move a step closer to the exit.

"Is this how things are going to be between us from here on out?" she asked.

"I don't know."

"You are a wealth of knowledge today."

"Who are you going to dance with?"

"What?"

"At the Saint Valentine's Day Ball," he grumbled. "Who are you going to dance with?"

"No one. As the dancing floor manager, I must see that the sets are full and that all persons wishing for dancing partners are supplied." Emmeline hesitated a moment, and then, despite the nervous pounding in her chest, replied, "I would dance with you, if you will ask me. Despite your aversion, I know you are well skilled at dancing and"—she offered a crooked smile—"you know, we are not really so much brother and sister as to make it at all improper."

He may have uttered an oath. "Brother and sister? Not in the least."

"Noah, what have I done to offend you?"

"Nothing," he said crisply.

"Then why won't you look at me?"

"Because when I do, I—" With a groan, he ran his left hand though his light brown hair, mussing it even more. He turned her way, yet his gaze seemed to settle on the pearls in her hair. "I have changed, Em, and I need to sort it all out. Take care of Hank for me while I'm gone."

"Of course I'll watch—"

Before she finished, he headed to the door.

Emmeline closed her mouth and glanced about the foyer. None of the dozen or so people milling about seemed to have noticed Noah's abruptness. That did not mean she had to tolerate his rude behavior. Lifting the front of her skirt, she hurried after him. While he may wish to end the conversation, she clearly hadn't made things right with him.

The navy-and-gold-suited doorman pushed the door back, stepped over the threshold, and held the door open. "Mr. Whitley, your bags have been delivered to the station."

"Thank you." Noah gave the man a dollar.

"Miss Travis," the doorman said, "your driver is waiting."

"Please have him wait. I need to speak to Mr. Whitley for a moment."

Noah gave Emmeline a sideways glance then walked outside. Emmeline hurried after him. They turned toward the corner where a street-car waited for passengers.

"Would you cover up?" he asked.

Even though his clipped tone vexed her, Emmeline flung the cape over her shoulders. With the sun nearing the horizon, the day was growing cooler. The tip of her nose and fingers already felt chilled.

They proceeded on.

They were halfway down the block when Noah abruptly stopped. He waited until the last of the pedestrians passed by, yet when he spoke, he still didn't look at her. "Since you're ready to spill...your thoughts, let's get this over with."

"I know how highly you think of Anne Fairfax."

"Everyone knows how highly I think of Miss Fairfax." He sounded surprised. "She's an accomplished young woman."

"I envy her accomplishments," Emmeline admitted. "Because of my envy, I've spoken ill of her. I've rebuffed her attempts at friendship. Though tossing the mallet at her was an accident, I am truly sorry for what happened and sorry for how I responded to your criticism. What can I do to stop you from being angry with me?"

"I'm not angry."

"Then what are you?"

"Frustrated!"

Emmeline winced. "With me?"

"Yes—no." He groaned. "I need to catch the train."

"I have one final question," she told him.

He nodded for her to continue.

Emmeline forced herself to sound calm. "Did you propose to Anne Fairfax?"

"You should have asked me this"—he gave her a frown—"before believing whatever gossip you heard."

"It wasn't gossip. Hattie said she'd found Anne crying. When she asked her what was wrong, Anne said she'd turned down a proposal from a wealthy and prestigious bachelor that all of Austin knows." Though saying the words should bring her pain—the very mention of him proposing to someone other than her—what she felt most was numbness, actually. "What other bachelor in Austin is as wealthy, prestigious, or highly desirable as you?"

The first blush she'd ever seen on him colored his cheeks. "Miss Fairfax wouldn't have me even if I were to ask her." He sounded hoarse.

"So you never proposed?"

"No, and nor do I ever intend on proposing to her." He resumed his path to the streetcar.

Emmeline hurried after him again, her heels clicking against the bricks underfoot. "Why wouldn't you propose to her?" She realized she'd raised her voice. She lowered it as she continued, "She's all that a man would want in a wife."

Noah stopped and swiveled to face her. "Miss Fairfax is a patient, kind-hearted, and *reserved* woman, but that doesn't make her a better woman than you." His brow furrowed. "If you take time to get to know her, you will discover you have much in common with her."

She couldn't help asking, "Such as?"

His gaze focused again on the fitted bodice of her gown. Mumbling to himself, he reached out, tied her cape closed, and drew back as if she was burning coals. "Such as being in love with the same man. Don't take that off during dinner. Churchill doesn't need any temp—" Whatever else he said ended in mumbles. Without another glance in her direction, he climbed aboard the streetcar. It pulled away.

Emmeline stood in the middle of the sidewalk, lost in her thoughts. Anne was in love with Noah too? Something seemed wrong. She looked to the corner where the streetcar no longer was. Only bicycles, wagons, and a few pedestrians. Noah clearly said Anne Fairfax wouldn't accept a proposal from him even if he offered. Indeed, Anne *couldn't* be in love with Noah. If she wasn't in love with him, then who?

Churchill doesn't need any temp—

—tations?

Emmeline touched the silky bow Noah had tied at her throat. "He thinks I'm in love with Garrison." She wasn't. Anne was. How she had missed what was right in front of her face!

She hurried back to the hotel's entrance. Before dinner was over, she'd know exactly where Garrison's affections lay. And she'd ensure he knew where hers didn't.

Take a little time, consider, do not commit yourself.
~ Jane Austen, *Emma*

College Station, Texas
February 14, 1882

"Perfect," Noah muttered, easing back from the rocking chair where he'd laid his three-month-old nephew in the arms of his two-year-old older brother. "Isabelle, make sure they don't move."

She stood to the left of the chair, while he stood to the right. Mr. Hilliard looked through the camera lens. With a click and a *poof*, he took another photograph of the boys. Good timing too because John Jr. was now putting his finger in his sleeping brother's ear. Noah handed Little Henry to his sister-in-law who looked, laughed, and spoke enough like Emmeline to make him regret thinking a holiday in College Station would be helpful. If she wore more elegant gowns instead of simple calico ones, she would look even more like Emmeline.

Seeing his brother and Em's sister doting on their boys—

He rather liked his nephews. He'd never really thought about having children of his own. Until now.

With a frustrated sigh, Noah scooped John Jr. out of the chair then gave them to his sister-in-law so she could change his nappy. "Hilliard, I want the photographs divided into two orders. One delivered to my brother's address at A&M, the other to Henry Travis at Hotel Brunswick in Austin."

The photographer smiled. "Certainly."

After Noah finished with the payment, he picked up John Jr. and waited for Isabelle to fit Henry into the carriage. They left the photography studio and walked down the street to where they were meeting John for lunch. Isabelle pushed the wicker baby carriage Emmeline had ordered direct from London upon learning of her sister's first pregnancy.

John Jr. stuck his finger in Noah's ear.

Noah said, "No," and withdrew the offending appendage.

"Emmeline's ball is tonight," Isabelle reminded him for the fourth time today.

Noah focused on gently nudging his nephew's finger away from prodding at his nose. They stopped at the intersection, waited for traffic to ease up, and then crossed the hardened dirt street.

Isabelle rolled the buggy onto the bricked sidewalk. She stopped near the entrance to the cafe and grabbed Noah's sleeve. "It is both your imperfections that make you and Emmeline perfect for each other."

"Distance makes the heart grow fonder."

"Oh Noah. My sister isn't that insufferable to live with," she advised, "once one learns to let her have her way on things that don't matter."

Noah shifted John Jr. to his other hip. "You sound like your father."

A glimmer of amusement flashed in her brown eyes. "Some days it's torture living with your brother, who is far more managing than Emmeline. Marriage is give and take, Noah, and when you love someone, you want to make the one you love happy. But you also have to know when you need to stand up for something that's important to you. Love does not give another permission to bully into submission." Her gaze shifted from him to her agriculture-obsessed husband who was weaving between pedestrians as he waved his white Stetson at them. "There's comfort knowing someone will always be here for me, and with me."

"I like my freedom," Noah put in. "Emmeline likes hers."

"That's justification for your selfishness?"

Selfishness? He always put others' needs before his own. Especially Emmeline's.

Although Isabelle was more than a foot shorter than him, the look she gave made him feel Leprechaun-small. "Noah, Noah, Noah. I'd hoped you'd come to your senses by now, but—" She gave her head a sad shake. "You are selfish. You also won't fight for the woman you love, and that makes you a coward."

John Jr. removed Noah's black Stetson. He waved it up and down.

"Sorry I'm late." John joined them at the entrance, grinning. "We'd gotten into a lively discussion on crop rotation. So who's a coward?"

Isabelle inclined her head toward Noah.

He shook his head. He wasn't a coward. He would fight for the woman he loved if he were in love. He wasn't. He wasn't in love with Emmeline. He'd been an older brother to her since she was born. True, he cherished her. Cared for her. Compared every woman he met to her, to Emmeline, to the woman whose face he wanted to see upon waking, who told him her every thought and opinion, who lived passionately in all she did. For the last four years, they did (almost) everything together. Being with her was right and good and—

His future.

His heart leaped in his chest.

Noah raked a hand through his hair, something he'd been doing a lot lately. He'd been managing Emmeline's actions, protecting her from unsavory suitors who wanted nothing more than her inheritance, and wanting her to marry so she'd be distracted from meddling. She'd helped him move past his grief after his mother's death and his father's grief-induced suicide. And all along, he'd kept her close because he wanted her for himself. And *how* he wanted and needed and loved her.

"I love Emmeline," he admitted, feeling rather numb actually.

"We know." John removed a folded paper from his coat pocket. "Here." He shoved the paper in Noah's hand then took Noah's hat from his son's grip.

Noah scanned the contents of the hand-written telegram addressed to his brother.

FAIRFAX AND CHURCHILL ELOPED STOP TELL COUSIN
NOAH COME HOME STOP MISS EM CRYING

Noah's gaze focused on the telegram's date. "Hank sent this *six* days ago," he said, his voice stiff and clipped as he glared at John. No telling what heartbreak Emmeline was suffering over Garrison Churchill's thoughtless action, and over what appeared to be Noah's callousness to her pain.

John and Isabelle shared glances.

"We were waiting for the right moment," John answered with an apologetic shrug. Yet his grin hadn't faded, so Noah knew he wasn't *that* sorry for meddling.

"Consider our actions a timely intervention," Isabelle added. "John insisted you'd come to your senses without our involvement."

Noah looked from one to the other. "You knew I was in love with Emmeline and didn't tell me?"

This time Isabelle offered an apologetic shrug, yet her smile was one of *I really can't be bothered with the denseness so common to those of your sort.* She was just like her sister.

Noah leaned away from John Jr.'s prodding finger. "I should have returned to Austin six days ago."

"Good for you to admit." John exchanged Noah's hat for his son. He then winked at his wife. "Go get your girl, and prove to the Travis sisters that the Whitley brothers aren't cowards."

Despite the absence of any marital proposals tonight, Emmeline glanced about the hotel's grand ballroom from her spot near the orchestra. She smiled. Gauze, tulle, and lace gowns in hues of pink, salmon, blue, maize, apple green, and white, as well as rich and brilliant colors, like her crimson gown, adorned the room. Austen Abbey's first Saint Valentine's Ball was a success. As Hattie walked onto the dance floor with Mr. Martinez, with ivory ribbons threaded through her blond curls, she looked lovely in her butter yellow dress. To think in two weeks, her protégé would be married.

To a well-educated and delightful beet farmer looking to grow strawberries, no less!

Emmeline sighed. There was no charm equal to tenderness of heart.

If she were counting—and she wasn't—with Hattie's upcoming marriage and Garrison and Anne's elopement, she now had four matches to her credit. Not that she'd actually matched Garrison and Anne. A week ago, she would have wagered them falling in love as unlikely as the ever-proper, ever-elegant, ever-British Mrs. Collins falling in love with, well—*hmmph.* She scanned the room for someone unsuited for the Abbey's headmistress. There! In the corner of the ballroom, near the balcony and by himself sat Garrison's father, Frank Mallory, looking as surly as the moment he had when she'd told him bringing his cat, Thor, to the ball was *absolutely* not acceptable. Sad to think, that forty-two-year-old man gave up *proper* years ago. He was quite handsome, though, if one liked rugged brawn.

Still—if she hadn't cajoled Garrison during their meal at the Imperial into confessing his summer meeting and subsequent courtship of Anne, the pair might still be deluded to think Emmeline loved Garrison and Anne loved Noah. Not even Noah could call her actions meddling this time. More like a timely intervention with a bit of disruptive honesty.

Per her dancing floor manager duties, Emmeline strolled about the room for anyone looking unattended.

While several younger Abbey girls sat alone or in groups, the older girls all were dancing, including Marion McDermott for the third time with that flirtatious Mr. Whelp, who at twenty-four was one of the oldest bachelors in the room; Eliza Branch with Hank, who clearly had worn her down with his repetitive asking; Jeanie Hale with the brother of an Abbey girl; and queen bee Edie Ellis—this time with Mrs. Collins's debonair nephew, Jonathan. Despite having obtained Mrs. Collins's promise that her nephews wouldn't come to fisticuffs like they had at the Christmas Ball, Emmeline glanced about the ballroom for where Mrs. Collins's other less-debonair-but-equally-attractive nephew, Harmon, was. His blond hair usually made him stand out in a room. While he'd yet to find a girl who interested him more than cattle, moonstruck girls continually sought him out.

She strolled casually yet quickly over to Mrs. Collins, so easy to spot in her standard white high-collared shirt and black skirt. In her upswept dark hair, she wore jeweled hair combs.

"Harmon is missing," Emmeline blurted.

Mrs. Collins's gaze stayed on the dance floor. She maintained a smile as she said, "I believe he can be found in the refreshment room."

"Of course." Before the night ended, she would ensure Harmon danced even if he didn't want to. Emmeline turned to leave.

"Miss Travis?"

Emmeline froze. She looked over her shoulder at the still smiling headmistress. "Yes?"

"Do be discrete." Her tone was so kind, it was impossible to take offense.

"As always, ma'am." Emmeline swiveled around and headed straight to the candle-lit side room where she fully expected to find Harmon and probably a few other wayward young men. Sure enough, there amid the tea, coffee, ices, biscuits, cakes, bonbons, and sandwiches, was Harmon and his step-cousin, Ford Winters.

"Don't—" she started.

Harmon, with that ever-charming smile of his, grabbed a handful of sandwiches and fled to the side door. Still only seventeen and wet-behind-the-ears, Ford froze like a hare in a trap.

Emmeline grabbed the sleeve of his gray frock coat and pulled him back into the ballroom. "You're duty, sir, is to dance with these lovely ladies, practice socializing, and be a gentleman any girl would wish to marry. One day you will thank me."

"Umm, Miss Travis, I doubt I will."

"Don't argue with your elders."

"But Harmon—"

"Oh, I'll find him, don't you worry." Emmeline stopped at the perimeter of the dance floor as partners were being exchanged. Surely some girl would appreciate dancing with a strapping young man. She glanced around. What girl truly needed to dance?

The crowd in front of them parted.

There sat little Annie Ellis looking lovely in her simple aqua blue gown, even though all in the room would say she was a faded image of her older sister, Edie. Annie was too young yet to attend Austen Abbey. But she would. For all of Annie's forthrightness and refusal to deal with idiots, she was devoted to her family, fluent in common sense, and had a passion for art that Emmeline found quite admirable. If anyone needed to dance—literally and figuratively—it was Annie.

"You will be a gentleman," Emmeline warned.

"If I don't?" Ford muttered, looking rather grim.

She gave him a slant-eyed glare.

The Adam's apple in his neck bobbed. "Yes, ma'am."

Emmeline placed her white-gloved hand on Ford's back and, with a bit of a forward shove, made him walk. He meandered over to Annie, his head shyly bowed. Whatever he said brought a glow to Annie's sweet face. She placed her gloved hand in his, and together they walked to the dance floor.

"Is this your *gift* in action again?"

Emmeline's breath caught. She didn't have to turn around to know Noah was standing behind her. Yet, as the music started for a lively waltz, she turned.

In his finest black frock coat and with his hair immaculately combed, there was not one man in the room who could compare to Noah—in appearance or character. Her heart felt as if it would explode from the love she had for him. She tilted her head and watched him watch her. Silently, she lifted a prayer that he wouldn't take five minutes to speak.

He frowned a bit. "I'm sorry I wasn't here after you learned of Churchill and Miss Fairfax's elopement." She knew what he truly meant was—*I'm sorry Churchill broke your heart.*

After all the meddling and matching and misunderstanding that had occurred over the last two weeks, now was not the time to be anything except candid.

"I am not in love with Garrison. Never have been. Never will be." She stepped closer so he could hear her over the music. "The tension between them was from lack of openness with each other. I have never been more miserable than I have since you left Austin. What must I do to rekindle our friendship?"

"Dance with me," he said, his palm open to her.

Emmeline stared gape-mouthed. He hated dancing.

Noah took her hand. Whether Emmeline had not herself made the first motion, she could not say; she might, perhaps, have offered it. As he held her hand, he pressed it gently and, she was certain, was on the point of carrying it to his lips, when—for some fancy or another—he suddenly stopped. In a moment's breath, even though the waltz was in full swing, she was swaying in his arms. For one who despised dancing as much as Noah did, he had a natural grace. Her body began to tingle, from her fingers to her toes. Everything was right and good and how it should be—with him holding her forever.

"I love you," she whispered out of the overflow of her heart.

Noah stopped.

The music came to an abrupt halt.

Emmeline looked to the orchestra.

The conductor pointed his baton at Noah and then bowed.

"What is going on?" she whispered.

"I can't make speeches," he said with such tenderness that it brought tears to her eyes. He claimed her hand and cradled it between both of his. "If I loved you less—" He shook his head again. "Emmeline LeNoir Travis, it's not possible for me to love you less. I've tried for the last thirteen days, and I was miserable. Took our meddling siblings to help me realized I don't want less. I want more."

His hands held hers a little more firmly. His blue eyes met hers. His lips parted. For a brief second, all air disappeared from Emmeline's lungs, and she stood there feeling, seeing, and knowing with all certainty the thoughts in his mind.

"Yes, my answer is yes," she blurted, smiling.

Noah returned her smile. "I had planned on going down on one knee and proposing properly. But my knees are still sore from the train ride, I don't have a ring, and you were so generous to agree already."

"Kiss her," Hank shouted from somewhere in the ballroom.

A few whoops and hollers rose about the room.

Noah swept her into his arms. Emmeline wrapped her arms about his neck and awaited her first kiss. Instead of kissing her, he carried her to the refreshment room. With the heel of his shoe, he kicked the door closed.

"Why are we in here?" she asked.

"Because some things don't need an audience."

There, with nothing but the tea, coffee, ices, biscuits, cakes, bonbons, and sandwiches watching, Emmeline enjoyed her first kiss. And second and third, and somewhere after she'd lost count—but before Mrs. Collins's interruption—she remembered that if anyone was to have known the best woman for Noah, she, Emmeline LeNoir Travis, his closest female friend, would have known it.

And she was right.

ROMANTIC REFINEMENTS

ANITA MAE DRAPER

Is not wisdom
found among the aged?
Does not long life
bring understanding?

Job 12:12

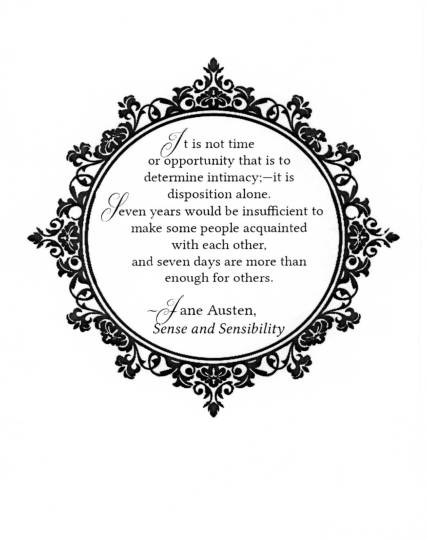

It is not time
or opportunity that is to
determine intimacy;—it is
disposition alone.
Seven years would be insufficient to
make some people acquainted
with each other,
and seven days are more than
enough for others.

~Jane Austen,
Sense and Sensibility

One

Marianne's abilities were, in many respects, quite equal to Elinor's.
She was sensible and clever; but eager in everything:
her sorrows, her joys, could have no moderation.
She was generous, amiable, interesting: she was everything but
prudent.

~ Jane Austen, *Sense and Sensibility*

September 1882, Texas Hill Country

Even the jerking and jostling of wooden wagon wheels travelling on uneven ground didn't drop Marion McDermott's gaze from the herd of rangy cowhands watching the action in the corral. Why, the thought that her future husband might be in the batch of hardened, heavy-working, hat-wearing men set her heart a-thumping—something the dandies back in Austin hadn't been able to achieve. Poppa's smile would surely shine when he heard how seriously she'd taken his warning about marrying a man for his good looks alone.

Yet as Aunt Mattie steered their outfit toward the white pickets which surrounded the familiar verandah-decked house, Marion nervously smoothed the lap of her periwinkle day dress. With its layers of ruffles and lace, it hadn't been the most practical choice for the hour trip from Austin, and as headmistress Mrs. Collins had repeatedly said, Marion should continue to work on virtues such as practicality even now that she'd graduated from the Jeannette C. Austen Academy for Young Ladies.

Over by the corral the cowhands gazed in Marion's direction even though the object of their recent attention still bucked with abandon in the corral behind them.

Spotting a familiar handsome face sent a hundred butterflies flittering in her stomach. Mr. Jeffrey Whelp could very well be the man to leave this ranch with a proprietary hand on her back.

As he left the rail and sauntered her way with the rest of the men, Marion faced the front, her gloved hands closing the silk parasol that matched her fancy travelling dress. Aunt Mattie reined in the team beside the fence where Marion's favorite yellow roses rambled along the white pickets.

Marion leaned down from her seat for a satisfying whiff of their heavenly scent. "Everything's always the same."

Aunt Mattie tied off the lines. "Not much changes on a ranch, except for the men. You'll recognize most of them, especially the ones your poppa sent over. My brother is as stubborn as they come, but he believes in family, and I value the support he has shown over the years since your Uncle Raith died. All his blustering at the beginning was only because that is what he thought a big brother was supposed to do. But he came around."

She nodded toward the outbuildings. "I don't think you've met my foreman yet."

A tall cowboy in a black hat stood on the stoop of the foreman's quarters. His off-white shirt and denims were much like the clothes of the other cowhands, but when he stepped down and headed her way, he lacked the rolling saunter of someone who spent hours in the saddle. Instead, his limping stride appeared jerky and torturous. Beneath a wide brim, his sun-creased face showed few signs of youth, and Marion guessed him to be about thirty or so. With his strong, clean-shaven jawline and wide shoulders, his overall appearance was that of a striking man any woman would have a hard time forgetting.

Their gazes locked, his directness questioning hers.

She looked away, annoyed that she'd been caught staring.

The cowboys drew near with Mr. Whelp in the lead, but the foreman was closer. Avoiding his eyes, she stood to greet Mr. Whelp.

An excited cowboy let out a sharp whoop and threw his hat in the air. One of the still-harnessed horses reared his head. The wagon jerked, tipping Marion off the edge of the open seat and sending her into the air. Balance. She caught the foreman's determined look as he stretched his arms toward her—

Marion flailed her arms in an attempt to fall away from the foreman. Even if he tried, she'd probably fall through his arms and land at his feet. She closed her eyes, unable to stop her downward movement.

Strong arms caught her and lowered her to the ground. How could he—?

"I always imagined you back in my arms, Miss McDermott."

Her eyes flew open at the velvety voice of Mr. Jeffrey Whelp. Tall, blond, and blue-eyed, God had truly blessed him with fancy facial features. He held her close. Too close for propriety—not close enough for scandal.

A delicious dilemma.

She peered up at him coyly. "Mr. Jeffrey Whelp, of all people. Do you still work here?" His muscles tensed beneath her palms, and she imagined the perfect picture they made with her blond hair inches from his chest as he gazed down at her in ardent admiration.

On the other side of the wagon, a man cleared his throat. "That's one way to make an entrance."

The gravelly voice held no disrespect, yet Marion's merriment diminished, instinctively suspecting the voice belonged to the ranch foreman. Did he think she'd fallen on purpose? Mr. Whelp's warm hands pulled her closer. Aghast that he—or anyone—would think she was a wanton, she pushed out of his arms. "Thank you for being a gentleman, Mr. Whelp."

The foreman and Aunt Mattie walked around the cowboy calming the jittery horse. With their heads bent together, their words were too low to catch.

As they approached, Aunt Mattie looked up. "Mr. Whelp, bring Miss McDermott's things to the house. Serelli will show you where to put them."

She beckoned Marion forward. "Marion, I'd like you to meet my foreman, Mr. Brandon Tabor."

The Rocking R's foreman tapped the brim of his hat. "Miss McDermott."

She tipped her head with all the elegance taught at the Academy. "Mr. Tabor."

"I understand you'll be staying with us for a month." His voice rasped across the dry air without a speck of emotion, although his turbulent green eyes reminded her of Travis Lake in a storm.

"Yes, I've completed my studies at the Jeannette C. Austen Academy for Young Ladies and have one month to spend with Aunt Mattie before going back to my father's ranch."

Jeffrey Whelp passed them, his arms full of travel bags. "I'll be back for the trunk, Tabor, since I don't suppose you'll be able to carry it." He nudged the picket gate open with his hip then strode up the walk with long, even strides.

Aunt Mattie *tsk*ed. "Brandon, I don't know why you keep that young man. If it weren't for you, I'd have fired him months ago."

Fire Mr. Whelp? Marion bit her lip to curb her outburst—something she never would have done before attending the Academy. Although Poppa would be pleased at her restraint, something more important had come to light in that exchange—the confirmation that Aunt Mattie had handed control of the ranch to Mr. Tabor. Who was he that Aunt Mattie would place in him the trust of everything she owned?

Mr. Tabor shifted his weight. He grimaced and shifted again, his palm pressed against his hip. "Can't fire a man for speaking the truth, Aunt Mattie, and it appears he's right." His rueful gaze settled on the lone trunk in the wagon, but he made no attempt to get it.

Used to Poppa's hard-headed need to prove himself better than anyone else regardless of his age and health, Marion stared in wonder at Mr. Tabor. Was he truly a man who understood his own capabilities and was confident enough to step back when required? If so, she owed Aunt Mattie credit for her choice, because a ranch foreman needed wisdom above all else.

Aunt Mattie looped her arm through Marion's. Instead of escorting her through the gate, however, she drew her toward the group of cowhands loitering nearby. "The men are waiting to meet you. Come along and put them out of their misery."

As they approached, the cowboys who still wore their hats yanked them off with sheepish looks. Their humble gallantry touched her heart. In turn, she didn't rush the introductions, giving equal time to each regardless of their age.

At the end of the line, an older-than-Poppa bandy-legged cowboy crumpled his sweat-stained hat in his hands. "Name's Ned, Miss McDermott. I worked yer Pa's ranch when you was just a squirt no bigger'n my knee."

A pleasant feeling warmed her as his old-timer's voice coupled with his lopsided grin tickled the edges of her memory. She tapped her forefinger on his arm. "Why, Ned, you're the one who told me all those Bible stories."

He seemed to grow taller before her. "Yep, that was me. Telling them stories was the only way to keep ya outta trouble."

Still smiling, she lowered her tone. "Shhh...it wasn't the stories, Ned, it was the peppermint you sweetened every story with that did the trick."

"Now don't go telling yer Pa 'bout that. But even with all them sweets gummin' up yer teeth, you've growed into a fine lookin' lady." He nodded as if that said it all.

Marion ran her tongue along her white teeth. She'd missed Ned when he'd left their ranch, but perhaps it had worked out for the best.

"Ned, I swear you wear my patience." Aunt Mattie turned Marion away from the blustering old cowhand. "Don't give him another thought, dear. Your poppa's always been proud of your pearly teeth. And you *have* grown into a beautiful woman."

Marion basked in the loving attention.

That is, until she saw the foreman waiting for them with only one side of his mouth turned up in a smile. Did that mean he approved? Or he didn't? The thought of either answer warmed her cheeks. Oh, bother, she had no wish for Mr. Tabor to see her red-faced like a schoolgirl.

At the gate, she unwound her arm from Aunt Mattie's, saying, "I want to take in these wonderful roses. Go on, I'll be along soon."

Mr. Tabor bestowed a full-fledged smile on Aunt Mattie and offered his arm.

Alone, Marion leaned in to inhale the fragrance of the yellow beauties. If Serelli remembered, there'd be a vase of them waiting in her room.

The front door banged as Mr. Whelp hurried through. He leaped down the steps, passed Aunt Mattie and the foreman, and stopped near the gate beside Marion. "Did I hear Miz Mattie say you'll be here for a month?"

Marion swayed one way, then the other. "Yes, that's correct." She dipped her lashes, peering up at him. "And will I see you often, Mr. Whelp?"

"As much as Tabor will allow." He looked at the foreman, then back at her. His chin notched up an inch. "As much as *you* want."

She brushed a wisp of hair off her ear. "I doubt I'll have much say in the foreman's decisions."

"You'll have him wrapped around your little finger if you keep looking like that."

Warm pleasure flowed through her at his obvious appreciation. She began to sway again.

"Marion?" Aunt Mattie called from the foot of the verandah steps,

Mr. Tabor by her side.

Mr. Whelp lost his grin. "Much as I'd like to spend the day staring at your beauty, I can't have Miz Mattie thinking the worst of me. You'll find your things in that pretty room upstairs." He flashed another grin before heading back to the group of cowboys hanging around the corral.

Marion tried to pay attention to Aunt Mattie and the foreman's discussion on a sick calf, but her thoughts centered on the man who had been upstairs in her room. Mr. Whelp's easy familiarity wouldn't have met the approval of Mrs. Collins, the Austen Abbey's headmistress, yet it filled Marion with the same excitement as she'd experienced during their dance at the Valentine's Ball when he'd crushed her against him, then let her go so fast she thought she may have imagined the momentary contact. Again, her cheeks flushed at the thought.

She watched him stride away with Poppa's directive on her mind. A month with Aunt Mattie was time enough to see what kind of man Mr. Whelp was both on the range as well as after a full day of riding. Someday her husband would inherit everything Poppa spent his life working for, and that man needed to do the same for his own children. Was Mr. Whelp as strong inside as he seemed to be on the outside?

The opening door drew Marion's attention. A slim woman with greying hair emerged from the house carrying a tray with a pitcher and three empty glasses.

Aunt Mattie patted Marion's arm. "There's Serelli and our tea. Will you stay for refreshments, Brandon?"

"Thank you, but not this time, Aunt Mattie." He nodded at Marion. "A pleasure to meet you, Miss McDermott."

Her gaze followed the foreman as he limped across the hard-packed yard to the line of outbuildings. Without pausing, he wiped his brow with the back of his hand before he made it halfway across. Her heart tightened as if she, too, could feel his pain.

Brandon sat on his cot clenching his jaw. He adjusted his clothing to expose the mass of scar tissue covering his right hip. The salve wouldn't stop the pain—only make it more bearable.

He reached for the tin container, keeping his hand clear of the small brown bottle standing innocently behind it. As he massaged the gooey stuff into his scars, his gaze swung back to the bottle. Although fifteen months had passed, Doc's warning about the addictive powers of modern medicine had taken root, sending shoots of fear through Brandon's brain. He'd seen what cocaine, laudanum, and other opiates had done to others in the hospital—others who either didn't know God or didn't trust Him enough. Brandon did. And if this was how God planned for him to live the rest of his life, he'd live with it, pain and all.

Except it rankled that he'd seen Miss McDermott flailing her arms like a windmill and instead of allowing him to catch her, she'd closed her eyes and given up. Since Whelp had appeared beside him ready to catch her too, Brandon had backed off and walked around the outfit to help Aunt Mattie down instead.

He couldn't decide if he felt worse about backing away, or because of the way she'd looked at him. One thing was for sure—he would never have forgiven himself if Whelp had missed.

With the salve already working, he stopped his ministrations and dropped his head back against the scratchy, woolen blanket.

Miss McDermott sure was a lively one. Full of fire with enough breeding to keep it bridled. The moment he'd seen her up on the wagon sitting pretty-as-you-please, his tattered Texas Ranger's heart had leaped off a cliff. He patted his chest, guessing it was for the best that she hadn't reciprocated any such feelings. Her brown eyes had questioned his familiarity with her aunt. And they'd softened dreamily when they looked at Whelp.

Aunt Mattie'd said her niece was all of nineteen. *Nineteen.* An old geezer like him had no business thinking of a nineteen-year-old's eyes— or any other part of her. Just as well she'd fallen for Whelp's charm like a flower in a drought.

After capping the salve, he slid it on the dresser. The little brown bottle appeared bigger and closer. He should empty it in the pig sty and be done with the temptation.

Three sharp raps interrupted his thoughts. "Boss? That sick calf ain't lookin' so good."

"Hold on to your hat, Ned." Brandon adjusted his clothes. "Come on in."

Ned stepped in, his face furrowed with worry. "She's scourin' something bad. Thought I'd check the rest of the herd." He extended his right hand.

Brandon accepted the offer and allowed himself to be hauled off the bed. "No, I'll do it. You stay here in case the ladies need something."

A light flared in Ned's eyes. He headed for the door without a hint of argument. "You're the boss. I think I'll let Miz Mattie know where she can find me."

Brandon caught the extra spring in the older man's step. "You do that, Ned." If the old cowhand wasn't careful, the whole Rocking R would discover his little secret, and he'd never live it down.

With the salve working to deaden his pain, Brandon eased toward the door. Time to get back to work. And those hotheads better be at it, too, because he'd be full of steam if he caught them lounging around and drooling at their guest.

He snorted.

Their guest. As if he owned the place. A ranch like this deserved a big family to fill the house and lots of little feet running through the yard. The merest twinge tightened his chest at the thought of his Savana. He'd had his turn at wedded bliss and enjoyed every second while she'd been alive, even though their union hadn't been blessed with offspring. And as damaged as he was, no woman in her right mind would consider him for a mate now, so he'd better stop pining about it.

Two

*I wish, as well as everybody else, to be perfectly happy;
but, like everybody else, it must be in my own way.*

~ Jane Austen, *Sense and Sensibility*

On Sunday morning, Marion splayed her hands across her waist and turned sideways to the mirror to check the back of her new Sunday-best dress. The two months she'd spent visiting Emmeline and Noah Whitley after graduation had given her a heady taste of social and financial freedom. As an Austin socialite, Emmeline, a hotel heiress and former Academy student, knew the best dressmakers for the latest yet most practical fashions.

Once more, Marion faced the mirror and smoothed her palms down her hips. Emmeline's taste had been impeccable when she'd spotted the display for the mint-colored shirtwaist and dark green skirt, saying the outfit would have accentuated Marion's attributes even without the aid of the required boned corset.

Marion hoped so. It seemed the perfect outfit to catch a certain cowboy's eye. Contrary to Mr. Whelp's prediction, work had kept him on the range for the majority of her first week on the ranch, but with it being the Day of Rest, she expected to see him later on in the day, if not at church. Satisfied she looked her best, Marion left her room, Bible and gloves in hand.

Downstairs, she laid her things on the sideboard before crossing the dining room to where Aunt Mattie sat alone at the table. She placed her arms around Aunt Mattie's neck and kissed her soft cheek. "Good morning. How are you?"

Without waiting for a response, she took her place across the table. Aunt Mattie's eyes strayed to the cabinet card on the mantle where an image of Uncle Raith standing close to a younger Aunt Mattie occupied the spot beside the mantel clock. "I'm comforted knowing we'll be going to church today."

Marion knew the reason was to visit the church cemetery as much as listen to the service inside the church building itself.

Serelli entered the room carrying a steaming plate which she set on the table in front of Marion.

Already feeling the constraints of her corseted clothing, Marion eyed the plate of poached eggs, toast and hash. "Really, Serelli—"

Serelli dashed over to the window as if she'd heard something outside. "They're bringing the surrey out, Miss Mattie."

They all knew that bringing the surrey out signaled the intent to leave in thirty minutes. Aunt Mattie waved Marion back in her seat. "Go on, eat your breakfast."

Marion picked at her food and managed to get a minimal amount down before Serelli, thankfully, whisked her plate away.

At nine o'clock, Marion closed the door on the chiming mantel clock. She followed Aunt Mattie and Serelli down to where Ned had parked the surrey near the picket fence, expecting to see Mr. Whelp striding across the yard. She had been sure he would take the opportunity to spend time with her on the way to and from church, but the only man in view was the foreman entering the barn.

"Isn't anyone else coming?" Marion asked as Ned handed her into the backseat beside Aunt Mattie.

"Brandon usually rides alongside. And the hands—well, after painting the town red on Saturday night, some of them don't come back until later in the day." She folded her hands around her handbag and rested them in her lap.

Marion looked across the empty yard. Not a cowhand in sight. She wondered if Mr. Whelp had stayed behind on a Saturday night, or if he enjoyed ripping the gut, as her own cowboys often said. The knowledge that he might be sleeping it off somewhere dulled the brightness of her day.

Yet it couldn't diminish her desire to go to church. Before arriving at Aunt Mattie's ranch, Marion had known what she needed to do. Now that she was here, her path didn't seem as clear. She needed God's reassurance that His hand was on her life, and what better way to feel that than to go to church?

The next morning, Marion sat across the dining room table from Aunt Mattie and buttered a roll with thick, creamy butter. "Going to church and then visiting yesterday was nice, but today's a working day and I don't want to be cooped up in the house. At home, I'd be out riding or working in the barn."

Aunt Mattie set her cup down. "You know I promised your poppa—"

"—that I'd act like a lady. Yes, I know." Marion reached for the juice pitcher, but tight lacings wouldn't allow her to stretch far enough.

Serelli rose from her chair. "I'll get that, Miss Marion."

"Thank you, Serelli."

Aunt Mattie smiled. "Have you finished the needlework project you started at that Austin Academy? If you win the blue ribbon at the state fair, you can take it home and wave it in my brother's face."

"I'd do better showing off a husband on my arm." Marion picked a crumb off the table and dropped it on her empty plate. "Needlework is boring. If only there was a category for music."

"Perhaps someday there will be," Aunt Mattie said. "But I'd like to get back to your comment about a husband. Do you have anyone in mind?"

Mr. Whelp's attractive features crossed her mind. "There may be." She twisted her napkin as if squeezing the cowardice out of her body. She hadn't questioned him about Saturday night because she hadn't seen him yet. And with only three weeks left before returning home, she was running out of time to get to know him better. "Do you remember the Valentine's Ball? I danced with a refined man with a debonair personality and fine features."

"That was Jeffrey Whelp." Aunt Mattie stood and gathered the cutlery. "You watch yourself around that man. I hear he turns into a tom cat at night."

"Aunt Mattie! What a thing for a lady to say."

"It's because you are learning to be a lady that I'm telling you to keep your distance."

Disbelief stunned Marion. How could it be? No one had said a word about an errant reputation. Surely even the foreman would have sent him away if such a thing were true.

And yet, when Mr. Whelp gazed at her with pleasure and promises in his smiling eyes, how could she not believe–

"—Tabor."

The foreman's name on Aunt Mattie's lips jerked Marion out of her dream state. "Pardon me?"

"Take my foreman. Now he's the type of man you should be considering for a husband."

"But he's old," popped out before Marion could curb her tongue.

"He's only thirty, and he's as trustworthy as they come."

"And he's injured, too. I need someone I can depend on to get the work done. Mr. Tabor doesn't look like he can pull a half day's job, never mind a full one."

"Jeffrey Whelp isn't the type of man to work if he doesn't have to. A ranch needs an owner who's willing to get down and do the work himself because it needs doing, not because there's no one else to do it but him."

Marion couldn't argue with that statement. Yet, if Jeffrey Whelp was that kind of man, why was he tolerated at the Rocking R? And where did that leave her?

"Are you saying that if Mr. Whelp comes calling, I can't receive him?"

Aunt Mattie sighed. "No. You're old enough to know your own mind. All I've heard are rumors, and for whatever the reason, Brandon won't let him go."

Appeased, Marion hugged her aunt. "Thank you."

Aunt Mattie pushed her gently toward the door. "Go on and take a walk before it gets too hot out there. But remember this…men who make good husbands aren't always the ones who set your blood thrumming the first time you meet. Make sure he's God's choice as well as yours."

Marion had an urge to skip merrily down the path toward the rose-covered fence. She curbed the feeling as her gaze fell on the cowboys gathered near the corral. Little girls skipped. Young ladies of refinement floated forward in a haze of nonchalance.

To appear disinterested, she walked along the fence perusing the rich pasture grasses, yet it wasn't long before the rancher in her noted the forage thinning beneath the hot Texas sun. The process was aided by strong winds that blew against her face, bringing with it the acrid scent of fresh horse manure. She wrinkled her nose instinctively, although she really didn't mind the familiar scent of ranch life.

She walked past the open doors of the darkened barn where the only light came from the wide doors on either end and the cracks in the walls. The stillness of the interior was disrupted by the cowhands' cheers and pounding hooves. She rounded the corner of the barn and found the railing filled with men, their eyes on whatever was happening in the corral. As if sensing her presence, they turned as one and watched her approach.

Without looking at anyone in particular, she climbed the fence and peered over the top rail in time to see the bronc buck off his burden.

The fallen cowboy picked up his hat and tapped it on his head. "I'm done." He swaggered toward her, grimacing. "Ma'am." He tipped his hat to her in passing.

He wasn't the cowboy she sought, but she smiled at him anyway.

She waited, eager to see who would ride next.

Trusting the fence to hold them up, they stared at her with a mixture of expressions.

She pointed to the corral, hoping to see Mr. Whelp subdue a mustang. "Who's up next?"

"I am!" Two young men hurled themselves over the fence. They strode toward the horse, elbowing and pushing each other. The taller one reached the horse first. He grasped the horn and cantle, but before he could mount, the shorter, more muscled cowhand rammed him against the saddle. His hat flew through the air, landing on the other side of the wild horse.

The mustang danced away, snorting.

The taller cowhand turned, his hand on his cheek. "Why you—" He finished his sentence with a jab to the shorter man's jaw.

"Enough," roared through the corral. Mr. Tabor leaned over the top rail and glared at the combatants. "In my office. Now!"

Hats in hand, the two men trudged toward the fence.

Mr. Tabor set accusing eyes on Marion.

She arched her brows as high as she could. What? Why blame her? He turned and limped away.

Fire burned in her veins. Just like Poppa to always put the blame on her whenever he found his hands fighting. She whirled back to find the fence empty of men. If only she could pry up the top rail and throw it after the foreman. She gripped it and tugged, if only to make herself feel better.

The sound of footsteps eased her grip.

"Ahh, the lovely Miss McDermott. A delightful rose in a garden of weeds." Jeffrey Whelp pulled off his hat and leaned forward, his face aiming for her neck. "Do you smell as good as you look?"

"Mr. Whelp!" She jerked back in shock. "Mind your manners, please." Her heart raced from his nearness, titillated by his behavior.

He bowed low before replacing his hat. "I couldn't help myself. You are truly exquisite."

His breeding shone with every word, yet for the first time she questioned his motive. "Tell me, sir, why would a man of your apparent breeding work on a common ranch?"

"Aren't you the inquisitive one?" He tapped his chin as if trying to decide something. "The fair is in town this weekend. Fun, games, and a Saturday night dance. Perhaps I'll answer your questions if you allow me to escort you."

Marion hesitated, mindful of his fresh approach just a minute earlier, coupled with Aunt Mattie's warning. Surely she could trust Mr. Whelp enough to spend the day with him. However else would she get to know him better?

He looked over her shoulder, and his expression hardened.

A shuffling step announced the return of the foreman. A quiver of energy rippled across Marion's back.

"It's not Sunday," Tabor said. "Why aren't you fencing the western ridge?"

"The boys are just heading out. Another minute with Miss McDermott and I'll be right behind them."

"You've had your minute."

Marion whipped around to face the foreman. "We were merely having a word. A moment more, and Mr. Whelp will catch up to them."

The muscles beneath Tabor's eyes tightened. "Now, Whelp."

His attitude was incomprehensible and inexcusable. With her gaze locked on Tabor, she raised her voice. "Mr. Whelp, I shall be pleased to accompany you to the fair."

Tabor's mouth opened and then closed.

Jeffrey stepped in front of her, blocking the foreman from her view. "I'll bring the buggy around at ten o'clock."

"Whelp!"

Brandon turned his back on Marion as soon as Whelp rode off whooping. He limped into the barn, thinking of how he'd have to work out a plan with Aunt Mattie so that Marion was never alone with Whelp at the fair. The dance would be especially challenging.

At the last stall, a soft whinny greeted him. He dropped his hand over the partition and scrubbed the filly's face, his anger fading. It'd always been that way between him and horses. He was supposed to be the one caring for them, and yet they eased his mind with their touch alone. If only their healing could work on his hip. The little palomino blew across his hand. With a final pat, Brandon turned away.

In the room that served as his office, he tried to work on the ranch receipts but instead of focusing on the numbers, he remembered how Marion had looked in her stylish green outfit. And then his pencil snapped in half at the memory of her face when she agreed to go to the fair with Whelp. He tossed the pieces onto the ledger. How could she trust Whelp? He rubbed his jaw. Apparently, she only saw his good looks and hadn't dug any deeper. Would she? Did she even want to?

He walked to the window and looked out at the verandah-wrapped house, thinking of his promise to keep an eye on Marion. No matter which way he looked at it, he was going to the fair.

On Saturday morning, Marion was adjusting the angle of her hat for the third time when she heard the unmistakable sound of brass fittings jingling in a harness. A quick look out the window confirmed Mr. Whelp had brought the double-seated surrey to the gate.

Marion set her hatpin in place and then sailed out the door in her green linen outfit with its matching parasol.

"Right on time, I see," Aunt Mattie announced from behind her.

Marion eyed Aunt Mattie's fine stepping-out ensemble, also with matching parasol. "You're coming?"

Aunt Mattie descended the steps. "Of course, dear. There's no reason why we shouldn't all go together."

"We?" Marion parroted, trying to keep the disappointment from her voice. She followed Aunt Mattie to the surrey.

"Brandon and I will accompany you and Mr. Whelp." Aunt Mattie accepted Jeffrey's hand into the backseat of the surrey. While she settled, the foreman approached, leading a saddled horse. He tied it behind the wagon before inspecting the team, his fingers trailing on the leather harness.

Jeffrey stood to the side, his face unreadable, ready to assist her. "Today will be one to remember, Miss McDermott. And to start it off—"

He brought one hand around, flourishing a yellow rose. "A scented flower that many consider the most exquisite of all, but it only pales in comparison to you."

She accepted the rose and allowed him to hand her into the front seat of the surrey. Although she knew he'd plucked the blossom from its rambling home beside them, delight that he'd even thought of it brightened her day. "Thank you, Mr. Whelp. I shall press the petals between the pages of my thickest book."

Her comment brought a low murmur from the seat behind her. Unable to hear the foreman's words, she knew it was going to be a long and trying drive to Austin.

Three

Marianne Dashwood was born to an extraordinary fate. She was born to discover the falsehood of her own opinions, and to counteract, by her conduct, her most favourite maxims.

~ Jane Austen, *Sense and Sensibility*

"I don't believe I've ever had a driver before," Tabor said from behind Marion. "Thank you for inviting me, Aunt Mattie."

Without warning, Jeffrey whistled and the surrey jerked forward with the team's movement. Marion grabbed the front rail as the memory of her tumble that first day filled her mind.

Jeffrey guided the horses through the yard, his shoulder brushing hers. "This isn't how I planned our day."

His voice held an unflattering whining quality which she supposed only reflected her own disappointment at having the foreman accompany them. Still, she wasn't about to let Tabor's presence ruin her day. She tipped her head and peered up at him through her long lashes.

"Oh? And what is the plan for today?"

Her coquettish manner hit its mark. His expression changed from surly to confident before she even finished speaking. He clicked his tongue and flicked the reins to increase the team's speed. "Patience, Miss McDermott. You'll find out soon enough."

The surrey bounced along the hard-packed road with the fringe dancing above their heads.

"Slow down, Mr. Whelp." Aunt Mattie tapped her parasol against the back of Marion's seat. "How you can tell my niece to have patience while you race down the road is beyond me."

Jeffrey's mouth tightened at her words, but he slowed the team a notch.

Instinctively, Marion changed the topic to the only personal thing she knew about him. "You mentioned an aunt in Austin, once. How is she?"

He angled his head in a quizzical look. "Why are you asking?"

"Because I'm interested in you—in your family."

That brought out a smile. "Then let me tell you about the time I hid my dear aunt's silver in the manure pile."

"You didn't," she said with mirth, not believing anyone would do such a ghastly thing.

Sporting the look of someone who wasn't one bit sorry for his misdeeds, he began to tell her of his naughty boyhood lived under the baffled gaze of a rich spinster.

Many story-filled minutes later, one of the wagon wheels dipped into a deep rut, halting Jeffrey's tale mid-breath.

A loud grunt followed by a groan escaped from the man in the seat behind Marion. Wondering if the foreman was in pain, Marion turned ever so slightly until she saw him in the corner of her eye. He lounged in the seat, knees apart, with his hands resting on his thighs, his face etched in a grimace of pain. If only she could ease his discomfort.

Jeffrey leaned closer, his sleeve brushing against hers, drawing her attention away from the backseat. "Tell me, Miss McDermott, would you like me to win you a prize today?"

She liked his deep, teasing voice...the way he focused his attention on her while waiting for her to respond. As if his world hinged on her answer.

Leather creaked. Tabor sucked in a rasping breath and in the next instant kicked her wooden seat.

Marion spun around, balancing on the edge of her seat. "Mr. Tabor? Are you all right?"

Aunt Mattie answered Marion's question. "Sitting too long in one spot doesn't do anybody a bit of good. He'll be fine."

Sitting in one spot? Marion stared at the foreman as he stretched his leg out over the side. He leaned toward Aunt Mattie and rubbed his hip.

Marion's thoughts swirled. How on earth could he run a ranch if he couldn't sit still—like on a horse—for more than an hour? An hour? Why, they hadn't even been on the road for more than thirty minutes even. She glanced at Jeffrey.

He looked at her and smiled.

She looked away. Whatever he was thinking wasn't nice, because his attempt to smile hardened his face so it wasn't as handsome as before.

She studied a passing ranch, aware that he was watching her. Another glance and their eyes locked. He winked, his blue eye flashing with merriment. Her heart flipped. How could she have thought for even a moment that he wasn't the most handsome man around?

Time passed and soon Marion spotted the tents and flags of the Austin Fair. Excitement welled up as the unmistakable sound of the calliope drifted across to them. She strained forward in her seat, eager to catch every nuance of the event.

Jeffrey parked amongst the teams and buggies in the area set aside for the purpose. He helped her down, his hand squeezing hers a bit longer than was necessary. His twinkling eyes proved he was eager to explore the annual delights with her.

Marion wondered if their chaperones would accompany them.

Brandon hadn't moved from his seat.

"Tabor, by the time you get down, the fair will be over," Jeffrey goaded.

Aunt Mattie waved them away from her side of the surrey. "You two go on and enjoy yourselves. We'll be along in our own time."

Marion ignored Jeffrey's snicker. Tabor's posture screamed anguish. She stepped toward him. "Are you sure? Would you like Mr. Whelp to help you—"

"No!" His hand shot out and stopped her forward movement. "Just go."

She ached from the rawness in his voice.

Jeffrey tugged her arm. "Come on, I smell food and my stomach's grumbling."

She didn't know what to do, and so she stood, undecided, while Jeffrey coaxed her forward.

Tabor's leg twitched.

Instinctively, Marion reached out, but he turned away, his face taut with raw pain.

So be it. Marion steeled herself against Tabor's rejection and allowed Jeffrey to pull her toward the sound of fun and laughter.

Four

I have not wanted syllables where actions have spoken so plainly.

~ Jane Austen, *Sense and Sensibility*

Pain shot through Brandon's leg as if he'd been seared by a branding iron. The embarrassment of his helpless state brought defeat to his mind. "I should quit so you can hire a better man."

Aunt Mattie tsked like she always did when the pain shot out of his mouth. "Brandon, you're the best foreman I've ever had. Now stop your wallowing. We'll have you fixed up in no time." Spry as a colt, she hopped off the surrey and climbed into the front seat. "Sit tight."

A snap of the reins and she'd turned the team away from the fair and toward Doc Abram's office. Brandon cringed as the surrey jumped and jolted over every rock and dip of the uneven ground. Yet instead of noticing the park-like setting around him, he kept seeing brown eyes ringed by concern. For him.

He snorted. More like pity.

"We're almost there," Aunt Mattie called over the sound of the clopping hooves.

He groaned. Nothing more ignoble than being carried into the doctor's office by a woman twice his age. Perhaps this time he'd accept the laudanum, because it couldn't get any worse than this.

Marion couldn't forget the anguish on Tabor's face. Nor the feeling of inadequacy which had poured out of him and seeped into her soul. As she strolled on Jeffrey's arm, she prayed for mercy for Tabor, as well as all the others who suffered such pain.

Jeffrey pulled her to a halt. "I thought we were here to have fun. You keep making a face like that and I'm going to assume you don't like my company."

He reminded her of a petulant child. She much preferred the adult version, and was womanly enough to bring it out. Turning sideways, she twirled her parasol over her shoulder and peered at him beneath the fringe. "How remiss of me. However shall I make it up to you?"

A gleam shot through his eyes. His arm slid around her waist. "Perhaps a kiss would soothe my wounded pride."

She pushed him away with a little laugh, shocked at the prospect of kissing him. In broad daylight, at that.

He acquiesced with a knowing smile. "Later, then."

Her cheeks grew warm.

Laughing, he pointed her toward a dining tent. "Would you prefer nourishment or"—he turned her toward the carousel with its ménage of animals—"a ride on a charging elephant?"

"A carousel. I've wanted to ride one since I first read about them."

"Then come, milady, your adventure awaits."

Determined to extract every bit of fun out of the excursion, she allowed Jeffrey and the gay music to draw her across the fairgrounds. However, as she circled and bobbed on the carousel, her thoughts turned to another man. If Tabor had escorted her, would he have been able to ride the carousel? With ease, or with difficulty, or not at all? Would he even have escorted her? More importantly, would she have accepted if he had?

The ride slowed, and Jeffrey leaped down. Bowing, he extended his hand. "Milady."

Marion faced the truth. Probably not. Especially not with the dashing Jeffrey around.

She forced a smile on her face and allowed Jeffrey to ease her off the ride. "Thank you, kind sir. And for your careful attention, a reward."

His head lowered.

"Food," she said in a rush lest he think she agreed to his other ungentlemanly suggestion.

They ate beneath a yawning white tent while sitting on a long, narrow bench. Half the seats were filled, and youthful sounds rebounded from the covering. Loud voices, clanging forks, clinking crockery, all blending into a fanfare of festivity.

Jeffrey proved himself a pleasant dinner companion and regaled her with tales of his own school days. She responded in kind with tidbits of information about social gatherings she'd attended while at Austen Abbey.

He searched her face. "Were you at the Bookman's Ball last year?"

"No, why? Were you there?"

An odd look crossed his features. He shook his head then looked away. "I don't believe I attended that one."

Something about his tone didn't match his expression, but why would he lie about being at a ball?

From somewhere across the way, a cow bawled its maternal cry.

"Oh, did you hear that?" Weary of the maudlin turn of the mood, Marion stood on tiptoes to look over the hats and bonnets of the crowd. "Let's go see the animal displays."

He pushed back his hat. "I can see all the animals I want back at the ranch. Miss McDermott—may I call you Marion? I'm here to have fun."

She stepped back, considering him. "Don't you want to see the prize winners? Poppa is looking for next year's herd sire. We need to know who has the best stock."

Jeffrey raised his brows. "And what would a lady know about herd sires?"

"I'm a rancher's daughter, Mr. Whelp. As a cowhand, you should be interested, too. Or am I not correct in assuming you want to own a ranch some day?"

Hands on his hips, he eyed her. "Oh, I'm going to own my own ranch. Make no mistake about that." He broke into a grin. "I only wanted to win a prize for you, first. But it's your special day. " He swept off his hat and bowed deep. "Lead the way, milady."

As they walked through the cattle shelter, Marion kept her eye on the bulls and steers. The new breeds showed a change in the Texas cattle industry. Northerners liked the tender beef from cattle shipped on the railroads. And if they didn't have to make the critters walk for weeks across the Texas landscape, they could raise breeds other than the rangy longhorns.

Jeffrey nudged her arm. "You're thinking about ranching again, aren't you? What's a poor cowhand to do when he can't even keep his girl's attention?"

Even though she had a parasol, she shaded her eyes for effect as she looked up at him. "Am I truly your girl, Mr. Whelp?"

"Call me Jeffrey." He leaned down, his lips approaching hers.

"Oh, look—there's Mr. Tabor," she blurted, nervously.

Jeffrey jerked back. He pointed in another direction. "And there's the lemonade booth." He tightened his arm around hers and guided her toward it.

Marion glanced over her shoulder.

Tabor had disappeared in the crowd.

Rivulets of condensation ran down the sides of the tall glass of lemonade Jeffrey handed her. She drank deeply, enjoying the tart, yet sweet liquid. Half done, she caught sight of Tabor, alone at a shooting booth. So, she'd worried about his leg for nothing. He seemed quite comfortable with his elbows planted on the thick plank serving as a counter while he sighted down the barrel. A second later, he sent the tin targets spinning, one after the other. The man was an expert shot! She couldn't hear what the booth operator said, but he laughed and handed over a blue ribbon. Tabor shoved the strip of silk into his back pocket before taking aim once more.

Jeffrey snorted. "A blue ribbon. It's not like he has anyone waiting for it."

"Why would you even say that? Some girls would say he's an attractive man." She sipped her lemonade.

Jeffrey threw her a funny look before grabbing her elbow. "Come on, I'll win you a ribbon."

She balked. "Wait! My drink." She gulped the rest of her lemonade and handed the empty glass to the booth attendant.

Jeffrey wasted no time weaving around people as he led her to the shooting booth. He stopped near one of the barrels which supported the counter.

Tabor laughed at something the operator said.

"Here." Jeffrey slapped a coin on the thick board.

The operator handed him a gun.

Marion stood next to Tabor. "You seem to be in better shape than when we left you."

He straightened and looked away. "I'm doing all right."

Bang, ping. Bang, ping. The targets spun around.

Jeffrey glanced over his bicep.

Marion smiled at him.

His eyes shifted from Tabor, to her, then back at the targets. He missed two, then hit the rest of them.

The operator handed him a red ribbon.

Jeffrey stared at it.

Marion reached for it. "Red! My favorite color. Thank you, Mr. Whelp."

Jeffrey passed the gun to the operator. "Reload it."

"You don't have to—"

"Wouldn't you like a blue ribbon to go with that red one, Marion?" He accepted the loaded gun, set his elbows on the plank and took aim.

She stood beside Tabor, her face warming at Jeffrey's familiar use of her Christian name, praying for Jeffrey to hit all the targets. When he did, she released her breath.

Blue ribbon in hand, Jeffrey presented it to her with a flourish. "Your prize, milady."

As she reached for it, he snatched the red one from her hand. "And now you no longer need this one."

Five

At first sight, his address is certainly not striking; and his person can hardly be called handsome, till the expression of his eyes, which are uncommonly good, and the general sweetness of his countenance, is perceived.

~ Jane Austen, *Sense and Sensibility*

Unable to take his cowhand's pretentious swagger for another second, Brandon walked away. There was something sad about a man who thought he needed to impress a woman by being better than anyone else.

Marion's laughter carried through the throng. He turned to look before he could stop himself. Her parasol permitted only a partial view of her face, but it was enough to see her enraptured face gazing up at Whelp.

And there was something sad about a woman who needed perfection in a man. He rubbed his hip, although it seemed his chest was the part that ached.

"Afternoon, Brandon," said a familiar voice behind him.

Smiling, he turned around, expecting to see Noah Whitley. Instead, he saw a fish pond kiddie booth. His gaze traveled until it landed on the banker, guarding the entrance. "Hey, Noah. I didn't expect to see you running a kiddie booth."

"You know, I could take that as an insult. I get along very well with my nephews."

"Oh, I know you do. But you don't exactly fit the image of a friendly uncle, you know." Smiling, he flicked his hand toward Noah's clothes. "You're the only man who'd show up at an agricultural fair wearing his Sunday best."

Noah brushed a bit of Texas dust off his twill jacket. "The booth is to raise funds for the church. I figured I ought to dress the part."

"Well, you're that, all right. Look, here comes a customer."

A few yards away, a little girl wearing a frilly purple dress strained toward them, pulling the hand of a young woman. But when she spotted Noah, the girl let go so quickly the woman stumbled forward.

"Eva, what on earth?" The woman hitched down the hem of her shirtwaist with one hand while patting her hair with the other.

The little girl—Eva—sidled past Noah. She stopped inches from the galvanized tub holding the fishing pond. Only then did she look at the water where a dozen wooden fish of all sizes floated along.

The woman approached, her appraising glance skimming over each man in turn. "How much to play?"

"A nickel," Noah answered.

"A nickel?" She looked askance. "What do you win?"

Noah didn't blink. "A licorice stick or a cinnamon stick, if you find the one with a star. A penny candy if you don't."

She shook her finger at him. "That's robbery. Where's Emmeline Whitley? Isn't she running this booth for the church?"

Unwavering in his look, Noah crossed his arms. "Which is exactly why it costs a nickel, since it's a fundraiser for Austin's needy."

Brandon straightened to take his weight off his good leg for a bit. His movement seemed to catch the woman's eye because she turned to him and smiled.

"Nanny!"

Keeping his hands in his front pockets, Brandon nodded to the little girl who'd been waiting so nicely. "Your daughter's getting impatient."

The woman laughed gaily, her hand near her throat. "Oh, she's not my child. Heavens, no! She's merely my charge."

"Mm hm." Perhaps that was why she seemed oblivious to the fact that little Eva was about ready to join the fish in the tub. He stretched the fingers of his right hand to catch the nickel he'd dropped in his pocket earlier. "Here, catch!"

Eva whipped her head toward him, auburn curls bouncing beneath her floppy flowered hat. She deftly caught the nickel he tossed at her and studied it.

"You give that right back. You can't go taking money from strange men."

Brandon limped over to the child, feeling and ignoring the woman's stare at his leg. Since he couldn't kneel, he stood back a few feet and bent down to her level. "Ranger Brandon Tabor at your service, ma'am." He swept off his hat, enjoying her giggle. "I believe your daddy is Mr. Bennet, which means you must be Miss Evangeline Bennet. Now I don't want you to get into trouble because of me, so I have a plan. How about if I take back my nickel, and then you help me win the game. Would that be all right?"

Nodding, she handed back his nickel, which he tossed to Noah. "Now which one do you think is hiding a star?"

Her hand shot toward the biggest fish in the tub.

"Whoa—"

She looked at him, her hand inches from the wooden floater.

"Just because that's the biggest fish doesn't always mean he's the best."

She bit her bottom lip, hand dropping to her side. "How do I know which one is the best?"

"Well, that's the hard part, you see. You never really know which one it is, but sometimes you get a feeling for it."

Her face scrunched up. "How do you do that?"

He held back his laughter. "Well, let's see...." He moved closer to the tub. "Give each of them a real hard look. Let me know when you're done."

She became very still.

Voices filtered into the booth, Noah's bride, Emmeline, among them. He closed out the sounds, followed his own directions, and concentrated on the wooden fish.

"I'm done," Eva announced, not taking her eyes off her quarry.

"Good. Which one is more special than the rest?"

"That one." She pointed to a medium-sized one, similar to the rest in every other way.

"Fish it out, young lady," Noah instructed.

Her hand hovered above it. She turned a questioning face to Brandon.

"Sure, go ahead," he encouraged. "If that's the one you want."

She lifted it out of the water.

Brandon blocked it from her view before she could peek under it. "Just one more thing. Sometimes we guess wrong because we can't know what's hidden underneath. That may be the fish with the star, or it might not. If it isn't, you're not allowed to throw it at me. Understand?"

She grinned.

He pulled his hand away.

She flipped it over. And beamed when she saw the yellow-painted star.

Half-hidden by a group of young women and children, Marion watched the little Bennet girl wrap her arms around Tabor. She'd been caught up in the whole exchange, drawn into it by Tabor's voice, devoid of the pain he'd displayed earlier. Marion knew him as a person who cared for others and his animals, but watching him with the little girl showed Marion how he would be with children of his own. It was something she had never considered before.

Emmeline strolled over to the fishing pond booth. "Somebody's earned a reward," she cooed. Threading her arm around her husband's she boldly kissed his cheek.

Noah grinned. "Keep that up, ma'am, and I'll have to marry you."

"You already did."

Marion blinked at the water in her eyes. She'd spent two months visiting the Whitleys, seeing them dote on each other, a perfect example of how God gives you the desire of your heart. What she'd give to have a love like theirs.

Curls flouncing, the little Bennet girl skipped past them out of the booth, waving a cinnamon stick. "Thank you, Ranger Tabor," she sing-songed.

Ranger Tabor? Marion briefly caught his eye before he headed to the Whitleys.

Tabor shook Noah's hand. "Seems you still owe me a 'thank you' for not marrying Emmeline for you."

Noah shrugged.

Marion gaped. In all the weeks she'd lived with Emmeline and Noah they'd never mentioned being friends with a Mr. Brandon Tabor.

Smiling, Emmeline rolled her eyes. She placed her palm on Tabor's arm. "Thank you for refusing his request, Brandon. Although, I do believe any lady would be honored to be courted by one of the noblest men in Austin."

Tabor gallantly tipped his hat. "I wish you all the best in your new life together."

"Thank you." Emmeline dabbed the corner of her eye. "The words take on a special meaning coming from you."

Jeffrey stepped in front of Marion. "There you are. Having fun?"

"Yes, I am." She sidestepped around him. What had Emmeline meant by that?

Tabor merged into the throng.

Jeffrey blocked her view again. "I apologize for leaving you like that. I'll make up for it, though." He tilted her chin up. "You don't appear to be wilting under this hot sun, but are you ready for another cool drink?"

She stared at the spot in the crowd where she'd last seen the foreman. She shouldn't care about a broken Texas Ranger who had nothing to offer a lady when there was a handsome young cowboy seeing to her every comfort. Surely, she shouldn't. Pushing Tabor from her thoughts, she tucked her arm around Jeffrey's. "It sounds divine, but first I need to say hello to Mr. and Mrs. Noah Whitley."

Although Jeffrey hadn't seemed interested in the agricultural aspect of the fair, by the time they arrived back at the carousel, he proved to be quite knowledgeable about the carnival side of it.

"Perhaps I'll win the brass ring, this time."

"What brass ring?"

He pointed to a metal box on the end of a wooden arm which was nailed to a post. "Grab the brass ring and you get a free ride."

Whee, whee, sang a whistle. A steam engine stood close to the brass ring post, smoke sailing from its stack. Wearing a leather apron over clothes streaked with grease smudges, a worker turned a knob here and a switch there. A wide belt began to wobble and bounce, moving from the engine's flywheel over to the carousel before disappearing beneath the flooring. Marion couldn't see where the other flywheel was, but assumed it was in the center of the carousel. Soon, the stitching that held the two ends together returned, zipped around the wheel, and headed back under.

Jeffrey led her into the line. "I'll sit on the outside this time."

"I didn't even realize before. I was too excited just to be riding around."

While waiting, she watched the riders. As the carousel moved, the people sitting on the outside animals reached out to grab the ring. It wasn't as easy as she'd first thought because the horses bobbed up and down as the carousel went around. A rider had to be at the top of the movement, and then lean out as far as they could to get a decent chance at grasping the ring.

Many riders tried, and when a long-limbed lad snatched the ring, the riders groaned as one. The ride slowed and stopped. The operator took the brass ring from the jubilant young man and told him to stay seated. The boy asked if his girl could take his place, and the operator agreed.

"I want another go-round," Jeffrey announced.

"No. I want to try." Marion picked an open-mouthed horse with fire in its eyes. She settled side-saddle, one foot angled into the stirrup, the other dangling over the outside edge. With nowhere to put her closed parasol, she handed it to Jeffrey. "Here. I can't try holding this."

He covered his heart. "I give you my heart and you give me your parasol." But he took it anyway.

With all the seats filled, the whistle blew and the steam engine started up once more. Marion started to rise as the carousel began its journey. The first time around, she'd passed the post before realizing it held the brass ring. The second time she was at the bottom of her ride. Around and around she went, trying to predict the perfect moment to stand, stretch and grasp.

A couple times, her fingers hit the ring but she couldn't grab it fast enough. And once, she almost toppled off her horse but managed to right herself at the last second. That time was scary because of the wide belt zipping beneath on its journey to and from the steam donkey.

Before she knew it, the carousel slowed and then stopped.

Jeffrey jumped off. Arms up, parasol leaning against his leg, he caught her around the waist and eased her to the ground. "You should have let me try," he teased, leading her off to the side.

She splayed her fingers across her waist. "And miss all that fun? Oh, but it was wonderful. Reminded me of roping a wayward calf."

"Don't you ever think of anything other than ranching?"

"Yes, but, ranching is my life."

The carousel started up again with a new contingent of riders. She wanted to see if anyone in this group managed to grab the brass ring.

"What about parties and social events?" Jeffrey asked. "And afternoon tea with the neighbors?"

"I'm not much of a social draw. Back home, I'd rather stay on the ranch." He didn't respond, and she was too excited to pursue the subject.

Her gaze landed on the pretty little girl in the lilac-colored dress from the fishing pond booth. Little Miss Bennet and her nanny, if Marion remembered correctly. The little girl was riding an outside horse, concentrating on the brass ring. Several times she stood to reach the ring, but even Marion could see she was too small. Where was her nanny?

Marion scanned the crowd until her gaze landed on the woman's back where she stood conversing with the steam engine worker.

Marion started toward the woman. After a step, though, she looked at the carousel and gasped. The little girl stood on her horse, leaning outward, arm raised. Marion stood transfixed, unable to take her eyes off the spinning carousel. Sounds faded away, leaving her caught in an eerie place where people talked and laughed, their mouths working normally, yet she couldn't hear a sound. Not the carousel music. Not the whirring belts of the steam donkey.

And then, as the girl in the lilac-colored dress came around for another try, Marion saw the determination in her eyes and she knew the child was going to jump, high above the bouncing belt, trying to grasp that brass ring.

With goose bumps riddling her arms, Marion lunged toward the carousel, pushing people out of her path, praying for a miracle.

The girl sprang from the horse at the same moment Marion howled, "No!"

Heads turned her way.

In horror, she saw the little fingers fly over the ring holder, grasping the air—someone blocked Marion's view!

Please, God, catch her in your arms of love.

The crowd gasped as Marion managed to shove the man out of her way and saw what everyone else saw.

Clinging to the ring's wooden support, the girl dangled precariously above the moving belt.

"Help!" Marion screamed. She threw a look back to the steam donkey worker who fumbled with the knobs and switches. The Bennet's nanny stood frozen—her face a sickly shade of green.

"She's a tough one, all right." A familiar voice broke through the silence, and she realized Jeffrey stood beside her, his arm possessively around her waist.

Marion wrung her hands. "We have to help her."

"Anyone trying to help her could get himself injured, or worse, killed." He tightened his arm on her waist. "No need for you to see this. Let's go."

"No!" She twisted from his grasp, pushed forward, and took a stand beside a young dark-haired woman she recognized as Eliza Branch, one of the newer students at Austen Abbey. Eliza's face reflected the horror Marion felt at watching the scene.

A few yards away, Tabor broke through the crowd, his face grim, eyes glued to the girl. "Hang on, Eva," he called. "I'll get you down."

"I want my daddy!"

"I know, sweetie. I wish he were here, too." Tabor moved close to the belt, arms raised.

Marion's pulse pounded in her ears. Only a couple more inches and his trousers would brush the belt—maybe pull him off balance on top of it—or under it. Yet he seemed uncaring of his own danger.

"Trust me, Eva. Remember how we worked together at the fish pond?"

"Y–yes." She tried to turn, and her body swayed.

"Don't move, honey." Tabor's hands were inches from her knees, but if he grabbed her, the shift of balance could send them both down.

Eyes wide open, Marion continued to pray.

Tabor took a little step forward with his injured leg, followed by a quick one with his good leg. Intuitively, Marion knew he was in pain.

"We're gonna play another game, Eva. Do you know what a fairy is?" Perspiration beaded along his hairline.

"Uh huh. F–fairies fly."

"That's right, sweetheart. And you're going to fly down to me when I give you the secret word, all right?"

The steam donkey quieted. The belt slowed but kept going.

"My arms are getting tired," Eva whimpered.

"I know, but it's real important for you to listen. When I give you the secret word, open your hands and drop straight down with your arms out. Don't bend at all. Do you understand?"

"Like I'm f–flying? What's the s–secret word?"

"Remember, straight as you can. Here we go, the secret word is... princess."

Marion held her breath.

Eva didn't move. "Mr. Ranger?"

"I'm here, Eva. You have to fly now, Princess."

She let go so quick, a look of surprise crossed his features a second before he caught her around her legs.

The belt continued to slow. Marion wanted to rush up and pull Eva's dress down because it bunched over Tabor's arm, but she wouldn't intrude for anything.

"Keep flying, Eva." Brandon rasped as he stepped back from the belt, his face contorted in pain. He managed a half step back with his injured leg before taking a longer step with his good one. The farther back he stepped, the closer the crowd advanced until he was several feet away from the belt.

"A heroic rescue," Eliza said in breathy admiration. She reached into her bag for a small notepad and pencil and began scribbling notes as if she were a newspaper reporter instead of a girl in finishing school.

Jeffrey rushed forward as well, elbowing the young woman out of the way. "Here, I'll take the girl." His arms encircled Eva's waist, and he pulled her away from Brandon.

Shrieking, she kicked with both feet until Jeffrey lowered her to the ground, a dark glower across his features.

"Eva!" The Bennets' nanny rushed up and shook her finger. "You naughty girl. Just wait until I tell your father."

Tears streaming down her face, Eva hung her head.

The nanny grasped Eva's hand and pulled, almost dragging her in the process.

Eva sent a tearful look at Brandon before being swallowed by the crowd.

Eliza rushed to Brandon. "You're a hero, sir. May I have your name?"

He grunted. With his injured leg extended sideways, he bent his right and tried to grab his fallen hat, missing by inches.

Marion hurried over and picked it up without thought.

He straightened, a flush to his cheeks.

"Here." She held it out to him.

Hesitating, his flush deepened.

It dawned on her that his reaction may have been caused by her quick action in front of the young woman, and not from his exertion.

"Obliged," he murmured. He placed it on his head and turned to the pretty reporter. "Please excuse me, miss. After such a harrowing close call with death or disfigurement, I'd rather not relive the experience."

"Of course. Forgive me." Eliza nodded at Marion and stepped back.

Jeffrey must have heard the last of it because he approached saying, "You can question me, Miss Branch, I tried to help—"

"Let it go, Jeffrey." The steel in Marion's voice brought Jeffrey's head up in a flash. She pushed past him toward the food tables, her hand clenched in a very unladylike fist. Taut nerves, frazzled feelings, thunderous thoughts on things out of her control. All she wanted was to sit with a cool drink and not think about anything. Or how Ranger Brandon Tabor pulled her heart in his direction when she wanted to go in another. And speaking of the man...what other compelling secrets was he hiding?

Jeffrey jogged beside her fast pace. "You called me Jeffrey. Do I detect a change in our relationship—Marion?"

Something *had* changed, although she wasn't sure what. She needed time to think about the events that had transpired.

Fiddle music filled the air. The perfect distraction. There'd be time enough to dwell on the day later, when she was alone.

She looped her arm through his. "Come on, let's go dance."

He was not an ill-disposed young man, unless to be rather cold hearted, and rather selfish, is to be ill-disposed....

~ Jane Austen, *Sense and Sensibility*

The sounds of lively music and gaiety pulled Marion toward the evening's entertainment. She led Jeffrey to the edge of the flowing dancers and waited their turn. Skirts swirled around dark trousers. Feet moved in time with the music. On a hay rack near the dancers, the musicians played their tunes.

Marion had attended many local fairs, but this was the State Fair. Red, white, and blue bunting and banners decorated the barn in abundance—more than she'd ever seen at one time. The colors were glorious and would be more so when looked at while spinning around on the dance floor.

The music stopped. Couples left the dance floor. Jeffrey led her forward. She took her place in a square, and then she was off, laughing and swirling as the colors flew around her. When it was over, she begged him for another. And then another, still. Finally, he led her to an empty chair in an area where several other ladies, old and young, sat fanning themselves.

"Rest here. I'll be right back." He smiled, and she melted under his appreciative gaze.

A hot Texas breeze blew in through the wide door opening. It sailed through the crowd and kept going out the door that twinned the first. Twilight when they arrived, darkness had spread across the land while she'd danced in wild abandon. But it had felt good to be back in her natural setting. The cotillions she'd attended at Austen Abbey couldn't match the exuberance of a country dance.

Her gaze roamed the crowd and settled on Jeffrey at the refreshment table. He appeared to be conversing with a girl her own age, with ginger-colored hair and a rather plain face. The server dipped her head and batted her lashes. Marion couldn't see Jeffrey's response, but the action amused rather than worried her. Why was that?

Movement at the door caught Marion's gaze. She didn't know why, except she felt disappointment when she didn't recognize any of the newcomers. And then her heart gladdened when she spotted Brandon arrive with Aunt Mattie on his arm. Marion looked away, her hand on her bodice. Surely her heart's fast beat was due to the increasing heat of a hundred moving people.

"Looking for me?" Jeffrey approached, both hands holding a glass of punch.

"Yes, of course. I'm positively parched."

He handed her a glass and then sat on the edge of the seat beside her. "I see Miz Mattie has arrived." He pointed in Aunt Mattie's direction with his glass.

"Yes, just now." She sipped the burgundy liquid, enjoying the respite away from the crowd. "It's quiet over here."

Reflected light flared in his eyes. "All the better. I don't want to share you with anyone." He leaned toward her, one arm behind her, his other crossing her front to grip the side of her chair. "I think a kiss is in order."

"Jeffrey, not here." She pushed his arm. It didn't budge.

"Later, then?"

"Ahem," announced the crisp British voice Marion would forever equate with Austen Abbey.

She almost laughed at the slow closure of Jeffrey's eyelids. Peering around him, she smiled at her former headmistress. "Good evening, Mrs. Collins."

Although she wore an ivory high-collared shirt instead of her standard white one, her black skirt and upswept dark hair with jeweled hair combs was the same Mrs. Collins who had turned a headstrong girl into the genteel young lady Marion hoped she portrayed.

Jeffrey's arm fell away from Marion's chair. "Mrs. Collins." His exaggerated bow didn't bring a smile to either woman.

"Later, yes," Marion said in response to his question. Her voice tight, she wished he wouldn't draw undue attention. "I'd like to *dance* again, later."

As he headed to the refreshment table to get the headmistress a cup upon her request, Mrs. Collins's looked at Marion with concern. "My dear, that young man is Mr. Whelp, the nephew of an old friend, Gertrude Baines. He has caused her nothing but misery."

Thinking of the exploits Jeffrey had detailed to her on their way to the fair, Marion couldn't disagree. But before she could respond, a gray-haired gentleman strolled toward them. She thought he would ask Mrs. Collins to dance, but his eyes were on Marion.

"And who is this, Mrs. Collins? One of your young ladies, I presume?"

The headmistress introduced him. "Mr. Schmidt, Miss McDermott."

Mr. Schmidt clicked his heels together. "A pleasure, Miss McDermott. May I have the next dance?"

"You may, Mr. Schmidt."

No sooner had they gained the floor than a shriek turned Marion's head in time to see an explosion of burgundy liquid hurl in the air. It landed on the white shirt of a gentleman. The ginger-haired girl stood on the other side of the punch bowl, her hands empty, a horrified look on her face.

"You idiot!" the man screeched at the girl. "Look what you've done!"

She leaned toward him, cloth in hand, and even from the distance of sixty feet, it seemed like tears filled her eyes.

The man pushed her clumsy hands away.

Jeffrey approached the man and spoke close to his ear. The man stopped glaring at the server. Head cocked, he listened intently to Jeffrey.

"There now. A silly accident." Mr. Schmidt turned Marion away from the scene. "Some men are like the steam engine under pressure. One little mishap and boom!" He spread his arms, fingers splayed. "Tell me, Miss McDermott. Would you prefer a boiling kettle, or a simmering pot?"

"I—" She closed her mouth. What was he asking?

He smiled benignly at her.

She glanced in Jeffrey's direction but couldn't spot him through the crowd around the refreshment table.

"Come now, Miss McDermott."

Had the music stopped? She hadn't been aware. Mr. Schmidt eased his hand around her waist and held his other one out. She placed her hands in position and waited for the next song, her gaze looking past his ear.

Brandon stood in her line of vision, his head tipped slightly forward and to the side, his eyes capturing her own. She sucked in a breath and held it, mesmerized.

The haunting sound of a violin disrupted Marion's focus.

Mr. Schmidt stepped sideways, dragging her with him. "Come now, Miss McDermott." He readied himself once more. "There aren't many steps to remember in that pretty head of yours."

All thoughts of Brandon fled as she concentrated on Mr. Schmidt. She ignored his snide remark only because he seemed to be a friend of Mrs. Collins's. As she danced, her eyes searched the crowd for her tall, blond escort. She couldn't see him, but she seemed to locate Brandon with unerring aim.

Mr. Schmidt danced her away from the view, his gloating expression and sweaty palms making her uneasy. Two more minutes and she could flee without making a scene. Until then, she closed her eyes and allowed the music to carry her away.

Brandon watched Marion waltz by in the stranger's arms. With her head tipped back, and her eyes closed, she appeared to be enjoying the moment. For the first time in fifteen months, he wished he'd been far away when the explosion damaged his leg. But if not him, then one of his men would have taken the worst of it.

Marion sailed past once more, sparking his anger. He'd been content with his lot before she'd arrived, and he'd have to live with it after she left. He headed for the door, unable to watch her float dreamily across the dance floor.

Outside, he moved out of the light cast by a dozen lanterns. As his eyes adjusted to the starry night, a young man approached, his light-colored hair gleaming from reflected light. "Going home, mister? I'll get yer rig for ya."

"Nope. But I'll let you know when I am."

The young man's shoulders dropped along with his smile. He'd probably hoped to make a few bits for his trouble.

"What's your name?" Brandon asked. "I'll be sure to ask for you."

His face brightened. "Harmon Gray, sir. Jonathan's working with me, but I'd appreciate it if you'd mention my name. That's Harmon, sir, and I'll be around until the last wagon leaves."

An elderly couple exited the barn, drawing Harmon's attention.

Brandon wandered off in the direction of the parking field. After searching for several minutes, he found a flatbed wagon. He hitched his good hip up on the deck and leaned back on his elbows. The pain wasn't so bad without the weight on his bad leg. Not if he ignored it.

Tipping back his head, he gazed at the stars. The familiar sight of the Big and Little Dippers always made him feel better. He pushed himself back until he was able to lie flat with his feet dangling over the edge, like he used to do on clear nights when Savana was alive. Hands tucked under his head, he searched the heavens until he found his favorite constellation, Orion.

Like a cat chasing a string, his eyes swung to Cygnet, Savana's favorite.

"See how she takes care of those around her. She'll never leave them. Never." Savana's words ricocheted through his head. And yet, she'd left him and gone to play among those very same stars. Music drifted on the breeze, reminding him that Savana had loved to dance. They'd danced in the meadow. They'd danced in the barn. And they'd danced in the cabin on a chilly winter's night. Pain crept through his body from his hip, from his heart, from every part of him that remembered her... aching for her touch.

Someone giggled.

Savana never giggled. Her memory floated away.

Brandon struggled to a sitting position, the cold shadow of loneliness slowing his movements.

A few wagons away, a silhouetted couple spoke together in low murmurs. Something about the man niggled at Brandon. Tall, he looked down at the woman and spoke in a low tone. She giggled again, a distinctive sound.

Brandon recognized her as the girl who'd accidently spilled punch on one of the richest ranchers in the area.

The man straightened, and in that moment, Brandon recognized Jeffrey Whelp. Where was Marion?

He held his breath, knowing a confrontation could ruin the social event of the season.

Whelp lowered his head, the woman raised hers, and their lips met.

Unable to watch, Brandon shimmied to the edge of the wagon and slipped off with a grunt. He glanced at the couple. They'd moved closer, if that was possible, and hadn't seemed to notice anything other than themselves.

Disgust churning his gut, Brandon skirted the wagons. Horses left standing in their harness nickered as he passed. Giving a pat here and a stroke there, he took the long way around in an effort to diffuse his riled emotions. He stopped beside the outfit closest to the barn to catch his breath and hope the searing pain in his hip died down for a bit.

The sound of horseshoes hitting the hardened ground reached him before the wagon pulled into view. A dark-haired youngster set the brake on the phaeton and sprang down. He waited, his eyes on a small group of people standing beside the entrance.

A rotund woman in her middle years turned and peered into the dark. "Where is that girl, Osgood?"

The bulky man beside her patted her arm. "Now, now, Pearl. She's probably off with some of those friends of hers."

Brandon recognized Pearl and Osgood Nelson. Approaching footsteps from behind turned his gaze to the sound. Through the darkness, the serving girl appeared. Alone. She stopped before reaching the light cast by the open doors and tried to fix her mussed hair. As soon as a distraction drew the attentions of the waiting people, she slipped into the light and around the corner.

Mrs. Nelson turned. "There you are, Beatrice. Come along, now."

Mr. Nelson herded them into the phaeton. At the last moment, he flicked his wrist and a silver coin flashed through the air. "For you, Mr. Wellington. Find yourself a nice lady."

The boy—Jonathan, he would bet—caught it and grinned. "I will, Mr. Nelson. Good evening to you, sir."

Beatrice smiled coyly at Jonathan.

Brandon wasn't amused. Didn't she know that men don't take kindly to having their affections played with?

As the phaeton disappeared into the dark, Whelp strode into view, grinning. "All the action's inside, Tabor. Or are you bored watching everyone else have fun?"

Brandon blocked the spiteful words with practiced ease. "A man finds action wherever he wants to look for it. And sometimes where he doesn't." He leveled his look at Whelp.

It had the intended effect. Whelp's composure dipped, his eyes questioning.

Aunt Mattie and Marion chose that moment to make an appearance. They stood in the entrance, two slender frames of the same height, their faces half in shadow. "We'd like to go back, now," Aunt Mattie said. "Are you ready, Brandon?"

Whelp stepped between them. "It'll take a few minutes to bring the wagon around. I wouldn't mind a final dance with Miss McDermott." He moved to her side.

Aunt Mattie looked at Brandon.

He shrugged slightly.

She shook out her shawl. "All right, Mr. Whelp. The music's just started. Bring her back the moment it stops."

Whelp's face darkened as he stared at her.

Marion grabbed his arm. "Come on, Mr. Whelp. We're missing the dance." She tugged his sleeve and stepped inside.

He followed, yet he didn't seem eager to dance.

Brandon mentally applauded her for pulling Whelp away before words were said that couldn't be taken back.

Harmon approached, and Brandon sent him off for their wagon. He nodded toward the dancers. "I'm beginning to think you were right, Aunt Mattie. He's trouble."

She stared into the darkness. "I just don't know anymore, Brandon." She sighed. "I want what's best for her, but if she has her heart set on him..."

Brandon kicked a stone out of the dirt. It pattered along the ground. "Do you think her pa would approve?"

She rolled her eyes. "Her father gives her whatever she wants, and that's the truth of it."

Harmon arrived with their wagon. Reaching up, he caught the coin Brandon flipped into the air. "Thank you, sir. Pleasure doing business with you."

As Whelp appeared with Marion, he nodded to Brandon. "You two know the way better than us. You should probably sit up front."

Brandon raised one brow for emphasis and looked at Aunt Mattie. She strode toward the backseat. "I don't think so, Mr. Whelp. Come, Marion, sit back here with me."

Grinning, Brandon untied his horse from the back of the wagon. "I think I'll ride along for a bit. Me and that wagon don't get along too well." It wasn't just the cramped wagon that bothered him...it was the ability to move fast if needed.

Wild boars, feral dogs, cougars, and other creatures roamed the Texas night. He may have been lackadaisical heading into town, but he was on the job now, and his horse would run where he couldn't.

Seven

Know your own happiness. You want nothing but patience—or give it a more fascinating name, call it hope.

~ Jane Austen, *Sense and Sensibility*

A week later, Jeffrey's breath warmed Marion's cheek. Thin streams of light leaked through tight wall planks, allowing her to see the dust motes dancing in an otherwise dark barn. At any moment, the huge door could slide open and Brandon, Ned, or even Aunt Mattie could walk in and see her embracing Jeffrey. They wouldn't know she'd just arrived and he'd surprised her, but the rumors would start.

"Come ride with me," he repeated.

After not seeing him for several days, she yearned for time alone with him, without the fear of getting caught. She missed the way his words and eyes expressed his appreciation for her. What could be more innocent than a ride in broad daylight to show her the sights?

"All right. I'll go tell Aunt Mattie."

He grazed her cheek with the back of his knuckles. "I'll get the horses."

She ran back to the house, changed into gauchos, and hurried back to the barn. Two horses stood by the hitching rail, one with a side-saddle. Assumptions. "Mr. Whelp, I ride astride."

"What?" He looked her up and down, taking in her riding clothes. "What in the world?"

"Switch the saddle, Mr. Whelp, or I'll not accompany you."

With a rakish look, he did as she asked.

She clasped her hands behind her back for fear they'd start clapping on their own. Oh, the joy of an afternoon of freedom. Even Aunt

Mattie's stipulation that she be back within three hours couldn't quell her happiness. The acquiescence hadn't come easy though, especially since Aunt Mattie didn't like Jeffrey's attitude, but she had no reason to distrust him. And, as Marion had pointed out, making her own decisions was part of becoming a woman.

With the saddle cinched, Jeffrey bent to receive her boot in his threaded hands. She mounted and waited for him to do likewise.

He threw her a grin. "I promise, this is one ride you won't forget."

Marion's heart jumped. She glanced at the house to see Aunt Mattie hurrying down the front walk. Fearing she'd changed her mind, Marion spurred her horse into action.

Brandon rode into the yard and reined in beside Aunt Mattie. He'd seen two figures riding off but had been too far away to make them out.

Groaning, he eased off his horse. "Company?"

Other than a look back when she'd heard the sound of his horse, she hadn't moved from staring after the two riders.

"Marion went riding with Whelp."

Brandon's heart fell into his stomach. Contrary to what his eyes told him, he'd hoped Marion had discovered Whelp's true nature. "Alone?"

"I couldn't hold her back, Brandon. If I had tried, she would have snuck out." With the pair no longer in sight, she turned to meet his gaze, worry bringing her brows together and washing the youth from her face. "Maybe even at night."

"You want me to follow them?" His hip flamed at the thought, but he tried not to show it.

"No." She glanced away. "She'll never trust me again if she found out. And Brandon, as much as I respect your skill as a ranger, I really don't want to take that chance."

He nodded, knowing she was right, unable to think of an alternative. "If it's all right with you then, I'll go address my pain and maybe do some praying while I'm at it."

She smiled, but it wasn't her normal happy one. More like a brief upraising at the corners of her mouth. "Thank you. I think I'll take a glass of tea and sit on the verandah." She made her way slowly to the house as if she'd suddenly grown twenty years older.

Stubborn as she was, she would probably sit there until her niece rode back into sight. He had a mind to ignore her words and ride out anyway.

And what about Me?

The question jiggled in his mind as it usually did after making a rash decision. If he was going to pray about something and hand it to the Lord, why would he take it back?

"I hear you, Lord. Seems I'll be too busy praying to do much riding anyway."

Ned exited the barn with an acrid-smelling wheelbarrow. "You say something, boss?"

Brandon passed him. "Talking to the Lord, Ned. Just talking to the Lord."

Marion's face warmed—partly from the blazing sun, partly from the affectionate looks Jeffrey cast her way.

They'd been riding abreast for an hour when Jeffrey stopped at the top of a small hill. "You're a good rider."

She admired the valley below where a lazy creek meandered through a valley of light green grass. "I'm a rancher's daughter. I'd better be a good rider."

He pointed to a grove of trees on the far side. The branches hung so low, she couldn't see the ground beneath them. "See those trees down there? Wanna race?"

Not only did she see the trees, she knew the fastest way to reach them. She kicked her heels, and leaned back as her horse took off down the hill. At ground level, she leaned forward across the horse's neck and crooned to him. The gelding wasn't familiar to her, but she knew horses, and the farther she leaned, the faster he ran. Instead of making a straight run for the grove, she cut to one side or the other as the hazards appeared.

Jeffrey stuck to her horse's tail like a pack animal on a rope. As if he too, knew the land intimately. Side-by-side they raced until the final hundred yards when he pulled ahead by a length before pulling up and springing off.

He faced her, arms raised, jubilation showing. "I won!"

With her chest rising and falling in quick succession from the exertion, she looked around, pleased to see the grove hadn't changed much in the two years since her last visit.

His hand on her knee brought her around. "Yes?"

"I thought we'd rest here awhile."

Beneath the weight of his hand, her skin burned as if the heavy layers weren't sandwiched between their flesh. Her pulse raced.

He raised his arms, a teasing smile on his face.

She leaned into his waiting arms, knowing he wanted to kiss her. A quiver ran through her. After thinking about it for days, she wanted him to kiss her, too.

He lowered her down until the toes of their boots touched. "I want my prize," he murmured against the side of her neck.

She tipped her head, gave him greater exposure, as tingles zinged through every nerve ending of her body. She couldn't answer. Didn't even try.

He trailed fiery kisses along her neckline, and when she thought she'd die from the torture, his lips sealed themselves over hers.

Her knees buckled. He held her tight, and yet she felt herself falling. The sensation piled on the others, sucking the air out of her. In a haze, she felt his hand on her back, roaming across it. He growled, deep in his throat.

Through a fog came the memory of her taking the wretched corset off before putting her riding clothes on.

His hand moved to her front and drifted to her—

"No!" She pushed him away and scrambled to the creek's edge. Kneeling over the water, she saw a wavering face with hair sticking out in all directions reflected back at her. She plunked her hand in the middle of the image, distorting her image. Her cupped hands gathered cold water and she splashed it on her face and neck before using her wet hands to press tendrils of hair back into place. With her palms on her cheeks, she prayed all evidence of the incident would fade as fast as the ripples had disappeared into the creek. Between her hat and the wind, Aunt Mattie wouldn't suspect a thing. Or so she hoped.

Jeffrey stood where she'd pushed him.

Without speaking, she picked up her hat and untied her reins.

"Marion, wait."

With one hand on the pommel, she faced the rear of the gelding and then swung herself up into the saddle.

His eyes widened. "I—" He picked up his hat and fingered the brim.

"I just couldn't help myself. You're a passionate woman, Marion."

She bit her top lip as his words reached her heart. No one had ever called her a passionate woman before. No one had even called her a woman before. Like a salve, pleasure soothed the cracks he'd placed there earlier.

He walked toward her, hands out as if calming a skittish colt. "I want to marry you."

"Marry me?" Her mind stumbled over the words.

"You must have considered it."

She stared at her stirrup. An image emerged of facing Poppa at the station with the most handsome man on her arm. The same image had once filled her with pleasure. Yet, she hesitated.

He took a step closer. "Isn't marriage what you want?"

Was it? She wasn't sure anymore. "I—I don't know."

He snorted. "You responded to my advances with passion. Marion—"

"No. I need to think." She wouldn't allow him to goad her into an answer...because he hadn't said a word about love.

Eight

The more I know of the world, the more I am convinced that I shall never see a man whom I can really love. I require so much!

~ Jane Austen, *Sense and Sensibility*

Marion peered over the boards at the foreman ministering to the quiet calf. Since she'd arrived at the ranch, Brandon had cared for the ailing critter, yet its health hadn't improved. This morning was no different. Brandon's sun-beaten hands, roughened by days of gripping leather and wood, had stroked the calf's neck, his sweet speech encouraging it along. Nothing had worked. No signs of injury, no erratic breathing, no bawling for its mother. And no one knew the reason.

The peace pervading the barn was in complete opposition to her emotions. She rested her cheek on her crossed arms and closed her eyes. The barn odors didn't bother her, nor the rustling in the corner since smells and mice were part of ranch life. And she loved everything about it, except death.

Brandon rose and retreated out of the stall to stand beside her in the aisle. "I've done all I can. Only God can save him now."

"What does God care about a poor animal? He didn't keep my momma from dying on the day I was born."

His expression deepened with sorrow.

"Don't pity me," she lashed out, cutting the air between them with her open palm. She marched outside, feeling his gaze following her, wanting to run, but too much of a lady to do it.

How dare he blame the decline of an animal's health on God, when he was the one caring for it!

She ran into the house and found solace in the only thing she knew that could bring her comfort—Aunt Mattie's piano. She played until her hands hurt more than her heart.

As the next few days passed, Marion divided her time between playing the piano and wandering the ranch yard. Jeffrey had vanished. Sent to the far reaches of the ranch, or so she suspected. No one talked about him. Not even her.

Several days after Jeffrey's proposal, she sat at the piano when movement in the corral caught her eye. Since it usually meant some measure of excitement, she finished her piece and headed down to find out.

As she neared the corral, she made out Brandon standing in the middle, alone. About to speak, she swallowed her words at the sight of a golden palomino in the corner to her right.

The horse pawed the ground. When it didn't bring a response, he trotted to the next corner, away from Marion, and waited.

Brandon made a quarter turn as well.

The horse ran back.

Brandon turned back.

Marion couldn't figure out how something so ordinary could be exciting, yet her adrenalin pulsed as she watched the action between man and beast. When she thought she'd burst with questions, the palomino's pattern changed. He walked over to Brandon and stopped a couple feet behind him.

Marion assumed Brandon would turn and reward the animal.

He didn't.

With Marion gaping, Brandon walked to the rail fence across the corral and opened the gate. The palomino followed, but when both were through, Brandon made a wide circle around and returned. He closed the gate behind him.

"What are you doing with him? Are you not breaking him normally because of your le—" She slapped her hands over her mouth.

One side of his moustache tipped up. "It's all right. You can say *leg*. On second thought, society dictates that you can't." He tipped his head. "Are we being dictated by society today?"

Before Jeffrey had used their kiss to shame her into accepting his proposal, she would have jumped at a chance not to be dictated by the confines of society. But that humiliation would stay with her for a long time.

He glanced over at the palomino grazing amongst the short grass of the home pasture. "They tried to break him for days, but I called them off. He's one of the rare ones who refuse to submit. Sometimes you can teach them it's not so much submitting as cooperating."

His words helped her decide to forgo the rules of society. For a while at least.

She scratched at the railing, not speaking until she pulled a loose sliver off of the board. "It's like marriage, then?" She waited for his answer with her breath held.

He chuckled, a warm, deep sound that caressed her heart. "Yep. One of the first things you learn."

Confused by the way her nerve endings tingled when he looked at her, she sassed back, "I guess I'll learn it then." She spun away, throwing over her shoulder, "Nice work."

Later that afternoon found Marion sitting on the verandah with Aunt Mattie when Ned and Brandon rolled in with the hay rack. Ned pulled up to the barn below the loft door and disappeared into the dark cavern.

Brandon stood and stretched languorously like a cat, paying special attention to his leg. He didn't glance in her direction.

Ned swung the loft door open and pushed the hay carrier out to the end of the beam.

"You clear, boss?" Ned yelled from the loft.

Brandon cupped his mouth. "All clear."

The sound of the squeaky pulley reached Marion as Ned lowered a wooden platform. Brandon used the tip of his pitchfork to guide it down beside him. Brandon made short work of filling the carrier.

As the pulley whined its protest, Marion held her breath. From her location, it looked like Brandon stood beneath the carrier, steadying the load as it rose above his head. If a line snapped, or his injured leg gave out—

"You care for him, don't you?"

"Pardon?" Her response was automatic, for she couldn't pull her gaze off Brandon until the load of hay drifted into the loft. The words sank in. She stared at Aunt Mattie. "I'm not sure what you mean."

Aunt Mattie picked up her needlework. "I think you do."

Marion crossed her arms as if to ward off the assessment. "Jeffrey asked me to marry him."

"Have you given him an answer, officially?" she asked, her voice soft as if she was afraid to speak the words aloud.

"Not yet, no, but—"

Aunt Mattie leaned forward in earnest. "For the love of God, don't decide until you know him better."

"But—"

"Wait a week, is all I ask."

Marion didn't answer. She wasn't sure she wanted to marry Jeffrey Whelp. But neither was she sure she didn't. And for all Aunt Mattie had done for her, the least she could do was honor her request.

Marion reached over and clasped her aunt's hand. "Yes, of course, if it means that much to you."

Aunt Mattie covered Marion's hand with her other one and patted it. "Thank you, dear. Stay here while I go to check on Serelli."

Aunt Mattie went inside, and Marion turned her focus back on the men, who worked without incident. After Ned drove the empty hay rack away, Brandon headed to the house. He glanced up and caught her watching him. Instead of turning away as he'd done in the past, he approached.

Anticipation filled her without knowing his intent.

As he neared the rose-covered fence, he tapped the brim of his hat in greeting, and kept walking until he reached the well. With a bucket of water before him, he plunked the dipper in.

The trials of his life showed through the lines on his face—fascinating avenues she wanted to explore. Where once his injury seemed an impediment, he'd proven otherwise. He was wise, interesting, and calm.

Jeffrey was handsome and attentive, but every time she thought back to the fair, she remembered how he'd wanted to walk away from that child in danger. Was that the type of man she wanted to bring home to her father?

Brandon rested, his back to the well. He held her gaze. In that moment, she knew he would never lead a young lady to a secluded alcove, kiss her senseless, and take liberties he shouldn't. In that moment, she knew he was, as Emmeline Whitley had said, one of the noblest men in Austin.

But would Poppa approve? Would he relinquish his legacy to a man who didn't look capable in his eyes?

Marion fled. Through the door. Up the stairs. Into her room. She plopped on her bed backward, arm on her forehead. "What am I going to do?"

In her confused state, she lost all track of time and lay there until the sound of hoof beats pounded on the road. She raced to the window, surprised and eager to see Jeffrey leading the crew, his eyes searching the windows of the house. Looking for her.

How could she think of Brandon when her heart pounded in her throat at the sight of Jeffrey? She snatched up her shawl and ran downstairs.

Jeffrey's face lit up when he spotted her in the foyer, his hat in his hands. He looked over her shoulder before settling on her face. "Would you care to take a walk, Marion?"

He took the shawl from her hands and placed it on her shoulders. Opening the door, he led her out, his large hand on the small of her back.

She probably didn't need the shawl, except it gave her something to hold as they walked along the fence. Across the hills, coyotes lifted their voices in chorus, heard far across the distance without the wind to carry it away.

"I've missed you, Marion," he said, his voice low, as soon as they'd passed the buildings.

She tucked a wisp of hair behind her ear and answered just as low, "I've missed you too. What have you been doing?"

He groaned. "Herding cows. Chasing rustlers. Fixing fence." He found her hand and swung it gently between them. "Everything but being here with you."

"I've been so bored without you."

"Well, I'm here now and we're wasting time." He continued walking, faster now, almost pulling her toward a grouping of cottonwoods a quarter mile down the road.

Giddy from his nearness, breathless from the exertion, she ran beside his long strides.

At the trees, he pulled her around so they were hidden from the buildings. Letting go of her hand, he pulled her close and kissed her.

She felt the pressure of his mouth, the warmth of his arms, the tension of his fingers on her back. And she waited for the explosion of exhilaration like the first time. It didn't come.

She pushed against his chest. "No."

"What?" He loosened his arms, his breath unsteady.

She scrambled for something to say to explain what she was feeling—or the lack of it. Her mind was blank.

He pulled a folded paper from his back pocket. "I was going to wait to tell you this, but I may as well tell you now."

"Tell me what?" She stared at the white paper that gleamed in the fading light.

He waved it between them. "It's from my aunt. There's an urgent matter than needs my attention. As I'm her only heir"—he puffed out his chest—"it stands to reason that I need to go when she needs advice."

Desolation filled her at the thought of his leaving. "How long will you be gone?"

"I won't know until I see her, but you can bet it won't be a second more than it has to be."

When he took her in his arms again, her head swam with sensory details, yet they didn't reach her heart.

His ardor increased, as if sensing her lack of passion.

She wiggled free, her hand straight out between them. "No, Jeffrey. That's enough."

"But I want to love you, sweetheart," he wheedled.

"Then respect me, and wait."

Nine

If I could but know his heart, everything would become easy.

~ Jane Austen, *Sense and Sensibility*

A thundercloud blacker than pitch followed Brandon back to the ranch the next afternoon. His hands itched with the need to wrap them around Whelp's neck, and his continual prayer was to take away his anger before he did something he'd regret. The best that could happen was for Whelp to be gone by the time he got back, because he'd never felt such rage.

He passed under the Rocking R Ranch sign and scrutinized the yard. Aunt Mattie waved from the verandah.

He tipped his hat and headed for the barn, eager to check the calf before things got rough. The critter had been on the mend ever since Marion had taken to bottle-feeding it. But even the thought of how cute Marion looked while tending the calf couldn't calm him this time around.

But the thought of her imminent devastation did. No matter what he thought of Whelp, Marion didn't deserve this.

She closed the stall door and looked up as he moved down the dimly lit aisle. He tried to walk with a smooth gait, but the ride from Austin had done a job on his hip.

Her gaze swung from his leg to his face. Concern covered her face.

"Where's Whelp?" he demanded.

Her brows drew together. "He's gone home for a few days. Didn't he tell you?"

"Oh, I know, all right." No sense denying the truth. Brandon limped past her to a high stool sitting near the back. He hitched himself onto it and extended his leg. The stalling tactic wasn't only to figure out what he would say, but to contain his emotions while saying it.

She moved to the closest stall and leaned her arm along the top board. "Mr. Tabor—Brandon—what aren't you telling me?"

A thrill coursed through him as his name passed her lips. She'd put a little inflection on the first half that sounded different. If she only knew how long he'd waited for her to call him by his given name.

He covered his mouth with his open palm as if to stop from uttering hurtful words. But they had to be said. "What's going on between you and Whelp?"

"He proposed days ago," she finally admitted.

The air thickened. A band constricted around his heart and tried to squeeze the life out of him. He leaned forward, hands on his knees and forced air into his lungs. "So you're getting married."

She flicked at something on her skirt. "I haven't answered him yet." She crossed her arms and leaned back against the stall.

Life fizzled back through Brandon's veins. If she hadn't said yes, she wasn't beholden to him. Strengthened by the thought, he motioned in the direction of Austin.

"I saw Noah in town today."

Delight crossed her face. "How's Emmeline?"

"She's in the family way."

"Oh, how wonderful!"

He took off his hat and swiped his palm around the leather sweatband. "It wasn't a social visit. Noah had some other news he wanted to impart."

"Oh?"

"Seems there's a young spinster in town who...ah...is also in the family way." He twirled his hat, unsure of the state of her sensibilities, wishing he'd brought the smelling salts.

Her eyes opened as wide as a new moon. "Not one of the girls from Austen Abbey?"

It was his turn to shrug. "Noah didn't say."

She glared at him, "Well then, what *did* he say?"

"Apparently, the gentleman," he spoke slowly, emphasizing each word, "is Mr. Jeffrey Whelp."

She jerked back as if slapped. "No! You lie!"

Tears flooded her eyes, glistening in the streaks of light coming through the wall cracks. With a sob, she spun and ran from the barn.

Marion ran past Aunt Mattie and Serelli and straight up to her room, only stopping when she'd fallen to pieces on her bed.

No, it wasn't true. It couldn't be true. Jeffrey would never—he couldn't ever—he was a gentleman through and through. Brandon had never liked Jeffrey, and this was his way of retaliating.

Emmeline would know the truth. She was just the person to reassure her.

Marion pushed off the bed and quickly changed into her riding clothes. As long as she was quiet, she could saddle a horse and make her way to Austin before anyone noticed she was missing.

Fearful that Aunt Mattie would be on the verandah, she made her way out the back of the house. As she passed the door to the summer kitchen, she heard the grating sound of a metal pot sliding across the iron stove. Glass clinked. The pungent smell of cooked beets filled the air.

Serelli's voice filtered through the open door. "What will we tell her?"

"We won't tell her anything," Aunt Mattie said firmly.

"But James said the Wellington boy, who was helping with the wagons, spread it all across kingdom come."

Goosebumps rose on Marion's arm, sending ripples cascading throughout her body.

"It was too dark to see for sure," Aunt Mattie reprimanded. "Jonathan Wellington may have seen two people kissing at the dance, but he guessed who they were." Something metal rang as it slammed against the stove. "Why would Whelp go after Beatrice Nelson when Marion's wearing her heart on her sleeve? It doesn't make sense."

Marion's knees wobbled. Her fist found its way to her mouth, a knuckle pressed against her lips, as her body trembled with indignation. They were wrong. A bolt of conviction shot through her. Straightening her spine, she marched into the summer kitchen.

Aunt Mattie stood by the table slipping skins off bloody beets.

At the stove, Serelli ladled clear liquid into jars of ruby slices.

Both gaped at her.

"You're all listening to hateful gossip, and I won't have it." She headed for the door, stopped halfway over the threshold, and turned back. "I won't have it, you hear?"

She spun back around—and slammed into Brandon.

He held her close, one arm around her waist, the other cupping the back of her head, holding it against his chest. "Aw, Marion," his gravelly voice rumbled against her temple. "It'll be all right."

She shook her head with what little movement he allowed. Unable to hold back her emotions, her tears streamed down her cheeks. Sobbing, she pulled back.

He let her go.

Grasping a handful of her skirt, she brushed past him and ran toward the house. Once again, she lay in bed encircled in confusion. Yet, one clear thought shone through—the feeling of security she'd experienced in his arms. His strong arms. And the whole time she'd felt his arms around her, she hadn't considered his injury once. She'd simply accepted him as a man.

Ten

From a night of more sleep than she had expected, Marianne awoke the next morning to the same consciousness of misery in which she had closed her eyes.

~ Jane Austen, *Sense and Sensibility*

Brandon waited at the hitching rail, watching the lone rider approach the ranch. He'd rather be working the palomino, but considering the envelope in his back pocket, this confrontation couldn't be avoided.

Whelp reined in and dismounted. "Morning, boss." He hitched his reins to the rail, acting as if nothing untoward had happened.

"What are your intentions toward Miss McDermott?"

"I'm going to marry her."

The words hurt more than Brandon expected, but he pulled himself together, a picture of cool nonchalance. "Will she marry you knowing you're destitute?"

Whelp threw a sneer across the space between them. "Why would you say that?"

"Because the day you received your letter from your aunt, Aunt Mattie received one from her as well. It said she's leaving her estate to the young lady you wronged, and she thought your employer should know what kind of man you are."

"Miz Mattie won't turn me out. She's too kind hearted."

"You're wrong." He withdrew the envelope from his back pocket and handed it to Whelp. "Pay for two weeks. Aunt Mattie insisted you get double what you earned. You're done here."

Whelp folded the envelope and shoved it into a pocket in his denims. "Where's Marion? I need to see her before I leave."

"She doesn't want to see—"

"Yes, I do." Marion left her sheltered corner and showed herself to the two men.

Jeffrey's face lit up. "Sweetheart!" He took a step toward her.

She stepped back.

He didn't press. Instead, he sheepishly rubbed the back of his neck. "I need to go back to Austin for a while, but I'll be back for you."

"No."

His face darkened. "You said you would marry me."

She clenched her fists in the folds of her skirt. "No, I never said I would."

His chin jutted forward. He took several deep breaths, his chest rising and falling as if with a huge effort. He untied his horse with jerky movements. "Whatever the lady wants."

Marion crossed her arms to keep her heart from jumping out and trailing him. He'd made her laugh, showered her with affection, and treated her like no other man had done before. In return she'd fancied herself in love with him. A girl's first love.

She looked at Brandon.

He stepped forward as if he'd been waiting for her. The strong, silent Ranger, always ready to rescue someone in distress. She'd been gullible when it came to Jeffrey, but at least she'd risked her heart for love. Practical, sensible Brandon Tabor would never do that.

Raising her skirt off the ground, she ran for the security of her room.

Marion snapped beans, helped prepare meals, and spent time socializing with Aunt Mattie and Serelli. Jeffrey's leaving had shown her how self-absorbed she'd been since arriving. When she wasn't working, her fingers flew across the piano keys, bringing Aunt Mattie's favorite music to life, allowing the melodies to soothe her. And yet she didn't feel healed.

Wondering if the calf had relapsed, she wandered through the barn. His stall lay as empty as it had the morning they turned him out with the herd. Her nurturing had worked, and there hadn't been any reason to keep the healthy animal in the barn.

In the corral, Brandon saddled the palomino as it pawed the ground.

"Easy, boy." His soothing voice carried in the breeze.

Marion slid into her corner. Watching Brandon had become a highlight of her day. The man who lumbered along on flat ground moved in fluid motion when working with the palomino—until his leg ached. Over time, she'd come to know exactly when the pain sharpened. He wasn't at that point yet.

With the cinch tightened, he slipped his boot into the stirrup and rose into a standing position, his body slightly leaning forward so that all his weight wasn't hanging on one side.

The palomino flared its eyes. His forelegs quivered. Brandon soothed him with a low voice, watching the ears swivel round to listen. When the horse stopped trembling, Brandon swung his bad leg over to the other side, found the stirrup, and stood motionless once more.

She held her breath. He'd never gone farther than this stage. Was this the day?

As if he'd heard her silent question, he caught her gaze and held it with his own. She saw the moment his eyes confirmed it, seconds before determination hardened on his face.

Her pulse pounded in her ears as she imagined him lying in the dust, unable to rise, unable to walk.

Brandon nodded as if sensing her fears. He lowered his seat to the saddle, all the while murmuring to the palomino and stroking his neck. Agonizing minutes passed until the horse's head lowered. Brandon stilled, hands on the reins before him, ready for action. He clicked his tongue. The palomino took a step. Then another, and another. Man and horse broke into seamless motion. They rode around the corral. Sometimes this way, sometimes that. Teaching and learning. Giving and receiving. Wild and wonderful. And beautiful.

When they stopped, Brandon patted the horse's neck. "Well done, boy."

She caught his grimace, heard his breathing change, and ached for him. If only she could take away his pain—heal him the way she'd tended the calf. She dropped her hands and swiped them against her skirt as if preparing for—what?

Anything he might need.

She crept out of her corner and ran lightly through the barn. By the time she reached him, he was alone. Behind him, a flash of gold raced across the pasture, free once more.

His tense eye muscles gave him the appearance of an angry man.

But she knew better. And she knew better than to offer assistance.

He braced his arm on the nearest railing. "He's got an easy stride. Well-tempered. By week's end, you can ride him."

She felt his restraint, as if breathing in more than quick, shallow breaths would hurt more than it did. Her fingers itched to smooth the lines across his forehead. She gripped her skirt to keep them still.

"I leave before then. In two days."

He brushed his palms against each other. "Right." With a nod, he walked on without her, his limp pronounced.

Even with his injury, Brandon was the better man. She'd played love like a game and lost because she'd gone after fancy and lost out on forever.

Eleven

Extravagance and vanity had made him cold-hearted and selfish.
Vanity, while seeking its own guilty triumph at the expense of another,
had involved him in a real attachment, which extravagance, or at least
its offspring, necessity, had required to be sacrificed.

~ Jane Austen, *Sense and Sensibility*

Marion paused her hands over the piano keys and watched the buggy carrying Aunt Mattie and Serelli pull out of the yard. She needed the music to soothe her turmoil more than she needed to socialize. Yet after an hour more of playing, she closed her piano. Her music had flowed, but not with its usual calming effect.

The empty house pressed in, hot under the afternoon sun. Perhaps she could convince Ned to accompany her on a ride. Minutes later, she stepped out onto the verandah in her riding clothes, spry for the first time that day. A four-inch rock lay on the top step with a folded paper flapping beneath it. She tugged the note out and scanned the contents, her heart beating a fast refrain.

Meet me under the trees by the creek.

It was signed with a big, bold B.

Brandon had ridden off earlier, tall and straight on the palomino, a musical movement across the Texas landscape. Had he planned a picnic? Her heart surged with joy.

She ran to the barn, not encountering anyone on the way there or inside. Moving quickly, she saddled the mare she'd ridden before, her ears tuned to any hint of Ned's approach. Other than a barn cat, the area was empty.

As she neared the grove, she spotted the silhouette of his horse on the far side. Closer, she made him out sitting with outstretched legs at the base of a tree. Her heart hammered at the sight of him. Was he sleeping? Hurt? Unconscious? Guesses tumbled in her mind as she raced the final distance.

Reaching the trees, she jumped from the saddle, unable to contain her exuberance. Every nerve in her body tingled with life. Something was amiss. Beneath the shaded canopy, she took a good look at the man lounging against the tree. Even with his hat shielding his face, she knew it wasn't Brandon.

The man raised his hat—

"Jeffrey! What are you doing here?"

He rose and walked toward her, contempt marring his face. "Looking for your cripple?"

How had she ever thought him handsome?

"I'm done with you." She turned and reached for the reins of her horse.

He clamped his hand around her wrist. "Where do you think you're going?"

"I'm leaving."

He swore. With his free hand, he stripped the reins from her hand and then pushed her toward her saddle. "Get on your horse."

She mounted while her mind scrambled for ways to escape.

Grabbing one of her hands, then the other, he wove a rawhide thong around them and the pommel.

"What are you doing?"

One side of his mouth curled up in a sneer. "I'm taking you to our wedding."

Bile spiked up her throat. She forced it back. How could she have considered him a gentleman? "You can't make me marry you."

Laughing, he led her horse toward his gelding. "We're heading to Mexico, sweet Marion, where no one cares about one little *chiquita.*"

Brandon practically fell off his horse after three hours of riding. For nothing. He should have stayed back and waited for the boys, but as soon as he'd found the note about the cougar tracks on the north range, he'd high-tailed it up by himself.

Fool. He'd been trying to prove that he could do the job on his own. Prove it to himself. Prove it to *her.*

He tied his horse to the hitching post in front of his cabin, too much in pain to take care of him at the moment. Hating that he couldn't do the job, he stumbled inside. The note still lay on the table. He passed it, his attention on his bed.

Only after he finished massaging the salve over his scarred hip muscle did the pain diminish. As it faded, his brain started to work again. Where was everyone?

He searched the yard and barn, the summer kitchen, and finally the main floor of the house. No one. He couldn't find a soul. With warning bells clanging in his ears, he headed for his horse.

A body lying prone near the corral caught his attention. "Ned!" He hoofed it to Ned's side, noting the patch of dried blood on his head. They both groaned as Brandon turned Ned onto his back.

Ned gripped a handful of Brandon's shirt. With surprising strength, he pulled him down close. "Thunder's rollin' in my head, boss. Whelp pistol-whipped me."

The hairs rose on the back of Brandon's neck. He sent a glance around the yard. "Where is he?"

"Saw him ridin' out yonder. East toward the grove." He eased his grip on Brandon's shirt.

"Where's everyone else? Mattie? Marion?"

"Mattie and Serelli took the wagon to Olive's." He pulled Brandon back down. "Marion. Saw her riding east. Toward the grove."

Brandon went cold. He stared at Ned. "You think they were meeting?"

"Wouldn't have to whack me for that."

No, Whelp wouldn't have had opposition if Marion wanted to go willingly with him. "How long ago did she leave?"

Ned peered at the sun. "Two hours. Maybe three."

Two hours? Brandon's rage crashed to dread. When Marion had continued to watch him work with the palomino, he'd begun to hope she cared for him.

"Whatcha waitin' fer? Help me up and git goin'."

The green-broke palomino rode swift and sure as if knowing the importance of his mission. Brandon praised God for the horse, for its stride was the smoothest of any horse he'd ridden since the explosion.

At the grove, he studied the ground until he saw their tracks heading south. Why south? The Rocking R was north. Only two things lay south of Texas—Mexico and the Gulf.

He urged the stallion into an easy lope. The horse's stamina was unproven, and a long ride lay ahead.

As they crossed the Rocking R's southern boundary, Brandon realized that he'd left his salve behind. Once he caught up to Whelp, could he manage to stand long enough to confront him?

Twelve

I come here with no expectations, only to profess, now that I am at liberty to do so, that my heart is and always will be yours.

~ Jane Austen, *Sense and Sensibility*

Brandon smelled the smoke first. It could have come from anyone's fire, yet his heart pulled him forward. Practically falling from his horse, he mentally kicked himself for not remembering to bring the tin by his bed. He tried to walk off the pain, yet it hurt more when he stopped than when he started. Grabbing a branch, he pulled himself toward a tree and leaned into it, allowing the tree to take the weight off his hip.

"I need help, Lord. I never knew the reason I survived and some of my men didn't, but if it was to be here at this time, I readily accept the challenge. But you have to help me. I'm in dire straits and can't do it. I'm not asking for healing here, but just a little touch from you to numb the pain awhile."

He stepped back from the tree. Pain shot up his back and down his leg. Well, all right then. He labored to the stallion and unsheathed his rifle. With extra bullets in his pockets, he headed for the camp. Halfway there he crouched low, amazed at his progress. Without thought, he'd been skimming across the landscape like the old days.

Marion sat cross-legged by the fire, every part of her aching. She

151

never thought she'd live to see the day that riding tuckered her out, but after a year of studies at Austen Abbey, her body wasn't up to the challenge of continuous hours in the saddle.

Jeffrey reclined by the fire a few yards away with his head resting on his upright saddle. The gentlemanly thing to do would have been to give her a saddle too. What a fool she'd been.

She eyed the position of his saddle with the soft inside padding lying on the dirt. A smart rider knew it'd collect grit that way, and when saddled, it would scrape against the horse's skin like a burr. Horses became ornery with scratchy saddle pads and tended to fight for control.

If Jeffrey's horse went awry, it could be the distraction she needed to escape.

Or would he just take hers? Or worse, share hers? She shuddered.

The incongruity of the situation almost made her laugh.

His snores urged her to action. She shifted, trying to loosen the rope around her wrists, already raw where her gloves didn't cover her skin.

One of the horses nickered. She paused at her task and stared into the darkness. Since she hadn't been staring at the fire, she could make out vague shapes of trees and brush. And then she saw him. A man crouched low, running between the trees.

Friend or foe?

He stepped closer to the fire and she gasped. Brandon? How could it be?

He placed his finger to his lips.

She nodded. Her greeting could wait.

He set down his rifle. With a gentle pressure, he angled her so that the fire's light fell on her wrists. A quick jerk and her bonds fell away. Leaning back, he searched her eyes. She didn't know the question, but flashed a tentative smile. He grazed her cheek with the back of his hand then picked up his rifle. With the tiniest grunt, he rose and disappeared into the darkness.

The snores stopped.

She pushed her hands behind her, intent on looking the same as when Jeffrey had gone to sleep.

He shot to his feet, hands buckling his holster. "Who's there?"

Click.

Jeffrey spun to the sound of the cocked weapon.

"I am." Brandon stepped into the firelight.

Marion's heart nearly burst with pride.

Jeffrey gaped. As it sank in who was there, he drew his gun.

Two flares lit the night—one a split second before the other. Only one grunt.

Her eyes flashed between the men, her heart in her throat, blocking her scream. She rushed to Brandon, straight and tall, and then turned to face their adversary.

Jeffrey cradled his bleeding hand. "You shot me!"

"And I didn't need two good legs to do it." He tied Jeffrey's hands behind his back. "Put out the fire, Marion. We're going back to Austin."

By some miracle, Brandon sat tall in his saddle when he and Marion rode into the yard of the Rocking R after leaving Jeffrey with the law in Austin, yet she could barely hold her seat.

Aunt Mattie and Ned waited by the water trough near the barn, having seen them from a distance.

"Marion, my dear, are you all right?"

Wearier than she'd ever felt, Marion nodded. "Yes, but only because Brandon rescued me." She gave him a wan smile.

He tapped his hat brim. His eyes searched hers, and she felt her cheeks warm. Something had changed between them as they rode the endless miles. She couldn't put a name to it, but clearly, he wasn't adverse to her company. Her heart fluttered with hope.

Ned tied her reins to the hitching rail and turned to help her down. "No, I'm fine," she whispered, flicking her head toward Brandon.

Yes, he'd been straight in the saddle, but she felt it had more to do with his attitude and responsibility than anything. After almost a full day of continuous riding, he had to be hurting something fierce.

He dismounted before Ned reached him. Once on the ground however, he limped to the front of his horse and braced himself on the hitching rail. Ned and Aunt Mattie gathered around him while Marion eased herself down.

Ned laid his hand on Brandon's shoulder. "How'd you manage it?"

"I prayed for a miracle," Brandon said, his words coated in wonder. He chuckled, and shrugged. "God gave me the strength to do what I had to do."

Aunt Mattie beamed. She beckoned for Marion to join them.

Marion stepped into the empty spot at Brandon's side.

Aunt Mattie laid one hand on Brandon's arm, and the other on Marion's. She bowed her head and began to pray.

Brandon hunched lower as if the weight of the world rested on his shoulders.

Ned drummed his fingers on Brandon's back, nodding along with Aunt Mattie's words.

Marion wasn't sure what to do. No one prayed like this back home.

Aunt Mattie's words drew her attention. "We can't know the reasons why this happened, Lord, but thank you for seeing Marion and Brandon back home."

"Yes, thank you, Father." The words sprung from Marion's lips without warning. Her eyes flew open to gauge the response. No one had moved.

But Brandon echoed her sentiment with fervor.

A minute later, Aunt Mattie ended the prayer.

"Come on, old man." Ned took Brandon's arm. "Let's get you worked up and feeling better."

The men left, the older aiding the younger. Marion felt compelled to go with them but knew it wasn't the time. "You should have seen him, Aunt Mattie. It was like he never had an injury."

Aunt Mattie patted her arm. "The Lord's hand was on you both. Now, let's go draw you a bath."

An hour later, Marion snuck downstairs, clean, dressed, and restless. The house lay quiet. Taking a chance that the ladies were in the summer kitchen preparing breakfast, Marion slipped out the door and sank into the most hidden chair on the verandah. Silently, she prayed for Brandon to find her.

No sooner had she opened her eyes than he emerged from the foreman's quarters. His eyes swept across the verandah and landed on her.

Her heart beat faster with every step he took in her direction. His face showed strain, lack of sleep, and something else she couldn't define.

As he came up the walk, she crossed the deck to meet him. Swiping her hand down the back of her skirt, she sat on the top step, giving him the option of not climbing the steps.

He placed one boot on the bottom step and stopped there, his arm along the railing. "I figured Aunt Mattie would've had you down for a nap."

She steepled her hands together and tucked them beside her neck, resting her head over them. "She did. I snuck out."

He chuckled. "I'm kind of wound up myself." He looked off toward the east, away from the buildings. "How about we take a walk?"

She rose and floated down the steps. She wanted to wrap her arm around his, but he didn't offer. Instead, she clasped her hands in front of her. They strolled across the yard without speaking. She didn't feel the rush of excitement—like she was standing on the edge of a cliff—that she'd always felt with Jeffrey. Instead, peace surrounded their unhurried pace.

By the time they reached the fence, Marion was experiencing small waves of anticipation, flavored with the assurance that she'd found the place she was meant to be.

They walked along the fence line, her hands swinging gently by her side, content.

He cleared his throat. "I understand your father arrives tomorrow."

Her heart sank to her stomach at the thought. "Yes, in the morning."

"When will you leave?"

"Most likely, immediately."

He kicked a rock. It skittered across the ground until it lodged in a clump of grass.

They reached the grove of trees where she'd shared a second kiss with Jeffrey. The memory flitted through and left without sparing a single emotion.

Brandon walked to the widest tree and leaned his back against it, his eyes intent on her. A thin white line framed his mouth, denoting his pain.

"I'm sorry he broke your heart."

She held her breath, unsure how to admit she'd been a fool. Breaking eye contact, she wandered to the edge of the grove and faced the house. Aunt Mattie stood on the steps looking their way. A quick wave, and she went back inside.

Her honesty was more important than her pride at this point. "I was a fool in regards to Jeffrey."

"Why did you agree to meet him?"

She swirled around to face him. "But I didn't!"

"Ned saw you riding off. Alone."

"I found a note on the steps and thought you'd left it there for me." A lump formed in her throat. "I thought you wanted..."

"Wanted what?" he asked oddly.

Feeling tears well in her eyes, she looked down. "Maybe some time alone with me."

"Have I given any indication I wanted that?"

"No, you've been quite the gentleman."

"Then why would you throw propriety to the wind for a clandestine meeting?"

Using both hands, she brushed away the tears streaming down her cheeks. She was leaving tomorrow. She'd already tossed away her pride where he was concerned. This might be her last chance to tell him how she felt. She took a deep breath and then admitted, "Because I wanted to be with you."

Brandon eyed her for several moments before breaking eye contact. What was she saying? That she had feelings for him? How could she love an old broken Ranger with only dreams and his good name?

With her face reddening, she blurted, "I'm sorry for presuming things that don't exist." In a flurry of skirts, she spun away from him and headed to the yard.

"You didn't presume wrong."

She stopped but didn't turn.

He'd realized his error as soon as the words slipped out of his mouth and now he didn't know how to explain what he had to say. Ross McDermott would never see him as a suitable husband for his only daughter. And if Marion had a falling out with her father, it wouldn't be on Brandon's account. He loved her too much to cause such a split. But how to turn her away without bringing her father into it?

Her shoulders trembled as if she was crying, yet she didn't make a sound.

Every part of him wanted to go to her, wrap her in his arms and tell her life would be whatever she wanted. Except it couldn't. He prayed for strength, gathering his arsenal of questions to put her off guard—and keep her there—doubting.

"You're saying you wanted to be with me, yet at the same time you had made it clear that Whelp was everything I wasn't."

"I was confused."

"You're too young to know what you really want."

"No, I—"

"Admit it, Marion, you chose Whelp because you thought he was a better man than me."

"But that was—"

"And you were right. He was younger, stronger and more agile. Just the kind of man your father needs to run that ranch of yours." He'd said too much. Once started, he'd gone on like a charging bull, unable to stop without tripping and falling to his knees. And that was one place he couldn't be when she was standing there in her fashionable, womanly dress with her hair swept up to show the perfect curve of her neck, and the total look of abandonment splashed across her face.

"Go back to the house, Marion." Closing his eyes, he leaned against the tree, determined not to give in. Minutes later, his heart thudded to the rhythm of her pounding feet as they took her away from him. He shoved his hands in his back pockets, wishing he could ride away and hide.

After a night of bawling like a calf that had just been separated from its momma, Marion had to use several cold compresses to smooth her puffy, red face. Thankfully, when she met the train with Aunt Marion and Ned, Poppa didn't let on that he suspected anything out of the ordinary. Once they got back to the Rocking R though, she caught him watching her with a keen eye.

The hardest part of the day was sitting across the table from Brandon during the evening meal. Marion would have preferred him by her side so she wouldn't have to look across at him, but Aunt Mattie had put herself and Poppa at the ends, and Brandon and Ned on one side. That left Marion feeling like she was alone on a stage looking out on an audience who expected something from her.

As soon as Poppa said the blessing, though, he addressed Brandon. "I know I said it earlier this afternoon when we met, but I can't thank you enough for rescuing my daughter."

Marion's hand twitched halfway to her mouth, allowing a splash of broth from her spoon to spill over the side and land on the napkin in her lap.

Poppa's eyes darted in her direction.

Brandon kept his fixed on Poppa. "My pleasure, sir. Your daughter is unique and quite head-strong, if I may say. She'll need a strong husband to keep her in check, but I have no doubt you'll find someone suitable."

His stoic voice drew Marion's attention in spite of herself, sure she'd see something in his attractive face. But his passive features matched his tone.

Poppa looked at her, then at Brandon, then back at her. Finally, Poppa looked at Aunt Mattie.

With a lump growing in her throat, Marion reached for her tea. Better to swallow tea than spout her anger and frustration. Over the rim of her glass she caught a twitch along Brandon's jawline. Why? Was he trying not to laugh? She set her glass on the table, overcome with an urge to dump it over his head—or better yet, she'd use the pitcher. With a sigh, she picked up her spoon. Mrs. Collins would never approve of such behavior, and Marion would never let Poppa think anything but the best thoughts in connection with Austen Abbey.

Suddenly, Brandon scraped back his chair and labored to his feet. "Thank you for the meal, Aunt Mattie, but I'll be heading to my quarters now."

Poppa stood as well. "I'll see you to the door."

"But you haven't eaten anything," Aunt Mattie protested.

For the first time that evening, Brandon glanced in Marion's direction. "Good-bye, Miss McDermott. I pray you find what you're looking for."

And then he was gone, and she knew in the deepest part of her heart that when it came time to leave in the morning, Brandon would be long gone, working in some remote corner of the ranch. Like the previous night, she stared across the table trying to imagine life without him. His respect and gentle touch—with her, Aunt Mattie, and the stock—had left an impression of how he would be with children. She had begun to imagine him with their own little ones, teaching them the same values as he had. Except there would be no children. And never again would she feel the soft caress of his eyes on her face. She sniffed. His empty chair wavered before her eyes. Rising, she asked to be excused more from habit than permission.

"Sit down." Poppa's firm voice plopped her back in her chair. "You have some explaining to do, and Marion, tears aren't part of the conversation."

Aunt Mattie clasped her hands together on the table, seemingly determined as Poppa.

They held her within their loving and wise gazes. Reaching for her napkin, she waved it once as if it was a flag starting a tournament. "Explain what? You know about Jeffrey. That B–Brandon saved me. What else is there?"

"You and Tabor are both carrying a world of hurt, and I want to know why."

Marion ignored social convention and wiped her wet cheeks with her napkin. How could she respond without putting blame on Brandon?

Poppa leaned across the table. With his large hand resting close to hers, he sighed. "Do you love him?"

She clenched the napkin into a ball with both her hands. "Yes, Poppa."

"And he hasn't offered for you?"

"No, Poppa, except—" She paused, suddenly unsure of anything anymore.

He leaned back as if he saw everything better that way. "Except he loves you enough to give you up."

"What?"

"That's what I'm thinking," Aunt Mattie said. "He's a man of principle, Ross."

"I don't understand," Marion said, wiping her eyes before looking from Poppa to Aunt Mattie. She ignored the little bubble of hope that tried to work its way into her consciousness.

"Marion," Aunt Mattie's caring voice commanded her full attention. "Do you believe that Brandon loves you? Really, truly loves you as a husband should?"

"Yes," she answered without any hesitation. And then she held her breath and pressed her lips together to stop them from quivering.

"That's good enough for me," Poppa said. "Marion, help Serelli clear the table. Your aunt and I have some scheming to do." He beckoned his sister to follow him out to the verandah.

Marion moved so fast that Serelli asked her to slow down. But between hope and distress, she had to do *something*.

Several minutes later, the front door opened and closed. "Marion?" Aunt Mattie called.

Marion stood before her, hands at her throat.

"Are you willing to be Ruth tonight?"

"Ruth? Who's Ruth?" Her thoughts scattered as she wondered what game they were playing.

"Ruth from the Bible. You must remember—Naomi sends Ruth to lie down with Boaz during the night."

Marion's face flushed. "Aunt Mattie! I would never—"

Poppa walked in. "Quiet, girl. I can hear you shrieking outside." He held his hands up as if in defense. "We're not asking you do anything immoral. If you don't want to try, we won't. We'll go on home and you can find someone else."

"No, I want him, but—"

"But nothing, the man needs a push. For all his intelligence and integrity, his pain is so deep he doesn't see himself as a strong husband like we do. Someday he will, though, so we have to do our part to help him get there. Now here's the plan..."

Brandon lay in bed wishing he didn't have to wait until dawn to saddle up and ride away. All he needed was a bit of moonlight to guide his path, except the clouds weren't cooperating. Darkness filled every corner of his quarters, matching the heaviness of his mood.

A board creaked outside his door. Probably just Ned coming to borrow something like he often did. Sometimes Brandon lit a lamp and they talked awhile. This was not one of those nights.

The door opened, someone entered, and the door closed.

Brandon pretended to be asleep.

Footsteps padded across the floorboards toward him.

The hairs on his neck stood up. "Ned?"

Soft breathing reached his ears. He grasped his blanket and was about to throw it off when he smelled something floral. For an instant he thought it was a dream and Savana was back in his bed. He lay in the dark, trying to pull his senses into order as the heady scent of roses filled his being. She lay on the bed without touching him.

Awareness crept upon him through the haze. His steady heart began to pound, shooting blood through his veins until his fingers and toes tingled. He knew it was Marion, but why now when her father was here? Or was she walking in her sleep without conscious thought of what she was doing?

Keeping his voice soft so he wouldn't wake her in terror, he whispered, "Marion?"

"Uh-huh," she murmured.

A light flared through his window, followed by the throwing open of his door. Ross McDermott marched in, Aunt Mattie close behind him.

Brandon pushed himself up, bracing himself on one arm. He tapped his index finger to his lips. "She's sleepwalking, sir. She doesn't know what she's doing."

Wide stanced, McDermott jammed his hands on his hips. "And does she often sleepwalk into your quarters?"

Marion giggled.

Brandon couldn't see her face, but he could see the other two. And they were grinning.

"What's going on here?" he demanded with all the dignity he could muster, considering he was wearing his Union suit underneath the blanket.

McDermott rubbed his hands together. "You got a shotgun, Mattie? Looks like we're having a wedding tomorrow."

"A wedding!" Aunt Mattie tucked her clasped hands beneath her chin. "I'll send someone for the preacher first thing in the morning. Come on, Marion, let's check your wardrobe."

Marion rose from the bed still wearing the dress she'd worn at dinner. Brandon thought she was going to leave without a word, but at the door she turned and blew him a kiss. McDermott winked then pulled the door closed behind the lot of them.

In the dark, Brandon fell back against his bedding. What was that? A dream? No, her scent still filled the air. He tucked his hands behind his head. It appeared that McDermott wasn't opposed to him marrying his daughter. Nor Aunt Mattie. And Marion? He smiled, recalling her giggle.

He tried to picture them five years down the road with a child or two. Would his leg be better or worse? Would Marion still love him if he was too feeble to teach their kids to ride or go out and do the work a rancher ought to do? He strained to see her by his side and failed.

Marion rubbed her eyes. She'd been staring in the direction of

Brandon's quarters for so long that in the gray minutes before dawn she couldn't tell if it was really him or merely her imagination.

He stepped off his stoop and headed to the barn without looking in her direction.

Relieved that she'd changed from her dinner dress to more sensible clothes, she charged down the steps and across the yard.

He stopped to turn at her approach, his face unreadable.

After planning her speech for most of the night, she was suddenly at a loss for words. Where were his open arms? His announcement of undying love? She waited. Her hope fell as an idea formed. What if he truly didn't love her and now she'd backed him into a corner?

"They won't call the preacher if you don't want to marry me," she finally blurted.

He jerked as if she'd slapped him. Shaking his head, he took a wobbly step toward the barn.

She wasn't ready to let him ride off alone without an explanation. Determined to follow him until he talked to her, she bumped into his chest when he abruptly turned back. He raised his hands and held her there.

His dark, intense eyes roamed freely across her face before a strangled sound escaped from deep in his throat. He pulled her to his chest, his lips close to her ear. "You're making me crazy."

She felt his heart beating through his shirt, a rapid thumping that brought a welcome surge to her own pulse. He raised her chin with his fingertips and lowered his lips to hers. Closing her eyes, she gloried in the warmth of the morning sun on her lids—a warmth that matched the sweetness of his kiss.

Too soon, he pulled away from her.

"I love you, Marion. From the first time I saw you, you've been here." He tapped his finger over his heart. "I just didn't think I had a chance."

She tilted her head, solemn because she had to be. "You didn't back then, and neither did I. We both had some growing to do. But I do love you, and I don't want you to think you've been roped into marrying me."

"No shotgun wedding? But sweetheart, look at them." He flicked his head toward the house.

Poppa and Aunt Mattie stood on the verandah watching them, their eyes shaded from the rising sun.

"And think of the tales we could tell our grandchildren." A strange look overcame his face and he looked down at her. "We can have children, Marion, if you want. I know I'm—"

"Brandon, I've been mad at God for a long time because he took my momma the day I was born, but you've taught me that God knows best." She stroked one of the weathered lines on his cheek. "You are the man God planned to be my husband, and I'll take whatever our future holds, as long as you are by my side."

His brows drew together as he swallowed. "Someday I'll try to explain how much I love you."

"I'll look forward to that. And speaking of the future, if we're blessed with a little girl, can we name her Ruth?"

He grinned.

Her heart swelled with profound joy. Looping her arms around his neck, she pulled his head down close, lips almost touching. "I hope that preacher gets here soon, but for now, my love...let's give the folks something to talk about."

Colonel Brandon was now as happy, as all those who best loved him, believed he deserved to be;—in Marianne he was consoled for every past affliction;—her regard and her society restored his mind to animation, and his spirits to cheerfulness; and that Marianne found her own happiness in forming his, was equally the persuasion and delight of each observing friend. Marianne could never love by halves; and her whole heart became, in time, as much devoted to her husband, as it had once been to Willoughby.

~ Jane Austen, *Sense and Sensibility*

ONE WORD FROM YOU

SUSANNE DIETZE

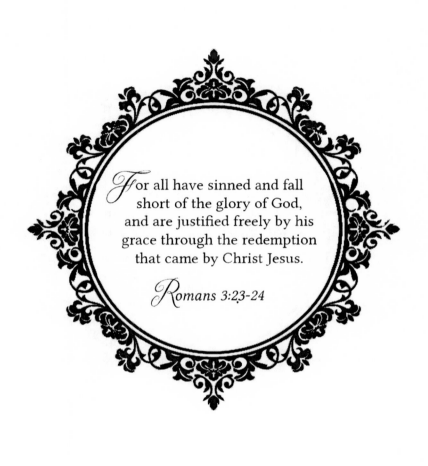

For all have sinned and fall short of the glory of God, and are justified freely by his grace through the redemption that came by Christ Jesus.

Romans 3:23-24

My affections and wishes are unchanged, but one word from you will silence me on this subject forever.

~Mr. Darcy,
Pride and Prejudice

One

October, 1883

"If it is indeed a truth universally acknowledged that a bachelor in possession of a lucrative cattle ranch must be in want of a wife, then Mr. Cray will be swapping vows before calving season." Merriment pulled at Eliza Branch's lips as she gazed past her parents at the darkness beyond the carriage window. "He doesn't need our assistance to find a suitable bride."

"This is no time for your odd sense of humor, Eliza." The carriage bumped over a pothole, and Mother sucked in a hissing breath. "This headache!"

"I'm sorry, Mother. I didn't mean to upset you. Are you ill?" Eliza bit the finger-seam of her glove and tugged, baring her arm to the evening cool. She cupped her hand over Mother's smooth cheek. "You don't have a fever."

Mother's head jerked back. "Still a hoyden after months of finishing school. Can no one persuade you to stop undressing with your teeth?"

"I didn't rip the seam this time." Eliza patted Mother's knee. "Let's turn back home. The Hales will understand if you're too ill to attend the gala."

"Your mother's fine," Father drawled. "Hot with determination, is all."

"No thanks to you, George." Mother's eyes flashed glossy as ink in the moonlight. "Now Eliza must wed Hezekiah Cray with too much haste for a proper society wedding."

"I—*what?*" A nauseating sensation coiled in Eliza's stomach, just as it did during her recurring nightmare of arriving tardy for a French exam at her finishing school, the Jeannette C. Austen Academy for Young Ladies. In those dreams, she couldn't recognize the conjugations on the chalkboard. But Mother's perplexing words boded a far worse fate than poor marks.

"*Marry,*" Mother reiterated, as if she were about to spell the word. "You're nineteen. Plenty old enough."

Eliza stifled a snort. She'd marry Mr. Cray, with his oily black hair, overlong mustache, and unsavory habits when his cattle sang in the church choir. "He gambles, Mother."

"He can afford to. He has the touch of Midas with livestock."

"And I do not." Father sighed and stared out the window at the dark street.

Eliza's mouth filled with fearful questions, cold and metallic as coins on her tongue. "What's happened?"

"The cattle are diseased." Mother massaged her temples. "Your father bred good stock with feral cows to produce some new kind of Longhorn. But he failed. The drought hasn't helped, either. We must sell the ranch to keep the house here in town."

Eliza touched Father's arm, willing him to look at her. "It's not so bad, is it, Father?"

He shrugged, but whether his action bespoke apology or resignation, she couldn't tell. The thick silver sideburns curving down his lean cheeks couldn't hide the clenched set of his jaw.

Mother stifled a sob. "We'll have to let Marta Fleischer go from the kitchen."

"You can't. Her pa just died. Her brothers are struggling with their farm. The Fleischers need the money."

"So do we. If it matters so much, then wed Mr. Cray and you can hire all of Marta's kin."

No need to go *that* far. "I'll pitch in to make up the shortfall with my earnings from the *Texas Star*. Mr. LeShand, my editor, said my advertisements bring customers to the clients, and—"

"Money isn't short. It's *gone.*" Mother sniffed. "We don't need pitiful contributions from your embarrassing hobby. We need you wed to someone who can support us and your sisters."

Eliza shut her eyes. *Honor thy mother and father. But Lord, how can a marriage lacking love and respect be your will?*

"You'll be leaving school at Christmas, when tuition runs out. But I'll not have it known that you left mid-year over *money*. For appearances' sake, you'll move home to prepare for your wedding. A wedding," Mother said, "that will save our family."

Eliza allowed the carriage's motion to slump her against the squabs. The closed-up odors of leather and Mother's violet perfume brought little comfort, for she preferred the book-and-ink smell of Austen Abbey, which was so much more than a school to her—it was a haven, full of friends and gaiety. And the ranch, her family's livelihood and lifeblood, had always been more of a home than the house in town. Vast and grassy and clear, it was the one place she could run and think.

She always knew she'd have to leave school and the ranch behind someday. But never like this.

"We should return home." Her voice sounded flat in her ears. "The gala tickets are dear in price—"

"Our donation to the hospital fund was made weeks ago. Besides, tonight is an investment in our future. Where else can you flirt with the wealthiest men in Austin?"

Whatever that meant. Austen Abbey didn't offer courses in flirtation.

"I thought you selected Mr. Cray for me." At once, Eliza regretted her sarcastic tone, but her mother's words both confused and vexed her.

"I prefer him, but if you find someone more to your liking, fine, so long as he's wealthy. Remember to smile, and use that gown to advantage." Mother plumped the pink and cream satin roses sewn onto Eliza's left shoulder seam.

When she donned the gown earlier, twirling for her reflection in her bedroom at school, she'd felt like a princess. Her roommate, Jeanie Hale, said the mist-green silk complemented Eliza's dark hair and blue eyes. *We'll be the prettiest girls at my parents' gala*, Jeanie had said.

Now the gown felt heavy, the bustle too large and the roses an extravagant, foolish frippery. Her fairy-tale dress was nothing but a lure to catch a deep-pocketed bachelor.

Gravel crunching under the wheels, the carriage slowed to a halt. A twinge twisted in Eliza's chest as she peered out the window. She'd always loved the Hales' home, a blue painted lady with a deep porch.

Tonight, laughter and light spilled out its square windows onto the well-manicured yard and into the street, but Eliza didn't feel like joining in the revelry.

How could she act as Mother expected when her heart was breaking?

With a groan like a bullfrog's, the carriage door opened.

"Fix your glove, Eliza. You've work to do. And if a marriage for money's sake offends you, try to fall in love tonight. With someone rich, of course."

Fall in love, indeed. She'd never fallen into anything in her life. Not mud puddles, not a gopher hole, and certainly not love. And she didn't expect to start now.

Eliza yanked the glove to her elbow and followed her parents into the house. There was only one person she wished to see tonight, and it wasn't Mr. Cray. Her gaze scanned the crowd for silvery-blond hair and a pink dress. Ah, Jeanie chatted across the dining room. Eliza hastened toward her—

Smack into a solid wall of man, all dark wool and spicy aftershave. Firm arms captured her in a steadying hold.

"Miss? Are you hurt?" His voice, honey-thick with a southern drawl, drew her gaze upward. The gentleman scrutinized her with concerned eyes the shade of fresh-turned earth, a touch darker than the hair curling over his collar.

"Not at all. I'm...fine." Gazing up at him, she forgot whether she was in the process of inhaling or exhaling. How ridiculous, gasping like a moon-eyed miss as shivers traversed her arms. No doubt she was addled by the collision.

Her gaze fell to the empty cup in his hand and the damp spots speckling his sleeve. "I cannot say the same for your punch. Forgive me, sir."

She tugged a handkerchief from her bag and blotted the damp spots on his forearm, accidentally whacking his abdomen in the process. At his wince, her hand lowered. He must think her a dolt. Or worse, forward.

Maybe Mama was right about her after all. But then he smiled—a look that was polite, if not warm. A good-bye, then. "Pleasant evening to you, then."

He turned but couldn't step away, not with Jeanie and her mother closing in on him, Eliza's mother at their heels. Considering the dark-haired gentleman was under thirty and had sufficient funds to attend tonight's gala, Mother must have deemed him worthy quarry for the Marriage Hunt.

"Mr. Delacourt." Mrs. Hale's plump cheeks framed her warm smile. "I see you've encountered our Miss Branch."

At Mrs. Hale's introductions— *William*, Jeanie mouthed at Eliza and blinked her eyes, as if prepared to tease her later with his Christian name—Mr. Delacourt bowed over their hands in turn, unsmiling.

"Mr. Delacourt visits from Memphis." Mrs. Hale gave Eliza a knowing look. *Unmarried*, it said. "He's the owner of the Tennessee-North-Texas rail line, which will be connected to Austin within the year."

Mother's eyes lit like a match strike. "Owner, you say? Why, Eliza has never traveled by train. Perhaps she'll have her first journey on yours."

"Mother, I don't think—"

"Actually, the line—"

The strains of violins and enthusiastic murmuring sounded from the parlor. Mrs. Hale clapped. "You will dance, won't you, Mr. Delacourt? Jeanie is promised for the first set, but Eliza is a skilled dancer."

Mother made a sound similar to a purr.

Eliza's stomach squelched. After such a request from their hostess, William Delacourt couldn't refuse. Neither could she. But to her surprise, Eliza realized she must not mind too much, since her foot tapped to the music's beat. She smiled up at Mr. Delacourt, ready to take his arm the moment he offered it.

His gaze skipped over Eliza and flicked to his hostess.

"I'm afraid I must beg off. A thousand pardons, ma'am. Miss Branch." He dipped his head in a curt nod and turned on his heel.

Explanations for his behavior knocked about Eliza's brain like moths against a window pane. Perhaps he was spoken for, or had an objection to dancing. But all he had to do was say so. There was no need for him to embarrass them both by refusing.

Mrs. Hale pinked. Jeanie's lips parted. Mother's ample bosom heaved. "Well, I never!"

"But it seems that I have, thanks to William Delacourt." He might be powerful and wealthy enough to own a railroad, but he was a rudesby, plain and simple. And utterly beneath her notice from now on.

Eliza's chin tilted up. "Go dance, Jeanie. Then you must tell me all about your partner."

"Are you certain? I could sit with you, if you need me." What a dear Jeanie was.

"Pah. I'm fine." A lie if one had ever passed her lips. But one of them should have fun at the gala, at least.

Fall in love, indeed. Tonight, the only thing Eliza had staggered into was the prospect of losing her home. And rejection, with its shameful sting.

A fresh throb of pain spread through Will's lungs and around his back. Were there no available chairs in this house? Merely breathing was difficult since his accident yesterday, but his injury was downright excruciating when touched.

Which Eliza Branch had done. Twice. Perhaps on purpose, just to get his attention.

Even a schemer deserved more courtesy than he'd shown, however. He hated the hurt he'd brought to her bluebonnet eyes by refusing to dance. But he could hardly speak, much less tap his feet, after she'd knocked into his battered ribcage. He might humiliate himself by passing out if he didn't sit down.

Halfway down the hall, a florid-faced fellow hailed him. Recognizing him as a local politician, Will forced a smile and prayed it didn't look too strained. *God, help me get through this night.*

"So, it's official now." The politician's white brows lifted. "The nation's about to be divvied up into time zones next month, thanks to you railroad folks, Delacourt."

"Three hundred time zones is a bit much for one country, even one so grand as ours." Will joked, trying not to grit his teeth from pain. "Life will be easier for everyone, not just for the railroads."

A pale green swirl caught his eye. Miss Branch swished past, accompanied by a stout gentleman with greasy black hair and a limp mustache. She didn't meet Will's eyes, but the tilt of her chin and pursed lips attested to her displeasure. Later, he'd apologize for his brusqueness. But she had replaced him with another dance partner just fine.

"Come meet Sanders." The politician beckoned him into an oak-paneled library. "He's interested in expanding his market north."

"The Tennessee-North-Texas might be the perfect vehicle for him, then."

Ah, thank heaven. An empty chair, plush with crimson velvet padding, awaited Will's aching bones. Far easier to expound on the benefits of his rail line from a restful position, propped against a pillow and in no danger of anyone knocking his ribcage. He should have remained in the hotel, perhaps, but that would defeat the purpose of coming to Austin. At least discussing the railroad distracted him. By the time they finished their discussion, the pain in his ribs eased enough for him to venture from the library.

It wasn't difficult to spot the freckled face Will sought. "Convincing folks to utilize the rail line, Charlie, or were you dancing?"

"Both." Charlie Bingham's face flushed a ruddy hue, a stark contrast to his carroty hair. "I danced with the hosts' pretty daughter, Miss Jeanie. See her there, in the pink?"

"I do." She was arm in arm with Miss Branch, whispering through their frowns. Discussing his rudeness, no doubt.

"You aren't even looking at her. You're watching her friend in green. Do not say Will Delacourt fancies a girl at last."

"Watch your tongue, or I'll remove you from the line's board of directors," Will teased. "The girl in green, Miss Branch, appears to be a fortune hunter. Her tactic was to bump into me, spill my drink, and wipe the punch off my coat. Sound familiar?"

Charlie tapped his temple in an exaggerated display. "That lawyer's daughter in Nashville. Not quite as imaginative as when the female 'fainted' in your arms in Arkansas. But Miss Branch might not have been devious in her intentions, you know."

"Perhaps, although such a tactic was employed with perfection by my stepmother. And Miss Branch's mother literally licked her lips once she learned I own a railroad." Like a dog eyeing a pork chop.

Shame warmed under his collar. A poor comparison. But enough ladies had tried similar schemes once they learned he was rich that his stomach soured to female company. He'd no patience for it, with his throbbing chest and back.

"Some of us wouldn't mind being appraised with such admiration." From the direction of his gaze, it was clear from whom Charlie desired such an assessment. Jeanie Hale's eyes lifted.

Miss Branch's gaze did, too, meeting his square. Were her eyes really the color of bluebonnets or had he imagined it?

He'd find out when he apologized. But then he'd walk away from her. He'd not fall into a trap, no matter how fetching the bait.

Perhaps Charlie needed the reminder, too. He gave his friend a gentle nudge with his elbow. "We're in Austin to promote the TNT, not court ladies. The enterprise will fail if nobody ships goods on our line."

Charlie spared him the briefest of glances. "You're not going to attract merchants if you look like you're about to eat them along with the canapés. Your scowl could scare small children."

He forced his gaze away from Miss Branch. "My ribs ache. The doctor said they're not broken, but still."

"You should've said so." Charlie's brows lowered over his light eyes, his attention free from Jeanie Hale at last.

"And admit I hurt myself falling from a horse? My father'd take a riding crop to me if he heard. Delacourts breed thoroughbreds. They don't fall off them."

"Your secret is safe with me. I'll say naught to your father other than to boast of our success with the TNT."

A smile pulled at Will's lips. "He'd be shocked to hear I've succeeded in anything."

"He'd best prepare himself, then. But you're paler than milk. Let's get you to the hotel."

A guest spun into Will, sending a fresh shaft of agony through his ribs. His next breath almost cleaved him in two. He could apologize to Miss Branch later.

"Fine. But tomorrow we start the next phase of our plan, sore ribs or not."

The grandfather clock in the downstairs entry pealed twice, piercing the silence blanketing Austen Abbey. Eliza could just make out the white pouf of Jeanie's bed cap in the darkness.

"What a dismal night for you," Jeanie whispered.

"The combination of my parents' news, Mr. Delacourt's snub, and the advances of Mr. Cray did not make for a pleasant evening. At least you had fun."

"You've something to give thanks for, too. You only had to dance *once* with Mr. Cray." Jeanie's quiet giggle subsided. "Oh, Eliza. I cannot survive without you. Perhaps Daddy could pay your tuition."

How sweet. "Thank you, but my parents would never accept it. Still, I'd like to graduate before I seek employment."

"Speak to Mrs. Collins in the morning. She's a fair headmistress. Perhaps she'll have an idea." Jeanie's voice sounded weary.

"It's late. Go to sleep."

"Tomorrow," Jeanie promised. "We'll do something about it then." She rolled toward the wall. Within moments, the soft sounds of her deep, even breathing stirred the silence.

An envious twinge pricked Eliza's chest. After so topsy-turvy a night, sleep hovered over her like a cloud, too flimsy and distant to grasp.

Lord, I know I should obey my parents. But if I can convince them there is another way, would that change anything? Will you show me how?

Eliza shoved back her coverlet and donned her room-cold wrapper and yarn slippers. God *had* given her a tool to survive this mess. Perhaps she should use it.

She withdrew a pencil and scrap of paper from her desk, and in the silver moonlight streaming through the window, she began to write.

Dear Mr. Editor....

Two

Wiping the smudge of pencil lead from her thumb, Eliza nodded in satisfaction. "Done."

"Did you put me down, too?" Jeanie peered over her shoulder.

"I did." Eliza pointed to their names, scrawled in her spidery penmanship on the sign-up sheet. They stepped aside, allowing the others assembled in the parish hall the opportunity to volunteer for the Harvest Fair. Eliza shivered as the street door opened, admitting more helpers and a rain-scented chill into the crowded chamber. While not ideal, the parish hall was the best space available for the fair preparations, considering the inclement weather. It was large enough to hold both people and supplies. Wood beams were propped against the far wall beside tools and stacks of used lumber, and barrels of supplies waited near rows of plain oak benches.

"Praise God for this rain." Eliza rubbed her arms against the cold. "I hope it means the drought is over—although I wouldn't mind sunshine and a dry wagon seat next Saturday, when we're out collecting donations."

Jeanie brushed something off the braid trim of Eliza's chestnut serge jacket. "Gum eraser," she explained. "I read your editorial this morning. You didn't name names—yours or Mr. Delacourt's—but do you think he'll recognize himself?"

Guilt swelled in Eliza's throat, but she swallowed it down. "If he's too good to dance with the local ladies, I imagine he won't read our papers, either."

"Just because he snubbed you doesn't mean he's a dime-novel villain. Father said Mr. Delacourt made a grand donation to the hospital fund. Forgive him and forget the whole thing."

Eliza couldn't meet Jeanie's eyes. Mr. Delacourt's actions, good or ill, shouldn't dictate whether or not she forgave him. Forgiveness was the right thing to do. Still... "I think I could more easily forgive his display of pride had he not decimated mine."

Jeanie gasped. "You *fancied* him. Oh, Eliza. Poor dear. Tell me everything."

Why, oh why, had she said anything? "There's nothing to tell—"

"Why, hello, ladies." The confident soprano of Emmeline Whitley interrupted, sparing Eliza from what was sure to be a vexing interrogation. As long as Emmeline didn't catch the rosy scent of romantic sentiment from Jeanie, that is. Although the young matron had put her matchmaking days behind her, nothing escaped her notice for long. Emmeline eyed Eliza and Jeanie with an eager expression. "I hoped I'd see you two here."

"You look well. How is your darling baby? Is she here?" Eliza peeked around Emmeline, searching for a perambulator or a cluster of cooing females.

"Larissa's home, dandling on Noah's knee. Both miss me, I'm sure." She grinned. "Guess what? I'm starting up our book club again in the New Year. You're an admirer of Mark Twain, aren't you? We'll be discussing *Life on the Mississippi*."

The group hadn't met in months, breaking for summer and remaining on hiatus while Emmeline settled her cousins in Austin. Eliza had long anticipated resuming the group, but now, her future was as clouded as today's overcast skies. Would her parents—and her finances—force her to give up everything she loved?

She'd best be noncommittal. "It sounds delightful."

"I shall procure a copy," Jeanie said.

"Wonderful. See you both soon." With a squeeze of hands, Emmeline bade them farewell and joined the other matrons across the room.

"Let's sit, too." Eliza indicated a bench where their fellow Abbey students conversed.

"Not yet." Jeanie's tone brooked no argument. "I asked you a question before Emmeline found us, and you'd better answer it. You fancied Mr. Delacourt, didn't you?"

"Him? Ha." The lie bit like a mosquito, and would likewise pester her until she confessed. "Very well. I thought him handsome and would have gladly danced with him."

"But he rebuffed you, and that is why you've punished him with that editorial."

The room felt close, stuffy. "My editorial wasn't *personal*. 'Tis my obligation as a journalist to inform the public of news, and the truth is, the railroads and their plump-pocketed owners intrude into many facets of our lives. Writers should draw attention to things that go unnoticed, like the railroads' high-handed bossiness." Eliza folded her arms. "And other things, too, like the troubles this drought has caused families."

Families like Marta Fleischer's, who worked a farm outside town. How could the sweet *fräulein* no longer work for the Branches? Times might be difficult for Eliza's family, but Marta's kin would starve far faster than Eliza's.

"Noble sentiments," Jeanie said. "But shouldn't you concentrate on making money by writing advertisements so you can stay in school, rather than writing unpaid editorials?"

"I finished two ads this morning. One for the new gentlemen's store on Pecan Street. The other ad extols Dr. Barclay's Cough Tonic. I compared a child's cough to a dragon devouring the peace of health and home. And the weapon of choice—Excalibur, if you will—is the tonic."

Jeanie burst into laughter. "Well, that should sell a few bottles."

"I hope so." Eliza spied more eraser bits trapped in the box-pleating at the front of her copper overskirt. Oh well. "I have to do something. I won't marry Hezekiah Cray."

"Eliza?" Mother's high-pitched call beckoned behind her.

Jeanie patted Eliza's arm and glided away. Eliza turned, ready to embrace her mother. They hadn't seen each other since the gala last week, after all.

But Mother couldn't return her hug, not with her hand resting on the arm of a gentleman in a rain-spattered blue coat. Unlike Mr. Cray, the young man was golden-haired and lanky. A half-grin split his classic features, giving him a roguish air.

"I must introduce you to Mr. Jacob Wicks. He's an *entrepreneur*." Mother drawled out the word like an endearment.

"Hello, Mother. Mr. Wicks. Welcome to Austin." She inclined her head. "How kind of you to help with the Harvest Fair."

"I confess to ulterior motives. Church is the best place to make new friends. And please, call me Jake." His eyes were warm and green as Christmas velvet.

"Jake is a railroad man from Tennessee." Mother batted her eyes.

Another one? "Austin must be the center of the world."

"I'm an investor, and there's a new rail line coming this way. The track's half laid, and it won't be long untill the Tennessee-North-Texas will be running goods to points north."

Mr. Delacourt's line. That man was everywhere these days. Except here, thankfully.

The street door opened, admitting a fresh gust of air and two men. Both shook rain from their sleeves and removed their dripping Stetsons. One man reminded her of a marigold—not a masculine comparison, but Charlie Bingham's sunny smile and orange hair brought the flower to mind. The other fellow boasted curls dark as loam and an even darker scowl, but despite his unfriendly air, he sent her stomach swooping like the dive of a hungry hawk.

She'd given thanks too soon. What was William Delacourt doing here?

In the days since his horrid first impression, she'd determined not to waste any thoughts on him. Her resolve hadn't held up well. She'd dwelled on him plenty. She didn't like it, but when she first saw him, she'd lost her breath. And it wasn't because she'd knocked into him.

"We have too many railroad owners in Austin at the moment, to my thinking." Mother's words drew Eliza back to the conversation.

Mr. Delacourt hung his coat and Stetson on a wall peg behind Mother. Pinpricks of embarrassment attacked Eliza's skin. The man may be arrogant, but she wished he hadn't overheard Mother. Then again, she wished a lot of things that couldn't be undone.

The Reverend Thaddeus Grimm, the church's new pastor, raised his arms to quiet the group and indicated they should take their seats. Jake nodded and melted into the bustle of volunteers, but Mother gripped Eliza's arm, holding her fast.

"Don't squander the opportunity presented to you today. I can hear the coins jingling in Jake Wicks's pockets—coins we need, missy." Her countenance brightened. "Oh, Mr. Cray has arrived."

Eliza glanced to where the mustachioed rancher paused in the door, expectorating a stream of tobacco into the street.

"I will not marry Hezekiah Cray."

"Foolish girl. He doesn't mind your opinions or plain looks, but if you're so repulsed by him, I suggest you get to work this afternoon. And I do not simply refer to fair preparations." She mouthed *Mr. Wicks*, as if to be certain Eliza understood her meaning.

Mother sat with the other matrons, leaving Eliza alone with her pitching stomach. Mr. Cray wiggled his brows in invitation, but she turned to search out her fellow Abbey students. Squeezing past sweet Colette Luce, Eliza sat between Jeanie and Liddy Duncan, whose mouse-colored hair did not reflect her exuberant personality.

"Sit, sit!" Liddy patted the seat and giggled, eyeing the gentlemen at the same time.

Despite her heavy skirt and layers of petticoats, the oak bench felt cold against Eliza's backside. Winter was on its way. And with it, Christmastime and Eliza's final days at school. Her already-queasy stomach flopped over.

"It's a pleasure to see so many people here." The pastor grinned, and Eliza forced herself to cast aside her gloomy thoughts. "We need all sorts of help preparing for the Harvest Fair, which will benefit our new hospital and the missionary school under construction in Kentucky."

Everyone clapped, even Mr. Delacourt. Eliza hated that she'd checked.

"Next week, we'll gather clothing for the missionary barrels, but today will be spent in committee and going through supplies." Pastor Grimm gestured toward several barrels and boxes. "Ladies, if you are not on committee, there are linens to sort for booths. Gentlemen, due to the inclement weather, we've stacked the donated lumber inside."

As the men moved to the far corner of the hall, the matrons circled to discuss the fair's dinner, bake sale, and entertainment. The Austen Abbey students sauntered to rummage through supplies, but Eliza followed the gentlemen.

"Pastor Grimm? May I speak to you of something troubling?"

His pale brows puckered. "Would you care to go into the sanctuary?"

"Not that kind of trouble." Her gaze flickered toward William Delacourt, who stared at her as if she were a puzzling item on display in the front window of Berryman's Dry Goods. "It's about the recipients of the mission barrels. I wondered if one could go to the Fleischer family."

His brows lifted. "They aren't parishioners, are they?"

"They attend a German church, but I didn't think it mattered. With the drought, their farm has suffered. Recently, Mr. Fleischer passed away and his daughter Marta lost her employment in town." *Thanks to my family.* "May we designate some of the clothes from the mission barrels for her use? Not just to Marta, but to the other immigrants who find themselves in need."

"I don't see why not. Now, why don't you get back to work with your friends?"

Work seemed an odd term to describe what the others were doing. Jeanie examined a bed sheet for holes, true, but Liddy, Colette, and the other girls stood and whispered, eyeing the menfolk. The few young fellows present set to work sorting lumber, including two Eliza recognized as Mrs. Collins's nephews, Harmon Gray and Jonathan Wellington. Both unmarried gents called upon the Abbey from time to time to visit their aunt, much to the students' delight. Harmon and Jonathan seemed to enjoy the feminine attention, too. But now, they and the other men seemed ignorant of the ladies' twittering. Except Mr. Delacourt. Hammer in hand, he worked a nail free and tossed it into a coffee can, watching her all the while.

Vexing man. She snatched up a square of cotton from a faded oak barrel. After examining the sheet for rips, she folded it into a lumpy polygon.

"What's wrong, Eliza?" Jeanie laid her neatly folded sheet on a bench.

Liddy perked up, like a dog hearing the word *walk.* "Something amiss?"

Eliza wouldn't give Mr. William Delacourt the satisfaction of reading his name on her lips. "It's the German immigrants. With this drought, they're in a bad way. I'm worried about Marta."

"Not that again." Liddy chose a sheet with a large tea-brown stain, glanced at it, and threw it on top of Jeanie's tidy pile. "*Les émigrés* are all you write about in your French themes at school, when the rest of us write about *l'amour.* Speaking of love." She peered over Eliza's shoulder. "Who's that?"

Eliza retrieved Liddy's blemished sheet. "You mean Jake Wicks?"

"Oh my." Liddy patted her hair and sashayed toward the men.

Jeanie sighed.

With sure steps, Liddy strolled into a pile of lumber next to Jake Wicks. She shrieked and tumbled forward, but Jake reached out a steadying arm before she landed.

Nervous laughter and twittering erupted as the volunteers watched Jake assist Liddy to her feet. All but Mr. Delacourt. His gaze fixed over their heads at the wooden beams propped vertically against the wall.

They'd been wedged against the pile Liddy walked into. As one, they began to slip down the wall. The women circled in their committee would be struck.

"Mother!" Her feet moved, but not fast enough. The beams fell.

Will couldn't catch them all.

He lunged, seizing an armful of the falling beams. With his shoulder, he deflected the rest, and they landed with a crack at the ladies' hems. The force of the wood stung Will's cradled arms, but the weight was nothing compared to the blast of pain reverberating through his bruised ribcage. He might as well have fallen off the horse again.

"Anyone hurt?" He managed not to grunt as he lowered the beams to the floor.

"Thanks to you, Mr. Delacourt, we are unscathed." A gray-haired lady in spectacles laid her hands over her heart. "That was a brave thing you did."

Her friends—except Mrs. Branch, who fussed under her daughter's ministrations—murmured in agreement.

"It was nothing." Although his ribs cried otherwise.

The woman in spectacles patted his hand. "I'm Honora Layton. My son Johnny told me he's curious about shipping his beef on your line. Why don't you come to supper so I can thank you? I'll invite Johnny, too."

"I'd be much obliged, ma'am." A customer *and* a home-cooked meal. *Thank you, God!*

Mrs. Layton batted her eyes as he took his leave. He chuckled despite the ache it caused his midsection. She must have been trouble in her day.

Charlie helped him remove the beams and lay them flat on the floor. "Your plan to integrate into the community couldn't have unfolded better. That accident may have just saved your reputation, after that unfavorable letter to the editor this morning."

Will snorted. "We're here to help industry in Austin, not destroy it."

"Speaking of destruction, what's Jake Wicks doing in Texas?"

"I think we know the answer to that." Will couldn't keep the acid from his tone.

"Do you think he persuaded your father...?"

Will shook his head and touched his aching side. The pain faded, but some wounds, like those inflicted by his father, never seemed to heal. "It doesn't matter. Right now I need to focus on the TNT."

"Just watch your back." Charlie clapped his shoulder. Then his demeanor brightened at once. "Miss Jeanie's alone. This is my chance to converse with her."

Besotted fool. If Charlie weren't careful, he'd never leave Austin. They were here to ensure the TNT's success and make a positive impact on the town. Not find wives.

Although a certain female had been on his mind. Eliza Branch returned to her post at the sheets. Loose strands of dark hair curled over her cheeks, much as they had the night of the gala. She was pretty, for sure, but shortly after he'd arrived today he'd overheard her mother urge her to find a wealthy man, verifying his instincts. She was out for money.

Nevertheless, he'd behaved poorly when he'd first met her and refused to dance. Time to make things right. He stepped toward her.

"May I help you with that?"

Her bluebonnet eyes hardened into sapphires. "That's not necessary."

"Work is more bearable when shared."

Her scowl softened, but she didn't relinquish the sheet. "That was a brave thing you did, catching that lumber. Were you hurt?"

"No splinters." Just agony in his ribs. He reached for the sheet hem trailing from her hands. "What are these for, anyway?"

"We drape them over the framed lumber, to make booths. Or to cover tables for games like the Glass Pitch." Her brow furrowed. "Laundry isn't a masculine occupation. Aren't you concerned what others will think?"

"I don't pay a lot of mind to what folks think of me."

This wasn't going right. He wanted to apologize, not argue. If he had a silver-dipped tongue like Jake Wicks, he'd have astonished her with his flowery apology by now. But he wasn't Jake, not in any way.

"I want to apologize for my behavior at the gala. I shouldn't have been so, er, curt."

Thick lashes fanned her cheeks as her gaze stayed downcast. Then she stepped away from him, still holding the sheet. Oh—he was supposed to mirror her movements to fold the sheet. Lengthwise, then crosswise. She stepped close, smelling of lemon and lavender like a breath of summer, and she took the sheet from him without touching his hands. Then her gaze lifted and he almost lost his train of thought. And the fact that she was a fortune hunter.

She smoothed the sheet. "It is forgotten."

"Not by me. You see, the day of the gala I sustained an injury. I wouldn't have been so brusque had I not been in pain. Truth be told, I hurt now." He hated admitting it.

"I'm sorry about your injury." Her pink lips twisted, as if the words behind them wouldn't form. "I owe you thanks for apologizing. And for your help today."

Why wasn't she sidling up to him now that he'd given her an opening? He'd expected fawning. Batting lashes. He must have gaped for too long, because her brow quirked and she handed him a musty-smelling sheet.

Two gentlemen carrying flat planks walked behind her. "Interesting dig against railroads in the *Texas Star* today," one said.

"You waste your coin on that rag? It's hard to find the news among the advertisements." The second man's voice faded as they moved on.

Eliza's cheeks bloomed pink. "I read that editorial, about the railroad presuming to divide the nation into time zones for its convenience. I thought the anonymous writer expressed her view—*his* or her view—well enough."

"He or she did. But I disagree with the piece. Regardless of who instigated the time zones, railroads or private citizens, regulation is a necessity."

She looked up at him with eyes so azure they weren't like bluebonnets at all. More like the blue of a candle flame. And just as mesmerizing. "But why must *trains* dictate the structure of our days?" Her practical question dragged him from thoughts of candles.

"Not trains. The railroads may be behind it, but even the federal government thinks it's a wise change." The folding became like a dance, lengthwise, crosswise, meet in the middle. "And a month from now, every train in Austin will run on the same time schedule. Surely you can see the value in that."

"Yes." She sighed. "I just don't approve of railroads dictating the change."

She was thoughtful, that was for sure. He admired the quality. "Your opinion is shared by many. Including the author of the editorial. He'll be happy when I leave Austin, I suppose."

A sly-looking grin pulled at her lips. "At least you don't care what anyone thinks of you."

Laughter burst from him, loud and unfettered, making his ribs throb. Not enough to stop laughing, though. He hadn't laughed like this since—

What was he thinking? Last time a woman made him laugh, more than his ribs ended up bruised by the time she was finished with him. He stepped back. "I'd best get back to pulling nails."

Her smile froze then melted away altogether. "Thanks for your help."

He returned to his stack of lumber, unease churning in his gut. He'd started to like talking with her. But the woman was a fortune hunter. Which made her no better than his greedy, money-minded stepmother.

He'd best not forget it again.

Three

"Sneaking out, Miss Branch?"

Eliza's shoulders sagged as her feet flattened. Clearly, her attempt to tiptoe past the headmistress's office hadn't been as silent as she intended. "I thought I'd take a short walk."

Mrs. Collins's head tipped to the side. "I'll only forestall you a minute. Come in, please."

Eliza trudged into the office.

Mrs. Collins took her seat, a tidy woman behind a tidy desk. Not a single brown hair escaped the neat bun at her nape. Her crisply pleated white blouse and gray skirt bore no wrinkles or lint. Likewise, nothing in the emerald-papered chamber was askew or dusty. Not even the potted ferns in their white wicker baskets dared wilt or fade.

If only Eliza's life were as uncluttered.

She perched on a chair of tufted brown velvet under a portrait of Queen Victoria, setting her satchel on her lap. Behind Mrs. Collins's desk, blue sky beckoned through the half-moon window, reminding Eliza she should be at the newspaper office by three o'clock. She forced her fiddling fingers to be still.

"Miss Branch, I cannot help but feel as if something is amiss." Compassion, coated in an English accent, was present in every syllable.

Had her parents written to the headmistress already? Eliza swallowed hard.

"Miss Lambert reports of your continued excellence in writing and literature. You are knowledgeable with globes, and your marks in French and domestics remain unchanged." Still just better than average, in other words. "But your instructors note your characteristic enthusiasm has not been present of late. Not even in music or art. You haven't touched the lyre in weeks, not unless asked to do so by an instructor."

So it had shown, then. "I shall endeavor to better apply myself."

"You're not disappointing *me*. The one failing to reap the benefits of this school is *you*."

Eliza chewed her lip. The time had come. Jeanie had suggested Eliza speak to Mrs. Collins from the start, but she'd resisted, wanting to accomplish the near-impossible on her own.

"About school, ma'am. I will be leaving." She proceeded to inform her headmistress about her family's financial issues, as well as her advertisements for the *Star*. "I was on my way to the newspaper office just now to deliver a few ads. Perhaps the income could help pay my tuition. Not all of it, but I cannot sit by and do nothing."

"I understand. Still, I cannot have my students skulking from the premises like felons." If possible, Mrs. Collins's rigid posture grew straighter. "Therefore I require you to inform me when you must visit the newspaper office, so I shall know your whereabouts."

Relief flooded Eliza's chest. "Thank you, ma'am."

"I'll do all I can to keep you here through graduation. Perhaps there is a scholarship opportunity I missed." She glanced at a neat stack of papers at her elbow. "In the meantime, hadn't you best be on your way?"

"Yes, ma'am." Eliza clutched her satchel and hopped to her feet.

"Take Miss Hale with you. A young lady such as yourself knows better than to run about alone, lacking wit and propriety that could so easily be found by simply employing a companion."

"Oh. Of course." Although Eliza tromped about Austin by herself all the time, selling her ads to Mr. LeShand and taking constitutionals in the park. But it wouldn't do to argue with the headmistress, after she'd been so generous. And Jeanie made most congenial company.

But she did not require a chaperone. What possible trouble could she get into?

"Ah, Will?"

Will pivoted on his boot heel. Charlie stopped on the boardwalk, one hand fisted at his waist, the other gesturing behind him with his thumb. "The hotel is this way."

"Sorry." He backtracked, sidestepping an oncoming gaggle of beribboned, twittering schoolgirls. "I was woolgathering."

A half-grin tugged at Charlie's lips. "So I noticed. I had to do all the talking in our meeting, thanks to your inattention. If left to you, the TNT would be carrying nothing back to Memphis but Texas air."

"You *are* the spokesman in our partnership."

"And you're the one who pushes pencils and loves the locomotives like pets. I know how our enterprise works. But you seemed preoccupied. Is your ribcage aching? Or is it something else?" His eyebrows wiggled like ginger caterpillars. "Something feminine?"

Not again. "Just because you're infected with love fever doesn't mean I've succumbed."

"Ah, Miss Jeanie." Charlie sighed as if he'd just caught a whiff of spring blossoms, and Will congratulated himself for diverting his friend's attention. He wouldn't fib and blame his still-tender ribs for his distraction. Neither would he admit he walked too far down the street because he couldn't get the blue-eyed fortune hunter out of his mind.

He forced his brain to consider Miss Branch's friend. "Miss Jeanie still delights, then?"

"Our conversation at the Harvest Fair preparations was delightful. Do you think she'll consent to speak with me again? Or perhaps take a drive?"

"I don't know." At Charlie's crestfallen look, Will snorted. "She's in finishing school. I doubt the ladies are allowed to leave the premises."

"Maybe I can call there. Oh, I say." Charlie faltered and gripped Will's bicep, something he'd never done before and probably wouldn't remember, judging by the addlepated look on his freckled face.

"Um, Charlie?" But one peek in the direction of Charlie's gaze, and Will's ribcage ached at his sudden suck of breath.

Three ladies conversed farther down the street, two in colorful garb, the other drab as a sparrow. Miss Jeanie's pretty face peeked out under the brim of a beribboned hat. The other well-dressed woman's back was to him, all blue bustle and bonnet, but he recognized her bearing, the tilt of her head and the way her foot tapped at her hem.

Eliza Branch.

Charlie's hand released Will's arm only to thump it, a mimic of the sudden pounding in his chest. "I must speak to her. Come. Or don't come. I don't care."

He was already darting across Congress Avenue.

Will sighed. "Hold up, Charlie." Charlie paused but cast Will a puzzled expression, so Will hastened across the limestone street and gestured at the ladies with his chin. "Looks important. Like they need a minute of privacy."

Miss Jeanie and the other woman bore funereal expressions. Eliza Branch shook her head, as if sad. Clearly they needed to finish their conversation—and he needed Charlie to focus on work, not women. But that wouldn't happen overnight. From his years on a thoroughbred ranch, he knew what went into corralling a stallion with a mare on his equine mind. Attention. Mastery. Solid boundaries. He'd have to employ them all to keep Charlie on task for the TNT.

Good thing he wasn't similarly tempted.

Then Eliza Branch turned her head to the side, her profile revealing her straight nose and dark, thick eyelashes. And he couldn't blame Charlie a whit for wanting to talk to the ladies.

"I suppose you're right," Charlie said. "Soon as they're done talking, then, we'll say hello. Hope nothing's too wrong, though."

"If something is amiss, we'll offer assistance." It was the proper thing to do. For the sake of fostering relations between the folks of Austin and the TNT. His strong desire to be near Eliza Branch had everything to do with being friendly for the sake of manners and business.

At least, that was what he kept telling himself.

The coins weren't even in Eliza's purse yet. Mr. LeShand had dropped them into her hand, leaving her too upset to secure them before she rushed from the *Texas Star* office. It turned out to be a good thing, though, because it was far easier now to press them into Marta Fleischer's palm.

"*Ach, Fräulein*, I cannot." The Branches' former servant shook her head with such force that her calico bonnet wiggled over her braided blond tresses. "I no longer *verk* for your family."

"By no fault of your own." With gentle pressure, Eliza folded Marta's fingers over the coins. "You were so good to us."

"And you vere good to me, *Fräulein*." Marta shifted the basket over her arm, clanking together its jarred contents. Sauerkraut? Eliza's mouth watered remembering the tart cabbage, served alongside Marta's ginger-seasoned pork roast. The jars should fetch a good price from the general store. "I pray for you, Miz Branch."

Eliza smiled. "You have my prayers, as well."

Marta bobbed her head. "*Danke, Fräulein.*"

As Marta disappeared into the crowd, Eliza's shoulders slumped. "First her father's death, then the lack of rain, and then my parents' dismissal. Poor dear."

"None of it's your fault." Jeanie's touch on Eliza's arm was gentle. "That was good of you to do, but now you won't have coins for Mrs. Collins."

Oh. True. Eliza sighed and initiated their walk back toward Austen Abbey. "God provides. Isn't that what we've been taught? Perhaps this is the time for me to put my faith into practice. I've never relied on God much before."

"But what if God doesn't provide? You'll have to leave school."

"Then I suppose I've got to accept He knows best." There was peace in the acknowledgement, if not joy. Maybe she should pray for that, too.

"But what about further money from the *Star*? What did your editor say?"

Eliza's jaw clenched. "Mr. LeShand is still willing to pay for my ads, but not for my articles. Remember last year when that rancher Brandon Tabor saved that little Bennet girl? He published a third-hand exaggerated piece written by a *man* over my eyewitness account. The plight of Marta and the drought is not 'newsworthy' enough for him. Neither is the upcoming Harvest Fair. 'Church newsletters,' he called my ideas. If he's going to publish something by me, a woman, he wants articles of a more scandalous nature."

Jeanie had the grace to gasp. "Mercy. We don't know of any scandals."

"He thinks I should find one. Or perhaps make one. He liked my editorial alluding to Mr. Delacourt and other railroad men. When I said I shouldn't have jabbed at Mr. Delacourt like that, he said I should have jabbed more."

"More?" Jeanie gaped.

"Articles with bite sell papers." Eliza's chest tightened, as if her corset shrank a size. "If I write something shocking, he'll print it and pay accordingly."

Jeanie frowned. "Prayer's our best bet, then, because you'd never do something so outrageous."

"Speaking of outrageous, I shouldn't press my luck with Mrs. Collins. We'd best head back."

"Oh, at once, of course." There was no one sweeter or more thoughtful than Jeanie.

A tall figure slipped in front of them, halting their progress down the street. Jake Wicks, a half-grin on his handsome face, beamed down at them and tipped his Stetson.

"And here I thought I wouldn't see you ladies again until Sunday. Who set you pretty birds free from your cage?"

Despite her anguish over Marta's predicament, the admiring way he looked at her made Eliza's hand fly to her chest. "We're students, not prisoners, Mr. Wicks."

"I'd never mistake such loveliness for common criminals." His gaze took in their ensembles, and even Jeanie giggled at his complimentary smile. After Mr. Delacourt's rejection, a handsome man's attentions soothed like butter on a burn. Though why she kept thinking of him irritated, like a pesky horsefly.

Eliza made introductions.

"Are all Austen Abbey students so pretty?"

"They are all accomplished in their own rights." Eliza had never flirted, but this was somewhat fun.

"Even Liddy Duncan—is that her name? I met her at the Fair meeting."

Jeanie nodded, shifting to make way for a man carrying a crate so she now stood facing the direction they'd come. "She's one of our friends."

Jake winked at Eliza. "Liddy's a flighty one, don't you think?"

Before Eliza could fashion a reply, Jeanie bounced on her toes. "I declare, is that Mr. Bingham?"

Eliza's throat thickened as she turned. Mr. Bingham and his frowning friend Mr. Delacourt strode toward them. Her hand dropped from her throat to her abdomen, offering light pressure against the dust devil of nerves swirling inside.

Such silliness, especially when she could work some good out of another meeting with William Delacourt. She turned back to Jake. "Didn't you say you wished to invest in the TNT? Now you can speak to its owners."

"Owner." Jake clarified. "Bingham is Delacourt's lackey, no more."

Lackey? The word jarred Eliza and set Jeanie's brow in a pucker. The wrinkle erased the second Mr. Bingham arrived and greeted them, his rapt gaze fixed on Jeanie as if she were a glowing pink sunrise.

It was nothing like Mr. Delacourt's intense stare for Eliza. He doffed his Stetson, allowing wavy brown curls to spill over his broad brow. Why must so arrogant a man be so handsome? Although he'd be even more so if he smiled on occasion.

"Running errands?" Mr. Bingham's eyes gleamed, as if Jeanie's had informed him President Arthur himself was in town. "Splendid."

Jake cocked a brow. "You ladies seemed so serious when I found you."

"Nothing upsetting occurred, I hope." Mr. Delacourt frowned at Jake.

Eliza toyed with the velvet drawstring of her purse. It wouldn't do to burden the gentlemen with Marta's story, and with it, her own tale of financial woe. "We ran into a friend."

"You've time for an ice cream, of course." Jake jutted his cleft chin, indicating the parlor across the street. "It's a warm day, perfect for a quick dish of strawberry ice."

Oh, how appealing ice cream sounded, cool and sweet and rich. And Jeanie seemed so eager. Maybe even Mr. Delacourt would smile—not his polite, cool smile but something warm and real—and she could see if it transformed his already handsome face.

Eliza shook away the absurd thought. Mrs. Collins had already shown leniency today. Eliza wouldn't test her headmistress. "Tempting, but we must return to the Abbey."

Jeanie wasn't the sort to pout. She was too well-bred. But her lower lip trembled.

"Haven't you business to attend to, Wicks?" Mr. Delacourt's brow quirked. "That's why you've come to Austin, isn't it?"

Mr. Wicks's laugh didn't sound the least amused. "It is."

"He'd like to invest in the TNT, wouldn't you, Mr. Wicks?" Eliza prompted.

"Call me Jake. And yes. That's why I'm here."

Mr. Delacourt's eyes darkened to jet. "My answer's the same as it was in Memphis."

Eliza bit her lip. Mr. Delacourt seemed well versed in saying no. She scrounged for something to say to poor Jake—he'd asked her to be familiar, after all—but Jeanie turned back.

"Come, Eliza. If we cannot have ice cream, Mr. Bingham insists on escorting us back to school."

"Allow me."

"May I?"

The two gentlemen at Eliza's sides offered their arms at the same time, Jake's brown sleeve to her left, Mr. Delacourt's of midnight blue on her right. Neither looked at her, but glared at each other. Jake's lip twitched. A muscle clenched in Mr. Delacourt's cheek, where a hint of stubble had begun to form.

Why did Mr. Delacourt detest Jake? He seemed a pleasant enough fellow. Perhaps the problem was not Jake; it hadn't been Eliza, when Mr. Delacourt was rude to her. No, perhaps the issue was Mr. Delacourt's character.

Oh, he'd apologized for rebuffing her at the gala, and he'd helped with the Harvest Fair. He'd made a point of being at all the right places and saying the right things, but warmth never touched his eyes.

Nevertheless, his proximity made her insides quiver like tomato aspic. But he still disliked her. Why else would he stare at her with such gravity? He only offered his arm because he had to. To be polite.

Still, her chest ached like something inside her broke when she ignored his proffered arm and took Jake's.

Four

Two by two, the Harvest Fair volunteers exited the stuffy parish hall to execute the tasks they'd signed up for last Saturday—all but Eliza, who felt a bit like a runt piglet trying to squeeze between its siblings at the trough. Nobody needed her assistance. Emmeline Whitley took a pretty Abbey student to request food donations from the kitchen of the Hotel Brunswick, and Liddy corralled Jake into partnering with her to solicit baked goods.

Eliza was to have collected clothes for the mission barrels with Jeanie, except her poor roommate hadn't made it to church this Saturday afternoon. She was huddled under her quilts at Austen Abbey, with Dr. Barclay's Cough Tonic and a bowl of chicken broth, leaving Eliza the odd one out for fair preparations. A group of men outside declined her offer to help frame booths because they didn't think she'd want to dirty her pretty dress. She snorted.

"Bye, Eliza!" Liddy called from the threshold of the street door. Eliza waved back, just as Jake looked over his shoulder and wiggled his brows, as if to say he'd rather be with her.

Balm. A little smile pulled at her cheeks.

At least she was free to visit with her parents, who'd just appeared in the doorway carrying an old quilt—a donation for the barrels, no doubt. Mother presented the thin coverlet to Pastor Grimm while Father rocked on his heels. She hurried toward them.

Hezekiah Cray stepped in front of her from out of nowhere,

like a cockroach scuttling from under a piece of furniture. A smirk formed under his long, stringy mustache. The flowery-sweet odor of the Macassar oil in his black hair almost masked the tobacco and perspiration reeking from his grease-stained plaid suit. "Miss Branch."

She inched back, but he forestalled further movement by placing his hand on her elbow.

"Mr. Cray." She glared at his hand. "You take liberties."

His hand dropped. "Your demure manner is one of the things I like best about you."

Did the man need spectacles? She, demure? Eliza choked a laugh.

At the sound, a hopeful gleam sparked in his little eyes. Her smile fell, swift and final as an ax to a chicken's neck. "How kind of you to describe me in such terms. I cannot say I am oft referred to that way. Alas, I must beg your pardon, for I see my parents. Good day."

Rather than step back, he slid forward. "Not yet, Eliza."

"I do not recall granting you permission to address me by my Christian name, sir."

Dear heavens, did he giggle? "Such fine manners, indeed. A true lady." Why, oh why, was he leaning so close?

"Mr. Cray," she warned.

His beady-eyed gaze raked over her figure as he stepped closer. "Yes?"

"Step away before I push you."

"That is no way to speak to your fiancé." His breathy tone sent shivers crawling over her skin. Like she'd disturbed an ant hill.

"My *what*?" Surely the whole room heard her shriek.

"You'd like me to ask you, even though it's all arranged?" That giggle again. "Very well, for formality's sake. Marry me."

That was *asking*? Bile shot up her throat. She swallowed it down. *Be polite. Be polite.* "Thank you for the, er, honor, but I cannot accept."

"Wicked vixen." The words were an endearment. "So coy."

Any intention she had to remain polite melted in a wave of anger. She counted to five. "I assure you, I am never considered coy."

His pink lips popped apart. "But your mother said—"

Of course she did. "I'm sorry you were misled, but we wouldn't suit."

A flutter of movement caught her eye. Mother stared at her. Beyond her, William Delacourt stood, hat in his hands, watching from the corner of his eyes.

"I see where this is going." Mr. Cray's voice pulled her gaze back to his beady-eyed inventory of her features.

"You do?" Thank heavens.

"You'd like me to get down on one knee and all that emasculating nonsense."

"Oh, please do not do that." Panic welled under her ribcage.

He swiped perspiration from his brow. "Then let us tell your parents the good news."

"There is no news." How else to communicate her answer? She'd tried courtesy. Even blunt honesty. Perhaps he'd hear her clearer now. "You can ask me until your cows churn their own cream into butter. The answer is now and forever will be no. I will not marry you."

His jaw slacked. "No?"

"No."

He stepped back to a proper distance. "Oh. Well then." He turned on his toe and all but ran out the street door.

The scent of tuberose replaced the sweet scent of his Macassar oil. "You jilted him?"

Eliza sighed. Her parents—Mother flushed, Father looking bored—cornered her, much as Mr. Cray had. "*Jilt* implies I accepted him in the first place."

"Too good for him, are you? Too proud?" The ruffles of Mother's purple bodice fluttered over her heaving bosom. "Mark my words, missy. If you don't cast aside your foolish notions and marry Mr. Cray, I shall never speak to you again."

"You can't mean that." Eliza couldn't close her gaping mouth.

"I can. I *do*. You will no longer be my daughter."

Tears pricked at Eliza's eyes like pins in a cushion. "Mother."

Father's bony fingers patted Eliza's forearm. "It's no use arguing with your mother. If she says she won't speak to you unless you marry Cray, then she won't. But bear in mind, I shall never speak to you again if you *do* marry him."

Something inside her burst into sweetness, like the first taste of a June strawberry. Was it relief? Or Father's blessing? Her fingers closed over his. "Thank you."

He shrugged and removed his hand. "The man's a no-account gamester. Who's to say he won't gamble away his ranch? Then you'd be right where you started. Broke. Except you'd have to look at his limp rope of a mustache for the rest of your sorry life."

Mother stifled a sob behind her hand.

"Everything will work out, I promise." Eliza would write ads forever if she had to. And she'd trust God to provide for them. She *would*. "I will help. I can."

A moan escaped Mother's throat.

Mr. Delacourt approached, his brows lowered as if he were concerned. Could this day get any worse?

"I beg your pardon." He nodded at Eliza and her parents. "Is everything all right?"

"Splendid," Mother snapped, her anguished expression shifting to one of haughty disdain. Father nodded his greeting with scant eye contact.

That left Eliza to be the voice of good manners, no matter how thin her nerves. Her forced smile stretched her lips with unnatural strain. "And you, Mr. Delacourt? How are you today?"

"Quite well." His lips twitched, but not enough for her to tell if he was amused or dyspeptic. "Pardon my intrusion, but it seems you and I are the only two left lacking partners, Miss Branch. Since Miss Hale is indisposed and my friend Charlie has taken ill, the reverend thought I could accompany you to collect the donations. If that's acceptable to you, that is. I've hired a wagon."

Apparently, the day could *indeed* worsen.

"Quite acceptable." She had no other option. She kissed Father's cheek and reached for Mother, but Mother jerked her head back.

"Oh, I did not know what you were doing, silly girl."

Eliza sighed but didn't try to kiss her mother again. "I won't see you until the Harvest Fair, I suppose. Tell the girls hello."

"We shall." Father shook Mr. Delacourt's hand. "Good luck with the collections."

Mr. Delacourt set his Stetson on his head and gazed down at her with eyes soft with, what, pity? She needed no such thing, from him of all people. With her shoulders squared and chin tilted up, she strode from the parish hall out onto the noisy street.

Sharp-smelling dust swirled around her, kicked up from traffic flowing in both directions. Sunlight pained her eyes for a moment, causing her to squint, but she should have guessed she'd have no difficulty identifying Mr. Delacourt's rented wagon. Everything about him bespoke wealth, so was it any wonder that even his rented wagon, its fresh parsley-green paint as glossy as the matching chestnuts it was hitched to, was finer than a regular old wagon should be?

"Shall we?" He spoke as if she were a grand lady ascending a carriage.

She climbed onto a wheel spoke. He took her elbow, but she still plopped like a weak-legged colt on the hard wagon seat. Some grand lady she was.

His hand didn't let go. "All settled?"

Looking into his eyes, his hand on her arm, she was suddenly back at the gala when she first saw him, caught to his chest, breathless, her pulse skittering like a rabbit's.

Answer his question, you ninny! The words didn't come, so she nodded. He tipped his hat brim and released her arm, leaving it tingling and icy. Ridiculous. She busied herself with smoothing the wrinkles from her salmon-hued skirt while he moved to stand at the horses' heads. Murmuring lyrical words to them, he inspected their bridles.

Eliza flinched. Mr. Delacourt was sweet with the horses. There was no other word for it. He might be arrogant, but he all but sang to the creatures, as if he were a different man altogether. Like Father, whose affections for animals seemed far stronger, or easier, than those he harbored for people. She'd always loved to watch Father with the cattle, or horses or dogs, for that matter. Once he was with anything with four legs, his heart shone through his eyes. Perhaps Mr. Delacourt was the same way, although she couldn't see his eyes under the shade of his hat brim. But his smile was wide. The first true smile she'd seen from him, and oh, she'd been right. The effect was dazzling.

He clambered up beside her, sending the wagon rocking on its springs.

Or perhaps that was just her spinning head, dizzy with confusion. *Don't you dare start to like him, Eliza! He didn't treat you half as well as he treated the horses. It's one thing to find him handsome. Like appreciating art. But don't go thinking more than that.*

If it wasn't too late. Why else would she have been so stung that he wouldn't dance with her at the gala?

"Do you have a list of where we're supposed to go?" He released the brake and directed the horses onto the street, his head turned so he couldn't see her flush. Thank the Lord.

"Mrs. Layton has some donations for us. Head north to Mesquite and turn right."

"I've been to her house for supper. A dear lady." He flicked the reins.

So he'd made one conquest in Austin. Eliza kept her gaze on the street, where shoppers strolled and children gathered outside Lundberg's Confectionary, divvying up sweets. Clattering wheels and clopping hooves filled her ears. All around was action and noise.

Yet she and Mr. Delacourt sat side by side, still and silent as gravestones.

She chanced a peek. He sat straight and held the reins loosely in his gloves, confidence emanating from his posture. Since when did a railroad owner drive a wagon with skill?

Not that she could ask, although propriety demanded she make small talk. She could almost feel Mrs. Collins nudging her. "So what do you think of the weather?"

"The weather?" He glanced at her, a brow quirked.

Genteel conversation was not nearly as easy as Austen Academy taught, and she couldn't ignore a scrape of irritation. "Isn't that what people discuss? The weather, or the progress being made on the new capitol building, or who's calling upon whom, or the quality of the rented horseflesh."

Another smile pulled at his lips, and despite herself, she rather liked it when he smiled.

"These horses seem to be good stock, I'm pleased to say." Most men of her acquaintance would have missed the edge of sarcasm in her question, but he hadn't. And it seemed to amuse him. "What else was on your list? The capitol? Progress is slow but sure. I cannot comment on any romantic attachments in Austin. Nor am I an expert on its weather, but it's a pretty day. I've heard tell it's too dry for October. Do you agree? On the weather, I mean?"

A smile pushed past her pursed lips. If he was going to make an effort at shallow conversation, then she would, too. "I do."

"Then there's something." He slowed the horses to allow a fringe-topped surrey to pass.

It was quiet a moment while Eliza's fingers fidgeted. If they could only safely discuss the weather, she should probably keep at it. "Last week's rain gave me hope the drought would end, but it did not last, more's the pity. I pray for rain every day."

"That's a prayer many of us share." He looked over his left shoulder, straining the fabric of his coffee-brown coat. It was a good color for him, with his dark hair and eyes. A coat of moss green, however, would look even more pleasing than the brown.

Eliza grimaced. She sounded just like the women in her ads for the gentlemen's stores. *Keep your mind on business and civility.* With the topic of weather exhausted, she searched her mind for other safe topics.

"It's kind of you to help with the mission barrels. Especially since you're only in Texas to work."

"One can't—shouldn't—do nothing but work. Or disregard serving the Lord. He has to be first, every day, in everything. My mother taught me that." Affection coated his words with sweetness, like maple syrup.

He loved his mother and horses. He wasn't all bad. And the closeness of his clean scent made her a little light-headed. Perhaps that explained her twisting toward him on the wagon seat.

"I ignore the Lord too much. I shouldn't, of course, but of late, it's been on my mind to let Him work some things out." Her fingers twiddled. She hadn't meant to say something so vulnerable. Mercy, she needed a safer topic of conversation. Fast. "She sounds like a wise woman, your mother. What else does she say?"

His smile faded. "She went home to the Lord six years ago."

Eliza's fingers stilled. "I'm sorry."

"Thank you. It's been hard, but our family's trudged on without her. Some of us faster than others."

A whinnying squeal from one of the horses drew her gaze forward. A phaeton hurtled toward them, driven by a laughing youth. He held an amber bottle in one hand and yanked the reins with the other, but the two horses under his lead charged on as if spooked. Mr. Delacourt pulled on the reins and spoke clear, calm words to the team. The wagon jolted to the side, and Eliza gripped the edge of the seat.

The phaeton careened past them. Its driver tossed the bottle in the street.

Mr. Delacourt shook his head. "Aren't there laws against such behavior in this town?"

The hairs at her nape stood to attention. Did he insult her city? "Austin has its share of trouble, just like everywhere else. Even Memphis, I am quite certain."

"My words didn't come out as I intended." There was that intense look again. "Austin is a fine city. That's why I'm here. It's the state capitol, a center of industry and agriculture, and it's still growing. Just think of the new University of Texas. The young men who study there—"

"And young women."

"Pardon?"

"The university boasts a female student." Her pulse ratcheted as she awaited his judgmental glower. Maybe he didn't intend to disparage Austin, but that didn't mean he wasn't arrogant. He was in Texas for one purpose. To make money. And he seemed to think higher of himself than anyone else, except perhaps his friend Mr. Bingham. He certainly didn't like Jake Wicks. Or her. She twisted back to face fully forward on the wagon seat. "Are you one of those who disapprove of women in college? Lacking sufficient intelligence and wit, perhaps?"

"Hardly." He smiled at her barbed questions. With a *gee*, he turned the wagon down Honora Layton's street. "I know one female who surpasses me in almost every aspect, intelligence and wit included."

He spoke with humor and something more. Admiration? Did he have a sweetheart in Memphis? Eliza fussed with the finger seam of her glove.

"My sister, Ginny," he said. "Ah, there's the house."

A sister. For some inexplicable reason, Eliza smiled. "How old is Ginny?"

"Sixteen. She's home with our father on the thoroughbred ranch."

Ah. "No wonder you were so good with the horses." She could have smacked her forehead for speaking it aloud.

"I may not want my father's business, but I share his affection for horses. Do you enjoy riding?" He stopped the wagon and set the brake.

"I don't know. I've never done it."

"Never?" At her shaking head, his brows rose. "Would you like to?"

Horses were so big. So unpredictable. The team hitched to the out-of-control phaeton had seemed wild, all snorting nostrils and thundering hooves.

Her father's ranch came to mind, all green meadows and wildflowers. Her favorite place in the world. What would it feel like to race over the grass, the wind in her hair? "I think I would like to ride at the ranch before—"

Oh mercy! She almost admitted their financial difficulties. At that blessed moment, Mrs. Honora Layton opened her front door.

"Mr. Delacourt." The way the elderly widow batted her eyes reminded Eliza of Liddy. He was handsome, and yes, he'd saved the ladies from a pile of lumber, but really. Mrs. Layton could be his grandmamma. The woman beckoned him with her gnarled hand, ignoring Eliza. "I made those molasses cookies you like."

"Why ma'am," he drawled as he climbed from the wagon. "I'm honored."

Eliza grunted then covered it as a cough when Mr. Delacourt reached to assist her. His large hands circled her waist, and he lifted her down, a quick, proper gesture from a man who didn't like her. Yet the touch, and the scent of his clean aftershave, left her swaying on the street.

Mercy. She was as bad as Mrs. Layton.

Homes of grand construction on either side of the street cast long shadows as Will turned the team onto a quiet avenue. He chanced a glance at Eliza. "How much farther to Austen Abbey?"

"The next street on the left is Chawton Circle, and you can't miss the Abbey. It's the only mansion on the street with a turret, of all things."

Her smile was slow, weary after such a long afternoon. But it spread to her eyes and made him wish the day wasn't yet at an end. He liked sitting by her, liked how the pinkish-orange of her dress brought out the roses in her cheeks. And he appreciated the spark in her blue eyes, and in her wit. Eliza spoke her mind, as his sister did, as his mother had. He valued her forthrightness.

He shifted his weight on the wagon seat. This line of thought was not good.

Best say something. "I've eaten more molasses cookies today than I have in my entire life." A lame effort at conversation, but it was true. He wouldn't need supper from the Hotel Brunswick kitchens tonight. Although he should order Charlie some soup. His brows scrunched. He hadn't thought of his ailing friend all day.

Come to think of it, she hadn't mentioned her ill friend, either. "Are you sick of molasses?"

"Don't tell Mrs. Layton." He laughed. To his relief, she did too.

"At least we accomplished our goal. Four full barrels for the mission school. And maybe for others, too." Her tone turned wistful, but before he could ask what she meant, she shifted toward him on the bench. "You met a lot of people today. Few menfolk, but hopefully today was good for business anyway."

Ah, the TNT. He hadn't thought much of it today, either. Although she was right. That was why he was in Austin in the first place. Yet somewhere between Mrs. Layton's cookies, taking tea with two other widows, and visiting a young family, thoughts of business had fallen from his mind like autumn leaves from the bare-limbed trees they passed. "I suppose."

"It was kind of you to oil Mrs. Elton's door hinge."

"It squawked like a crow. How could I not?"

"That squawk was nothing compared to the Price's baby. You did just fine with him, by the way." Her eyes flashed gray in the dimming light.

"I doubt that. He caterwauled the whole time." Bouncing a very small, squalling infant had felt unnatural and awkward. But it had also felt surprisingly agreeable.

"Nehemiah's colicky. I'm certain the Prices appreciated you cooing to him. And I know they were pleased when you took little Ronald outside to play ball."

"Now that was real fun."

And it had been, especially when Eliza joined in. Flouncy gown, gloves, and all, she'd lunged to catch Ronald's throws, and when she tossed the ball to Will, there was force behind it to match her mischievous grin.

There was something admirable about Eliza. He'd been vulnerable today, confiding in her about his mother, speaking of God, finding joy in service. She hadn't made him regret his vulnerability, as his father often had. Rather, she encouraged it. She'd been vulnerable, too.

He turned the team onto Chawton Circle. What had happened today? All his good sense crumbled, like sod under a pick axe. He admitted what he'd tried to stifle since he met the woman. Eliza Branch may be a fortune hunter, but he no longer cared.

He had feelings for the girl.

"Why are you staring at me?" She blinked.

He hadn't realized he had been. But he wasn't concentrating on his driving, either. He'd almost passed the circular brick drive to the Austen Academy. He turned the team onto the drive and stopped in front of the three-story mansion of red brick and cream limestone—and yes, there was the turret. Like a castle in the middle of Austin. Staring at the rich architectural features gave him a minute to summon his courage. "Eliza. I mean Miss Branch."

"You're pale. Are you ill, Mr. Delacourt?"

"Perhaps I am." He removed his Stetson. "Don't wed Mr. Cray."

Her eyes narrowed. "I don't plan on it."

"You may not, but I heard your mother. It's not my business...."

Her hand flew to the high neck of her gown. "No, it is not—"

"But you can't wed Cray. Or Jake Wicks. You wouldn't be happy."

Red splotched her cheeks. Not a sweet blush. An angry flush. "You presume to know what makes me happy?"

His throat thickened. He said everything wrong. "I'd like to. Know what makes you happy, that is."

"You would?" The livid line of her shoulders softened.

"I would." He clung to the reins so he wouldn't clutch her fingers.

The mottled color in her cheeks faded to a becoming pink. "Mr. Delacourt." The name on her lips was like a breath of breeze.

"My name is Will. And I'd like you to use it." He licked his lips. Was he really doing this? "I'd like to court you, even though I planned not to."

Her brow furrowed. "Planned not to court someone in Austin?"

"That. You, despite the temptation. Everyone knows I have money. I know you feigned falling into me at the gala to get my attention." Her eyes narrowed again, but he pressed on. "I overheard your mother last week, insisting you marry because of...certain financial issues. I resisted, not wanting to join myself to a fortune hunter."

Eliza stood, rocking the wagon on its shocks. She hoisted her skirt and climbed over the side, hopping to the ground.

He wrapped the reins around the brake and scrambled from the wagon. Didn't she understand? "You're wonderful. So wonderful you made me forget my determination to be removed from your charms. But I cannot help it." Shouldn't that make her feel good?

Not according to the scowl she tossed him. "So I bewitched you?"

"Yes." No, that didn't sound right. "What I mean is, I came to know you."

"Pity you came to know me after misjudging me. I did not throw myself into you at the gala, and you may take *that* with you back to Memphis when you shake the dust of Austin from your boots. Alas, my first impression of you, as a rudesby, can never be shaken."

She stomped into the mansion and slammed the front door.

Will marched behind her, his fist raised to hammer the door, but the fluttering of a curtain stopped him short. Girls. Watching. He spun on his heel and climbed into the wagon.

His father was right about him. Now the whole world knew him for a fool.

Five

" *Fortune hunter.* That's what he said." Eliza plopped the hat box on her bed and tugged out her rose-colored bonnet. It was her favorite, with a pretty red hue that suited her complexion, and she could use the boost it would provide to her confidence when she spoke to her editor, Mr. LeShand. She'd felt off since Will Delacourt's insulting proposal last week.

"Unbelievable." Jeanie's voice rasped, still raw from her illness. She'd gone home for a week to recuperate under her mother's ministrations, and had just returned to the Abbey this morning. "I cannot fathom why Mr. Delacourt despises you so."

"That is the worst part. He does not despise me, or rather, he wishes he could, but cannot. He is willing to overlook my greedy fingers because I have bewitched him, despite his 'best attempts' to wish otherwise. He'd like to court me, Jeanie. Court." Eliza's gestures were too large to be ladylike, but no one could see her but Jeanie in the privacy of their shared bedchamber. "And oh, how I would have agreed to it if he hadn't first said such ugly things, despite my own hesitations. My first impression of him was as vile as his of me, but I thought things had changed. We had a lovely afternoon. He was so..."

She was about to say endearing, especially when he held colicky Baby Nehemiah, but she chewed her tongue.

"He was so, what?" Jeanie's eyes were wide.

"Sincere. And I suppose he was. Poor conflicted man." Her tone was icy with sarcasm.

"It might be understandable he drew that conclusion." At Eliza's gape, Jeanie shook her head. "Not based on your behavior. But if he overheard your mother, what else could he think?"

Eliza didn't want to think of that now. She shoved her bonnet atop her head and pinned it in place. "Speaking of Mother. She told me she'd disown me for not marrying Mr. Cray." She turned away from Jeanie and pinned her hat into her coiffure.

"She does not mean it, dear. I'm certain."

Eliza laughed, but there was little humor in it. "She repeated her threat in a note she sent this morning. I must wed at once. Not Mr. Cray, of course, now that he is betrothed."

"He is?"

"I thought you'd have heard. To Colette Luce. Our Colette, whom we've studied with the past year. She had the sniffles last Saturday and went home, same as you. Turns out she ended the day an engaged woman."

Jeanie gasped. "I didn't even know she knew him."

"Me, neither. We heard Monday when Colette came to collect her things. I don't know how Mother heard, but she fell into a fit of the vapors, and she says my last chance to restore her to health is to snare Jake Wicks."

"Oh, Eliza." Jeanie offered her hand. It was warm and smooth, clasping Eliza's. "I wish I'd known. Not about your Mother. You're accustomed to such wounds. The other. You should have told me right away about Mr. Delacourt."

"I didn't wish to upset you while you were ill."

"Sufficient reason for me to accompany you now to see Mr. LeShand. You've much to tell me. Besides, Mrs. Collins asked me to go along for the sake of your reputation, didn't she?" Jeanie stuffed two hankies in her bag and pulled on her coat.

"Not when you're ill, goose."

"I require fresh air." Jeanie's mouth set in a mulish expression.

Eliza hesitated then withdrew her warmest muffler from her dresser drawer and wrapped it about Jeanie's throat. "Fine, then, but you'd better not relapse."

Arm in arm, the ladies bade Mrs. Collins adieu and strode out the Abbey down the circular brick drive. A gust of wind pushed a tendril of Eliza's hair over her eyes. Turning her head to the side to repair the damage, she saw a flicker of movement in the corner of the Abbey's front lawn. A lanky male figure, his well-fitting coat the same gray-brown hue of the tree behind which he stood.

"Mr. Wicks?" Eliza hastened toward him, pulling Jeanie with her onto the grass. "Is that you?"

Jeanie leaned into Eliza. "Why is he lurking behind trees on the corner of the property?"

"He's not lurking. He's probably gathering his courage to knock on the door of our imposing Abbey." Mayhap to visit Eliza.

Sure enough, Mr. Wicks's grin was wide as he strode toward them, as if he were truly pleased to be spared the gauntlet of asking Mrs. Collins to call on her charges. Eliza grinned.

Mr. Wicks bowed, his smile never slipping. "You ladies escaped the cage yet again. Another errand? Or are there more of your number about?"

"Just us." Eliza let go of Jeanie's arm. "Jeanie hasn't been outdoors in a week." Nor had she seen Jake in that amount of time. But he was here now, and his presence lightened the heaviness pressing into her chest. A pleasant reminder that Will Delacourt was not the only man in the world who seemed to like her.

Perhaps Mother was right—or at least on the right track. Perhaps it was time to invest more in her friendship with Jake Wicks.

The telegram crackling in his fist, Will shook his head. He hoped the gesture appeared dismissive to Charlie. It wouldn't help for Charlie to guess how he really felt. Like he'd fallen from the thoroughbred and had the wind knocked from him all over again.

"He won't come."

"I'm sorry. But can you say you aren't surprised?" The lines around Charlie's eyes, usually creased in laughter, deepened in sadness.

The soft plunk of the telegram hitting the bottom of the waste can was the room's only noise for a full minute. "I expected Father's refusal to visit, to see firsthand how the TNT's track is progressing, how exciting this is for me. But I hoped he'd come, anyway."

"Did he—" Charlie coughed from deep in his chest. In the past week, he'd convalesced in the suite to recover from his illness, but a few symptoms lingered. Not that he'd admit it. All he'd spoken of was how he must recuperate so he could call on Jeanie. "Did your father offer a reason for his refusal?"

Will arched a brow in answer.

Charlie sighed. "You don't need to prove anything to him. You're a visionary when it comes to investments and machinery. Yet you still crave his blessing."

"Do I?" He stared out the window, seeing no farther than his own blurred reflection.

"We all crave our fathers' blessings. Yet yours withholds it, time and again."

"He didn't used to."

"He expected you to take over the ranch one day. When you didn't, he refused to consider your affection for all things mechanical. For trains."

"It's more than trains, Charlie. You know it's more." Will dropped into an upholstered chair and rested his elbows on his knees. He felt sore all over. His ribs. His head. His heart.

How could everything have gone so wrong?

He'd thought he was doing the right thing, being honest with Eliza. He admired her, from her fine eyes to her mind, but how could one court a woman when there were unspoken things between them, like her desperate need of his money? Look where it had gotten his father.

Unless he'd gotten it all wrong. Eliza wasn't his stepmother Claudia, after all.

He gripped his hair, tugging the roots. "I've made a mess of everything."

"Not everything. The TNT track is over the Texas border now. And we've gained new investors." Charlie withdrew the wadded telegram from the waste bin. "This is not a reflection of your worth or success, my friend."

"No. My own actions do a fair enough job causing rifts." He didn't want to enlighten his friend to what he'd done to Eliza. Not yet.

"Do you mean what happened with Claudia? I thought you were over it, but I can see why you're still stung. She cast you aside for your father, all for money's sake. But I think you were even more hurt by the cold treatment that followed from your father, how all of his approval went to Jake Wicks instead of you. Your father views you as a rival, you know."

"I was nineteen. Hardly an opponent. I wanted his approval, not his farm or his house or his money-hungry wife."

Claudia. What had drawn him to her, anyway? She was pretty, but there was nothing admirable about her that he could recall. Especially when she lured him only to marry his widowed, vulnerable father.

No, she was nothing like Eliza.

Eliza, who tried to show her parents affection despite her mother's repeated rebuffs and her father's apparent lack of interest. Eliza, who wouldn't marry a wealthy rancher she didn't respect. Who gave of her time to help others in need. Who rocked colicky infants with a smile on her face.

He stood, sending the chair scraping over the oak floor. "Fortunately, I learned from my mother to seek approval from my heavenly Father, not my earthly one. But she also taught me to make things right when I've erred."

"A decent plan, to be sure, but I don't see where you've gone wrong with your father in inviting him to Texas."

"Not that. Not today, anyway. While I do need to reconcile with my father, today I must apologize to someone else." He donned his coat. "Are you well enough to go outside? Good. Make sure you look presentable, should you come across Miss Hale."

"Why should we see her?" The look of shock and giddy hope on Charlie's face was worth a boot-full of silver dollars.

"Because we're calling on Austen Abbey."

Eliza held Jeanie's arm while her roommate succumbed to a coughing fit. "Perhaps you should go back inside."

"Miss Hale?" Mr. Wicks held Jeanie's other arm, his brow creased in concern.

"I've been ill," Jeanie explained to him, "but I'm much improved. Although I find myself in need of a brief respite."

The racket must have drawn Mrs. Collins's attention, however, for she appeared on the front porch, her eyes wide in the look Eliza had come to know as a command. "Miss Branch, why do you not escort your caller 'round the house. The three of you might take air in the back." Directly in line of sight of the entire house.

At least Jake was accommodating. He offered both Eliza and Jeanie his arms, walked them through the side gate near where he'd been first standing, and settled Jeanie on a plump-cushioned wicker chair on the screened back porch.

A good thing, since Jeanie's cheeks blotched red from her coughing. Eliza touched her cheek, satisfied to find it cool. "Poor dear. Are you certain you do not wish to go inside?"

"No. Just a moment is all I need."

Jake smiled. "While you recover, then, Miss Hale, perhaps I might convince Miss Branch to take a turn about the yard?"

"Go ahead." Jeanie waved her handkerchief like a white flag.

"I won't be far, if you need me." Eliza's ruby dress rustled as she and Jake moved to the perimeter of the dormant grass. "So how goes your business in Austin?"

"Slow." He laughed.

"It's clear you know Will Delacourt." She couldn't pry, but maybe he'd enlighten her why Will was so sour.

Jake gave her a sheepish grin. "We grew up together, Will and I. On his father's property in Memphis."

Eliza shivered, but not from the stiff breeze scuttling leaves over the yard.

"My father was in Old Man Delacourt's employ. I didn't come from money." His brows rose as if in apology.

"Money is no indicator of a man's measure. Loyalty, courtesy, and honor are better gauges of a person's worth."

"So says a lady with plenty to spare." His teasing smile seemed flirtatious.

"Not exactly," she said without thinking. A shadow flickered across his features and then disappeared. Or maybe she imagined it, for in a moment he was smiling again.

"My father would do well in your book, then, because he worked with Mr. Delacourt, breeding thoroughbreds, for years. They served together in the War Between the States. Mr. Delacourt repaid my father's devotion by keeping him on, despite his loss of a limb at Shiloh. And he promised him he'd always have a place for me in his employ."

She couldn't help noticing curious faces peeking through the Abbey's rear-facing windows. Gentlemen callers were oft relegated to the backyard and were quite the cause of excitement among the students.

"The senior Mr. Delacourt sounds to be a generous man."

"He is. That is why he is so disappointed in his son."

"Will, you mean?"

"He has no other." Jake sighed. "It almost broke Mr. Delacourt when Will rejected him to start a railroad. It did not help matters when Mr. Delacourt appreciated all my years of labor for him. I thought if I invested in the TNT, showed Will I was interested in helping him, he might receive my hand of friendship. What else can I do? Yet reconciliation might be impossible. He's not the same since the person he loved most rejected him."

"His mother, or his sister, Ginny? He speaks so well of them."

His lip curled. "I refer to Claudia. He was too addlepated to see it was his father, not him, she admired. She was courteous to him because she was going to be his stepmother, but he misinterpreted it. To embarrassing results."

Will loved his stepmother? Eliza's stomach soured.

"Mr. Delacourt has no patience for this train, er, hobby of Will's. Not that it's the old man's money, no, Will's purse comes from suspiciously good luck, if you catch my meaning. Investments that just happen to work out every time. Dodgy, perhaps. Still, I'd like to make things right between us, but Will's too proud to accept my money."

From across the yard, Jeanie laughed, a hoarse but happy sound, and Eliza turned. Her friend perched on the porch, looking up at—oh, mercy. Charlie Bingham and Will Delacourt were here, Will's expression as cloudy as Charlie's was bright.

Steeling her spine, Eliza waved at the newest gentlemen callers as if their presence didn't bother her a whit, but her innards quaked. How dare Will Delacourt show his face here, after what he'd said? And how dare her traitorous heart beat faster upon seeing him?

She spun her back on the porch and glanced up at Jake. "Did you say the TNT is a hobby? It's a business, isn't it?"

"Oh yes. But I expect he'll soon be off to the next thing."

"Next thing?" She glanced at Will. His arms folded over his chest.

"He likes toys. He gets bored. He'll leave the TNT for someone else to run. Why shouldn't it be me?" Jake smiled. "But I'd much rather use our last moments together to talk about you and what you like. What you think about."

All she could think about now was Will Delacourt. Rich. Bored. Misjudging her. *Fortune hunter*, indeed. She folded her arms, swinging her purse—the empty bag where she'd planned to put the coins Mr. LeShand would hopefully pay her. It reminded her of what she liked, as Jake had put it. She bit her lip.

"I—I write."

"Stories?" His eyes widened.

"Yes. But mainly articles. Words that matter. Sometimes I see things that are unjust, and I know of no other way to do something about them. Like the German immigrants in the settlement just north of town. They've suffered like everyone else in the drought. Sometimes worse. But the editor at the *Texas Star* won't publish an article that doesn't *have teeth*."

"Ah." He took her elbow and halted their steps. "Well, if it's the immigrants you want to write about, and you need teeth, perhaps I can help you."

She knew without looking that Will watched her, but she didn't dare tear her gaze from Jake's. "What do you mean?"

"Those German immigrants?"

Marta's tear-streaked face flashed through her mind, and she nodded. Jake increased the pressure on her elbow. "That settlement is in the direct path of the TNT. Will's got the power of eminent domain to buy those folks out of their land. Except he's not paying the minimum price. Don't ask me how he's getting away with it, but he is. Now there's a story for you."

Numbness spread up her arms and down to her boots.

"Eliza?" Jeanie's hoarse voice called across the grass.

Eliza couldn't speak, couldn't manage to do anything more than return to Jeanie. Who sat beside Will.

His brow furrowed. "Are you unwell, Miss Branch?"

Jeanie stood. "You're pale. I hope you didn't catch my cold."

"Perhaps." The word sounded thick.

Will offered his arm. "Allow me to escort you inside."

"No, that's all right." If she touched him, she might cry. He may be arrogant, but she hadn't thought him capable of cheating immigrants.

"Leave her be," Jake drawled. "She's fine."

Will's jaw clenched. "She's not fine. Clearly."

"She's not a machine, not some engine you can tinker with." Jake rolled his eyes. "You don't understand people at all."

His harshness jarred the numbness from Eliza's limbs, and she caught a sneer of utter hatred on Jake's face. She shook her head as if clearing off a spider web. Maybe Jake was tired of bearing the brunt of Will's jealousy even after he'd extended a handshake of peace. But maybe she should ask Will if Jake spoke truth. Tilting her head to the side, she leveled Will with a look. "I find I would appreciate a moment with you after all, Mr. Delacourt. I beg your pardon, Mr. Bingham, Mr. Wicks."

Jake's half-grin iced as he tipped his Stetson.

Her jaw ached as she stomped back to the yard, ignoring Will's arm. "Let's go, then."

From the corner of her eye, she saw Liddy burst out the back door and grip Jake by the arm. She tugged him around the side of the Abbey, toward the street. Oh, Liddy. So forward with men, and poor Jake wasn't interested in her that way. He'd called her flighty, hadn't he? She'd have to speak to Liddy about it, perhaps, but right now, she had to speak to Will. Without being overheard.

Eliza marched toward the back fence. With his long strides, however, Will kept up with her unladylike pace, while Jeanie and Mr. Bingham followed behind, but at a much slower speed. Would the girls spying from the house see her half-jog and tattle to Mother? If Mrs. Collins were watching—oh, of course she was watching.

Will was at her side, peering down at her. "Your color is returning. Do you feel better?"

"What I feel is unimportant." Although he still drew her like a moth to flame, and she hated it. "There isn't much time and I'd like to speak to you in private."

"As would I." His Adam's apple jerked. "I botched everything. Wicks is right, I am better with machines. They either work or they don't, and you can fix what's broken. But people, well, sometimes the broken parts never fix. That's why I handle the trains and Charlie deals with people. Everything I say comes out wrong."

"Not quite." He'd said plenty of sweet things to the horses. And the church's elderly widows. He'd encouraged little Ronald when they'd played ball, and he'd cooed for the colicky baby Nehemiah.

Then again, he didn't think *they* were after his fortune.

The thought brought a stab of pain to her chest, but she shoved it away as they reached the corner of the yard. She stopped in a brushy spot less visible from the Abbey and spun to face him, her ruby skirt swinging in an arc. *God, help me do this.* "I must ask you something. A simple yes or no question."

"Anything." His fingers twitched.

"The immigrant farmers displaced by your use of eminent domain. Did you pay them what the law dictated their land was worth?"

His jaw went slack. "That question is not so simple—"

"A yes or no is all I require." *Please say yes.*

He looked away. "I have to explain."

She folded her arms over her heaving chest. "Did you or didn't you?"

"Did Wicks put this in your head?" His eyes darkened to flint.

A hot flush washed over her arms and legs. "Do not involve him."

"Wicks is already involved." His lips twisted, as if he'd eaten unripe fruit. "Did he tell you about Memphis? What happened there?"

"To make you hate him? He said enough. He said your father preferred him." At the clenching of Will's fists, Eliza shook her head. "But this isn't about Jake Wicks. I ask you again. Did you pay the farmers the minimum specified by law? Yes or no?"

A muscle worked in his cheek. He looked away. "I wish you would listen to me as you've listened to Jake Wicks."

"I wish for the truth." *And for you to be the man who I started to feel something for, the one who coos to horses and babies.*

"No, you don't. You've already judged me." His eyes softened. He reached up a hand as if to cup her cheek, and then let it fall. "No. I did not pay the minimum."

Was this what triumph felt like? This buzzing in her head, making her unsteady on her feet? This bitter taste curling her tongue? She covered her mouth, just as Jeanie and Mr. Bingham caught up to them.

"Oh my," Jeanie said. "You are ill. Let's get you back to the Abbey."

Eliza nodded. She wanted nothing more. She needed to be alone in her chamber with her thoughts. And a pencil.

Eliza's gaze fixed on the half-moon window behind Mrs. Collins's desk, watching the high, oyster-white clouds float against the cerulean November sky. She couldn't bear to look at her headmistress.

"I'm to understand," Mrs. Collins began, her tone as crisp as the snap of the *Texas Star* as she lay it on her desk, "that you wrote this?"

Eliza licked her too-dry lips and lowered her gaze to her fidgeting fingers. "Yes, ma'am."

The clock ticked. The muffled chatter of girls playing croquet on the expansive back lawn carried through the window. Liddy's voice was easy to identify, wailing that her father didn't like her beau—but which one? She'd had so many. It was no secret she fancied Jake Wicks, but he hadn't come by the Abbey again. Eliza had half-expected it, due to their camaraderie.

Not that Jake Wicks mattered right now. Not with the *Texas Star* lying in its inanimate innocence on Mrs. Collins's desk. She couldn't look at it. "The article, as you see, is anonymous."

"The notoriety of its author does not concern me. Rather, I'm troubled by the content." Mrs. Collins steepled her fingers under her chin. "You were paid, I take it?"

Eliza nodded. "More than I receive for my ads."

"And you came by the information from a source?"

"Yes." A relieved breath escaped her tight chest. Thank goodness

Mrs. Collins hadn't asked Jake's identity. "Mr. Delacourt has the authority to displace homesteaders in the path of his railway for fair compensation. That's public knowledge. Yet he didn't pay the lawful price."

If she spoke the words enough, perhaps one day, they wouldn't sting. How she wished he'd paid what was due, and not just for the immigrants' sake. For her own, too. She hadn't realized how much she wanted to believe the best in him.

"Did you verify what your source told you? Speak to Mr. Delacourt? Someone in the land office? Anyone who could confirm or deny the facts?"

"I lacked the luxuries of time and authority to do so." Even if she could investigate without concern for her anonymity, how could a finishing-school student interview businessmen and be taken seriously? "But my source has known Mr. Delacourt for years."

"Yet he was willing to indict him with ease." Mrs. Collins's brow quirked. "And now, guilty or innocent, Mr. Delacourt has become a pariah in Austin."

"If he swindled the immigrants, perhaps he should be."

"*If* is the key word, isn't it? I understand your motivation, dear. Financial need. Your concern for your German friends who have suffered. Your sense of justice. Seldom have I seen such a strong sense of fairness in one of my pupils. I admire it. But I fear you've erred this time. You've allowed your pride to mar your journalistic integrity."

"Pride?" That had nothing to do with this. Didn't darkness need to be exposed to the light? "Forgive me, ma'am, but I don't know what you mean."

"I didn't think you took me for a fool, Eliza. I've seen how Mr. Delacourt looks at you. As if you pain him, and I suspect you do." She chuckled, as if remembering something fond, but tears pricked the backs of Eliza's eyes. He thought her so horrid she *pained him?*

Maybe she *was* horrid, after all. She'd written grave things about him, which, if true, needed to be said. It didn't have to do with how he felt about her, of course.

Except she couldn't separate her emotions where he was concerned.

Will admitted he hadn't paid minimum. But why hadn't he? Her stomach clenched with nauseating intensity. She should have tried to investigate. Should have spoken to Mrs. Collins about it. Should have *prayed* before she acted. But she'd felt so hurt, and writing the article had made her feel powerful. Vindicated. Helpful.

Had her desire to write those words stemmed from her sense of injustice? She'd thought so. Now, however, she wasn't so sure.

"I am sorry for causing trouble when you were gracious enough to allow me to write for the *Texas Star* in the first place. And I'm sorry for writing about Mr. Delacourt without complete facts. I'll investigate further. I'll write a retraction, if necessary."

"A wise course. But as you explore his use of eminent domain, take the time to examine your heart, dear. Did Mr. Delacourt's actions toward you, or lack of them, influence your article? Even if you are correct and he broke the law, did you handle the information in a manner beyond reproach?"

"No." Eliza's whisper was no more than a breath.

"Pray and consider, my dear. Remember when we err, we can be forgiven. Perhaps you should write on the subject of grace for your next French theme." A faint smile lit her eyes. "Now, hadn't you better get changed for the Harvest Fair?"

"I can still go?"

"Why shouldn't you? Others rely on your assistance tonight. Besides, moping here won't solve anything. This evening, you may find an opportunity to make things better, if not altogether right."

Mrs. Collins waved her hand in dismissal, and Eliza stood. Her fingers fumbled with the clasp of her satchel.

"Here." With the clatter of silver on wood, she laid the coins on the desk. "My earnings."

"Oh, no." Mrs. Collins's mouth pinched. "I can't take those."

"Please." Eliza didn't want them back. Couldn't look at them.

"Just this morning, a donor provided scholarship funds for one worthy student." The way Mrs. Collins said *worthy* made a shiver scuttle over Eliza's spine. Such a description no longer applied to her. "The Lord saw fit to provide."

But Eliza hadn't trusted Him. And look what she'd done.

With trembling fingers, she reached for the coins.

"You're asking for my two cents' worth?" The pennies clanked as Eliza dropped them into the metal box. Then she tapped her chin as she scrutinized the cookies and candies on display. Her one-hour shift at the Harvest Fair baked goods booth was almost over, and many of the treats had already been purchased. "I would go with the divinity. White and soft as snow, with English walnuts to give it texture. Definitely worth two cents."

"I'll take it." Seven-year-old Mary, Eliza's youngest sister, giggled, revealing a gap where her front tooth used to be. Eliza had missed that particular milestone, as well as several others of her younger sisters' changes, since moving to the Abbey. Why, June's hair was pinned up, Laura had grown two inches, and Kit's gaze followed groups of boys. Her sisters were growing up fast. One good thing about leaving school early would be spending more time with them.

She wouldn't accept that scholarship Mrs. Collins mentioned. She didn't deserve it.

Mary nibbled the candy on the side of her mouth with a full set of teeth. "Good choice."

The air nipped now that the sun had gone down. Eliza was glad for the high collar of her chocolate silk gown, but Mary's cheeks flushed pink from activity and excitement. Who could blame her? It seemed half of Austin was present for tonight's fun. Abbey students, present and past, strolled about. There went former Abbey student Marion Tabor with her husband Brandon, wearing matching grins, and oh, it appeared she was going to have a baby. Soon.

And in the Glass Pitch booth next to the baked goods, two young men close to her age scooped coins from their pockets. Ah, Mrs. Collins's nephews, Harmon Gray and Jonathan Wellington. A younger Abbey student, Glenda Cole, stood between then, eyeing the vases, bowls and dishes placed on tables inside the booth. With a wide smile, Glenda pointed to a piece Eliza couldn't see, and Harmon and Jonathan tossed pennies in its direction. Which competitive swain would win the dish for Glenda? Either way, tonight's victory wouldn't quell the rivalry between Mrs. Collins's nephews.

The tuning strains of a fiddle carried on the autumn breeze, signaling the dancing would soon start. What a pleasant night for a dance, not too cool or warm, with a soft breeze. The decorations were beautiful, too, with beribboned cornstalks and sheaves of wheat tied to the booths and posts. Torches stood in bright sentry at even intervals through the empty field chosen for the Fair, illuminating the booths and plank tables where diners devoured the savory-smelling supper of fried chicken, roast potatoes, yeast rolls, and pickled vegetables.

Not that Eliza had been able to do more than pick at the food on her tin plate before her shift started. She wasn't even tempted by the cookies and candies surrounding her now. Her stomach twisted like a sodden washrag when she thought of her article about Will Delacourt. True or false? And if true, did the result justify her methods?

"There's Mother. I need more pennies. Bye, Liza." Mary darted off.

If Mother had more pennies to give. One more thing to fret over. Eliza shook her head. *God, I trust you to provide. For everything, even the chance to fix my article if I need to.*

The sheet at the side of the booth flapped as Jeanie slipped inside. "Surprise!"

"What are you doing here? You're supposed to be with Mr. Bingham."

"I could ask you the same. I thought Liddy was relieving you at seven."

"She is, but you know Liddy."

"I'll keep you company until she comes. Charlie knows where I am." Jeanie's eyes twinkled in the torchlight. "He had an opportunity to talk business. He was too much of a gentleman to take it, but I insisted. Besides, I wanted some of Mrs. Layton's divinity." Her brows furrowed as she handed Eliza some coins. "I don't see any. Did it sell out?"

"My sister took the last one."

Jeanie selected a piece of fudge and Eliza rearranged her wares on a platter to make it appear as if she had more to sell. "From the looks of all of the booths, I'd say the Harvest Fair has been a success all-around. It's wonderful news for the mission school and the hospital."

"Um-hm," Jeanie said around her mouthful of fudge.

Despite the darkness and the distance, Eliza recognized the figure in brown passing the other side of the dining tables.

"Jeanie, would you mind watching the booth until I get back or Liddy arrives? I need to speak with someone."

Still chewing, Jeanie waved her hand. Eliza gave her friend a quick squeeze and hastened from the booth, weaving through tables.

"Marta." She caught up to the German immigrant. "You've been on my mind."

"*Jah*, you too. I'm glad I get to say good-bye." Marta's looped braids bobbed while she nodded. "Ve're leaving this veek for a new farm for my brothers to verk."

"I'm so sorry you have to go."

"Jah, but it vill be better."

The poor dear put on a brave face. Perhaps too brave, with that wide smile. Eliza bit her lip. "So you've found good land?"

"Jah." Her eyes brightened, but not with unshed tears. Joy shone from her countenance, more dazzling in the dark night than the torch beside her. "Thanks to Herr Delacourt."

Eliza shook her head. "But he didn't pay you the minimal amount."

"No. He paid three times more." Marta held up her fingers.

"He gave you more money today?" To make up for his publicized misdeeds, perhaps?

"*Nein*. He offered vhen ve signed papers, veeks ago. Find *gut* farm, he said, and ve did, vith all our kin. Much better than ve have now. That land is dry. *Gut* for nothing but train track."

Eliza's deep, steadying breaths did little to slow the shock coursing through her body. "He didn't swindle you."

"*Ach, nein*. Whoever said so is the *schwindler*." She took hold of Eliza's hand and squeezed. "You *gut*, Miss Eliza. May *Gott* bless you."

"May He bless you too." Eliza's voice cracked, but the music swelled and Marta didn't seem to hear her. With another squeeze, the immigrant disappeared into the crowd.

Three times more. Will Delacourt had been generous with the people displaced by the TNT. Perhaps through him, God provided for those families. Marta Fleischer seemed to think so.

As if her half-boots were lined with lead, Eliza hobbled to the darkness outside the fair's perimeter where conveyances parked, horses nibbling on the dry grass underfoot. All was still out here, nothing but the soft sounds of horses shuffling and a bat flapping overhead. The distant strains of the fiddle and banjo carried over the gentle breeze, along with laughter and cheers.

A happy evening—a blessed evening—for many. But not her.

She sniffed back tears, filling her lungs with the odors of dying grass and horse. Craning her neck, she stared up at the stars until they blurred and tears spilled down her cheeks.

She was supposed to be a good Christian woman. What had she done?

Too much to list. She leaned against a stranger's wagon and shut her eyes.

"I'm sorry," she whispered. Pride colored most every decision she'd made of late. She'd said she'd trust God but she ignored Him, disobeyed her family, spread gossip, and falsely accused Will, all to protect her injured pride and take control of her future.

For what? To stay in school? To protect people she cared about like Marta? She may have had good intentions. But none were worth the agony of sin gnawing away at her bones.

Eliza's eyes shut. Amazing that even when she was a sinner, God still offered Jesus for her sake.

A peace she didn't deserve enveloped her, warmer and sweeter than the sage-scented spring air on Father's ranch. She didn't deserve clemency, yet God offered it time and again. *Help me to always come to you first. To better trust You.*

She opened her eyes and swiped her cheeks. She needed to find Will Delacourt. Now.

"Eliza!" A figure in a pale gown rushed over the grass. "Are you here? Eliza!"

Jeanie. Eliza hiked up her skirt and ran. "I'm here. What's wrong?"

"Liddy." Jeanie panted, her hand on her stomach.

"Is she hurt?" What else could explain Jeanie's behavior?

"I don't know. She's gone." Coughing in a remnant of her illness, Jeanie thrust a paper at Eliza. "Lila Wentworth wanted to wear her paisley shawl tonight, but Liddy had borrowed it. She went into Liddy's room and found this on her pillow."

Eliza couldn't make out much of Liddy's loopy scrawl in the dark. Something about unfairness and meeting somebody at the fair and then—

"I need a torch."

"No time." Jeanie pulled her forward. "It says she's run off. Her father cautioned them to wait before granting his permission, and oh—we've got to find her before it's too late. If Jake Wicks hasn't compromised her already, that is."

Eliza thought for a moment she'd tripped over a gopher hole. But she'd just stopped, no longer able to control her feet. "Jake Wicks?"

He'd done plenty of things to make her think he liked her. Flattered her. Appealed to her wounded pride. How she'd swallowed his deceptions.

Especially his lies about Will.

But Will would have to wait. Foolish Liddy.

"We'll find her." Eliza stomped toward the booths, her bustle thwacking her backside like a bell clapper. "I'll look around the western half of the fair. You take the eastern."

Jeanie nodded and scurried off. Eliza scrutinized faces, looking for Liddy or Jake, whom she wouldn't mind taking by the ear and shoving headfirst into a watering trough. Hastening from booth to booth, she whispered prayers for help.

The hairs at her nape prickled, and she turned around. Will stood in the shadow of a booth, a plate in his hand. The look on his face startled her with its intensity.

She stirred up dust, running to him.

"Miss Branch. Is something wrong?"

How she wished she could take his hands. "I am so happy to see you."

"You are?" His brows shot up under the curls at his brow as he set down his plate.

"I am." And she didn't care how improper or forward or crazy she looked, not to him or her mother or the rest of Austin. She had to tell him, now, before she lost the chance. She touched his coat sleeve, as if the light contact could tether him to the spot.

"I was wrong. I believed you all but stole the land from the Germans to build your line. I believed every ill thing I could conceive about you, but I should have spoken to you, shouldn't have judged you before I assumed the worst. You have no reason to forgive me, but I hope you will. I'm so sorry for the trouble I've caused you and I hope I didn't ruin your business."

His eyes deepened to something wet and dark, like looking down into the depths of a well. "I forgive you. And I hope you'll forgive me. I misjudged your intentions. And then with Wicks." He stopped, as if fighting with himself to continue.

"Oh, Will." Her fingers tightened on his sleeve and his eyes went wide when she used his Christian name.

"Eliza!" Mother's sharp voice beckoned, and the scent of tuberose filled Eliza's nostrils. "What is the meaning of this, consorting in the shadows with...*him*? Haven't you read the *Texas Star*?"

Her fingers fell. "Yes, Mother. In fact, I wrote—"

Will held up his hand. "I mean no impropriety, Mrs. Branch."

"I should hope not." Her bosom heaved. "Eliza, be mindful of your beau, Jake Wicks, seeing you like this." Her brow arched at Will at the word *beau*.

"He won't. He's, well, I'll just say it. He's run off with Liddy Duncan. Jeanie and I are searching for them right now, hoping to stop them in time."

"Eloped?" Mother flinched, as if she'd smelled a rotten egg.

"Liddy may be foolish, but I love her." Eliza shook her head. "She deserves better than to end up with a liar. I've got to find her."

A muscle clenched in Will's jaw. "Pardon me, ladies." He tipped his Stetson and was gone, like chaff in the wind. Something in her heart tore off and went with him.

"This is terrible." Mother choked back a sob.

"I know." Eliza patted her mother's arm. "Liddy made a dreadful choice."

"Liddy?" Mother gaped. "You think I'm on the verge of apoplectic shock because of Liddy? She's the smart one here, missy. At least she has a husband now. Jake Wicks, no less. One more wealthy man out of your reach, just like Mr. Cray. And from what I just saw, you could have had Mr. Delacourt and his fortune, after all. You ruin everything, Eliza, and now our family has nothing!"

Grief and shame unspooled inside her like a spilled bobbin. But ultimately, she had to believe Mother was wrong. God wouldn't leave them with nothing.

She would rely on Him this time. She had no choice.

Seven

With a *clitch*, Eliza fastened her trunk and then wedged her Bible into her overstuffed brocade satchel. A hasty scan about the bed-chamber assured her none of her personal effects remained scattered about her room at the Abbey, except for the heavy tan gloves she'd chosen to protect her from the December chill outside. She scooped them up but didn't slip them on just yet. Donning them would be her final act as an Austen Abbey student, and she wanted to prolong the moment as long as she could.

In the three weeks since the Harvest Fair, word spread that Liddy eloped with Jake Wicks and they'd fled to Memphis or Mexico, depending on who shared the gossip. After the last words they'd spoken to each other, Eliza expected a call from Will, but Charlie alone had called at the Abbey, repeatedly, and it hadn't take him long to deliver the news that Will was settled back in Memphis with his family. Or to declare himself to an ebullient Jeanie.

Life moved on, and for Eliza, it seemed as if she'd lost many things these past three weeks. Her ability to stay in school. Her good graces with the newspaper for her libelous article. Closure with Will. But she wouldn't fight the changes. She had to trust God for her future.

Jeanie slumped on her bed. "I'm pretending this is just another school break. You're going home for Christmas, and you'll be back in January. Which you could, you know."

"I have no money to pay for school."

Jeanie folded her arms. "So *The Star* won't take any of your ads anymore, much less articles. But what about the scholarship?"

"Mrs. Collins tried to persuade me to stay, even last night, but I couldn't take it." Eliza shrugged. Her chest felt heavy, but a sensation of rightness tempered it. She was doing the correct thing. "A new student matriculates in January, a young lady of exceptional intellect and grace, but whose family has been hard-hit by the drought. The scholarship will bless her, I'm sure of it. Don't worry," she teased, "you still get your own room."

"I don't care about that." Jeanie's eyes filled with tears. "I hoped we could plan my wedding together, late at night when we're supposed to be sleeping."

Eliza clutched her friend in a fierce embrace. "Do you think you can cut me from your wedding plans? After we used to play bride in your parlor? Your poor little brother was a most reluctant groom. Good thing Charlie isn't so grumpy at the prospect of standing up with you."

The mention of her new betrothed brought a wet-sounding giggle to Jeanie's lips. "He seems as eager as I do. Although I'm nervous about moving to Memphis."

Eliza released her friend and scrounged through her satchel for a lace-trimmed hanky. The act provided an excuse to avoid Jeanie's too-discerning gaze. She may be leaving school, but things would be very different soon, anyway. Jeanie would marry in early June, and her life would be full of new dreams, new family, babies. And Jeanie's life would be forever linked to Charlie's best friend, Will Delacourt.

Would Jeanie write about him? Eliza both hoped for and dreaded it.

"You know, Will Delacourt will be back from Memphis before the wedding." Jeanie's mention of him couldn't be coincidental. "Perhaps you two will run into each other."

"But I won't be about Austin much." Mother didn't want her girls seen once their clothes went out of fashion. And what could Eliza say to him that she hadn't said already?

"Come visit us in Memphis." Jeanie hooked her arm through Eliza's.

"Bombard the newlyweds? How gauche!" Did her teasing smile fool Jeanie? She couldn't visit Will's best friend. Couldn't chance seeing him. She'd fallen for Will Delacourt, railroad tycoon, awkward rocker of colicky babies, sweet-talker to horses. She hadn't wanted to, but despite herself, she'd stumbled headlong into love after all.

The chamber door swung wide on its hinge and Liddy burst into the room, a whirl of rose perfume and emerald silk. "Surprise!"

Did one congratulate the runaway bride of a scoundrel? Eliza hugged her anyway. "How are you?"

Liddy yanked off her glove and revealed a garnet ring on her fourth finger. "I'm here to collect my things. I couldn't leave my diary. What a horror that would be if anyone found it. The secrets inside!"

"Vibrant reading, I'm sure." Eliza shuddered.

"I hear you're engaged." Liddy patted Jeanie's hand. "We're brides to Memphis men together."

"You're settling in Memphis?" Jeanie's brow knit.

Liddy waved her hand. "Oh, no. Austin. Jakey is an important person at the TNT office here and earns a wagon-load of money. Not that I should speak of such things, but look at the dress Jakey bought me. He spoils me so."

Eliza's knees wobbled. "Did you say, TNT?"

Liddy offered an affirming hum. "Jakey's plans were in a bit of a rough spot, you see. We thought Papa would bring Jakey into the law firm, but Papa said Jakey just wanted our money, which was the meanest thing to say, so I said good riddance to my family and Jakey took me to Memphis. We were in the ugliest house and I almost wondered if I'd made a mistake when who knocks on the door but Mr. Will Delacourt? He gave Jakey a job."

"How grand." Jeanie's eyes shot Eliza a pointed message.

"Everyone loves Jakey. Except for Papa." Liddy pulled a face. "Well, I must get that diary, but congratulations, Jeanie. And Eliza, best of luck."

"My prayers go with you." Eliza meant it.

With that, Liddy was gone.

Eliza gaped at Jeanie. "Why did Will do that? Not that it matters. He's a good man. I wish I'd figured it out earlier."

Jeanie's smile was sad. "I just hope Liddy and Jake don't squander his gifts."

"I was so wrong. And there's nothing I can do to make up for what I did." Eliza paused, tossed down her gloves, and dug into her satchel. "Unless—"

"What are you looking for?"

"My pencil. I have one more thing to write." Eliza stuck it between her teeth while she found a scrap of paper and plopped down at Jeanie's desk. Her hands shook when she began scribbling.

The deed was done. He'd done all he could now. And Will felt weary to his bones.

Shutting the door behind him, he hung his Stetson on the hat rack in the foyer and smelled the changes wrought in the house during his absence. Pine and cloves. In the hours since he'd stepped out this morning, his stepmother Claudia had been busy. Fragrant pine boughs looped over the staircase and clove-stuffed oranges nestled among fresh-cut greens on the gleaming mahogany entryway table. The smell of Christmas filled the house, but there was nothing of its spirit here.

As if echoing the lack of Christ present in the house, no lamps were lit against the night, but the golden glow of firelight spilled from the parlor. Will's boots thudded against the parquet floor as he crossed the grand foyer to step inside.

Blessed heat from the fire blazing in the hearth blanketed him, but he preferred the warmth in the welcome he received from his sixteen-year-old sister, Ginny.

She set down the volume in her lap, *Pride and Prejudice* by the look of it, and allowed him to kiss her cheek, but then she pushed him away with a playful shove. "Your lips feel like something from the icebox."

"It's cold out there." He held his hands to the fire. "Where's Father?" And Claudia, of course.

"At some party." His sprite of a sister yawned. "Did it work?"

"Yes, Wicks is officially settled back in Austin." At last. It had been a month since that scalawag's elopement, a month spent dwelling on Jake Wicks, first making inquiries to find him and his bride once they'd scuttled out of Austin when Liddy's father wouldn't hire him. Then time to employ the blackguard and set him up to work in the TNT office in Austin. Wicks was now making a good salary and had a stable job, so at least, this way, he couldn't hurt Liddy the way he'd hurt Ginny.

So it was done. Jake Wicks would never be gone from his life, but perhaps he could find closure.

He hoped. Will studied his dark-haired sister. "I'm certain this has stirred some unpleasant memories for you."

She shuddered. "It has renewed my sense of relief, for certain. Jake was so charming and witty and had a way of making me feel precious."

"You weren't alone." Eliza's face crossed his mind, sending his belly into a whirl. A month away from her, and she'd claimed most every thought he had. "He fooled everyone."

"But not you. That's why Father is so hard on you, you know."

Will shook his head. The fire couldn't warm the chill that pervaded his bones when he was in this house. Good thing he'd be settled in his own place soon. "I didn't start a rail line to rebel against Father, you know. I did it because—"

"Because you're a tinker. You like engines and that loud whistle the engineers sound when they come around the bend. I'm sorry Father can't understand."

"Me, too." But he'd keep praying.

Ginny's chin indicated a slim, brown-wrapped lump on the coffee table. "This came for you today. It's a package from Charlie. Maybe it's a Christmas present."

"Business, no doubt." Although Charlie had never sent parcels. Curiosity got the better of him, and he slid his thumb under a flap.

"Well?" Ginny leaned forward, her book forgotten. "What is it?"

Will couldn't stop smiling. It was something of a Christmas present, indeed.

Eliza rounded the corner of her parents' Austin neighborhood. She may no longer be able to tromp through Father's cattle ranch—although it had not yet sold—but she could enjoy taking exercise on the streets of Austin. Walking, thinking, dreaming, time alone just for her. So long as her steps didn't take her to Chawton Circle, home of Austen Abbey. Not yet.

Eliza blew on her fingers, a most unladylike gesture, but an effective one. Exercise may have stirred her blood, but her fingers and nose hadn't received much benefit.

But shouldn't the weather be cool at Christmas? In addition to the brisker temperatures, signs of the season were in evidence along her stroll through the neighborhood. Wood smoke and pine scented the air. Folks tipped their hats and wished one another Merry Christmas. Eliza loved the season of goodwill, but she cherished the holiday's true meaning. Jesus became incarnate to save humankind. To save her, while she was a sinner.

Offering a prayer of thanks for His birth and mercy, Eliza turned the corner of her street. Once home, she'd take out her lyre, something she hadn't done in too long. She'd practice some Christmas carols. But first she'd enjoy a fortifying cup of tea to warm her hands and bones.

Her steps faltered when she reached the front stoop. Hitched to the post, a pair of unfamiliar chestnut horses waited, snorting steam in the cold air. Visitors. A buyer for the ranch, perhaps? She hastened inside the pine-festooned foyer, banging the door and knocking over the umbrella stand with a clatter.

Eliza sucked in a pine-scented hiss and righted the umbrella stand. *Help me be more demure, Lord.* Still, she caught herself removing her gloves with her teeth while she followed the sounds of Mother's twitter to the parlor. A pair of masculine voices joined Mother's. One, Father's. The other's, deep and rich.

Oh!

His eyes were just as she remembered. Dark and soft as fertile earth, focused on her.

"There you are." Mother's eyes were bright as a candlelit Christmas tree. "Look who called. You remember Mr. Delacourt, don't you?"

As if she could ever—never mind. She licked her chill-parched lips. "Good day."

Will bounced to his feet like popping corn. "Good day, Miss Branch."

"We've been waiting an age for you." *Do not ruin this*, Mother's eyes said. "Tea, darling?"

Eliza's longing for tea dissipated like steam. Will was here, hale and smiling. She never thought she'd see him again. She took a step toward the chair across from his when he scooped a newspaper from the table beside him.

"Actually, Miss Branch, there's something I'd like to show you. Outside. I know you're probably chilled, though."

"No. I'm snug as can be." She didn't need fingers.

"Then let's—that is, if you don't mind, Mr. Branch?" At Father's nod, Will gestured for her to precede him. "We'll return directly," he said over his shoulder.

"No rush," Father said.

"Stay warm. Not *that* warm. Stay on the porch, Eliza!" Mother called.

Will shut the front door behind her and led her to the street. "No disrespect to your mother, but we won't stay on the porch. I want to show you the horses."

"They're lovely." Although why he wanted to show her horses, she couldn't fathom.

He rubbed the white blaze on the larger one's nose. "Phoenix here is my favorite, since I helped break him five years ago. And this," he said, patting the squatter horse, "is Daisy. She's as gentle as any mare

I've ever known. I brought her back from Memphis, just to meet you."

"Me?"

"Some weeks ago, I offered to teach you to ride. Do you remember?"

"I remember." *Everything.* With tentative fingers, she patted Daisy's head. The coat was sleek over Daisy's hard skull, soft to Eliza's bare fingers. "But with all that's happened, I didn't think—wait, you don't mean now, do you?"

He chuckled. "No, I just wanted you to get comfortable with the idea. Here." He pulled a chunk of carrot from his pocket. "Hold your hand flat, like this." He straightened her fingers, sending shivers up her arm that had nothing to do with the winter chill. "Let her do all the work."

Daisy's lips tickled Eliza's palm. "Goodness."

Will pulled more carrots from a pouch hanging off the saddle and they fed the horses. When he'd handed her the last of the chunks, his hand pressed hers. "I didn't just come for this."

Of course not. "You have a railroad line to open soon."

"And something else. I should tell you, I'm not alone in Austin. I've brought someone to spend Christmas here with me, and she's back at the hotel."

A woman? Oh.

"My sister Ginny." His grin turned her kneecaps to hot butter. "She's eager to meet you. But in the meantime, she gave me permission to tell you what I couldn't before, not without betraying her confidence. It's about Jake Wicks."

That scoundrel. He'd played her like the lyre. "I'd rather not discuss him, to be frank. Everything he said was a lie."

"Not everything. He held a favored position at the ranch. Until he persuaded Ginny to elope, that is."

She gasped. "But she's, what, sixteen, you said?"

"Fifteen at the time. You see, Jake incurred a lot of debts, more than he could pay off as Father's employee. But he reckoned if he married Ginny, he'd have a share in her inheritance. He flattered her and per-suaded her to elope, but we caught them in time." He stared at Phoe-nix's blaze for a minute. "He and I never were friends, but if he'd loved Ginny, really loved her, I could've accepted it. Once Father told him he'd never see a dime if he married her, though, he disappeared."

"Poor Ginny." The urge to box Jake's ears made her fingers twitch.

"When you said he'd run off with Liddy, well, I'd been through this before. She's a wealthy young lady, but I'd overheard at a business meeting that her father didn't approve of Jake. I suppose Jake expected he'd change his mind if they were man and wife. But he didn't."

"I heard as much from Liddy." She chewed her lip. "You hired Jake. Why?"

His brow furrowed, as if the answer were obvious. "Because you love Liddy."

Her chest filled with heat. "You followed them because of what I said?"

"She's your friend. If I couldn't stop them from eloping, at least I could ensure Jake wouldn't abandon her or let her starve." His chin tilted a notch. "I've warned him. If he hurts Liddy, he'll lose everything. You don't have to worry about her, at least in that way."

Hot tears stung her eyes. She'd judged Will as arrogant and prideful. But he was wonderful and—oh. Her arms strained to wrap around his neck. Instead she kept her wits in place. And her hands firmly on Daisy's broad neck, even though she still clenched a hunk of carrot. "*Thank you* sounds most inadequate."

"I had the same thought when I saw this." He tapped the newspaper against his thigh. "Charlie mailed it to me. It's quite an article."

Her last article for the *Star*, which she'd had to beg Mr. LeShand to publish. Since she signed her name, took responsibility for the libel, and called upon him to exercise Christmas cheer, he'd thrown up his hands and allowed it. And told her he'd miss her, but he'd never admit it again.

Heat prickled her cheeks then, as it did now. "I didn't think you'd see the issue. I hoped it would help things for you here. I'm sorry if it embarrassed you."

"Embarrassed me?" He shoved the newspaper into a leather pouch hanging off the saddle. "I loved every word of it. You are so brave, defending me, holding yourself accountable for the previous article. But your praise about paying the immigrants? Eliza, I paid what was fair."

"More than fair. You showed grace and mercy. To the immigrants and to Jake." He should know before he left Austin again. "At first I thought you just cared about your business, but that's just another thing I was wrong about. You've blessed people here."

"So have you. Which is why members of the community, like Noah and Emmeline Whitley and Brandon and Marion Tabor, pitched in for an Austen Academy scholarship for young ladies who strive to improve society. Your parents said Mrs. Collins wrote to them about it. You'll have to apply for it, of course."

"You had nothing to do with it?" If he'd orchestrated the opportunity, she'd not take advantage of it. She'd not allow a man to pay her tuition.

"Not a thing, but I can't say I'm unhappy about it. You want to finish school, and you should. I want you to be happy, and I feel like I've made you the opposite." He nuzzled Phoenix, shaking his head. "My father loves me, but he raised me as a Delacourt, better than everyone else. We don't make mistakes. And then I watched him become ensnared by a woman who wanted nothing but his money."

"Jake said you liked her." A fresh round of heat filled her cheeks. "Did he lie?"

"No, he spoke true about that. I was an idiot. And after, I wasn't prone to trust females. When you fell into me, I thought, well." His Adam's apple bobbed above his snowy shirt collar. "I thought it a ploy. But it was the best thing that ever happened to me. You and your bluebonnet eyes changed everything. You didn't stand for what you perceived as my dishonor."

"*Perceived* being the key word."

"I disagree. My request to court you was shameful. Calling you a fortune hunter?" His jaw clenched. "I'm sorry."

The heat in her cheeks spread to her toes. "I'm sorry too."

His hand lifted, large and smelling of carrots, to rest warm against her cheek. Then his thumb traced the line of her jaw to her ear.

"I went about it all wrong, but truth is, I cared for you. I can't say when I knew it. I was in the middle before I knew my feelings had begun. My affections haven't changed, but one word from you and I'll go back to Memphis and never bother you again. Charlie can handle the TNT down here. If, however, you can stomach me, I have to warn you, I'll wait for you to finish school. And then I'd like to court you, because I love you, and I think I'd like to marry you, Eliza Branch."

The last bit of carrot fell from her hand to the gravel with a thud.

"I bought an old plantation outside Memphis." Will spoke faster now, his honeyed drawl thickening to molasses. "The house lacks modern conveniences and the land's overgrown, but there's a huge meadow like you told me about on your father's land, and it's filled with the prettiest little blue flowers that reminded me of your eyes."

Her hands found his lapels. "I love you, too."

His eyes did that thing again, where they liquefied like the deep dark water at the bottom of a well. "Will you say yes, then? You don't have to answer me now about the courtship. Or the idea of marriage. But at least to taking a ride with me?"

"Yes. To the ride. To the courtship. To the m—"

He dipped his head and kissed her in front of the horses and the house and the entire neighborhood. Her breath hitched, holding in the spicy scent of him, and then she forgot about breathing at all. His kiss was wonderful, like the thrill of Christmas morning in every fiber in her being. She threw her arms around his neck and returned his kiss until her smile got in the way. Then they were laughing, until the horses nudged their shoulders and Mother shouted from the door.

"The porch, Eliza!"

Epilogue

Perfectly matching Eliza's bridal bouquet, clusters of bluebonnets and white roses adorned the gleaming red conveyance. So did streamers of white ribbon, their tendrils fluttering in the warm July breeze.

Eliza's hands flew to her cheeks. "It's the most beautiful caboose I've ever seen."

Will's chest puffed with pride. "You don't mind sharing your wedding day with the inaugural run of the TNT?"

"It depends." Eliza leveled her groom with a teasing gaze. "How much of our honeymoon do you plan to spend on business?"

He answered with a kiss. Short, but full of promises.

"That's enough, you two," Charlie's voice intruded.

"Don't you have a train to catch?" Jeanie Bingham, a new bride herself, teased.

Eliza winked at her husband. "Yes, let's do get going. I have a travelogue to write for the Memphis newspaper, you know."

"And every word will be a delight." He kissed her hand.

"Whose idea was it to stand at the back of the train?" Mother brushed her sleeve. "This soot will ruin my gown."

Father grunted and stared at the shiny, rumbling engine, several cars ahead. Perhaps he was thinking of returning to the ranch. After Will's investment, Father's business showed signs of once again becoming a flourishing enterprise.

Eliza kissed her parents and sisters in turn. Then Jeanie and Charlie. "Until next month."

Will assisted Eliza onto the caboose's platform. She adjusted the pearl satin train of her wedding gown—a little sooty, true—and tossed her bouquet into the crowd of revelers waiting behind the train, including Mrs. Collins and her friends from Austen Abbey. Marta, grinning in the back, caught it.

With a long *hwoo-oo*, the train whistle filled the clear afternoon, and the train lurched from the Austin station. Eliza waved until their family and friends disappeared from sight. Will captured her hand.

His eyes liquefied. "God is so good, my precious wife, to bless us even when we both made a mess of things."

"Indeed." She kissed the faint stubble on his chin. "But He has a way of fixing things, doesn't He?"

Despite her foolish pride and prejudice.

ALARMINGLY CHARMING

DEBRA E. MARVIN

For God has not given us
a spirit of fear, but of power
and of love and of a sound mind

II Timothy 1:7

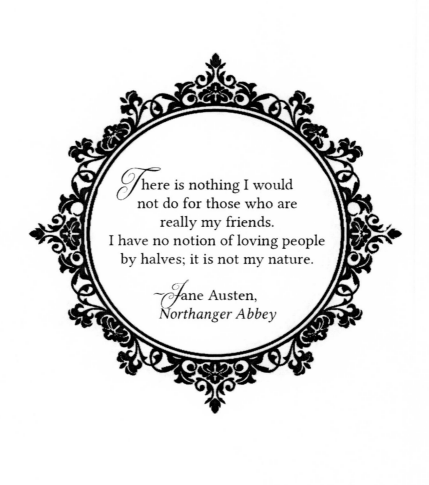

There is nothing I would
not do for those who are
really my friends.
I have no notion of loving people
by halves; it is not my nature.

~Jane Austen,
Northanger Abbey

One

Kathryn Morton turned the page....
We pulled the horses up near a small copse of woods, leaving Slim nestled like a snake between two boulders. The rest of us, including Jesse himself, piled large stones between the rails. At the mournful song of the whistle, we raised our masks, and I beheld the approaching locomotive's smoke in the distance. My heart pounded with anticipation.

Kathryn pressed her forehead to the train window and peered through the spot she'd previously wiped clean. Wide, scruffy land filled the endless horizon. Now that she thought of it, those trees did seem rather menacing. She nudged her glasses up her nose and returned to the dime novel.

We set about to make a great noise, firing eighteen or twenty shots, as the train came to a standstill.

The rattling rock of the railcar slowed, though they were still out in the middle of nowhere. A sudden clatter of footsteps on metal, and her mouth went dry as the landscape.

Train robbers.

On the roof.

One would shoot the coalman in cold blood. Then the driver, if he didn't act quickly. The train would stop. Mask-wearing, six-gun toting, sour-breathed bandits bent on thieving and destruction would appear, disproving Mother's insistence she'd surely be killed by Indians.

Kathryn's foot tapped as fast as her wild heart. Why hadn't she used the lavatory?

Cousin Jane, asleep beside her, remained blissfully unaware of impending doom. A faint glistening pooled at the corner of her mouth. She was too well bred to drool.

"Jane! Wake up!"

Another clink-clank. The robber might be Jesse James himself. No, she'd seen his death photo, and he had not looked well. Not well at all.

The railcar door flew open, intensifying the clackety-clack.

This was it.

Horrified, she faced the round, pink-cheeked conductor who paused by their seats.

He nudged his hat off his sweaty forehead. "Excuse me, miss, but we'll be arriving within the half hour."

Kathryn grasped the ruffles at her neck. "What about the bandits?"

The conductor cocked his head. "Are you all right, miss?"

Embarrassment warmed her face, and she moved her hand casually along her jaw. "Yes. I'm fine. Thank you." He appeared relieved to move on.

Jane rubbed her eyes. "Put that dreadful story away before you scare yourself senseless."

Kathryn complied. She always complied. Jane was five years her junior with ten times her spunk. Jane's future held a year of finishing school in Austin. Kathryn was along as companion for propriety's sake only—a brown mouse tagging behind a golden lioness. Jane was well able to take care of herself.

Cousin Jane fluffed the mounds of unnatural curls framing the only feature they shared—large amber eyes. "I hope you don't expect to read during your entire week's stay. I've heard there are many amusements around the city, and that we must avoid the riverfront." She opened her reticule and checked her face in a tiny mirror. "Which only makes me more anxious to go. I find I quite adore adventure."

"But your mother said—"

"Kathryn. Honestly." Jane sighed and shook her head.

Kathryn pinned her straw hat into her topknot and watched the countryside pass. Jane's frustration was just a reflection of what sat lumped inside Kathryn's chest.

Mesquite and Mexicans, cattle and cowboys. The trip from Philadelphia to Austin had been worth all of Jane's pitying remarks because she, Kathryn Patience Morton, would, in one short week, return home to her very proper Cheapside-born parents, a modern American daughter. Confident, brave, and independent.

She had no idea how she'd do it. But she'd try, by gum.

Well, she wouldn't take any risks. And she'd be very careful. Caution never hurt. There was no need to be foolish, of course.

Last off the train, Kathryn followed Jane down two narrow steps onto the platform. With one quick motion Kathryn checked her hat and adjusted her bustle.

And *then* remembered to survey for prying eyes. Not that anyone looked at her when Jane was around.

She hurried to catch up as Jane marched toward the shade of the station. "Is someone supposed to meet us, Cousin?"

"Of course."

A mustached young gentleman stepped forward, an older man trailing him. "Ladies, are you two by chance the Misses Radcliffe and Morton?" His gaze went to each as he named them, presumably advised of their descriptions. *Miss Morton will be the dull one with glasses.*

"Why yes, we are, sir," Jane purred. "How ever did you guess?"

Kathryn studied the station architecture, trying not to stare at the man who dressed and spoke as any fine Philadelphian, and appeared to be in his mid-twenties. She felt Mother's shove from a thousand miles away. A male with all his teeth? Perfect marriage material.

"There is no mistaking you have just come from the east, and"—he leaned closer—"quality always tells." After directing the older man away, he removed his hat, bowing his oiled, unmovable dark hair over Jane's hand. "I'm Jonathan Wellington. The second. My aunt, Mrs. Collins, has asked me to escort you back to the Abbey."

"The abbey, sir?" Kathryn asked.

"Oh, yes, forgive me. It's the name given the school by the girls. Now, let us be on our way."

Jane opened her parasol and stepped in the direction of Mr. Wellington's gesture, yet it was Kathryn whom Mr. Wellington's direct gaze sought out so that he might offer her his arm. "Allow me. I've taken care of everything. Frank, my aunt's handyman, will follow us with your trunks."

She accepted his escort out of the station, though it made no sense. Jane was the beauty in the family, the one with charm, confidence, and—the great equalizer—money.

"It is but a mile's ride, Miss Morton. Barely time to appreciate my new phaeton."

The red-spoked wheels must have inspired his choice of ascot tie. "You won't drive too fast, will you sir?"

Jane climbed into the seat, her *tsk tsks* finding their target. "Come along, Kathryn. Sit in the middle so I don't have to worry about you."

Bless Jane's heart for not voicing the *as you know how clumsy you are, dear.*

The space barely accommodated skirts and padding and bustles when she wedged herself between them. Mother would have an apoplexy at such intimacy. The buggy leapt forward, and he bent nearer. The coconut oil fragrance of Macassar Hair Tonic flooded her senses.

"It is best if you hold my arm, Miss Morton."

She abstained until one particularly jarring hole lifted her off the seat while she held down her wind-blown hat. Emboldened, she slipped her hand around his upper arm. The increased pounding of her heart, faster than the horses' hooves flying in front of her, made her woozy.

And that wouldn't do.

Determined to be the new, confident Kathryn, she breathed deeply and returned his next smile.

Then it was over. With an abrupt stop in the Jeannette C. Austen Academy for Young Ladies' circular driveway, her grip fell away.

"Ladies!" The enthusiastic welcome preceded the tightly corseted matron bustling down the wide stairs. "How nice to have you here. My, you look just like your mother, Miss Radcliffe. How fondly I look back on our school year together."

After introductions, Kathryn only half listened to her cousin's dramatic recounting of their journey and instead focused on their hostess. Mrs. Collins, her warm dark eyes twinkling, appeared younger than Aunt Cassandra, and maybe a bit more fun. Her lovely English accent seemed unaltered by years in Texas.

At the handyman Frank's arrival, Kathryn slipped away from the small talk, and despite his insistence, gathered her carpetbag. Her heart sank as she watched him hoist the weight of Jane's immense trunk, given the decided impairment in his shoulder.

"Please, sir, can't someone help you with that?"

He paused. "I'm fine, miss."

Her stomach clenched with instant regret. Her fussing had embarrassed him. She pivoted and promptly collided with a cowboy.

"Oh!" In a futile attempt to cover her gaping mouth, the bag dropped at his feet. "Oh!"

He tipped his hat as he dipped to retrieve it, barely breaking his gaze. "Miss."

She should not stare into such amused hazel eyes, or notice they were framed with dark lashes. She shouldn't notice that his brows and what she could see of his hair at his ears and collar shone a sun-bleached light brown. And she most certainly shouldn't stand there unable to speak or move.

Lizzie Bennet would say something clever. Fictional heroines always did.

He walked from the buggy to the building and placed the bag with the others on the verandah. Still she stood.

"Miss Morton," Mrs. Collins called. "Come join us. You too, Harmon. Frank will take care of the rest, but I appreciate your concern."

The handsome cowboy was already walking away. "Thank you, but I have to be getting back to the ranch."

Like a practiced sleuth, Kathryn oh-so-cautiously watched from the corner of her eye—only to be caught when he glanced back.

Did cowboys no longer have bowed legs? This man's legs...his...and his shoulders. There seemed nothing amiss. He disappeared around the massive gray stone building, and she'd taken two sleepwalker's steps to follow before she saw him mounting the back of a beautiful dark horse. Such strength. And ease.

"Kathryn! Come along."

"Be right there, Jane."

Within the hour Kathryn was seated in a spacious double parlor with Jane, Mrs. Collins, Mr. Wellington, and two students, Eleanor and Isabella. The girls were agreeable company, thankfully, for in one week, she was to companion Isabella as far as Richmond on the return trip.

The second time she noticed Mr. Wellington's blue-eyed stare,

Kathryn surreptitiously wiped her face, sure she must be wearing crumbs from the imported tea biscuits she'd presented their hostess. She removed her glasses, wiped at her face again, and closed her eyes for a respite.

"Miss Morton, I do believe you need some rest." Mrs. Collins's tone was warm but did not invite argument. "Please, do not stay for our ramblings."

"Thank you." The moment she stood, Mr. Wellington was at her side.

He took her hand and bent over it. "Consider me your guide to our city this week. Nothing would give me more pleasure."

"Thank you for your kindness." Her digestive biscuit threatened retreat. Nausea often accompanied a case of nerves, but honestly, one would think she'd never had a gentleman's interest before.

And they'd be right.

She tugged her hand from his and left the room, climbing to the second floor room she would share with Jane. At the top of the richly carpeted stairs, a broad window drew her, and she pushed the sheers back. Where had that cowboy gone?

Once behind the heavy oak door, she sighed at the gift of solitude. The spacious cream-colored bedroom offered a balcony, currently in shade. She removed her shoes and skirt, her petticoat and bustle, her stays and stockings, and lay on the canopied bed in her shift, the most luxurious comfort she'd had in a week's time.

She stretched and wiggled, unable to hold back a smile. What would mother think of her now? Paid such attentions by a very polite gentleman, but thinking more of the rugged man who had stolen her ability to speak. Was he no more than a cowpuncher? Such a distasteful term. A drifter across an endless sea of brush and Texas dust, fighting in the name of justice and all that was good in the world?

If they were to fall in love, would she have to ride a horse? Drive a wagon? Carry a pistol, a rifle? Would she have to save the ranch? Or worse? Learn how to cook?

She sighed and closed her eyes to sleep.

The Indians' war cries sent gooseflesh across her shoulders. Their horses pounded the parched earth, and her lungs burned as she ran for her very life. They were right behind her. She glanced back. She wasn't going to make it. She stumbled but was caught up by a strong arm, in a blur of dark fabric and dark horse. He'd come for her! She sat behind Harmon, clinging to his muscular body as they out-ran the Comanche raiders. Their lead lengthened until they were at the top of a scrubby rise. The horse protested when Harmon pulled him up to a sliding stop. Dismounting before the dust settled, he swung Kathryn down into his arms. His hands lingered at her waist, even after her feet were solidly on the ground, and he gazed at her with those unforgettable hazel eyes.

"Miss Morton, are you all right?"

"I–I think so."

"Then, I can wait no longer. I must know. Can you ever love me?"

"Oh yes, Mr. Cowboy." Her eyes flew open. Mr. Cowboy?

Kathryn let her head relax again into the pillow, more convinced than ever that locomotive travel addled the brain.

"Kathryn!"

The brisk shaking of her shoulder proved she'd finally fallen asleep. "Jane. Stop. I'm awake. What is it?"

"You must get ready."

It took her a moment to rise and dress. Her cousin's devoted assistance roused her suspicions.

"Do you have any idea of the conquest you have made, Kathryn?"

All that from just one of the cowboy's glances? Could it be? Her heart drummed in delight.

"Mr. Wellington made no doubts of his interest in you."

Oh. That. She turned away. "I'm sure he is just being kind."

"Don't be silly." Jane grabbed Kathryn's shoulder. "This is it. The chance we've waited for, and I'm not going to let you ruin it."

Kathryn pulled away. *Breathe. Slowly.*

She'd come here determined to make a change, and the first step was standing up to her cousin.

Only, not right now. Not when her head pounded at the thought of a suitor. Goodness sakes, she wanted a suitor—she'd long dreamed of a suitor. And now that he was here...

He didn't suit her at all.

Two

Do not trip.

With forced casualness, Kathryn trailed her hand along the smooth oak banister as she descended the stairs, praying each step of the way. She kept Jane's blond up-do and froth of curls in her line of vision to block Mr. Wellington's upward, and singularly unnerving, gaze.

The entryway was not so different from the one in Jane's home back in Philadelphia. An eclectic mix of furniture, paintings, and fixtures bore the fragrance of Uncle Frederick's old family money. Jonathan Wellington's demeanor quite suited the luxurious details.

Why hadn't she claimed a headache? She could no more eat a meal now than prepare one. Her insides buzzed like locusts at the thought of any man's attentions toward her, much less one considered eligible.

Could she grow to appreciate, even love Mr. Wellington? At four and twenty years, she'd determined the likelihood of marriage...unlikely.

She breathed in slowly and raised her chin. She could do this.

The bottom riser creaked just as he took her hand.

"Jonathan?"

She recognized that voice. He'd come back! Mr. Cowboy—Harmon—stood in the doorway, dressed for dinner. If she'd been able to take a breath, he'd have stolen it away. How could a man look so fine in a frock coat, vest, and black bow tie yet appear so discomfited?

He came forward, his lazy smile warm as the evening. "Please introduce me to your guests, Aunt Augusta."

The headmistress and her black taffeta swished across the two-story entryway. "I would have earlier, had you not run off. This is Miss Jane Radcliffe, a new student, and her cousin, Miss Kathryn Morton." Mrs. Collins turned to him and straightened his tie. "This is my nephew, Mr. Harmon Gray."

Kathryn looked back and forth between the two men. "Are they cousins as well?"

"No, but they are blessed to share the same aunt." She raised a jaunty brow. "Jonathan is my late husband's nephew, and Harmon is my sister's son. Between semesters, they dine with me on Sundays." She patted his lapel before releasing him. "Given your interests in the west, and we hope Texas in particular, Miss Morton, I believe Harmon may be able to show you something of a working cattle ranch, this week. If you are interested."

"Oh yes. Indeed I am, ma'am." Oh yes.

A lovely color rose on Miss Morton's dainty face when her cousin tugged at her sleeve, intent, he guessed, on upbraiding her enthusiasm for something so...common.

Harmon enjoyed her lack of pretense, but interesting as she was, he wasn't sure he had time to escort another wealthy easterner around.

Ahh, but that sweet smile, and those eyes—a golden brown—were a rare treat when she dared glance his way.

"Just name the day, miss, and I'll come collect you, if you don't mind riding on a wagon seat." So much for his intentions. He'd find a way to be free this week.

Jonathan snapped the cuffs of his jacket and glared. "I believe she'll be with me tomorrow, Harmon."

Jonathan wasted no time.

"I'll leave it to Miss Morton." Harmon turned to Aunt Augusta. The woman wore serenity like a perfume, and it was one sure way to beat a growing irritation with Jonathan before it ruined the evening.

He offered Miss Morton his arm; Jonathan mirrored the effort. Her face blanched at the doubled attention, and Harmon withdrew, turning to her cousin. "Miss Radcliffe?"

The pretty blond accepted his escort to the dining room, but her smile was as friendly as a cat's. This might be the first time she'd been second choice to her cousin. The five of them settled at one end of a table seating twenty. Having learned that an academy of young women was no safer than a church supper for a single man under thirty, he normally avoided meals during the school year.

They'd gone a second course before Jonathan ended a soliloquy on his favorite subject—himself.

"Miss Morton..." Jonathan said, touching her sleeve. An act that, if Harmon had been counting aright, numbered in the way-too-often range. "...Miss Radcliffe tells us you are an avid reader."

Miss Morton squared her fork across her plate. She'd barely touched her meal. "I do enjoy reading," she answered, with an underlying wariness Harmon admired.

"Aren't you the dark horse, with your taste in dime novels?" Jonathan declared. "I myself find the gothics morbid."

Harmon rolled his eyes.

"Too morbid," Miss Radcliffe agreed.

Aunt Augusta eyed Jonathan warily.

Miss Morton sat up straighter, opened her mouth, but nothing came forth.

"Seems to me," Harmon offered, "a wide range of reading material can't be a bad thing."

Miss Morton's gaze softened with gratitude. She really was a pretty gal.

"Then the quiet woman at my side outshines us all." Jonathan punctuated his remark with a wink in her direction.

Dandy Boy was outdoing himself tonight. He always had less tact than Harmon's gelding, but teasing a shy girl this way? Harmon scrubbed a hand over his face.

Aunt Augusta patted each corner of her mouth with her napkin. "Scripture says a gentle and quiet spirit is of great worth."

He'd heard this verse read in church this morning, just before a sermon demanding they *put away wrath, put away bitterness.*

Jonathan grinned before swallowing down the last of his dumpling. "I say. Given Miss Morton's interest in mysteries—"

"Not tonight, Jonathan." Despite her smile, Aunt Augusta's voice took on that calm before a storm tone they'd both heard before.

"But I'm sure our guests will be interested in our most famous unsolved crime."

If Jonathan had not failed out of law school, he might have known when to rest his case.

"I prefer you didn't."

"Oh, but he must tell us, now," Miss Radcliffe pleaded. "I will simply die of curiosity if he were not to finish. And my dear cousin waits on his every word."

They all turned as one to inspect Miss Morton's face.

What Harmon saw was her desire to flee the room and possibly Austin altogether. "Miss Morton, you do look played out." That didn't help. "I mean, you must be tired from your travels."

Her gaze momentarily shifted to Miss Radcliffe. "It was rather exhausting."

With a selfish chatterbox like that? "I can imagine."

The most delicate of guilty smiles brightened her face, and brightened his evening. Harmon chased the last three peas across his plate. What was it about her?

Miss Radcliffe's fan tapped against his arm. "About that unsolved crime..."

He glanced at his aunt, who gave him leave with a small shrug. "Miss Radcliffe," he began, "there are some awful events in Austin's recent history, and not topics for the dinner table."

"I agree." Jonathan groomed his mustache with all the drama he included in his tone. "I speak of our cemetery ghost. Not just any spirit, but the ghost of a murdered servant girl, rising up to warn of the Axe Murderer's return."

Miss Radcliffe squealed with delight. Miss Morton's eyes widened into perfect circles, much like the *oh* gracing her open mouth.

Harmon pushed his chair back to stand. Dragging Jonathan out by his eye teeth might just silence him.

"Harmon." Aunt Augusta kept her gaze to the table before her and rang the small brass bell.

He breathed in long and hard and released it just as slowly, eventually easing back into his chair. What was wrong with him?

When the maidservant Cora looked in, Aunt Augusta waved her over. "We are decidedly in need of some chocolate. What say you, Miss Morton?"

"Oh, it's my favorite." She gave Cora a generous smile, and at their maid's departure, she turned to Aunt Augusta. "If you please, ma'am."

Her voice was steady and warm, though she still fidgeted with her blouse. "I'm afraid our interest is piqued. Such stories are found in any town. It's no reflection on your lovely city."

Jonathan leaned closer. "Then you admit you believe in ghosts, my dear?"

She answered with a frown. "No, but I do believe in the power of a story to draw out feelings that we often find hard to express. But that's all it is. A story. Every cemetery has a ghost or two...if you believe in them."

Aunt Augusta folded her napkin in exacting measure. "It's true, girls,"—she cast a disappointed glance at Jonathan—"there have been disturbances to the nearby cemetery. Vandals, I'm sure. But we've lost one of our incoming students because of these ridiculous rumors."

"Oh, no. I'm sorry, ma'am." Miss Morton looked around the table. "Is the graveyard so very close?"

Miss Radcliffe caught Harmon's eye before looking across the table. "You were right about my cousin, Mr. Wellington. You have much in common."

Jonathan grinned like Mr. Lewis Carroll's Cheshire cat, while Miss Morton, lips clenched, sent her cousin a frustrated glance.

The chocolate dessert arrived, and might have just saved the evening.

The little missy, quite unaware of everyone's scrutiny, methodically claimed each bite and crumb off her plate. Harmon enjoyed his cake more, for the pleasure she took in such a treat.

When Aunt Augusta rose, signaling the end of the meal, they all stood. Miss Radcliffe caught Harmon unaware by appropriating his arm and pulling him to the hallway.

"Mr. Gray, would you be so kind as to show me the grounds of the school?"

He glanced over his shoulder to discover Jonathan propelling Miss Morton the other way. Jane Radcliffe's diversionary tactic could not have been more obvious.

He'd planned to speak with Miss Morton alone, and it wasn't just to stall Jonathan's flagrant play for her.

She peered back in confusion, adding to the tightness in his chest.

Somewhere between the gazpacho and Graciana's five-layer torte, he'd hoped Miss Morton's shy interest went beyond curiosity.

Unless she was here looking for a husband.

Harmon snickered. Marriage? She'd probably never spoken alone with a man, and that innocent, pert little blossom of a mouth had most certainly never been kissed.

"What's so funny, Mr. Gray?"

He'd forgotten Miss R at his side, though at one time, he'd have enjoyed her flirtations. "I'd rather not say."

"Then you should not, for I find I'm usually shocked by how a man thinks. But there must be something you can tell me about yourself."

Talk about himself? Admit he'd been contemplating her cousin's lips? He hid a grin. "Well, miss, being a cowpoke and all, I don't rightly know what to say."

His sarcasm was lost on Miss Radcliffe, who took it as leave to chatter on. Just as well for him, freed to remember how Miss Morton had gazed in gratitude at his encouragement. She needed a hero, all right. Someone to take her hand and ask her to dance, away from the shadow cast by her belle-of-the-ball cousin. And it wasn't going to be Jonathan.

Three

Kathryn rose early, relishing the quiet, and left Jane to her much-needed rest. Poor Jane. It required uncommon effort to be the most charming girl in the world.

Anxious for a taste of freedom, Kathryn pinned back just a portion of her hair and, with her small *New Testament* in hand, descended the stairs. Before heading out the back door, she peeked into the kitchen where three women buzzed about, chattering in cheery Spanish.

The warm air surprised her with its freshness, and she made a beeline for a bench shaded by a small-leafed tree. An unfamiliar yellow-headed bird hopped about at her feet. Everything was so different here. Just what she'd hoped for.

"*Señorita?*"

One of the young Mexican women presented a cup of hot coffee. Kathryn's attempt at one of her three new words, *gracias,* earned her a warm smile enhanced by the sparkle of beautiful, dark eyes.

Beyond twisted trees, scrubby brush, and scattered rooftops, the Texas morning sky filled her chest like a symphony. A song of new beginnings.

Kathryn blew dust from her glasses, intent on reading her verses, but her thoughts defied her, returning again to Harmon Gray. She closed the tiny book. "Lord, thank you for the beauty of your land and this trip. Bless Mrs. Collins and the students, especially Jane. And keep my parents from worrying about me. They mean well, but—"

A shadow fell over her, and she opened her eyes.

He was here. Her cowboy.

Mr. Gray's strong jaw shifted under a school lad's grin when he stopped in front of her. The sleeves of his crisp, white shirt were folded up his forearms.

Kathryn's backbone went all rubbery when he touched the rim of his hat.

"Beg your pardon, miss. I didn't mean to disturb you."

She took a deep breath. "I'm surprised to see you so early. Have you no chores to do at the ranch?" She cringed. Could she sound any more absurd?

"I did my chores, actually, but if you're thinking of our cattle, most are still out on summer range with our men."

"You're not a cowboy, then?"

He tipped back his hat, amused. "Around here I'd be considered a rancher. Are you disappointed?"

Disappointed? With perfection? She had to close her mouth and look away. "Oh, no, of course not. I mean, I find it all so interesting. So different from where I live."

"I don't think I could live anywhere else."

No, he belonged right here.

He removed his hat and rotated the brim through both hands, stopping once to push his hair back. "I meant what I said when I offered to show you the ranch."

An alarming pressure built up in her chest. She could only nod.

"Well, good. I'm glad. It's not much, but I think you'll enjoy it. Again, I'm sorry for the interruption. I thought I'd see if my aunt needed anything."

Father handled his hat the same way, and it made her miss him. "I didn't see her in the house."

"Then I'll wait. If you don't mind."

Dare she ask him to sit? No, better yet...she set down the cup and stood. "Might you walk with me, sir?" Before he could decline, she forged on. "I'm eager to see beyond the school, and yet I know it'd be wrong for me to go by myself. Because I'd like to—well, there's so much—and I've spent days sitting in the train." What in heaven's name was wrong with her? She lifted her chin. *Change the subject.* "I saw a woman riding a horse."

"And?" He studied her, grinning.

"I don't see many women riding...astride." Kathryn bit her lip.

He gestured, and they began walking. "Have you ever ridden a horse, Miss Morton? Riding sidesaddle takes more courage than I have."

Was he teasing her? "Oh, surely not."

"Oh, surely yes. They're downright dangerous, if you ask me. We have a real sweet mare you could ride, but we don't have a sidesaddle."

She could listen to him talk all the day long—rich, thoughtful, gentlemanly. If she could just stop rambling. "I read that a horse can tell if you're frightened. I'm afraid the truth is...I'm afraid."

"That's fine. I promise to be right there with you."

"You would?" Those eyes could make the new Lady Liberty drop her torch.

He reached for the tiny Bible in her hand. "May I?"

Confused, she handed it to him, and he promptly put it in his shirt pocket.

"Until we return."

She caught a soft mix of scents—leather and horse—and studied his profile before remembering to watch her step. "Mrs. Collins is your aunt? My parents are also English."

"Augusta Collins is—was—my mother's sister."

"You mean..."

"My mother passed away. It will be two years this week."

"I'm so sorry."

They walked on, and the silence worried her. *Think of something clever.* Something not so clever might even do. "Someone needs to find out who's causing the trouble."

"Trouble?"

"In the cemetery."

He glanced down the street and touched her elbow, directing her to cross. "The murders ended two years ago. I'm sure you'll be safe. It's not like you'll be out alone at night."

She felt his gaze upon her and reddened.

"You don't feel uncomfortable now, do you Miss Morton?"

Uncomfortably alive. Painfully aware what a sheltered life she'd been living. "No."

"Then we'll go on."

"Where is that cemetery causing all the fuss?" If she could just see it for herself, she would...what? Put on a Pinkerton badge and arrest the scoundrels?

"Over that rise a bit, but it's not much to see."

"Well, actually." *Stop being skittish, Kathryn.* "I do wish to see a place capable of keeping students from your aunt's fine school. Honestly! The ghost of a dead girl rises to warn the city of the murderer's return? It might make good fiction, but..."

But it was just what she needed to do to prove to herself she was every bit as capable as Jane. Oh, brains didn't seem to count like beauty, but some day they'd be saying... *There goes that plucky Kathryn Morton.*

"All right. We'll go."

She stole a glance. "You'd rather not. I can tell."

"I'm in no hurry to go back."

"Really?"

His gaze drew her to those eyes, light against the outdoorsy color of his skin.

"And leave a pretty gal like you?"

She had to look away but couldn't hold back a smile. Such soft words carried her up the path. Pretty girl? Even if he didn't mean it, she'd never heard that from anyone but her parents.

The cemetery was larger than she'd expected, rolling and dotted with trees. Tombstones and patches of grass drew her to walk on.

"Why, it's so spread out. Our Philadelphia cemeteries are crammed, head-to-toe. I like to read the names and dates and imagine their lives. We even have some famous Americans there, you know."

Bragging on cemeteries, now, Mouse?

"There's no one famous here, leastwise not outside of Texas."

"Well, it's perfectly lovely, and if I were a ghost, I'd be happy here and never frighten anyone."

Mr. Gray put his hand on her arm and stopped her. "We need to go back."

She turned at the sound of a horse shaking its head. Tts rider stood near a stone bench.

Mr. Gray's discomfort deepened, and he dropped his hand when the white-haired man spun around.

The stranger strode forward, his thick brows drawn in sharp disapproval. "What are you doing here?"

Kathryn's hand went to her chest. "I'm so sorry, sir. I apologize—"

"Not you, girl." He glared at Mr. Gray.

"Father, Miss Morton is visiting with Aunt Augusta, and I joined her on a walk."

"To a cemetery?"

What? She stepped back. Mr. Gray's father? Here? "I find them fascinating."

"You might think differently, if someone you loved were here."

Like my little brother? How would he know her heart ached every day with loss? "Actually, I believe the soul is—" No, she wouldn't start a discussion on doctrine here. To Mr. Gray, the son, she offered another apology and glanced across the head stones. His mother must be buried here. "Excuse me, please." She darted away, her eyes stinging.

"Father, you had no call—"

Her pounding heartbeats filled her ears, even as she rushed across hard, uneven ground. She'd ruined it all with her silly talk, and she could never face Mr. Gray again. *If I were a ghost...*

"Miss Morton. Wait up."

"I can't," she called over her shoulder. "What you must think..."

"If you slow down some, I'll tell you what I think."

She did. Roped in by the soft drawl of his voice.

He came to her side, his hand briefly touching the cuff of her sleeve. "I think you're about the sweetest girl I've met. And I'm sure there are very interesting stories here."

"But your father..."

"He didn't show my mother much care when he had the chance, and his regret has made him a miserable...old coot." He glanced back. "Don't mind him. He doesn't deserve your concern."

Her insides ached like a stubbed toe. She raised her gaze to him, but he was staring at the ground. "I'm sorry you feel that way about your own father."

"I don't come here often, because, well, I don't believe Mother's here." He looked out across the cemetery, his mouth tight.

She waited. What could she say now that would change anything? "I shall pray for your father. And you, if you don't mind."

He murmured thanks and something she didn't hear. It was a quiet walk back to the Abbey until he bade her good-bye. She dropped to the bench, watching him leave, and then stared at the spot on her cuff where he'd placed his hand. Given his father's reaction, it seemed unlikely she'd see their ranch now.

Instead, she'd relive that walk a hundred times.

"Miss Morton."

She startled, having missed his return.

Harmon Gray reached into his pocket and returned her New Testament. It was warm and, if she were alone, she'd bring it up against her cheek.

Would it be sinful to put it under her pillow tonight?

She watched him walk away before realizing she hadn't even thanked him. Bright color drew her eyes to the open kitchen door.

Jane marched toward her, stopping five feet away, hands on hips. "Kathryn, where have you been?"

"Giving my heart a little exercise."

"Well don't dawdle. We only have two hours to get you ready before he comes." She shook her head and then headed back to the house.

Kathryn leaned forward and dragged her boot across the thin grass. She'd forgotten all about Mr. Wellington.

Four

Movement in a first floor window caught Harmon's attention. Just as well given his stated excuse for the early morning visit. Aunt Augusta, in her ever-present high-necked white blouse, waved him in to her office.

Harmon removed his hat. "I wondered if Frank needed anything from the lumberyard."

She raised one brow and sat back in her desk chair. "Funny, I didn't see your wagon."

It had been a cockamamie idea. He studied his boots. "No, I guess you wouldn't." Aunt Augusta might smell of violet water like Mother used to, but she was sharp as a cavalry scout.

"What's bothering you?"

"I ran into Father at the cemetery."

"This morning? Why ever were you there?"

Good question. "Walking?" He shrugged. "I sort of agreed to escort Miss Morton."

"And your father? How does he come in to this story?"

"He was there. Darned if I'd expected that. But no surprise; he was miserable."

Aunt Augusta closed her ledger and stood. "It was good to see you in church yesterday."

Her words hit hard considering their soft delivery. They both knew he wouldn't have gone if she hadn't guilted him into it.

Never one to stand idle, she moved to the window and picked dead leaves off her beloved begonias. "When do your classes begin at the university?"

"Next week." He'd yet to remind Father. Did it even matter?

"There'll be plenty of engineering jobs here when they start work on that dam." She turned her attention on him, the look that had put fear in him since he was a tyke. "Are you still thinking of leaving town? You love that ranch."

"I just can't live there anymore, that's all." He went to her side and kissed her forehead. "I best be on my way."

"Harmon?"

"Yes, ma'am?"

"Miss Morton is a dear girl."

Harmon nodded and left the room. If anyone was going to break Miss Morton's heart, it wouldn't be him.

Harmon pushed the back door open and waited for his eyes to adjust to the ranch house's shuttered kitchen. Father sat in his chair in front of the unlit cook stove as if it were a cool January day rather than a sunny September morning. He probably was cold.

He is cold. I shouldn't have come.

The thirty-minute ride from the Abbey hadn't cooled Harmon's anger. No one knew better that Harmon Gray, Senior was best left alone, but Father's treatment of Miss Morton still needled Harmon—not that his temper required much of a push.

"How could you be so rude?"

Father rubbed at his whiskery chin but offered no reply.

"I'd planned to show her the ranch, but I doubt she'd come now."

Father chuckled. "I'm sure she's mighty impressed with a real cowboy."

"Don't speak of her like that. She's a kind girl, interested in seeing new things." Harmon's hands fisted at his side. "You—"

"What? Say it boy, unless you can't. You've made it clear enough you don't give a hoot about this place."

God help me. His chest heaved. It wasn't the ranch driving him away.

If it wasn't for the guilt, he'd have left long ago.

Father stood. His hair was in need of a cut. Deep lines and shadows surrounded the eyes staring long at Harmon. "I don't need you telling me what I already know. Now, go see what Ernesto's doing."

Emptiness replaced the anger, dissipated by Father's refusal to argue. When had the old man gotten so...old?

Dear God, I have to get away from this place...before I become just like him.

Kathryn watched Jane flip her parasol into position and walk away, the perfect feminine profile in a soft pink jacket and matching bustled skirt. She had enough silk roses on her hat to hornswoggle a hive of bees. Kathryn's hand went to her own plain, flat-topped straw with its single brown grosgrain ribbon, and wished she hadn't agreed to a trip to the park.

The hat had nothing to do with her dismay—rather, the eager gaze of one Jonathan Wellington and Jane's not-so-subtle prodding. Strolling on a man's arm evidently required patience. She'd seen her elderly neighbor move faster on an arthritic day.

"You needn't be shy with me, Miss Morton. I put it to you that I am your greatest admirer."

"Well, about that, I think it's only fair to—" She glanced up, drawn by the intensity of Jane's stare. Was her cousin's hearing that good? From under those fair, perfect brows, came a glare that could make President Cleveland cower.

Kathryn pressed her mouth tight. She'd have to tell him how silly this whole thing was, but for now she'd just try to enjoy the attention. "What were you saying, sir?"

He carried on, having the knack of providing both sides of the conversation. "—dinner on Friday evening, then?"

"What's that, Mr. Wellington?" Dinner? "I'm not sure it would be appropriate. Besides, Eleanor says the Hotel Brunswick is quite fancy."

"A fine establishment, yes, and I will ask Aunt Augusta to accompany us. She rarely has the chance to dine out when the Academy is in session."

Kathryn smiled. A genuine smile, because the idea of a real restaurant meal in Texas piqued her curiosity, and because a long green beetle inspected the brim of Mr. Wellington's bowler.

"Do you enjoy walks in Philadelphia, Miss Morton?" He left no room for an answer. "Because some girls are only interested in flitting between stores." The beetle opened its hard wings, fluttered them, but didn't rise. "One young woman was injured only last week while crossing Congress Avenue. All for a new flowered hat she saw in the storefront."

"Like a butterfly after nectar?" Kathryn clamped back amusement.

"Oh, I assure you it was quite serious."

The bug took flight. Right toward her face. With a shriek, she ducked.

"What is it, my dear?"

"Didn't you see that bug fly at me?" Her hands fanned over her head. "Is it on my hat?"

Jane popped up at her side. "Kathryn, whatever is going on?"

"Oh, my dear girl." Mr. Wellington shook his head and leaned closer. "You are so charming."

Not so his cigar-smoky breath.

Jane turned aside. If she'd winked any harder she would have injured her eye. "You two take your time."

"Wait. Jane, come back."

Jane didn't. Her look said it all before she continued on, her waddling backside stealing Mr. Wellington's notice until he cleared his throat and placed his hat over his heart.

"Miss Morton, do you believe in love at first sight?"

Mr. Harmon Gray's image came to mind faster than that bug had buzzed by. She swallowed hard and nodded.

"Good. Because I too am quite the romantic." He nestled her arm in his. "I will telegram your father, today, and ask if we might court."

She looked for signs he was teasing. "Would you repeat that?"

He only smiled.

"Sir, we've just met. Yesterday."

"I know. Glorious, isn't it?"

"It's..."

"Sudden. Yes." He straightened her hat. "I know you are a cautious person, and I'm asking you to give me a chance."

His sincerity and the tentative phrasing of his words brought a lump to her throat. "I do need time to get used to the idea."

He pressed her fingers. "Thank you."

Before she could utter a word, Jane was at her side, bursting with excitement. "Oh, Kathy, this is just what you wanted!"

It was?

Kathryn asked to be excused from dinner and slipped away and into bed early. Her stomach ached, it truly did. The ache of worrying she'd end up alone. Never special to anyone after her parents were gone.

Why did it plague her now?

The walk with her cowboy seemed like a dream. A schoolgirl's imaginings.

Mr. Wellington's interest was all too real.

Why wasn't this easier?

Jane entered the room. "Kathryn, are you awake?"

She didn't move.

"I need help with my dress. I'm sorry."

Kathryn pushed herself up and swung her bare feet onto the carpet. Jane could manage well enough if she had to, so the questions should soon begin.

"He's quite taken with you," Jane whispered. "You do like him? A bit?"

She tugged to release the last hook on her cousin's back. "I want to."

"And I want you to be happy. Mother's marriage began this way, and now she adores Father. Don't be afraid. And Mr. Wellington's willing to move to Philadelphia."

Kathryn stared at her in disbelief. "How? Never mind. I don't want to know." At that, she crawled under the sheets, keeping her back to Jane.

"I'm sorry, Kathy. You won't admit it, but I know you worried that you'd never marry."

Had Jane actually paid that much attention?

"Your mother worries for you as well. They want to see you settled and taken care of."

Kathryn pushed herself up on one hand and looked over her shoulder. "Of course they do, but I planned on learning how to take care of myself first. Just in case."

The next morning, Kathryn sought refuge on the shaded bench, watching the same birds hop about, though they didn't cheer her today. She'd hardly slept. Jane said Mr. Wellington asked that they keep his request a secret until her father gave his blessing. How overjoyed Mother would be to receive the news.

She had to try, had to give Mr. Wellington, and herself, a chance.

Harmon Gray's attention, exhilarating as it had been, would never amount to anything but fond memories.

She wandered to the stable and found Frank cleaning harnesses. If his arm bothered him, he did not show it. Sparkling flecks of dust and straw drifted across a shaft of sunlight. She approached the stall containing the darker of the two Abbey sorrels, but the familiar tightness settled across her chest. *Lord, I have to get over this fear of horses.*

All her fears, actually.

"Go on, Miss Morton. She'd love the attention."

Kathryn raised her hand, but jerked it back when the big nostrils sniffed. She tried again and succeeded at stroking the white patch between the horse's long-lashed brown eyes. It nodded in appreciation.

"Does your family have carriage horses?"

Kathryn turned to Frank, unsure he was speaking to her. "Why no, sir. We live in a small house and have no place to stable even one horse, nor store a carriage." And Father would never own a horse after—

She pulled her hand away from the warm, velvety muzzle. Her brother's death had been no fault of the horse involved.

"I see."

Frank's hesitant answer drew her attention to his face, lined with confusion.

"Have you ever been to the East, Frank?" She glanced down at the cat now rubbing against his leg.

"I'm afraid so. Though I wish I'd never left Texas."

"What did you dislike about it?"

"War."

The word was too heavy to bear and dropped between them. Frank tossed a rag aside and stood, stretching his back. "I'm proud to have been part of the First Texas. I did what I thought I should do and didn't turn tail, but war is never something to look back on fondly." His eyes held such sadness.

"Is that how you hurt your arm?"

"I'm lucky to still have it."

Together, they watched the cat wander ever closer, nonchalantly inviting Kathryn's attention.

Frank cleared his throat. "Dysentery kept me out of Sharpsburg, where I lost my brother. The worst wounds are the ones we can't see, I figger, and some never get over them."

"I do know a man like that back home."

"Keep it in mind if'n you go out to the Gray Ranch and meet Harmon's father. Appomattox broke his spirit, though he was decorated for bravery."

"Mr. Gray's father? You know him well?"

"Used to be my closest friend. But things change. I tried, well...I drank to stop the nightmares, bury the anger. Truth is, all I needed to do was face what happened, and let go of my regrets." He closed up the jar of thick yellow paste. "Course I couldn't have done it without prayer, and Augusta's husband willing to give me a second chance."

"Mother always says *kindness goes a long way*." Kathryn looked out from the barn into the bright morning light and squinted. "Has anyone been kind to the elder Mr. Gray, lately?"

"That's a good question." One of the horses snickered when Frank passed by the feed barrel. "Come on, Thor, and I'll get you some milk."

She turned to go.

"Miss Morton?"

Kathryn glanced back over her shoulder.

"You come and find me if you need someone to talk to, you hear?" His earnest gaze said as much.

"Thank you. I will." He was a nice man, and she tried to imagine Mr. Gray and him as young men. Friends going off to war.

She'd promised Harmon she'd pray for his father, and she would. If she did visit the ranch, she'd make a point of talking to him.

In fact...

Not just about the war, but about this ghost business. If he spent time there, he must have an idea what was going on. The New Kathryn was determined to find out what was behind the rumors affecting Mrs. Collins and the Abbey. And if doing so also meant more time with Harmon, all the better. She wasn't about to stop seeing him quite yet.

Five

High noon's heat enveloped the shaded porch. Not a breath of wind. She might have to fan herself. Next to her, a newspaper lay on the seat of a wicker chair. WARNINGS SENT FROM BEYOND THE GRAVE. Talk about a tasteless headline.

Kathryn was in danger of melting, right where she stood. And so was the generous square of chocolate she'd unwrapped to slowly savor. She pushed the last of it into her mouth and, before closing her eyes, noticed the gooey goodness on her fingertips. Mm. Excellent.

The door handle rattled, and she spun around. "Graciana, that was—"

"I've disturbed you again," offered Harmon Gray.

She turned away. "No, not at all." What was disturbing about having her insides rearrange themselves every time this man walked in the room? She swallowed again and imagined the chocolate clinging to her teeth.

"Did you enjoy your ride around town yesterday?"

She nodded while earnestly working her mouth and tongue.

"I hope you still want to visit the ranch before you leave."

She faced him but kept her hands behind her. "And your father?"

Mr. Gray removed his hat. "He'll be fine, but I don't know what you're expecting, miss. It's not up to a lady's standards. And now, with me taking classes the last year—"

"Classes?"

"At the University of Texas. I'm studying engineering."

"Really!" She almost grabbed his arm in her excitement, and his grin became a chuckle. "But does that mean you'll no longer be a rancher?"

"The ranch is my home, but I'm not certain it's my future."

"I used to dream of going to a university."

"You don't say." His surprise warmed into an encouraging smile. "And what would you study?"

"History. Science. Literature. Mother says I'm a flibbertigibbet. I have few skills, and should I find a need to support myself..." Mortified at what she'd admitted, she hurried to cover her mouth before remembering her messy fingers.

Mr. Harmon Gray stared at her mouth.

Oh no! The chocolate. She wiped her face with the back of her hand and studied his eyes.

"You don't want to marry, Miss Morton?"

Is that what he thought?

"Of course I want to marry." And not worry about how she'd get by on the little her parents could leave her. Back home in Philadelphia, she was a wallflower, with as much attraction as this old rattan side table. Her chest ached so, you'd have thought her corset shrank in the heat.

She wanted to be loved.

Mr. Wellington is quite smitten, cousin. Why couldn't she be smitten right back?

The reason was standing right in front of her.

She backed up, knocking her large Bible from the table. *Texas Jack,* her latest dime novel, slipped from his hiding spot between the words of the saints.

She reached for it but stopped short.

Bending down beside her, Mr. Gray's attention went from the dime novel, to her sticky fingers, to finally rest on her face.

His disappointment made her look away.

It wasn't fair. Those dime novel stories were her one small fancy in life. The only thing left to a woman her age if she didn't want to join the knitting circle or the garden club. Other ladies her age were busy being wives and mothers, and society had no use for her other than as a companion to interesting girls. She had no experience with children, nor could she cook. All she knew of life, and love, was watching the way her parents doted on each other and kept her safe and close.

Harmon's strong fingers collected the yellow-covered paperback, and then her brown leather Bible and placed them on the table when he stood. "You really do like those novels, don't you?"

Her throat thickened. "Yes." *Oh Lord, don't let me cry.*

"I'm all for books, but I hope you get out and enjoy yourself, too."

"I enjoyed our walk."

"Me too." He tipped his hat and turned for the door.

"Wait, Mr. Gray. Please."

He glanced back, his face cautious.

"Ah...would you wait here a moment?" Kathryn dashed toward the kitchen sink, licking the chocolate off her fingers.

She hurried back and stood right straight in front of him. What had Jane told her about Mr. Wellington? *Let him know you're interested.* How did one go about doing that?

"Mr. Gray? I'm interested..."

His eyes widened.

No wonder. "I mean..." She swallowed but the dryness in her throat didn't go away. Neither did the growing grin on his face. "I mean, I'd like to spend, oh, I'd enjoy...I'd be happy to go to your ranch with you. Or wherever you want to take me. Uh..." She closed her eyes and reached for the table to steady herself.

"Miss Morton?"

She licked her lips and opened her eyes. "Yes?"

He'd come close enough she could smell sunshine on his denim shirt, close enough she could see a small patch of whiskers he'd missed on his chin, right under his mouth.

He tipped his hat back a bit and moved closer, raising a finger to hover under her nose. "You have some right there."

One side of his mouth lifted before the other and he let his fingertip fall away. "Any more chocolate around here?"

She'd lost the ability to speak. A sudden warm breeze blew over her—except there wasn't a drop of wind, and the heat settled deep under her skin.

She stepped back and rocked the table again. "No. I ate it all. I'm sorry."

"Me too, because it looks mighty tempting." He kept his eyes fixed on hers while heading for the porch door. "Tomorrow, then?"

"Uh-huh."

When he was out of sight, she dropped to the wicker chair.

Harmon Gray, you do something strange to my insides.

Something new and not appropriate for spinsters. But if a man that good looking, and of the same age, wanted to flatter her, it would be rude to stop him.

She considered herself, mirrored by daylight in the window glass. She wasn't all that bad, was she?

She headed for the kitchen and requested a piece of string. After Graciana provided it, Kathryn returned to her room, gathered the seven dime novels she'd brought, thumbed through them one last time, and restacked them into a nice tidy, tied-up package for the burn bin.

Wonderful words. But imaginary lives. He was right.

She had a real life, a new life, spinning around her, and she didn't plan on going back.

Do not be afraid, nor be dismayed, for the Lord your God is with you wherever you go.

Kathryn tightened her bun and her resolve. No longer would she let willy-nilly-ness hold her back, not after seeing what a bit of gumption had garnered her with Mr. Gray.

Do not be afraid.

The Lord surely must be with her on this because He'd provided a clear, starry, moonlit night. Perfect for a walk.

In a graveyard? Yes. A graveyard. Where nothing was going to happen.

Well, if it was nothing, why did her legs feel like she'd had too much of mother's medicinal? Gracious! She hadn't even left the room yet. She hadn't even stood up.

It was this sneaking around nonsense. Sneaky felt like she'd put on someone else's shoe by accident. It just didn't fit.

With Jane asleep, Kathryn took a deep breath, squared her shoulders, and proceeded to dress in her darkest shirt and skirt. The door hinges whispered, the hall was silent, the stairs... The very top step squeaked as though she'd tripled her weight since dinner. If anyone asked, she'd say she was merely on her way to the kitchen.

Her stomach knotted up into a Texas-sized regret at the idea of making up a lie.

Mr. Gray felt assured she'd never be out at night, alone, but this was a safe part of town, and the axe murderer was long gone—she was sure of it. If cowardly vandals were willing to be out at night doing harm, she could at least be brave enough to spy on them, if it helped Mrs. Collins.

Lord, I know my fears hold me back in so many ways. I have to do this.

Outside, the gothic silhouette of Austen Abbey was the same lovely building that earlier glowed of sunlight and released the sounds of feminine laughter. Nothing was different except the sweet night air lacked the dusty taste of daylight.

There was absolutely nothing to be afraid of.

She'd pocketed a small matchbox and carried the back porch's lantern. Bright moonlight deepened the shadows and painted a patchwork before her. She darted from dark patch to dark patch.

This wasn't so bad.

Except for the cold chill rolling up her back and tickling the nape of her neck. She stopped.

And waited.

She swallowed—the noise so loud in her ears anyone would hear it.

She took another step and heard it again, and turned suddenly. Her heart thumped so in her throat, it frightened her. Another deep breath helped. No one was there.

But the clatter of approaching horses and wheels sent her for the shelter of the nearest tree. She yanked her hand off the bark. Who knew what creatures crawled there? She shivered. Something moved above her in the branches, but she stood completely still until the carriage passed.

A dog barked out a warning in the distance. She took a step. This time, rather than keeping to the shadows, she walked the middle of the street, accompanied only by the scuffling scrape of an occasional stone.

Something dipped past her head, a silent bird slipping through the dark. Then another.

She patted at her hair to chase the shiver across her scalp. Those were black, winged beasts, not birds.

Behind her...just the crackle of a dry leaf.

Except it wasn't.

Something, or someone, followed her. She walked faster.

Conscious of the white lace trim at her wrists glowing in the scrappy moonlight, she folded her arms against her stomach. Every muscle in her body was tight, every inch of skin prickled.

Another tree, a deeper dark. She ran to it, her heart pounding, and put the tree between herself and the assailant. She froze, watched, and waited. All she heard was rapid, heavy breathing. She covered her mouth. It stopped.

There was nothing there.

Something touched her skirts. She leapt back. "Go away. Whatever you are, go away."

Again the pressure. This time against her shin.

Her legs wobbled. She couldn't move.

Between the drumming of her heart, a cat's purring filled the silence.

Her breath escaped in a blast. "Silly beast. You nearly frightened me to death." For an elderly, oversized cat, Frank's faithful companion, Thor, moved fast. His ragged meow and pushy manners demanded a scratch between his ears. When she straightened again, she took three deep breaths and moved on.

There was nothing here now that wasn't here in the daylight. Including the arched cemetery gate—menacing in the moonlight. Time to light the lantern. She didn't need to trip over something and be found crawling around with a broken ankle.

Once struck, the match flared in a bright shower of stars, startling her and the cat.

If anything, the cemetery grew bleaker by lamplight. Every shadow crueler. Every stone colder.

And every direction seemed more confusing. Stillness moved with her. Despite her hope to catch sight of vandals in the act, she was glad to be alone.

She walked up the small rise and eventually found the tree and bench where Mr. Gray had sat. How often did he visit?

She might as well look while she was here.

Stone by stone, she searched and finally found it.

Harriet Gray. Beloved Wife and Mother 1840-1885

"Harmon says you're not here, ma'am, and I agree, but I wish you could tell me what to do because I really do care for him. How can I help things between him and your husband before I go?"

She sat on the bench. Despite its coolness, and the dark, Kathryn leaned back. Thor jumped up beside her, hinting at a place on her lap. She checked to see she'd returned the matches to her pocket, blew out the lamp, and allowed the cat to push against her hand. There were no ghosts in this cemetery any more than she was a detective in a paperback novel. And apparently, no vandals.

A gentle breeze played with her hair, cooling her before it stilled.

A hymn came to mind. The last one she'd sung in church before their trip. Would Mrs. Gray mind?

"Blessed assurance, Jesus is mine!" she sang softly. *"O what a foretaste of glory divine! Heir of salvation, purchase of God, Born of His Spirit, washed in His blood. This is my story, this is my song, Praising my Savior, all the day long."*

Thousands of stars sparkled in an indigo sky larger than any she'd ever seen. When was the last time she'd simply looked up into the night?

Today, she'd let her heart run free, and found it leading her away from fears and apprehension. The risks ahead might prove more than physical. *Guide me, Lord. Give me wisdom.*

Harmon caught his strutting-down-Congress-Avenue reflection in the solicitor's window. Here he was in his new, and first, pair of laced shoes, and sporting his fanciest Sunday suit and bowler hat. Determined not to let Jonathan manipulate Miss Morton. For her own good. Except the fact remained he was acting just like Jonathan. Blast this hat, he was dressing like him too, all bib and tucker.

Admit it, Junior, you fancy the girl.

Harmon couldn't ignore the tightness in his jaw. That weasel Wellington had always been a pain in his side. What did the dandy do other than preen—oh, and burn through his inheritance? Hadn't worked a day in his life.

But how could he say it? *By the way, miss, that feller is only after your money.* She looked mighty insecure already.

Aunt Augusta despised their rivalry—not that her nephews were related to each other, thankfully—but before Harmon spoke to her about Jonathan's motives, he must first examine his own.

Feminine chatter announced their presence before four Abbey girls, out for a morning of shopping, actually appeared. He'd been watching for them after seeing the school's carriage around the corner, and it might seem more casual to speak with Miss Morton now, rather than to call upon her as he'd planned.

"Mr. Gray!" Eleanor darted toward him, her feminine enthusiasm and form quite fetching. Unfortunately, she had that look in her eye.

That look in her eye. Had he seen it in Miss Morton?

Was he anything more than a flesh and blood link to a paperback hero? Kathryn needed to encounter life firsthand, not just through her imagination. And he'd like to help.

"Ladies." He tipped his hat to Eleanor, then Isabella, next, Jane and lastly to plain-dressed, so-shy Miss Morton, because he was drawn to her beautiful eyes first, and now could linger.

"What brings you to town, Mr. Gray?" purred Jane.

Why the little fox bothered with him at all was a mystery, as it was clear she didn't think him worthy. It must be some sort of female sport, like calf roping, and she was showing her prowess.

"Thought I might buy a new shirt for the barbeque on Saturday." His eyes traveled where they should not go. Not that it bothered Miss R a bit, from the way she kept emphasizing her assets.

Isabella and Eleanor traded gleeful glances. "You'll be there, then, Mr. Gray?"

"I expect so. I haven't missed one yet." He couldn't read Kathryn's wide-eyed reaction. Anticipation? Fear? "Miss Morton, might I have a word?"

Isabella squealed, suggesting she was not quite finished with finishing school.

Jane Radcliffe was at his side in a flash, turning him aside with a hand on his upper arm. She squeezed his bicep—actually squeezed it—and enlightened him. "I really think you should talk to Mrs. Collins about this plan to take my cousin to your ranch. I hardly think it proper."

He leaned closer to her ear. "You can rest easy. Aunt Augusta will be coming along as well."

Her surprise wore off quickly. "Even so, Kathryn is quite—"

"I'm a gentleman, whether you think so or not, and you must let her experience something of Texas." Harmon pulled away and glanced back at Miss Morton. Those big doe eyes, made bigger by corrective lenses, glanced down but returned to his and did not break away.

He was making progress.

The others moved on.

"Miss Morton, I'm glad I found you. I asked Aunt Augusta if I might walk with you again this evening. There's someone I'd like you to meet."

"I'd like that."

Her natural beauty bloomed with attention. Anticipation filled his chest with a stirring that Miss Jane's flirtations and impeccably packaged figure failed to ignite.

"I've also asked if the two of you might join me tomorrow at the ranch. Our cook is eager to fix you ladies something nice—he adores my aunt."

Miss Morton's brows lifted in concern.

"Now, don't you worry about Father. He'll be nothing but polite with Aunt Augusta around. You know, she lived with us after her husband died."

"Will I need to wear anything special?"

Something caused her cheeks to color nicely, but when she bit her bottom lip, he had to look away. "I can't say, miss. I don't know a thing about women's clothes, other than you look mighty nice today."

She glanced down at her clothing, her brows peaked.

"I hope you excuse my forwardness, making plans without asking you first."

"No, no, it's fine." Kathryn Morton's face brightened, and she glanced ahead to the girls. "I will see you tonight, then?"

"Yes. I look forward to it." Won't she be impressed when he took her to meet a woman who not only had gone to college in the east, but ran her own small business?

He remembered Miss Morton's hair loose down her back when they'd walked to the cemetery. He watched her hurry to catch up with the others. Why did a pretty gal like her dress like a matron schoolmarm? Probably the same reason she didn't expect to marry. What was it?

What she really needed, more than a riding lesson, was a kiss. Or two.

Whoa, Junior. Stop right there. That purity was part of her charm—that and an enthusiasm for life. Mother would have liked her, and it was the first time he could imagine such a thing. A broad smile lightened his step.

Until he looked up to see Wellington closing in.

Jonathan's mouth thinned as he studied Harmon's suit. "What are you about this day, cousin?"

"Shopping." *Cousin.* One day he was going to pop that popinjay right across his sarcastic mouth. Today he'd just walk away.

Jonathan caught up. "Take care you are not considering something that is already taken."

"Is that so?"

"Yes. Stop plying your cowboy charm on Miss Morton."

Harmon huffed at such bunk. "I'm just helping her see a bit of Texas before she leaves."

"I wish I believed you." Jonathan stopped at the entrance to Bennet's Boutique.

Given Miss Morton's eager acceptance of his plans for tomorrow, Jonathan had a surprise in store. With not so much as a nod, he darted into the haberdashery, and Harmon continued on his way. Good riddance.

Two blocks away, Frank—and the Austen Academy carriage—waited. The grizzly old cuss took one good look at Harmon's get-up and raised a brow. His lopsided, all-knowing grin said it all. This wasn't the first Abbey girl to catch Harmon's eye, but it had been awhile.

That one had been more like Jane. Pretty, wealthy, vain, and most importantly, a Northerner. The perfect choice to annoy his father.

Frank nodded but couldn't hide amusement. "Harmon?"

"Can't a man buy a new shirt? Dress up once in a while?"

"This better not have to do with Jonathan and Miss Morton."

"You think I should stand by and let him manipulate her just because he needs a wife with money?"

"Is that what he thinks?"

Harmon studied Frank's growing smirk. "What do you know about it?"

Frank straightened up and got right in Harmon's face. "Miss Morton's a fine gal. I don't want to see her hurt."

"Neither do I." What was going on?

"Then you'd better take a good long look at your reasoning. I expected more from you."

"I'm not going to hurt her."

Frank backed off. "Oh, I see. Tell me how that works, son."

Son? "I know what I'm doing."

"I'm sure you think you do, Junior."

Junior was worse. "Frank, I don't want to discuss it." A harmless flirtation was good for her, wasn't it?

The old soldier looked up and down the street before turning sharp eyes on Harmon. "Don't you think of bringing a wife home till you and your pa make peace."

Wife? He wasn't going to marry her, just win her affections, just... His head began to throb. He swore under his breath and hung his head. "Father started this a long time ago—"

"Did you sleep through Sunday's sermon, 'cause you just don't seem to get it, do you?"

Harmon shook his head and walked away. Frank used to be friends with Father, and Harmon didn't see him coming around to visit.

Put away wrath. Put away bitterness. Yeah, he'd heard the sermon all right.

Kathryn's legs felt like ants crawled inside them when she, Jane, and Mr. Wellington crossed the Colorado Bridge, rumbling along in his barouche—or was it a phaeton? To avoid the view of the river and the jelly-like sensation in her limbs, Kathryn focused on Jane's eyes and brows, which performed admirably over each of Mr. Wellington's witty remarks.

"Where are we going now, Mr. Wellington?" Kathryn asked, hoping they'd soon turn back for the Abbey.

"I have a surprise for you, though I think Miss Radcliffe has guessed."

Jane giggled. "Mr. Wellington has planned a picnic!"

"What? Now?" Kathryn's stomach sank. "But what about dinner? Does Mrs. Collins know we won't be there?"

Jane fussed with a finger curl at her temple. "I left her a note. She can't very well tell *you two* what you may do."

"But—" Kathryn swallowed back the taste of harsh words. No, no, no! Harmon Gray was coming for dinner and had asked to walk with her later. "When will we return?"

"Do you have plans, Kathryn?"

"I—" She squared her shoulders and clamped her mouth shut. Maybe frustration would shoot the words right out. "I do, yes. Mr. Gray is coming to dinner and asked if I might walk with him. He has someone he'd like me to meet."

Mr. Wellington sighed. "Oh, yes, with your interest in Texas... But I must tell you, my sweet"—he turned sad blue eyes her way—"the person in question is probably a lady friend. One of his many. All silly enough to find the idea of a cowboy interesting and...well, maybe he's finally picked one to make his wife. Heaven knows that run-down ranch needs a housekeeper."

She stared straight ahead, not daring to meet Jane's gaze, and blamed the jiggly tension in her stomach on the rough road. Had she only imagined a man like Harmon Gray could find her interesting?

Jane patted her arm with a *there now, there now* pity.

Did Jane know her just-so-pleased-with-myself smile thinned her lips dreadfully and would give her wrinkles some day? Right now, it felt good to think so, anyway.

And Mr. Wellington? He could just stop his pride-and-joy phaeton— or was it a surrey—and let her out and...well, she had no idea where she was, but she didn't want to be stuck here like the cucumber in a tea sandwich. A picnic? Jane would have a conniption fit if someone did this to her.

"Kathy, you mustn't worry about Mr. Gray. He's only trying to be a good host for you. I'm sure Mrs. Collins asked him."

"Yes, and I hate to say it, but I think you'd be sorely disappointed with a trip out to the Gray ranch." Mr. Wellington nudged her with his elbow. "We have so little time together this week as it is."

And precious little time with her cowboy. That cowboy, who, according to Mr. Wellington, wasn't interested in her after all. She raised her head, willing herself to act like the news meant nothing to her.

She was just too darn...mannerly. Mr. Wellington had gone to so much effort, she couldn't bring herself to complain.

"Come now, Miss Morton. A picnic along the river?" He nodded to a couple passing them in a similar contraption. "You'll enjoy it so much."

"Maybe the first of many." Jane's lily-of-the-valley fragrance was as soft as her whisper. "Unless—" She leaned in closer, and her whisper became a hiss of warning in Kathryn's ear. "Unless you choose to ruin the best chance at marriage you'll ever have."

Jane did have a way with words.

Kathryn sighed. No wonder she read so many books. In fiction, she could handle outlaws, ghosts, and the odd mountain lion attack, and not have to pretend her heart wasn't breaking. How could she face Harmon Gray when his attentions had been no more than pity?

Seven

Fresh coffee and bacon drew Harmon into the ranch house kitchen. The sunrise cast an orange glow over the scrub brush visible from the window where his father stood.

He'd loved this view all his life. A fading sliver of moon gave itself over to the day. "I don't believe we'll be having company today." It was bad enough Father was as pleasant to be around as a mule with a toothache, but after last night's failed dinner—Jonathan had euchred him out of a few hours with Miss Morton—Harmon had decided it had been a bad idea all around. He'd been playing his own game with her.

"I'm sorry, son." The old man almost sounded sincere.

"I thought you'd be relieved."

"Just as well, isn't it?"

"I don't really know."

"Your aunt hasn't been here in years."

And she'd be shocked at what they'd let this place become.

Yet, he regretted not seeing Miss Morton's enthusiasm for the ranch. Somehow he'd thought that seeing her reaction to his home might be just what they needed. But that was selfish. He went to the big cook stove.

"Son?"

Harmon looked over his shoulder.

"I'm sorry for more than that girl not coming."

Harmon filled his cup and walked outside without responding, knowing he couldn't swallow it anyway. Now? Now, the old man wanted to call a truce?

A week ago, life had been simple.

Last night, with Miss Morton and Miss Radcliffe absent, and after Isabella and Eleanor left the Abbey's dinner table, Aunt Augusta admitted her fear. Jonathan, anxious for an infusion of funds, had set his sights on what he perceived, wrongly, to be the wealthy girl most likely to fall for his charms. Where he got that idea about Miss Morton, Aunt Augusta didn't know, but she blamed herself.

As it seemed the lonely, naïve girl had never even had a man's attention before, Jonathan's plan should have been effortless. Harmon had gone from finding her charmingly amusing and in need of protection to competing with Jonathan. And being almost as thoughtless of her sensibilities.

Well, not *that* low.

His tenderness for her threw him for a loop. She was so unlike anyone he'd ever admired, and he wanted to be the one at her side as she discovered the joys in each new day. But she was a soft-hearted woman and somehow saw him as the man he used to think he was. That made him ready for a change.

Change must be that chisel in his chest, scraping away at his heart.

Unless he was way off, she had feelings for him, feelings that, with a little encouragement, might lead to more. But was it right to encourage her when he had no idea what he could offer? Miss Morton deserved a settled man from a good home. Not a shoddy imitation of *Texas Jack*. And not this strife-filled home. Frank had been right.

Forgive.

One of the few cattle in the pen bellowed from boredom, and Harmon tossed his coffee across the dry earth. "I can't do it, Lord. Not yet."

A fine Texas day to be in love, and oh, how Kathryn loved Austin. The fragrant southern air, the birdsong new to her ear, the color of the pale, rough soil, the open horizons, and a rancher named Harmon Gray.

It didn't matter that he didn't love her back. It was the gift of this trip. She'd awakened with a wild, new joy in her chest. She'd sat out every dance in her life. No more.

Yesterday's impromptu picnic had cost her time with Mr. Gray. He'd waited for her, polite as he was, but left before they'd returned. Polite, but not interested in her for anything other than to please his aunt.

This morning, Kathryn happened to be watching out the front window of the wide landing—happened to be, because she'd been standing there far too long—when Mr. Gray arrived on horseback. No wagon meant there'd be no trip to the ranch today. Her stomach had been so full of aching recently, she wondered if she'd ever feel like eating again.

She stepped back from the window and glanced down at her new split skirt. Practical yet modern, and modest given its fullness. The latest fashion for horseback riding, and she'd been so excited to find it.

Apparently only her wild imagination would be riding off into the sunset.

A knock at the bedroom door, and a cheery yoo-hoo proved to be Mrs. Collins, slightly out of breath but smiling. "Miss Morton, Harmon is here and asked to speak with you."

"I don't think I can." Her gut twisted like it was oral report day in school, but this time she was too old to hide under the bed.

"Last night was a simple misunderstanding. Come along." Mrs. Collins led, and Kathryn followed, tripping into her when the headmistress stopped and put a hand on Kathryn's shoulder. "Life, if you live it right, keeps surprising you, and the thing that keeps surprising you the most...is yourself."

"I so admire all the things you've done."

"Well, my dear girl. Those words came from the mind of Jane Austen. A bright, single young woman who never traveled anywhere, nor married. But she understood the human heart."

"Well, I sure don't." Kathryn pressed her hand against her stomach, but it leapt into her throat at the sight below.

Mr. Gray waited in the entryway, hat in hand, and turned at the creak in the steps.

Her mouth went dry. She clung to the banister, descending slowly, and stopped before him.

"I'm sorry I missed you last night, Miss Morton. Apparently you were unaware of Mr. Wellington's plans."

"Yes, I'm sorry too."

"As it turned out, I have to cancel our plans for today as well."

She couldn't read his face and didn't trust herself to speak. She found no anger there—not that she'd expected it, but, well, he wasn't dying on the inside, was he?

He stepped forward. "I hope you are not too disappointed. Let's try another time?"

When? The next time she felt like dropping in to visit from Philadelphia? There'd never be another time. She moved away, determined to admire the bright orange petals of a wildflower bouquet on a small marble table. Her fingers shook, and she pulled them to her side. "Thank you for your kindness."

"If I don't see you before you leave, I wish you well in your future."

Her hand went to her throat, where her pulse thumped a dirge for her romantic dream. She didn't think she could face the prospect of leaving town and not seeing him anymore, but she hadn't expected it to be now, rather than the end of her stay. She couldn't help but look at him.

His face brightened. "No, I was wrong. We have the barbeque coming up. I'll see you then."

But he didn't move other than shifting his hat from hand to hand.

Go, so I can breathe.

"Miss Morton, will you come with me? Outside. It won't take long." He put out his hand.

She took it.

He moved so fast, she followed without thought until they stood five feet from Mr. Gray's horse.

She squeezed her fingers into one tight fist under her breastbone.

"I can't have you going home from Texas without being able to say you rode a horse."

She gasped. "I can't." She'd planned to be so brave, especially with Mr. Gray at her side. Now, the old familiar fear filled her so completely, she was unable to move.

"Henry is the most reliable friend I have. You'll be safe."

"Henry?" She put a shaking hand to her mouth and took a step back.

"Don't be frightened, please."

She looked from the horse to Mr. Gray, and a hole opened up inside her chest. She never talked about it; how could she explain?

"I want to do this for you. I won't make you, but I think you're underestimating yourself." Mr. Gray's arm went around her back. "He's very gentle. I wouldn't consider this if I didn't trust him."

"Mr. Gray, when I was young..." Tears burned her eyes, and her nose filled with pressure. She averted her head and waited. The words were stuck, and she shook her head, pulling away. "You see...my brother..."

The beautiful horse waited, flicking one ear.

"Was your brother hurt riding?"

A whispered "No" accompanied a subtle shake of her head while she gazed down at the gritty soil. "Not hurt—killed. My brother's name was Henry. How do you like that?"

He slapped his hat against his thigh. "Why shoot. Forgive me. I had no idea."

When she could answer, she faced him. "Of course not, and you were kind to ask. My brother climbed up the harness of our neighbor's carriage horse and fell off. It really wasn't my fault." She kept his gaze. "I really need to do this. Will you help me?"

Harmon showed her once how to mount the horse, then enjoyed the determined concentration on her blotchy face. Not only was she nervous, and rightfully so, but she was hardly an outdoorsy girl.

"Remember, put your foot up here, Miss Morton. Grab on to the horn and pull yourself up. Take a little hop with the other foot. Your skirt is wide enough to work but—"

"It's a *riding skirt*, Mr. Gray." She smoothed her hands along her hips and smiled, and if he wasn't mistaken, there was some teasing on those lips.

"Go on. I'll catch you if you slip."

She lifted her shoe toward the stirrup, once, twice, and then, completely red in the face, succeeded the third time. With her left hand on the horn, and a little hop, she dragged herself up with her right hand and crawled up into the saddle without him boosting her bottom.

The curl of those sweet lips could not hide her elation when her eyes danced with victory. "I bought the new skirt yesterday."

He had to laugh. "You really did want to try this, didn't you?"

"Yes. But I had no idea—well, I didn't expect it to bother me so much. My brother was always so fearless." Her smile had faded, but she radiated delight at her accomplishment.

"Well I admire your courage even more, then." He checked the stirrups. "May I shorten this for you?" He tugged on the stirrup and rested his hand on her little boot where it met her ankle.

"But I'm not riding anywhere, am I?"

"After all this, I think you can at least let Henry take you around the yard here." He finished shortening the strap and saw to the other. "It's called riding, not sitting." He guided her foot in place and patted her leg, then glanced up. "There, how's that?"

She didn't seem affronted in the least by his touch.

He took the reins in hand and walked Henry about the yard. Miss Morton gradually relaxed and grinned broadly at him. He might well have stopped a runaway train for how good it felt to see her like this. After a few lengthy Texas minutes, he led her to the front of the house with its mounting block.

"Had enough?"

"For now. Thank you."

"Next time you can use the block."

"You mean I could have used that, instead of—"

"Yes. I forgot."

The corner of her mouth tipped upward. "Spontaneity is one of your charms."

"And the others?"

She looked him over, out of the corner of her eyes. "Not humility."

Harmon laughed. "You pegged me, there." He offered a hand. "You and your fancy skirt did fine. Real fine. Here now, get down. I'll help you."

She obliged, a bit less awkwardly, and he put his arms around her waist as she slid down, her hands finding his shoulders.

Harmon was in no hurry to give up his hold. Why had he canceled her visit to the ranch? They could have had the whole day together.

Because he'd thought it was for the best.

Because he wasn't supposed to want her company or want her looking at him the way she was looking at him. He'd only wanted her safe from Jonathan and to make her smile, to boost her confidence. Now all he wanted to do was kiss her.

She fluffed her blouse off her skin. "Whoo. It's gotten quite warm, hasn't it?"

"Mm, yes." He stepped back, releasing her. "I best be on my way. I'm sorry to learn of your loss, but I think your brother would have been proud of you."

She nodded. "Thank you."

Harmon reached for her hand and squeezed it, maybe too long. He considered pulling her closer. She didn't look ready to argue. In fact, she made no attempt to look away. He rubbed his thumb across her knuckles. "I don't know if you'll ever come back to Texas, and if you do, you'll likely be married. And...well, what I'm saying is I've enjoyed your company this week."

He led Henry away before mounting the saddle and removing his hat. "I'll see you Saturday, Miss Morton."

He only looked back once. She hadn't moved. He could turn around and go right back to her and kiss her like he wanted to. But this was supposed to be about her. Just because he'd gone and fallen for her and every beat of his heart said that was reason enough, didn't mean he was anywhere near the man she deserved.

He had some business to attend to first.

Eight

"The moment I saw you I knew."

Kathryn dragged her foot to slow the Abbey's back porch swing and looked up into Jonathan Wellington's earnest gaze. She'd been thinking of Harmon, and she didn't want to, because when she did think of him, she couldn't seem to think at all.

"Knew what, sir?"

Before he answered, Jane popped her head around the porch door. "Good night, Kathryn. You too, Mr. Wellington."

When Jane was gone, he cleared his throat and straightened his four-in-hand tie to line up nicely with his knobby Adam's apple. "Please don't leave on Saturday after the barbeque. I can't bear the thought."

Actually, the sooner she left...the sooner her feet would touch the ground again when she walked. She might never have a moment alone again with Harmon, but it didn't change the fact the sky was bluer and the birds sang truer today. She'd hummed her way through the afternoon and eaten two helpings of dinner.

Jonathan grabbed her hand with such urgency, she flinched—thank God she hadn't said *not that hand!* Harmon had held it so sweetly.

"Not leave?" she asked, but his eyes confirmed it. "My parents are expecting me, and I am engaged to act as Isabella's companion for her trip back east."

He stood and led her into the twilight. "From what I hear, Isabella now has plans to stay. You must ask Aunt Augusta."

"Really?" The darkening sky created a new shade of blue and held only one star bright enough to flicker this early.

"My dear Kathryn." Jonathan nested her hand in his.

He was beginning to get on her nerves, and the idea of it shocked her. *I'm lucky to have his attentions.* She didn't feel lucky.

He led her to the bench. Her bench. And it seemed a little wicked to be out in the dark with a man. She sat.

Still claiming her hand, he dropped to one knee.

"Mr. Wellington! Your pants will be ruined."

"You must have known this was coming. Has any man ever been as besotted with a woman as I have been with you? Your beauty and wit, intelligence, grace. Kathryn, please."

Had he been drinking? She tugged her hand free.

"Please consider being my wife. I know this is early—"

"Early? I barely know you, and my parents—my father—"

"And if you leave, it will break my heart. Unless I know we are pledged to spend the rest of our lives together."

Her head throbbed. She wasn't sure she could get through one more day with him, without losing her patience. A lifetime? *Oh mercy.*

"No. Father wouldn't—I can't stay. Besides, they won't believe me if I tell them."

"They'll believe it when they receive my request that they come to Austin. Please tell me they'll learn to care for me as much as you do."

That much? Hm.

Even now, she could hardly stop thinking of Harmon Gray instead. "I hardly think they could come to visit. The cost alone, when I have so little for—" Had Mother even planned a trousseau? "My father rarely takes more than a day off, much less a week and I couldn't bear to—"

"What do you mean?"

"I mean, his job at the newspaper. He's the senior typesetter." She leaned in to whisper. "I don't like to brag, but he runs the entire department and trusts no one to do the front page but himself. Except for Monday's paper because, of course, he doesn't work on Sunday."

Jonathan stood and turned away. "Are you telling me they couldn't come to meet me here?"

"I'm afraid so, sir. And I couldn't ask them." She mustn't tell him no so quickly. It seemed so cruel. "Mr. Wellington, your kind offer has... honored me, but I ask that you allow me a day to consider—"

He looked so stricken, poor man, holding his head in his hands.

"Until tomorrow, Mr. Wellington?"

"Yes, of course. You are wise to be wary of making a mistake, especially with someone you hardly know, and a marriage that would take you so far from your parents."

They'd be popping buttons to see her married, though not likely expecting her to live anywhere other than Philadelphia. "They'd be quite—" Shocked. But there was no need to boast of that bit of news. OLD MAID FINALLY RECEIVES PROPOSAL.

"Good-bye, Miss Morton." Jonathan glanced back during his hasty retreat.

How brave to throw caution to the wind for the leanings of your heart. If she hadn't met Harmon Gray, she might have learned to love Mr. Wellington and his passionate nature.

How could she explain to anyone why she'd have to say no?

Friday morning drizzled in. Kathryn stood on the sheltered balcony overlooking the front lawn. Such a shame. Austin Abbey bustled with preparations for Mrs. Collins's annual alumni barbeque the next day. A celebration of new beginnings.

Like this trip. She'd had so many expectations.

But never had she expected heartache.

Harmon.

And then there was poor Jonathan Wellington. Would he get over her upcoming refusal, as fast as he had fallen for her?

Soothed by the steady rain, Kathryn moved through her morning as though slogging through Pennsylvania mud. Even Jane seemed quite subdued—and very thoughtful. Perhaps she was coming down with a fever?

The servants Cora, Graciana, and her daughter Vicente chatted merrily in Spanish, with nary a breath in between a separate conversation in English with Frank. Kathryn caught mention of the cemetery, and learned a servant girl from a banker's home had gone missing yesterday, the anniversary of one of the notorious murders.

That poor girl. Kathryn quickly prayed for her safety.

Philadelphia's cemetery ghosts always proved to be young men with an excess of alcohol and time on their hands. Still, she couldn't blame Austin's citizens for their nervousness after such a brutal time in their recent past.

Somewhere down the hall, a bell trilled. No, it was a telephone. A telephone! Her parents certainly could not afford such a newfangled luxury. Mrs. Collins waved at her to wait, while the headmistress disappeared into her office. It was rather exciting. After a short conversation, Mrs. Collins called her.

"There's a young woman and her mother here to visit. Of course, it's not the best time, but I didn't want to send them away. Would you come with me? Perhaps you can speak to the girl while I show her mother around?"

"Yes, but I know so little about the Abbey."

"But you know how to make someone feel at ease."

That compliment stuck with Kathryn as she met Lady Wentworth and her daughter, Lila. Just as Mrs. Collins had planned, Kathryn found herself walking with the quiet, dark-haired girl. If it were possible, Lila Wentworth seemed even shyer than Kathryn, though she carried on a pleasant conversation as she became more comfortable. They were laughing when the older women met them outdoors.

"What did you think of her?" Mrs. Collins asked after the mother and daughter left.

"I think she'd be a lovely addition to the Abbey. She's quite interested in history and French."

"And you? Did you enjoy speaking with her and showing her around?"

"Ever so much. Yes! Thank you for asking me."

Kathryn felt a sense of accomplishment that brightened her afternoon. On her way to her room, she looked out the window of the small second floor room below the Abbey's turret. The crunch of an arriving carriage sent her inside to watch Jonathan Wellington step out. From the gloomy pace of his approach, face hidden under his umbrella, he must have an inkling of her refusal.

Rather than delay, she hurried down to the beautiful foyer. Today was a new day—a day to stand up and speak her mind. His broken heart could have been avoided if she'd been honest with him from the start, and refused Jane's meddling.

He smiled weakly and removed his hat. "I must first apologize for rushing you."

"Come in and sit. I have made a decision."

As she'd watched other women do, she preceded Mr. Wellington into the drawing room and sat piously on the edge of a chair.

Dark circles ruined his handsome face. He looked positively wretched. "Please end my suffering, Miss Morton."

"I am sorry to say this, but I am going to have to decline your offer, sir. I am not sure I could make you happy. I'm—" *Stop belittling yourself.* "It does not mean I don't appreciate it."

His hand wiped across his face, and the dear man forced a smile. "Unselfish as always, Miss Morton. My heart is broken, of course, but you give me the courage to go on." He stood. "And rather than have everyone see my despair, I will leave you now." Mr. Wellington bowed and turned for the door.

"Wait."

He froze.

"I release you from our dinner plans for tonight, but I hope to see you tomorrow, if I haven't ruined the party for you."

Confusion clouded his face but he kept his composure. "I will try to attend, but I'm not sure my heart can take it. You'll understand."

She did. All too well. Yet...what if she'd said yes? It would be her heart breaking now instead, and that was a terrible way to start a marriage. Especially when Mr. Wellington would always remind her of Harmon Gray.

Friday night's dinner was early and light, for the Martinez women and Cora had little time for anything but party preparations.

Kathryn needed busywork and buzzed down the hall toward the headmistress's office, only to stop at the rich sound of Harmon's voice. "I can imagine his face when he realized her situation." A sound tasting like chocolate. Too late, she backed away, trying not to eavesdrop.

His face appeared from the doorway. "I was just leaving, Miss Morton."

Yet he stared, holding her captive until turning back to his aunt. *Breathe in. Breathe out.*

He bade Mrs. Collins good-bye and Kathryn looked aside, unable to watch his exit.

"Come in, Miss Morton."

Kathryn steadied her nerves by focusing on this small, warm room she admired for its orderliness and Queen Victoria's portrait on the wall. "Is there anything I can do to help for tomorrow?"

"How are you at flower arrangements?"

"Awful."

"Tying bows and bunting?"

"Worse."

"Do you sing?"

"No, not well. I'm afraid I only excel at reading and listening."

"I forgot to tell you. Frank found your novels near the trash bin." Mrs. Collins leaned back in her chair, smiling. "He's been reading them this week."

A small thing, but it encouraged Kathryn's spirits greatly. "I must ask, ma'am. Is it true another student has canceled?"

"I'm afraid so. Memories of our city's dark days run rampant. But I hope her family reconsiders, as we've just heard the missing girl has returned. Married, not murdered."

Kathryn gasped. "Oh, that is a relief!"

Mrs. Collins rose and marched her tiny, practical feet around the desk. "You are such a thoughtful girl, and I insist your job here tonight, and tomorrow, is to enjoy what you can of our company. I'm going to miss you, Kathryn."

Kathryn's nose plugged up, and the rims of her eyes burned a warning. *Don't cry.*

"I'm sorry for that business with Jonathan. I'm sure you did the right thing."

"You are? He seems upset."

"Jonathan will bounce back. Don't be surprised to see him acting his old self tomorrow." Mrs. Collins's beautiful British vowels, and her caring eyes, made Kathryn long to be home, wrapped in her mother's arms.

"Really?"

"I expect he may have learned a lesson." Mrs. Collins brushed a loose wave back into place on Kathryn's head. "Don't fret. Relax and rest."

Kathryn returned to her room, relieved she'd handled the proposal well. Harmon's face came to mind, and then the words she'd overheard. *I can imagine his face when he realized her situation.*

The sharp crush of cold, hard truth stole her breath, and she sat abruptly on the edge of the bed.

No wonder Mr. Wellington's surprise when he'd learned her parents were good working class people with simple tastes. His nervousness this morning hadn't been fear of rejection but fear she'd accept his rash proposal.

Had Harmon Gray been similarly misinformed?

Kathryn leaned into her pillow, wrapping it over her aching head. She felt small and empty inside. How could she have been such a fool?

Nine

Hidden in the room's recessed corner, Kathryn waited in her darkest dress. She couldn't have slept if she wanted to. Her pride at having the courage to say *no thank you* to Mr. Wellington's proposal had disappeared in a flood of embarrassment.

Jane's sad eyes had confirmed it. Mr. Wellington, and likely Mr. Gray as well, hadn't been interested in her in spite of her mousy looks, bookish brain, and timid personality.

And certainly not *for* those reasons.

He'd thought she was Jane's wealthy cousin, a newspaper heiress.

As much as her heart ached, she wouldn't have missed this trip—the adventure of a lifetime. If she never married, she at least knew the excitement of attraction, the heart-racing nearness of a man who turned her heart to a steam engine, and the surprising sight of a gentleman on his knee asking for her hand.

The most remarkable man in Texas had put her on his horse and laughed along with her after tolerating her tears. She couldn't be all that bad.

Maybe she would find someone to love.

She'd learned courage on this trip. Courage to do something without knowing the outcome. Courage to risk a little pain or heartache.

She'd seen cowboys, and cattle, Mexicans and mesquite. It wasn't a complete loss.

At dinner, Isabella, the young Abbey graduate, had confirmed she was staying to pursue an education and marriage, leaving Kathryn to travel home alone on the train.

Now, in the dark of the evening, she closed her fingers around Frank's gift, the newest Beadles dime novel, and held it close. She'd no longer feel shame in the small distractions populating her unpretentious life.

Jane rolled over, mumbled in her sleep, and snuggled deeper under the sheet.

The servant girl's return gave further proof the streets were safe. It freed Kathryn, *the New Kathryn*, for one final challenge. For herself and for Mrs. Collins, she must dispel the ghost rumors and help Austin Abbey.

She could put it off no longer and descended through the silent house. She borrowed a rain slicker off the back room's pegs, lit the lantern, and left.

She had to get there first. The walk to the cemetery was quiet, with only the gentle taps of raindrops landing on her coat. Once inside the gates, and over the rises of the cemetery, she caught sight of a weak light under a tree.

Her heart began a booming call to action. Continue on, or go back? She mustn't confront the vandals, only observe them long enough to provide the information Mrs. Collins could give the sheriff.

She checked her pocket for extra matches and opened the lantern's small door to blow out the flame. Kathryn stood a long time before moving. The light hovered in the distance, and she moved closer.

A small breeze rustled branches, covering her footsteps. She heard no voices—unusual, she thought, as vandals often worked in groups. Young men were not known to be a quiet species; ghosts were notoriously silent.

The light flickered ahead and, this time, male laughter confirmed her suspicions. Young hoodlums. She tried to dry off her glasses, but it was useless. Picking her way forward, she slipped on a small branch, and it cracked under her foot. She didn't move.

Branches, or raindrops, or nuts plopped to the ground around her, at times mimicking footsteps. The voices had stopped or were blocked by the rushing blood in her ears. Every inch of flesh on her back told her to run.

Something solid shoved her between the shoulders, and she went hard to the ground. Her knee slammed into stone, her lantern and glasses flying.

"Don't come back or you'll never leave."

Her hand went to her leg. The attacker's footsteps pounded across the earth, disappearing into the night. With such stinging pain—*don't throw up*—it took a moment to realize she'd heard a gunshot. It couldn't be anything else.

She opened her eyes to approaching lantern light, carried not by a ghost but by the solid figure of a lone man.

Kathryn tried to push herself up to escape, desperate to avoid him, but he raised the light.

"Who's there?"

She scrambled to her hands and knees and dragged her already scraped hand across the rough grass and soil for her glasses. The lamplight grew until she was bathed in the yellow glow.

"Who are you?" he demanded again.

She sat back on her haunches and grimaced in pain. She squinted into the darkness and, although the light shadowed his face, knew it was the elder Mr. Gray. "It's Miss Morton. From the Abbey."

"Here? What in the world has you out here now, girl? You're that fascinated with death you come looking for it at night?"

"I came to find out who was causing trouble."

"You're either the silliest girl I ever met or the bravest."

Oh Lord. Humiliation shoved nausea aside.

"Did you see them?"

She wiped her eyes. "One of them knocked me down."

"Are you hurt?" He reached forward and took her arm. "Come under the tree."

"Wait. Don't move. I've lost my glasses."

He blew out a tired breath and dropped down to help. Lamplight and discomfort etched his face, and she realized it wasn't just impatience but actual pain. Few soldiers came home unscathed. They both patted around.

"We've checked enough. I'll drop my bandana here and look again in daylight. The grass is thick with all this rain." He gave her a hand up and, though her knee ached, she bit back a complaint. "I've started checking things over at night. Guess I was a bit late to help you. Walk over this-a-way and you should miss stepping on your spectacles."

Mr. Gray led her to the bench under the tree where she'd first seen him. "Weren't you afraid to come here?"

No. As a matter of fact, she hadn't been. "I know you think I'm a silly girl, but I'm tired of these rumors of ghosts hurting Mrs. Collins and the Abbey."

He took his hat off and wiped his forehead before returning it. "I don't know anyone else who has moved a muscle to help."

"So far, all I've done is manage to lose my glasses."

"We'll find them, don't worry."

Mr. Gray said no more, and Kathryn's body relaxed. The calming plop of fat raindrops striking leaves soothed her and gave her a sense of peace despite the fact her last effort to help Mrs. Collins and the Abbey had failed.

"I should be going, sir."

"You're not walking home alone. Can you even see where you're going?"

"I don't really need to wear my glasses all the time."

"So you hide behind them?"

Kathryn studied his profile by lamplight. "Is that what you think?"

"You wouldn't be the first person to do it."

That was true enough. If no one noticed her, no one would then find her lacking. "Frank told me about you. About the war. I can't imagine you need to hide from anything with all you did."

"I wasn't afraid in battle. It was coming home when so many better men didn't. Good men died." Mr. Gray stood and walked a few steps away, his oilcloth coat whispering in movement.

"I don't understand."

"I don't either. I wasted a lot of time and hurt the people I loved." He took his hat off and set it on the bench between them. "I admire your efforts, miss. Thinking of Augusta's school like that. Worrying about the graves. You're a right fine young lady, and you've been good for my son. I saw his mother's Bible opened up on his bed yesterday. I have to think it had to do with you."

Warmth flushed her face—not for any irrational hopes but for knowing Harmon was on the right track. "I've been praying for the two of you. I hope you don't mind me saying it."

Mr. Gray looked off into the distance, but she didn't think he was angry.

"I'm going home tomorrow. I'm sorry we didn't have more time to chat."

He turned to face her. "Let's get you back to the Abbey."

"Gray? Is that you? Miss Morton?"

They both looked toward the approaching light.

"It's me—Frank."

Mr. Gray lifted the lantern. "Watch out for the missy's glasses, somewhere over there. Go around to the left."

Frank came up to them and put his hand up while catching his breath. "Am I glad to see you, Miss Kathryn."

"Is something wrong? Is Jane ill?"

"No, it's you I'm worried about. After I saw someone down the street, I noticed the coat and lantern missing off the porch. Couldn't figure anyone but you out on a night like this." He stepped closer. "What are you doing here, anyhow?"

"You wouldn't believe me if I told you." Kathryn winced when she stood. Her knee would be bruised in the morning. "Can you take me back, Frank? It will save Mr. Gray the trip."

"I'd be glad to."

She turned to Mr. Gray. "Thank you for helping me." She offered a hand, and he covered it with a gentle squeeze. "I'd like to hear about the war, but I know it must be difficult to talk about. May I write to you?"

"That'd be fine, missy. I'll look for your glasses at daylight." He shifted his stance and looked at Frank. "One of those no-accounts knocked her down. I fired my pistol, and they took off."

Frank's mouth dropped open and then, frowning, he looked her up and down.

"I'm fine," she insisted. "Really, it's just my knee."

Mr. Gray rubbed a hand across his wet face. "I'll go to the sheriff's tomorrow and tell him what I know. For that matter, I'll go to all the papers and demand they issue an apology for the trouble they've caused."

"That's wonderful, sir. I hope they listen." Hearing it redeemed a dreadful day. She turned to Frank and realized the rain had stopped. He offered his arm, and she obliged. "Good night, Mr. Gray."

Three city blocks passed before she had the urge to speak. The Abbey's turret came into view against a sky full of moon-chased rain clouds. "I suppose you know about Mr. Wellington."

"Yes. You're well rid of him."

"And Harmon Junior? Was that all an act, too?"

"He's not perfect, miss. He and Jonathan have always been so—"

"Competitive. I see it now." Were any of his feelings real?

"He'll be here in the morning, and you can decide if he's sincere.

You're a smart girl. I think you'll know."

Kathryn stopped in her tracks. "Smart? After what I just did?"

"I don't rightly understand you, girl. You've got parents who love you?"

"They don't know any better."

"Now *that's* foolish. What makes you think you are any less worthy of love than anyone else? Did someone tell you different?"

"No, I've never fit in. God loves me too, but...oh, I do seem ridiculous, don't I?" She took a deep breath.

"I think you've been comparing yourself to others instead've accepting all the fine things you are."

Just like Mr. Gray. Was that what wearied him into such unhappiness?

At the back porch door, Frank helped her remove the oilcloth coat. "Now get yourself dried off and asleep, and no one needs to know about this little adventure of yours."

At least with Mr. Gray's promise, there might be an end to this ghost nonsense. "Thank you for your help, Frank. My adventure didn't end like I'd hoped."

"Your story's nowhere near done. Truth is, I've got my eye on a woman myself, and I'm determined to grow even older and grayer, with her."

"Oh, Frank. That's wonderful."

"You just wait and see, Miss Morton."

Ten

"What?" Kathryn's eyes opened the next morning to find Jane's too-close face.

"It's not like you to sleep so late," Jane said. "The meat has been cooking for hours. I can't believe you of all people would want to miss this. A real Texas event."

Sunlight burned around the edges of the drapery. "What time is it?"

"Nearly ten." Jane's voice faded away. "Kathryn, look at me!"

"What?" She didn't have to shout.

"Are you all right?"

"No. I'm not. I don't feel well." Though not enough to warrant bed rest, being under the weather did provide an option.

"I will tell Mrs. Collins and ask Cora to bring you something to eat."

"Don't go yet."

The mattress shifted under Jane's weight.

"Jane, Mr. Wellington's proposal—"

"It's all my fault. Mrs. Collins tried to stop him after she realized he had taken it that far." Jane's hand rested on Kathryn's arm. "I'm truly sorry I pushed you."

"Yes, but I know why, and it wasn't a selfish reason."

"Then you forgive me?"

It was Kathryn's turn to pat Jane's hand. "Of course, but will you let him know I have no ill thoughts toward him?"

Jane smiled, and, for the first time, Kathryn saw Mother's kindness in her cousin's features. Jane leaned closer. "When the heart is really attached, it's difficult to be pleased with the attention of anybody else." Jane's eyes widened at Kathryn's confusion. "Kathryn, I speak of Harmon Gray."

"What of him?" Hearing his name after the humiliation of yesterday was like re-injuring a bruise.

"Don't you want to see him on your last day? The train boards at five. The day is already short, and if I felt that way about a man, as you do for him—"

"How did you...?" Kathryn sat straight up.

Jane walked to the wall rack holding Kathryn's three dresses. "You don't suppose I haven't noticed. He is quite handsome, and thoughtful. I admit it now." She raised a brow at Kathryn.

"But he's a cowboy, Jane. And I don't know if his attentions were any less selfish than Mr. Wellington's."

"He's a gentleman and a rancher with hopes for a successful future. I don't believe he played you false."

"You admire him now?"

"Yes." Jane's shoulders rose and fell. "I was wrong."

Kathryn pulled herself around and propped herself up on elbows, schooling her face to say what she must say. "If you care for him, I wish you the best."

Jane tossed her dress choice for Kathryn across the chair. "Wear this one." Jane put her hands on her hips and stared intently at her. "If I'd been thinking clearly when we arrived, rather than judging him...Well, he'd never look twice at me now, and I deserve it. Why, he's already asked after you, all soft in the eyes..." Jane's own dreamy look faded. "Oh, I've been so awful. I wish I had half your goodness. Seeing Mr. Gray moping around makes me realize...I'm so sorry." Jane squatted down, face-to-face. "You are a lovely girl and you've got a special man waiting for you."

"I'm not going downstairs." Kathryn swung her legs around and sucked in her breath as she sat up, glancing at her black-and-blue knee before quickly covering it. "I can't. You must understand."

"I don't, honestly." Jane stood. "You've always been so smart, but avoiding that man is downright unreasonable." She scowled. "Whatever did you do to your hair?"

"It rained last night."

"Not in here."

"I needed some time to think. Go and enjoy yourself. Please." Kathryn grabbed Jane's hand when she started away. "I shall miss you, Jane, but I know you are going to do well here."

Jane leaned back and kissed Kathryn's cheek. "Where are your glasses, by the way?"

"Around. Somewhere." She hoped to never have to tell. In daylight, the fact she'd taken such a chance last night shamed her. Thank God she hadn't been severely injured. Would Frank and Mr. Gray really keep her secret?

That afternoon, Kathryn left her room only long enough to look out the back window. Harmon stood alone, watching the house, and she stepped back. Was his interest genuine, or purely offered on his aunt's behalf, or, like Mr. Wellington, had it been about some misguided notion that family money made her a good catch?

What was real? Only the hurt.

Minutes later, someone knocked at the door. It couldn't be him. Still... She dreaded it *not* being him.

"Miss Morton, are you awake?"

"Mrs. Collins?"

"May I come in?"

Kathryn opened the door, and Mrs. Collins reached up to lay a hand on Kathryn's forehead. "Are you feeling better?"

"Yes, but—"

"But not enough to come outside." The headmistress studied her carefully, her lips pressed in frustration. She went to the window and pulled apart the drapes. "There are many people I wished you to meet."

"And Mr. Wellington is here?"

"Yes. And Harmon, but I suspect you know."

Kathryn's face answered for her.

"Frank told me what you did last night."

"I figured as much when Graciana came in to ask about my knee." She let her hair cover her face. "I've been such a fool this week, this whole trip. Trying to make something out of it that it wasn't supposed to be."

"What do you mean?"

"I thought I could go home a better person than I left, and in trying so hard, I proved how right everyone has been about me." Oh, how she'd love to be cool and collected rather than a sniffly bundle of shaking hands and belly aches.

"Nonsense. I am proud of you. So many of our girls are interested in nothing more than finding a husband. An admirable goal for any young woman to be a mother and wife, but for some there is so much more. It is a true gift to put others first, Kathryn, though you did risk danger last night." Mrs. Collins tossed Kathryn her robe. "Here, put this on."

"But I fear I may live my whole life as nothing more than you see here."

"For someone as sweet as you, that can be enough, Kathryn, though I agree you have so much potential. But rather than hope to be someone else, there is nothing better than being the best you."

Kathryn crossed her arms over her chest and looked down at the floor rather than face the truth.

"Come to the back window." Mrs. Collins pulled her across the wide upper hall to look again over the activity below. Tables with festive cloths, chairs half-filled with partygoers, children running, mouthwatering smoke rising from the roasting meat. "Graciana's son Joe is here with his wife Hattie. She'd love to meet you. And Emmeline and Noah Whitley. Do you see her? I can't believe they have three children now. A dear, dear couple. The man with the limp was a Texas Ranger. I know you'd enjoy speaking with him."

Kathryn nodded.

Mrs. Collins put her arm around Kathryn's back. "The students who really excelled here found the courage to live to their full potential rather than conform to the expectations of others."

In the middle of the group, Harmon lifted a sun-kissed little girl. He smiled broadly until he glanced toward the window. Kathryn stepped back.

"He can't see you, but he'd like to. A good-bye at least?"

Kathryn's stomach set off an alarm. "I can't."

"All right. But I thought you'd like to know that his father came with him. A real answer to prayer. He went to the sheriff and the newspaper this morning with a full account of what's been happening at the cemetery." Mrs. Collins turned toward Kathryn's room. "You've done quite a bit in only a week's time."

"Thank you. You've been so good to me, ma'am. I'll never forget your encouragement." Kathryn's heart broke a little. The headmistress hadn't told her anything new, but coming from a confident, inspiring, no-nonsense version of her loving, but timid, mother had made the difference. *Oh, Mother. I owe you an apology.*

"Come down to the front door at four, and Frank will get you to the station. But I have an offer to make. Stay, and be my assistant for a year. Take some classes as well. Stay now, or go home and at least consider it." She paused at the door. "Do you know I never thought I'd fit in anywhere?"

"But you're so wise, and beautiful."

She smiled. "Thank you. But it's all because a certain handsome Texan rancher picked me—rather than one of the pretty girls—at a dance back east. Miss Radcliffe's mother could tell you I never had a chance at a beau. Too bookish. But when Mr. Collins looked at me, I felt beautiful in his eyes."

Tears threatened Kathryn's eyes.

"That's all it takes, my dear. Don't doubt the power of love, and never walk away from something because you don't think you deserve it."

Mrs. Collins hugged her as warmly as on Kathryn's arrival, but for much longer, and then left.

Stay here? She couldn't do that to her parents, could she? She'd certainly never get over her regard for Harmon if she had to see him every day. Her nose felt funny.

Wouldn't she soon be out of tears?

The door he'd watched all afternoon opened, and Harmon stood. But it wasn't her. Instead, Frank nodded to Aunt Augusta, signaling he was about to take Miss Morton to the railroad station.

"You'll never beat the devil around the stump sitting here."

"What's that, Father?"

Harmon's father slapped him on the back. "What are you waiting for, son?"

"How can she think my attentions were any more real than Jonathan's?"

"Were they?"

From the loss of sleep and the torn-up state of his insides..."Yes. But I can't say he didn't stir me to action."

"Anything else? Like me and the fact she's a Yankee?" Father laughed for the first time all afternoon. The first time in a long time.

"You really do like her?"

Father moved closer. "I do. And you care too much to let her go without setting things right."

"She doesn't need anyone else telling her what to think, and I can't very well ask her to stay." He'd prayed for guidance. Let her go, or speak up? He wanted her to stay all right, but the Gray Ranch had been no place for such a sweet girl.

"The girl has gumption, I'll say that."

"I didn't want her to think we could have a future, and I did a darn good job of it. She clearly doesn't want to see me."

"I think she needs you to prove she's been wrong about herself." Father put his hand on Harmon's shoulder. "You're might near as stubborn as I am, but I thought you had more of your mother's good sense."

Sad regret filled Father's eyes.

It had been there all along. When had he stopped hiding it?

"I'm sorry, son. I can't change the life your mother had any more than I can change the kind of father I was after she was gone. But I love you, and it took that girl of yours to show me I was holding on to the past."

That girl of mine? That kind, wonderful girl that I wish was mine?

"I'm sorry, too, Father." He stepped forward, wondering when the load of resentment he'd been carrying had fallen off.

"I'm proud of you. I want you to make your future the way you want it, not to worry about me and the ranch. It's yours if you want it. If not, I can move on. But right now it's time the Gray men did something right. Let's go."

Eleven

Kathryn shifted on the seat to take a last look as Frank's wagon rolled down the circular drive out onto Chawton Circle. The Abbey's gray stone facade blocked the view, but not the happy clamor of the party.

Her special, once-in-a-lifetime week was over, and she was going home changed, after all. That sense of a new beginning hadn't come with any promise of ease or enjoyment, just that it would be new.

And this raw pain in her chest was new.

The sky had cleared, but the air clung close and warm and thick like summer at home, calling Kathryn to finish her journey. She would treasure every mile of the United States going by her windows, talk with more people, eat more food, and enjoy every moment left of her great adventure. Mrs. Collins's gift of *Northanger Abbey* would have to wait. Without her glasses, and the need to filter out Cousin Jane's ramblings, there'd be no reading.

Frank placed her small trunk by those of other eastbound passengers and scuffed the soles of his boots as he waited with her. "They say the train will be on time."

"Thank you for everything, Mr. Mallory."

"You take care now, you hear me? I don't like you traveling back alone."

"I'll be fine. Really." She stared at him long enough to elicit a grin.

"Well, you're a brave girl, but I hope you don't get yourself into trouble trying to help every person you meet who needs a friend."

"Why would I do that?"

He raised his eyebrows and grinned. "I don't miss much. Just because I'm an old codger with manure on my boots. And you're no Texas Jack, so don't take on any train robbers."

"Not without my glasses." She laughed. "Why don't you get on back to the barbeque? I'm not alone now, neither will I be for the next week or more." She put her gloved hand out and shook his gently. "Please go. I appreciate your kindness last night."

"I'll be out in front until I see that train come and go. If you change your mind, I'll be there to take you back."

"That's not going to happen."

He nodded. "Good-bye, miss."

Kathryn turned, not able to watch the last of her Austin acquaintances walk away. Despite her harebrained ideas, a few new friends seemed to think no less of her, even had a good opinion of her. She held her head higher.

Lord, you've been telling me that for years. You and Mum and Father. What was I thinking to disagree?

A man resembling Jonathan moved past. Something about him disturbed her, and she immediately pulled her reticule and travel basket closer. Too many dime novels. He was no more a train robber than she was.

And cowboys weren't all heroes. Just some of them.

Harmon Gray. Stop making me think of you.

She might never read another western or romance again. *Lord, help me forget him.*

Nothing had ever hurt like this, and it wasn't Harmon's fault. She'd brought this on herself with dreaming things that could never be. Stretched her heart all out of shape. Maybe that was a good thing. It was part of change, after all. The biggest risks in life weren't physical.

She wandered to the far end of the building, one of fifteen or so people standing outside the terminal in its shade rather than inside.

"Stop! Come back here." A woman's shout startled Kathryn. "He took my bag!"

Kathryn wheeled around to face the Jonathan look-a-like dashing toward her, ready to run right through her. She shrieked and raised her arms to protect her chest and face. She couldn't let him get away. At the last moment she stuck out her foot. It was going to hurt.

It hurt.

At least the culprit's landing produced a convincing "umph" as well.

She spun around—saw a whir of shocked faces and rushed movements—and spun back. He scrambled to rise but she took two long steps and dropped directly to her knees, squarely onto his back, sacrificing her basket and reticule. Jane Austen soundly clumped him on the back of the head with two inches of English literature.

"Kathryn!"

"Miss!"

"Miss Morton?"

The hand on her arm was Harmon's, and she gazed into his anxious eyes while he raised her up. A nasty word startled her, and she caught sight of the thief glaring at her as he was dragged away by a railroad attendant and a rangy cowboy.

"Are you all right, little miss?" Harmon's father had gathered her belongings.

Frank, a bit winded, came to her side. "I can't leave you alone for a minute."

The realization of what she'd just done rattled through her and set her legs trembling. Harmon pulled her to face him, his hands on both her upper arms, and held her steady. "Are you hurt?"

Hurt? Was she? The concern on his face caught her breath. What was the question? "My knee hurts, but what are you doing here, and what will happen to that man?"

"Jail, I expect. Listen. You left something." He pulled a small brown paper package from his shirt pocket.

"What is it?"

"Father found your glasses. We brought them this morning, but in all the activity, Cora forgot to take them to your room."

"I'll put them in your little bag," Harmon Senior said, his eyes bright.

She looked to his son. "So that's why you came?" *Please say no.*

"Only one of the reasons, Kathryn."

Tell me.

The crowd's noise grew, and the train whistled its approach.

"Excuse me, sir, is this your wife?"

Harmon broke his gaze to glance at the man before returning to those big amber eyes. "No."

"Well, she's going to have a front page story in the paper. I'm Will Delacourt, and that man tried to steal my wife's purse. Miss, if you're not leaving on that train, we'd like to take you to dinner and—"

"Harmon Gray, is that you?"

He had to turn at that. "Miss Eliza?"

"You know him, dear?"

Her grin filled her face. "This is Mrs. Collins's nephew."

"Oh, yes. Of course. Harmon."

Harmon nodded politely, but there was only one person he needed to talk to. "Will you excuse us, please, Mr. and Mrs. Delacourt?"

Kathryn's eyes widened at what could be considered rudeness on his part, but she allowed him to pull her away from the couple, and the racket of the crowd. When he opened his mouth, the train whistle obliterated his words, then their laughter. Harmon shook his head, took off his hat with one hand, and tossed it to his father. He wasn't about to let go of *his girl* now.

His hand slid up her arm, to the line of her jaw. He turned his wrist, and his fingertips disappeared into the upswept hair behind her ear. He rubbed his thumb on her cheek and followed it with a brush of his lips, then pulled away.

She placed her hand against his chest, a light touch to his collarbone but otherwise she did not move or blink. Was she frightened, fearful it wasn't real?

It wasn't. Everything around them disappeared.

He leaned down and kissed her cheek again. Stepped closer, giving her time. Her eyes were wide, staring, while her pulse thumped against the palm of his hand.

When her eyes closed, he placed his mouth on hers, and his other hand sought her back. Her lips followed his, and he pressed against their fullness. He tipped his head and deepened the kiss, imploring her not to pull away. She didn't.

Her hand slipped higher and wrapped around his neck.

He stopped, took a breath, tasted coffee, and her mouth captured his. He heard a small groan—his—and knew he had to stop. He pressed his cheek to hers. "Are you sure you're all right?" he whispered, pulling his hand from her hair.

Kathryn's eyes opened slowly. She placed a demure hand on her neck and checked her collar before answering. Her soft "yes" lacked conviction.

He leaned back, and only then let the numerous voices and the train engine's impatient wheezing.

"That's not your wife, young man?"

"Can I get in line?"

"She's right pretty, that one!"

"She's got to be a Texas gal, for sure."

Her eyes were wild with this-can't-be-happening shock and the beat of her heart matched his—rapid against his hand. Harmon kissed her forehead before releasing her.

"Maybe we should get you to a doctor?"

"I'm fine. Really." Her laughing eyes approved when he took her by the shoulders.

"I have no right to ask you this after the week you had, but will you stay?"

"Stay?" some onlooker charged. "I thought you was gonna ask for her hand."

"Get out of my way and I'll ask."

Harmon silenced the men with a mischievous glare, and Frank and Mr. Gray took a step forward to reinforce the point, and the crowd broke up.

Kathryn looked over to Mr. Delacourt and his wife, and Harmon did as well. They were both smiling, and Eliza's eyes were red and teary.

"But I have a ticket, and the train is here." Kathryn looked beyond him to the boarding passengers.

"Kathryn Morton, you tell me what you want. You. Not what someone else expects, or what you feel obligated to do." He cupped her jawline. "You tell me now if you think you can stay a few extra days, or forever."

"Yes."

Harmon looked around at the crowd, lively with whoops and clapping.

"They understood me, Mr. Gray. I said yes. I'll stay."

"Father? My hat?" Harmon reached out an open hand and took the hat returned to it. Placed next to his face, it blocked the majority of gawkers.

She moved with no hesitation and directed her mouth to his. He pulled her to him, and his hand slipped to the small of her back. Harmon broke it off then offered a quick kiss at her ear. Her hand tightened on his arm.

"Are you ready to run away with me? I'll grab your trunk right now." His voice was hoarse with the effort to keep the words private and just for his enthusiastic little wallflower.

"Away? But Mr. Gray..." She smiled.

"If we took off now and rode toward that sunset, we'd be so far away I might never find my way back."

She giggled and effected shock, but her kiss had already said yes.

In truth, they could go anywhere. He could finish school here, or go east. There were good engineering jobs to be had everywhere. Rivers would always need bridges. They could stay here in Austin. She'd love the ranch.

"Don't worry, I just want to take you back to the Abbey, and let everyone know how I feel about you."

"And that is?"

He swooped her up into his arms. Kathryn's laughter was darn near as intoxicating as the delight they'd shared in their first kiss. He glanced from her face to the men at his side. Father held her frilly little bag and basket in one hand and slapped Frank on the back with the other. They both grinned from ear to ear.

"Does this mean no for that dinner tonight, Harmon?" Eliza Delacourt asked from his side.

"I'm afraid so," he answered her, then turned to her husband. "But why don't you join us back at the Abbey? It's the annual barbeque, and Father's brought some good Gray Ranch beef." That should seal the deal. "Been slow-cooking all day."

"This would have been our first time to miss it," Will Delacourt answered, squeezing his wife to his side. "Allow us to give you two a ride there."

"I thank you for the offer, sir, but no." Harmon strode out of the station with Kathryn in his arms and set her down just long enough to plant a kiss on the side of her cheek. "I'm going to put you up on Henry, so you can ride behind me back to the Abbey. You're small enough to sit square on rump," he told her, staring into her eyes. "And I know you're fearless enough to do it."

"Are you sure he's okay with this?"

"Oh, Henry's powerful okay with this. Do you trust me?"

Kathryn nodded. It would have to suffice. Her heart raced so fast, she could barely breathe. She was either going to expire right here, or she was going to take a bold—okay, shakey—step toward her future.

He lifted her up to sit sideways behind his saddle, and she clung to the back of it. The gelding harrumphed, and Harmon held her steady.

"You're fine. Just keep holding on and...yes, that's it. Okay, boy." He hoisted himself up in the stirrup, almost standing, and then carefully placed his leg astride before sitting. "Are you frightened?"

"No." But of course she was. Afraid now that the joy filling her might make her float up and away. "But can I hold on to you, now, instead?"

"You better. Why do you think I didn't go for the carriage?"

She threaded her arms around him just before Henry took a step. The big hips shifted under her and she tightened her hold. She could do this.

"You hang on to me like you don't ever want to let go, and we'll be fine." With a light flick of the reins, Henry began his walk down the center of the street.

But how tight was too tight? Mr. Gray had to be able to breathe, after all.

"Kathryn, I'm going to do everything in my power to keep you safe and happy. You know that, right?"

"Yes." She rested her cheek against his shoulder blade. "Harmon? Back there at the station..." Could she say it? "Why did you kiss me?"

He patted her arms, snug about his waist, and twisted around. "I had to play the cards I was dealt. I wasn't sure pleading would work. I hope you leaving with me like this means it worked."

She pressed closer against his back.

Out of the corner of her eye, she saw Frank's wagon pull alongside, her travel trunk in the back. Mr. Gray Senior shared the bench, and his horse followed behind.

"Gentlemen." Harmon tipped his hat.

Frank's boisterous shout startled Henry, and Kathryn clutched tighter. "Sorry!" Frank called, waving to her.

So that was a rebel yell.

Henry's smooth gait helped her relax, and she straightened, allowing herself to once more admire Austin and the big Texas sky. "I don't quite believe this is happening to me."

He caressed her hand. "I have to admit my face hurts from smiling. Now, let's stop at the telegram office. Your parents need to know there's been a tiny change in plans."

"And a big change in my story."

Then he turned his head. "Just when are you going to stop calling me Mr. Gray?"

"I'm not sure." She smoothed the back of his shirt collar, and touched the hair between it and his hat. "Harmon." She'd said it enough today, sitting in her room, but now it felt like a whole new word on her lips. "I hope to have the chance every day. Will that do?"

Harmon pulled her hand up to kiss it. "That will do nicely."

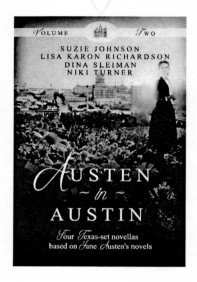

Simply Lila by Suzie Johnson
based on *Lady Susan*

Yearning to find a real-life hero, a wallflower must learn to live outside the pages of an Austen novel.

Fully Persuaded by Niki Turner
based on *Persuasion*

A brokenhearted artist struggles with the shame of her family s bankruptcy and the return of her first love whose proposal she d spurned because he was poor.

Mansford Ranch by Dina L. Sleiman
based on *Mansfield Park*

An aspiring novelist with a keen eye for character must determine who is worthy of playing her own leading man.

Sense and Nonsense by Lisa Karon Richardson
based on *Sense and Sensibility*